P9-CLS-827

Sundered

BETHANY ADAMS

Copyright © 2016 by Bethany Adams

All rights reserved. No part of this publication may be reproduced, distributed or transmitted in any form or by any means, including photocopying, recording, or other electronic or mechanical methods, without the prior written permission of the publisher, except in the case of brief quotations embodied in critical reviews and certain other noncommercial uses permitted by copyright law. For permission requests, write to the publisher, addressed "Attention: Permissions Coordinator," at the address below.

bethanyadams@bethanyadamsbooks.com

Publisher's Note: This is a work of fiction. Names, characters, places, and incidents are a product of the author's imagination. Locales and public names are sometimes used for atmospheric purposes. Any resemblance to actual people, living or dead, or to businesses, companies, events, institutions, or locales is completely coincidental.

Book Layout ©2013 BookDesignTemplates.com
Cover designed by Eve Milady, http://www.venetian-cat.com
Edited by Jody Wallace, http://jodywallace.com/
Interior image © kohy81, licensed through depositphotos.com

Sundered / Bethany Adams. -- 1st ed.
ISBN 978-0-9975320-3-6

To all who struggle with self-confidence:
Everyone has value.
You have value.
Never forget it.

Acknowledgements

As always, I would like to thank my family for their endless patience and support. My husband, who is my first reader (and plot-hole-spotter extraordinaire). My children, who say everyone should love Mommy's book. Mom, who has always supported my dreams. And my brother, Ben Adams, who is always willing to answer random graphic design questions.

Great big thanks are always in order for my critique partners and amazing friends. Jessica, Natasha, Catherine, Shiloh, Shantele, Jody—I love you guys! And there are so many writing friends I know I'm missing. I couldn't do without the support of MCRW and the Debut Collective. Our writing community is amazing!

I'm forever grateful to my editor, Jody Wallace. Well, okay, I maybe wanted to yell at Jody for some of her insightful editing questions. I got revenge by making her laugh with my return comments. Did you ever convince your family you were really working instead of watching cat videos, Jody? Hehe

Last but not least, a big thank you to my amazing cover designer, Eve Milady. How you create such magic, I'll never know. And congratulations on publishing your own debut novel! I can't wait to read it!

1

Lyr rubbed at his aching chest and then jerked his hand back before Arlyn could see. If his daughter had the slightest hint that he wasn't completely recovered, she'd insist on heading back to Braelyn, and he'd seen more than enough of the inside of his estate. He'd promised her a trip to the village once things settled down, and it was past time to fulfill it.

The last of the nobles under his command had gone home over two weeks ago now, their blood-oaths delivered. Lyr shuddered a little at the memory. His energy, both magical and physical, had been so low after his grave injury that standing on the hill taking oath after oath had been pure misery. But he hadn't wanted anyone to know how weak he was. Leaders didn't have the luxury of faltering.

Still, something must have shown, since Arlyn shot him a concerned glance. "Everything okay?"

"Perhaps not everything," Lyr answered, unwilling to fully lie. Not to her, though he had no qualms about evading the healer. "But I am well enough."

With a frown, she grabbed his arm, stopping him beside her. "What's that supposed to mean?"

"Just that it will take time for life to return to normal."

Arlyn quirked a brow at that. "You looked upset."

"Forgive me." Lyr forced himself to relax—as much as he could while scanning the forest path for danger. So far, he'd seen nothing but ancient trees and the occasional bird, but he had to remain vigilant. "My thoughts had wandered to less pleasant things. The village will make for an excellent distraction."

Arlyn stared at him for a moment and then shrugged. "If you say so."

Lyr gestured toward the path, and they started forward once more. He wanted to give her something for everything she'd been through since finding his world. Something for all the time he'd missed with her—twenty-two years by Moranaian time but twenty-six on Earth. That he hadn't known Arlyn existed until almost two months ago was irrelevant. He never should have left Aimee, his soulbonded, behind on Earth when he'd learned of his father's murder. If he'd just insisted she brave the Veil...well, he'd never know, would he? And Arlyn had paid for it.

What was a trip to the village compared to that?

He knew from Arlyn's gasp when she picked out the first building from the surrounding trees. His people didn't clear the land for their homes, choosing instead to build in and around the forest. The stones mined farther up the valley were perfect for blending in, the variegated shades of gray, green, and brown hard to discern from the tree trunks and the vines spilling over the walls.

A slow, delighted smile stretched across his daughter's face. "Is the stone carved, too?"

"Most of it," Lyr answered. "Much like the walls of the estate."

"How many buildings are down here? It's hard to tell from up on the ridge."

Lyr pursed his lips, thinking. He'd just approved the last of the building plans for the season, shifting the number upward. *Ah, yes.* "In the immediate area? Four hundred and thirty-seven, not counting businesses."

Arlyn's eyes widened, and her gaze shifted to the forest around them. "Where?"

For the first time in a long time, he found himself smiling. He shoved worry aside and gave into the urge to tease. "They could be invisible."

She let out a snort of laughter. "Yeah, right."

"How can you be so sure? You just started learning magic, after all."

"Because the way my life has been going lately, I'm sure I would've run straight into one by now," Arlyn answered. But she grinned as she said it, so he knew she was only teasing in return.

He grimaced at the reminder of how chaotic her life had been since arriving on Moranaia—and not just the adjustment from Earth to a new land. Stumbling into a conspiracy against him and almost being murdered hadn't exactly been the easiest welcome. He tried not to let the thought destroy his good humor.

"I can't fault your logic," he said. In truth, though, many of them are built around the trees near the village center. Larger, more obvious settlements are near the fields to the north."

They walked in companionable silence for a while, the gentle swish of the swaying leaves soothing them. The houses were spread thin here, and most of the occupants were away at work, leaving nothing but the forest's peace. Lyr had decided to come here for Arlyn's sake, but it was easing some of the heaviness in his own heart. He could push aside thoughts of all he'd failed to do. Protecting his own people, keeping his mother safe from injury, not noticing—

His fists clenched as he cleared his mind once more. Maybe he wasn't *quite* pushing it aside. Especially since the mastermind behind the last attack was still unknown.

"You're frowning again."

Clechtan, Lyr cursed to himself. "Sorry."

Arlyn gave him a sidelong look. "Are you sure you don't want to hold off on this?"

"I finally caught up on my paperwork." He forced a smile to his face. Anything to keep her from guessing how much he hurt, body and spirit. He'd recover soon enough. "In a couple of weeks, the earliest of the harvests will begin, bringing yet more work. We should enjoy the lull."

The trail opened into the natural clearing that held the village of Telerdai, and if Arlyn still had concerns about his mood, she let them drop as she took in the view. Stone paths meandered through flowers and shrubs to meet at a clear pool in the center. Around the perimeter, shops sat at the base of the largest trees, and stairs curved up the trunks behind them to a few homes built up in the canopy, most inhabited by the shop owners.

One of the generals of the army, Lyr commanded a large number of soldiers either at the estate or living in the surrounding lands, and the village reflected that. Circling the center garden on the way to the bowyer, they passed two types of armorers, a blade smith, and a leatherworker. He pointed out the tavern as they approached the bowyer's shop, more general offerings beyond. If he still had the energy, he'd take Arlyn there for the midday meal.

Since Arlyn was still uncomfortable with Moranaian greetings, Lyr entered the shop first. Only to pause just beyond the entry at the hum of magic filling the room. The bowyer, Leren, perched on a stool behind her workbench, her gaze never wavering from the wood beneath her hands. Arlyn halted beside him, a frown furrowing her brow as she took in the scene.

"*Isilai,*" Leren muttered to them around the file she gripped between her teeth.

He gave a short nod and moved to the small display of bows to the left of the entrance. Imbuing spells into an object was a delicate art, one he would not disrupt without great cause. And for once, he had no need to rush.

Arlyn hesitated, her gaze on Leren, before shrugging and joining him at the display. *"What's going on?"* she sent along their mental link. *"Why did she say 'in progress' instead of greeting us?"*

"She is in the middle of a spell-working," Lyr explained. *"The word has been used for so long that it is considered a polite way for artisans to warn patrons that it might take them a moment."*

"Ah." Arlyn ran a finger along the smooth edge of a small recurve bow. *"Fine craftsmanship. Does she work by commission?"*

"Most artisans do here."

"Forgive me, Myern," Leren said, addressing him by title. He turned to see her standing, the magic finished. "Welcome and good morn to you."

Lyr gave Arlyn a subtle glance as he started toward the bowyer. Though he knew his daughter was nervous, she followed after a moment. He held back a smile as he made the introductions and chatted with Leren about her family and business. Arlyn was going to have to get used to such things, for he wasn't backing down on naming her his heir. Fortunately, it didn't take long for Arlyn to lose her reluctance. After a few moments, he took a subtle step back as she and Leren discussed how bow-making techniques varied between Earth and Moranaia.

A door at the back of the shop opened, and Leren's young daughter stumbled through with a couple of boxes balanced precariously in her arms. As she struggled to close the door behind her, Lyr darted forward to help. He reached for one of the boxes, but it toppled free, knocking the lid loose as it hit the floor with a jarring clang. Lyr froze, and his stomach clenched at the sound.

His gaze fastened on the bits of metal spilling out. For one long moment, the world spun hazily around him. Arrowheads and files, all made of *peresten*. Not iron. Not even steel. He rubbed his wrist almost reflexively. Not chains. He wasn't bound in Allafon's home, his life bleeding away. The barely-healed wound on his chest burned in memory.

"Myern?" the girl whispered.

By will alone, Lyr forced his eyes from the scraps of metal. He took several long, deep breaths, the sound loud in his ears. Could the others hear it? He dropped his arms to his sides and straightened, only then taking in the girl's ashen face. "I'm sorry, Areth. I almost had the box."

She stared at him for a moment, and he could practically see the debate in her eyes. But at fourteen years old, she knew enough of formality and politeness not to ask about his reaction. He just had to hope the others hadn't noticed—especially Arlyn. He would not have her worried about him when he only needed a little more time to heal. He was the Myern—the lord of the estate. He would manage.

"I shouldn't have tried to carry it all," Areth finally said. The color had returned to her face, but she shot him a cautious look as she bent to place the contents back into the box.

Swallowing bile, Lyr knelt to help her. Not iron. *Not iron.* "Working with your mother today, then? She sends excellent reports on your progress."

"Thank you, Myern." Areth's face flushed with the pride that lit her eyes. "She might even let me make a bow on my own soon."

"Once you finish your analysis of the differences between Sidhe dialects," Leren called.

Some of Lyr's tension faded at Areth's exasperated expression as she stacked the last file on top of the box. A timeless reaction of child to parent, a look his own daughter had already worn more than once in the past month. Gods willing, he'd see many more. Even if he didn't deserve it.

"An important task," Lyr said. *They have no idea how much.* As the Sidhe became more stringent in their demands for aid, knowledge of their language was more crucial than ever.

Areth smiled as she picked up one of the boxes and carried it to a second worktable. "Then I'll make sure I do a good job."

Even as Lyr returned the smile, he detected a mental nudge. Kera's energy signature. Stifling a groan, he turned back to the display of bows as Arlyn and Leren continued their earlier discussion. Better to hide his expression while he answered his new assistant. *"Is something amiss at the estate?"*

"A messenger just arrived through the portal. He said he has urgent news, and from the look of him, I believe it."

Lyr ran his hand through his hair. Hadn't he known the peace was too good to last? *"We'll head back now, then. If you haven't already, offer the messenger refreshment and rest."*

"Of course, Myern."

So much for not needing to rush.

ꙮ

After all that had transpired over the last couple of months, Lyr was beginning to seriously dislike his study. It had become a place of uncomfortable, if not painful, conversations and unwelcome revelations. He glanced wearily around the long, oval room, the bookshelves along the walls lit by the midday sun streaming in through the windows and skylights. He should have been cheered by the beautiful sight, but his heart pounded with dread. An urgent messenger sent in person through the Veil could only be trouble.

Lyr stood in front of his broad, wooden desk, Arlyn just behind and to the right and Kai, his friend and Arlyn's mate, to the left. After an odd beginning, their relationship seemed to have settled. Not realizing she wouldn't understand, Kai had begun the bonding with Arlyn without her knowledge. None of them had been certain if she would accept Kai or have their bond broken. Surprisingly, she'd forgiven him. Lyr thought he'd managed to do the same. But, *clechtan*, he'd only been acquainted with his daughter for a couple of hours before his best friend had started the bond with her.

A month or two of anger was little enough.

The door on the opposite end of the room opened, and Kera escorted the messenger in. It took all of Lyr's centuries of training to maintain a neutral expression at the first sight of the other elf. The messenger's face was haggard, wrinkles set deep around his mouth and eyes, and he wore plain clothing. Nothing like the garb of an ambassador. The relative peace of the last month was indeed coming to an end. Lyr reinforced his mental shields to keep the others from sensing his concern.

Kera gave a small bow and tapped her chest twice in salute. At Lyr's nod, she turned to the messenger. "Honored visitor, I present to you Callian Myern i Lyrnis Dianore nai Braelyn, lord of this estate and liaison to all Earth-related realms of fae. Myern, I present to you Oberin Tesore, messenger of Queen Etora of the Colony of Neor."

Lyr considered the visitor bowing before him. Many of the Sidhe aligned with major factions, such as the Tuatha de Danann or the Seelie or Unseelie courts, but here and there a city would separate into its own governance. A colony fell somewhere in between, somewhat autonomous but still under the rule of another. Queen Etora owed allegiance to the Seelie court, though she largely ruled without interference. He'd never met her, considering she had last sent an ambassador when Lyr's father was alive.

"The House of Dianore bids you welcome, Honored of Neor."

"Thank you, Myern," the messenger said, his voice wavering with exhaustion. "The hospitality of your House has been most generous."

"It has been our honor." Out of the corner of his eye, he caught Arlyn's slight movement and held back a smile. Her human side emerged most often in her lack of patience. "Our House has not had the pleasure of a visit from one of your people in quite some time."

The messenger lifted his hollow gaze to Lyr's face. "I fear it will be no pleasure now. It is a grave problem that brings me here to a plane so far removed from my own. My words are too important for the bonds of politeness to be met. Please forgive my brevity."

"Then let us dispense with formality. What brings you here, honored messenger?" Lyr asked.

"There is no gentle way to say this." Oberin paused to take a deep, ragged breath. "Neor has fallen. The poisoned energies from surface Earth seeped into our realm, crossing the dimensional barriers. Our people, unable to replenish magical energy, began to go insane. Less than a month ago, violence broke out among the maddened. And last week…last week, Queen Etora retreated to a nearby dimension with the few who were still healthy while King Feron took the sick into quarantine. Our city has become a place of mob rule, as there are not enough among the healthy to restore order."

A wash of dread trickled down Lyr's spine, and his throat tightened around the curse he couldn't release. Just before Arlyn had arrived on Moranaia, he had sent Kai to the Seelie court to discuss the poisoned energy that had begun to create difficulties there. Though there had been cause for concern, there had been no indication that the problem was so severe that an entire city might fall into chaos.

That had only been a couple of months ago. What had changed?

"That is grave news, indeed," Lyr answered solemnly. "Tell me. Why have you journeyed so far during such a time?"

The messenger bowed slightly. "My lord, Queen Etora would like to formally request your aid in freeing Neor of violence and strife. The energies are too terrible for anyone to return for good, but those trapped in the grip of madness must be contained. And…there have been rumors of your discussions with some of the Seelie—the possibility of a return to surface Earth to fix the source of the problem. If Neor could someday be saved…"

Next to Lyr, Kai stiffened, but he didn't speak. Such negotiations were supposed to be secret, and his friend had to be displeased that there were rumors. Had Lord Meren allowed information to leak to others? Lyr shoved down his own rush of anger. What game did the Seelie play? They'd requested Lyr's help with the poisoned energy seeping into the underhill realms and then made all attempts at negotiation as difficult as possible. And now, it seemed, at least one of them was spreading rumors.

He'd be having quite a discussion with a certain Sidhe lord. Later.

Lyr struggled to keep his tone level. "Speaking of the Seelie, why have you come to us when your colony is under their dominion? A request of this magnitude should come through them."

"We have given up all hope of their aid, my lord. We have been petitioning them for some time, yet they refuse to send help, saying only that the humans are to blame and that we must relocate. After hearing of your discussions, the queen decided to appeal directly to you."

Oh, yes. A very lengthy conversation with Lord Meren. "You do realize the complications this brings, I presume? Aside from the diplomatic nightmare this could cause with the Seelie, I cannot dispatch our warriors without a clear and imminent threat to these lands except under order of the king. I am uncertain how long receiving approval might take."

Before the messenger could respond, the door to the study opened, and Ralan, heir to the throne of Moranaia, entered. "Do it."

2

The light never truly faded in Alfheim.

From the highest point of her home, Meli watched the last rays of the setting sun glint off the white stone of the city's walls and reflect from crystals on the tips of countless spires. Magical channels connected each crystal in the city, bringing that light into every home. The glow flowed around her silver robes and pale blond hair. It shone against the white floors and cream walls like dawn—but then, everything here was designed to heighten the effect of light.

Only the darkness creeping into the edges of the plains below marred the perfection.

At least Meli's window was too high up for anyone to see how she trembled. She gripped the edges of the windowsill to still her shaking hands, but it was no use. Her king was going to send her through that darkness, all on the word of a mad seer.

Meli was only twenty-five—years, not centuries—and it would be her task to guide the ambassador through the sick energy and into the Veil that separated dimensions. Since she was only one test away from being ranked an Unfavorable One, a person without useful magic, the seer's judgment had caused an uproar amongst the other noble houses.

Meli was nobody. A near-outcast who'd never been outside Alfheim, though she'd always felt the pull to...elsewhere, a place she could feel in her heart but didn't know how to reach. But someone like her, so close to being relegated to the fringes of society, would never be allowed to travel. Yet now she would be expected to lead a group through the mists to a place no one had ever heard of.

Her father had appealed to the king multiple times not to send his only daughter into the mists, and Meli suspected he'd even tried to seek an audience with Freyr, their God and High King, without success. It was no surprise. Her family had once been among the most powerful noble houses, but the more they'd used their influence to stall Meli's testing, the more tenuous that position had become. She'd have to submit herself for the test soon to save them ruin. If she had the chance.

The darkness that had been creeping into the surrounding land for fifty years had sped up markedly during the past year. Time passed so quickly here compared to Earth, where the sickness seemed to come from, that none were able to predict how long it would be before it crept into Alfheim proper. The king had grown desperate enough to consult the Ancient One, a seer so old that not even the long-lived elves had a record of her

name. Gods only knew what he'd had to offer her to earn her
aid.

Seek those cousins long departed for the land of Moranai, she'd said.

A strange command. Of all those to ask, why their distant
"cousins," a race of elves that they hadn't spoken with in millennia? The Ljósálfar, the Light Elves, barely even acknowledged their closer cousins among the Sidhe, much less these
Moranaians. Why not an appeal to the Vanir or Aesir? Though
not too far above some of her people in power, they were gods,
the strongest force Meli could imagine enlisting. But acting on
the advice of a seer rumored to be senile, the king had commanded otherwise.

And the king had commanded it be done with Meli the
Magicless in the lead.

Freyr above, Meli muttered to herself. She knew nothing about
crossing between worlds, and she didn't have the power to complete the task. Yet here she was, preparing for a journey across
the Veil. She was certain to get them all lost or killed. The stories
of the seer's madness were surely true.

Perhaps the gods wanted Alfheim to fall. Meli swallowed
against the lump forming in her throat. If so, the seer had done
a fine job of ensuring it.

Meli spun from the window and glared at the leather bag still
open on her bed. What did one pack for a journey to one's
doom? She wouldn't need embroidered court dresses to wander
between worlds, and if by some miracle they reached this land
of Moranai, anything formal would be left to the ambassador.
Others were responsible for preparing provisions.

At last, she shoved in three robes, a few shifts, and a couple of sturdy belts. Meli's hand hovered over the small silver knife her brother had given her before he'd left for warrior's training. She bit her lip. Would she need to defend herself in the Veil? Would it cause offense in a foreign land? Shrugging, she grabbed the hilt and slid her knife into a side pocket of her pack.

Duty might lead her forward, but she wasn't going defenseless.

∘⊙∘

"If you could excuse us, Messenger Telore," Lyr began calmly, but inside he seethed. "Perhaps you might enjoy a moment's rest while we discuss this matter."

They waited in silence as Kera escorted the stranger from the room. Then, with a shake of his head, Kai grinned at Ralan. "I thought *I* was the impetuous one. Your manners were certainly not improved by your time on Earth."

The prince gave a careless shrug, though Lyr suspected that the words stung. Ralan had spent over three hundred years on Earth after a serious argument with his father and had only returned to save his half-blood daughter's life. The experience had left him a fascinating blend of regal and casual. "I have Seen that it must be done. The violence of the maddened Neorans? won't be contained there for long. Other cities will fall in rapid order if this isn't taken care of."

"I must still seek permission from the king to send so many warriors, Ralan."

His friend stiffened. "I am Heir, and as such, I can speak for my father."

"You mean the one you refuse to talk to?" Kai asked with a laugh. "I thought you denied your place as his heir."

"I meant to do so." Ralan rubbed his hand over the back of his neck and sighed. "Then I opened myself to my talents once more. The futures where I renounce my position are…not to come to pass, if I can avoid it."

Lyr studied the prince's closed expression. He had little experience with seers, at least those actively working as such, but they tended to be enigmatic about their predictions. His long friendship with Ralan would give him no advantage in that regard. "I don't suppose you can tell us who is to blame for all of this?"

"Not if I hope to achieve a good outcome. The future is a tricky thing, changing with each action we take. The things you would do now if you knew… There are too many unfavorable paths from there."

Lyr's eyes narrowed as unexpected anger flowed through him. As far as he knew, his life had never been guided by a seer before, and he found he didn't like the feeling. But he couldn't deny his prince's command. "I'll send aid, provided you're willing to discuss this with the king. I'll let you be the one to tell him that a portion of his warriors have been dispatched without his knowledge."

Ralan winced. "He'll demand I return home, but if he thinks an apology—"

His friend's jaw clenched tight around words he wouldn't say, but Lyr understood. The king might regret the rift he'd caused, but Ralan wasn't ready to forgive him. He might never be. "You can't avoid him forever."

"I know." A scowl tightened the prince's face. "All too well."

ოჲ

Every dinner reminded Lyr of his own failure, and this one was no exception. His fingers tightened on the glass in his hand as his mother hobbled across the dining room with the healer's support. It would take time, Lial said, for her to recover from her fall from the library tower. Even for elves, a shattered spine was a serious thing. If his mother were human, she'd be ashes on the wind.

All because Lyr hadn't realized that the captain of his guard was a traitor.

None of the others appeared to notice Lynia's struggle. Ralan, Kai, and Selia, Arlyn's magic teacher, were discussing the day's events. Ralan's daughter, Eri, and Iren, Selia's son, leaned close, their voices too low to hear. Perhaps sensing Lyr's regard, Arlyn shot him a concerned glance, but Lyr ignored it. What was *wrong* with him? He forced his eyes away from his mother and set his glass on the table. *I can do this.* He'd succeeded in hiding his reaction to his mother's injury for several weeks now. *One more dinner,* he promised himself. *One more dinner without them knowing.*

At a whimper from his mother, Lyr looked up—just as she stumbled. Though Lial steadied her and she continued to her seat, Lyr stiffened against the urge to slam his fist onto the table. She'd never blamed him. Not once. She even gave him a tremulous smile as she settled into her chair at the other end of the table. But *he* could never forget.

"*Father?*" Arlyn whispered, leaning closer.

Some of his tension faded at the word. She'd begun to call him Father more of late, and Lyr didn't think he'd ever grow tired of hearing it. "Today has been unusual. But I'm fine."

One corner of her mouth quirked up. "I'm not sure I believe you."

Lyr only shook his head. What could he say? He didn't want to burden her further with things that would pass on their own. They had time—elves had nothing if not that.

"I can't believe the messenger insisted on going back right away," Kai said from his place at Arlyn's right. "At least there was a guide available to take him quickly through the mists. I'm not sure he would have had the energy to cross the Veil on his own again."

Ralan lifted a platter of meat and passed it to his left, serving Selia first. "I told you it was dire."

"My team will leave first thing in the morning," Kai said, causing Lyr's heart to slam hard in his chest. He hadn't had a chance to ask his friend who he'd take on the scouting mission, as Lyr usually trusted Kai to pick the best people for the job. But this time....

"You aren't taking Arlyn along, are you?"

Arlyn herself laughed, and Kai let out a sigh. But he shook his head. "No. I was afraid she'd accuse me of treating her as weak again, but no."

"I'm not stupid, either." Her grin lit her entire face as she gave Kai a nudge. "And I'd rather not be a stereotype."

Lyr's brow furrowed. "What?"

"You know," she said. "The barely-trained girl who rushes into danger and gets captured or killed? No, thanks."

Across from her, Ralan chuckled. "But they usually look good while doing it." Lyr gave the prince a blank look. "She's talking about movies and television shows. And sometimes books. It's a popular trope in Earth stories."

"I don't think you're at risk of being a stereotype, Arlyn," Lyr said with a smile.

Some of the humor faded from her eyes as she shrugged. "It's not like I need to go searching for trouble. Enough has found me of late without hunting for it myself."

Though he knew she hadn't meant it as a rebuke, Lyr stiffened. She didn't blame him, but she should. She'd had to cross the Veil to find him herself. She'd almost died more than once because he'd failed to recognize the traitors under his dominion. If trouble had found her, it was all on Lyr.

In the sudden silence, Lyr stood. Ralan's young daughter and Selia's son stared up at him, mouths agape, at the abrupt motion. Lyr glanced away from his mother's chiding eyes. "Forgive me. I just recalled an urgent message that must be drafted."

It was a terrible excuse for his rudeness, but no one challenged it. Lyr had to escape before his emotions spilled over and he lost control. Even if he had to come up with an urgent message to draft.

ঌ৩৫

"Dammit," Arlyn muttered as the door closed behind her father. "I didn't mean that the way I think he took it. I'd joked in a similar way earlier."

Kai's hand wrapped around hers, though he frowned at the door. "I've never seen him quite like this. Not even after he returned from Earth without your mother."

"He says he's fine, but…" Arlyn let out a long sigh. "I don't know."

She almost told them about the incident at the bowyer's but couldn't bring herself to do it. It felt too much like betrayal to reveal how he'd almost broken down. Really, Arlyn wasn't quite sure what *had* happened. His skin had gone white, his eyes almost panicked, when the box had clattered to the ground. But he hadn't been shot by an arrow, so she had no idea why arrowheads would have bothered him.

Could she have imagined it? Her father had recovered so quickly that she hadn't been sure, and her uncertainty had kept her from asking him about it. But his reaction just now? Everyone had seen that. Now Arlyn needed to figure out what to do about it.

∽⊚∾

The firelight flickering across Kien's face matched the anger consuming his insides without cease. For the first few days after his only living spy had returned from Allafon's estate, his fury had run red with blood. Literally. Kien had enjoyed decorating the camp with pieces of that idiot, a demonstration that subdued the recent grumblings of his followers. His body still trembled at the betrayal.

Allafon had sworn to him, *sworn,* that the portal would be theirs. For three hundred years, Kien had been exiled from Moranaia, and now his best chance to return was lost. All because his little puppet on the other side of the Veil had had a thing for their enemy's mother. Allafon could have eliminated Lyr and the House of Dianore in one easy blow, leaving Braelyn open and vulnerable. Instead, he'd chained Lyr and his daughter while trying to capture Lynia. What fool left his prisoners alone to go chase a woman?

Too bad they'd killed Allafon during the escape. His torture would have brought hours of enjoyment.

Kien was a prince, and he would not be denied the throne. He still had the half-bloods, his naive followers. A few simple magic tricks and tidbits of training held them in his thrall. Well, that and the promise of world domination. Kien could empathize. If he was born to rule, then perhaps these half-bloods were destined to control the humans, as well. Their success meant nothing to him past his own victory.

The spell that leached poison into the local energy fields was almost complete. As soon as it was done, they would find another place to set up camp. For ten years, they'd traveled around the world building the framework; now came the fine-tuning. The United States was a particularly obliging place, covered by miles of public parks where an enterprising magic worker could set up a cloaked camp that no one was likely to discover. And no one would hear their screams if they did.

The sound of hoof beats pierced through Kien's anger, and his lips curved into a wicked smile. Tucked into a small hollow deep in the Great Smoky Mountains, their camp was almost impossible to find and certainly would not be stumbled on by a random person out for a horseback ride. No, it must be his favorite pawn. If not for Naomh, the Sidhe would have destroyed Kien's plans long before. Good thing the fool still held sway.

Naomh rode through the camp straight to the fire without so much as a glance at the severed head spiked at the entrance. His long, pale hair flowed around his leather-clad form to blend with the creamy hide of his horse. In contrast, his companion, Caolte, tossed his fiery red hair from his eyes as he took in every detail of the camp from his midnight black steed. Ah, brotherly camaraderie. Didn't they realize one would inevitably betray the other? It was the way of siblings.

Naomh pulled his horse to a halt but did not dismount. "This has gone too far."

Kien's smile widened. "I am certain I do not understand. I am doing precisely what you wanted. Hasn't the surface become too poisoned for your kind to remain here for any length of time?"

"We were supposed to convince the restless among the Sidhe to stick to the underrealms," Naomh bit out through clenched teeth, "but your poisoned energy is seeping into our homes. Now my own brother is in talks to return to the surface to fix the problem. I like to ride the hills, not live on them."

"I have had…complications. Perhaps even heightened by *your* incompetence. My enemies have strengthened, and the portal remains out of my reach." Kien let some of his anger flash in his eyes, though his voice remained smooth. "Care to explain why the Moranaian diplomat is still alive?"

Naomh's aura sparked with energy. "A failure that will not be repeated. Keep the poison from spreading below, and I will see to his death myself. I care not who you purge from above so long as I am free to roam the twilight."

"I will see what I can do," Kien answered with a sharp, humorless chuckle. *If only Naomh understood who was really in control.*

Without a word, the pair turned and spurred their horses to a gallop. Just as they reached the outer edges of the camp, Caolte looked over his shoulder, tossing hair that flickered with the hint of true flame. His cold, blue eyes promised certain death as he held Kien's gaze. Though Caolte never spoke, Kien understood the warning. Hurt Naomh and die.

3

With one last wave for Arlyn, Kai stepped through the stone arch and into the mists of the Veil. He kept careful hold of the spell linking the two other sonal to him lest they get lost in the endless gray as he searched for the strand that would lead him to his destination. The task took longer than a trip to Earth, a path he traveled often, but Kai hadn't visited Neor since his training over three hundred years ago. As soon as he found the pale orange strand, he used it to pull himself and the others to the correct portal. With the energies thankfully calm, it took little time to reach the opposite side.

The group emerged into a sparsely illuminated cave, and Kai shuddered. He wasn't usually bothered by being underground, but there was something about the sterile, industrial feel of the Neoran settlement that bothered him. They weren't called the

People of Order for nothing. A sick jest that they'd fallen into this level of madness first.

A strip of mage light imbued into engraved metal panels ran up each side of the short tunnel leading out of the cave, the eerie glow fading into black just beyond. As on his previous trip here, the engravings triggered a sick feeling of dread. He'd forgotten the sensation after so long, but now his body tightened with more than just worry for the mission.

With a shake of his head, Kai suppressed his unease. He gripped the hilt of his sword and reinforced the magical shield that protected him from non-physical attacks. Then he gave a quick hand signal, and the three *sonal* crept to the end of the tunnel that opened onto the main thoroughfare to the city. Light globes, once gilding the road with a cheerful gleam, now dangled dark and lifeless from their metal poles. The only illumination came from the occasional flash of lightning and the false, magical moon shining at the top of the giant, hollow cavern. Would it have been better to arrive when their magic sun rode the sky? A gust of wind shifted one of the light globes, and Kai flinched at the hideous scrape of ruined metal against metal. *Probably not.*

Their gray-and-black clothing faded into the shadows as they darted away from the entrance to the portal room. Whispers and groans echoed from somewhere in the distance. Flickers of mage energy shot through the sky, punctuated by the occasional scream. Kai's worry amplified. The Neorans prided themselves on their control. What kind of poison could lead them to such insanity?

Miaran, Kai cursed. He and his scouts were at a disadvantage, unable to pull in extra energy without risking madness themselves. Unhampered by such concerns, the tortured few running rampant through the fractured city could replenish any spells they created until their innate energy stores ran out. By the looks of the lightning splitting the sky, their power was far from drained.

The road was almost certainly a trap for the unwary. The Neorans had arranged their city to mathematical perfection. Their sense of order was habit, so ingrained that it would likely last through madness. If there were magical sensors alerting anyone to an arrival through the portal, the main route would be watched. With a quick mental command, Kai directed the *sonal* to leave the tunnel and blend into the cliff face to the right of the cavern as he ducked to the left. They crept a few yards before stopping to observe the city in more detail.

The harsh, perfect angles of the buildings were not softened by the light of the imitation moon. From a small pocket in the stone, Kai scanned the metal structures. No sign of movement, but...

He caught his breath as the hair on his arms lifted and his shields shrilled an internal warning. An orb of condensed lightning crashed into the rock wall a few body lengths away, and his throat convulsed around the cry he held back. *Close. Too close.* A sudden yelp of pain sounded nearby, followed by shrill laughter, the sound just as much a weapon as the orb. Both were near enough to knot Kai's body with tension before the thud of running feet signaled the Neorans' departure.

"Have you been attacked, Taysonal Kaienan?"

Focused on scanning the area with his senses, Kai sent the other scout a feeling of reassurance. He expanded his magic in slow stages, like a toddler testing uneven ground. After several moments, he was satisfied that no one wandered between his current position and the portal. Although Kai could shield himself and perform some combat magic, he was no mage and wouldn't last long in a battle with several maddened ones. Of the other two *sonal* with him, only Belere was more proficient, but her skill wouldn't be enough to make a difference, especially since none of them could pull in energy.

Kai sent the other two a quick mental nudge. *"We need to return to Moranaia. I was not attacked, but that fight came perilously close. We dare not go farther without mages."*

They slipped back to the portal with as much speed as possible and rushed through. Kai could tell at once that something had changed, as the energies of the Veil were no longer calm. The mists roiled like clouds before a storm, and the strands of magic he needed to follow tumbled and snarled. Nevertheless, he led them in, searching for the strand that would return them to Moranaia. Time meant little here, but experience told him that half the day passed before he finally found it. Sweat rolling down his back and limbs heavy, Kai pulled them through. He could hardly *wait* to repeat the process with an entire troop.

∾ଡ଼ଢ଼

Meli stood before the giant stone arch of Alfheim's portal and fought to control her agitated stomach. The breakfast her worried mother had forced on her threatened to return, risking further humiliation. Most of the elves gathered around her small party thought the king was mad to rely on one so young and low in rank; in truth, she agreed. The ambassador, a severe female over a thousand years old, would hardly deign to speak to her. Surely the seer was wrong. And yet…

Something pulled at her. Meli had always had a feeling of business undone, images of places she had never been. As a child, her parents had worried over her strange dreams, though they were mostly a blur to Meli. Except the eyes, emerald green and filled with pain—those she saw clearly. She had long felt that if she just stepped through the portal, she could find them. Perhaps she could at least solve that mystery with this insane trip, provided she didn't get the whole group of them killed.

Vionafer, High Mage of Alfheim herself, strode forward and held out the crystal that Meli would need to bind her group together in the mists. Taking a deep breath, she accepted the offered stone. Her hands trembled around the smooth piece of crystal, and she struggled not to drop it as a tingle of energy washed over her. As far as she knew, she had no gift for traveling through the land between worlds. She had no gifts at all, magical or otherwise. Her power was minimal at best, barely enough to attune to the stone. If she were to lose or break the crystal, the entire group would be lost. Acid rose into her throat until she thought she might choke.

"Relax, Ameliar." Vionafer smiled, one of the few friendly expressions Meli had seen that day. The mage brushed aside her golden brown hair to lift a chain from around her own neck. From the end, she unhooked a net of fine silver mesh. "Place the crystal in here and wear it on your journey. You needn't hold it the whole time."

Meli exhaled in relief. "Thank you, Lady Mage."

"The chain and net are spelled against breakage, and once you slip it on, it will not fall off unless you pull it off with intent. I have added a spell connecting the magic of the crystal to the enchantment holding your supply cart aloft."

"My lady, I—" Meli stumbled over her words, stunned by the wealth being given to her so casually. She wouldn't have been able to afford such elaborate spell work for centuries. Custom work by the High Mage herself cost a fortune. "I am honored beyond telling to be entrusted with this. I only hope I prove worthy."

Vionafer leaned close, her expression solemn, though her voice was light when she spoke. "I also added a beacon. If you find yourself lost beyond hope, it will activate and alert me. It wasn't part of the king's orders, but I refuse to send you out without some kind of safeguard. And do not worry—the king paid quite handsomely."

The twinkle in the mage's gray eyes surprised Meli. They'd never spoken a word before this day, and yet it seemed she had an ally. She found her mouth curling up in her first smile since the king's decree. Hopefully the High Mage had charged the king triple. "Words can hardly express my thanks, Lady Mage."

"Reward me with your safe arrival." Vionafer held open the net for the crystal and then sealed it closed with a few muttered words. As Meli lifted the chain over her neck, the energy of the completed spell pulsed around them. She had enough of her own magic to sense the threads binding the other four and their supply cart to her. With one last smile, the High Mage left Meli to face the portal once more.

Bolstered by the mage's words, Meli took her first tentative steps towards the giant stone arch. Just before passing through, she glanced back over her shoulder. At the edge of the crowd, her parents struggled to maintain their calm façade. Nearer, the ambassador and her three attendants—Berris, Pol, and Orena—followed, their faces carefully blank. But it didn't take much to imagine their consternation and fear at someone as worthless and young as Meli leading them into the unknown. She had her own share of those feelings herself.

ஓலௌ

"In short, we're going to need more mages," Kai said, concluding his formal report.

Lyr shoved down the urge to drop his head into his hands. Though Lyr was a general over a contingent of their army, the Callian side boasted those most skilled in *physical* combat. Their true mages worked under the generals of the Taian branch. If Ralan insisted that they aid Neor, then Lyr would have to negotiate with the Taians for a small troop of mages. To think he'd almost been caught up on paperwork.

Usually, his role as Myern, third duke of the Callian branch, fulfilled him, but Arlyn's arrival had upset the balance of his life and his work. Dealing with attacks on their House and finding a teacher for Arlyn's unexpected magical abilities had been disruptive enough. But Lyr's injury had sapped most of his energy. He could only sigh at this newest development.

"*Miaran*," Lyr muttered, though the expletive hardly satisfied his frustration. "How many and what type do you think we'll need?"

"At least five, possibly ten," Kai answered. "We need mages capable of shielding a large group and containing the Neorans we apprehend. They must also carry energy crystals since the energy there is too poisoned to draw on if they run out of reserves."

"Wait a second." Arlyn turned from where she stood at the window. "What are you going to do with the Neorans you capture?"

Kai shook his head. "That's not my call."

Lyr tapped his fingers on his desk as he considered the question. What would be safest for all? He thought back over Kai's report. "We'll contain them as best we can until we find the source of the poison. Then hope we won't be forced to kill them.".

Arlyn's mouth fell open. "Kill them? You're joking, right? You can't just murder these people, insane or not."

"If we cannot properly contain them or get them to cease attacking, we'll have no choice. They've already turned on each other. I will not allow my own people to be in danger."

"Of course not, but…" Her brows scrunched. "Can't they be cured?"

Lyr glanced at Kai in surprise. Hadn't he given Arlyn more details about the missions he'd been on before her arrival? "According to what they told your bonded when he visited the Seelie court, the Sidhe have been unable to cure the madness caused by the energy poisoning. I don't believe the Neorans know how to do so, either, or they wouldn't be seeking our aid."

"Maybe you should talk to Lial. Just because the Sidhe haven't found a way doesn't mean we can't," Arlyn said.

Despite the serious discussion, Lyr couldn't hold back a smile at hearing her say "we." Besides, she had an excellent point. "I will do so. Until we can find the source of the poison, removing and curing those affected would certainly be the best solution."

Kai cleared his throat. "But what about the mages? Ralan can petition his father, but that will take time."

His daughter's concerned expression reminded Lyr of at least one set of paperwork he was working on, and his smile broadened. Though Arlyn's mother had been from Earth, they had discovered that Arlyn's grandfather had been the abandoned half-blood offspring of a mage on the Taian branch— Selia's father, Loren, in fact. Lyr was in the process of negotiating the connection between their two families. Considering Loren's guilt at neglecting his son and losing track of his bloodline, Lyr might just be able to finesse a few mages from him. Especially since Selia was on Lyr's side.

"I'll see what I can do."

"You could ask—" Arlyn spun to the window, her gaze darting to the trees beyond. "Did you feel that?"

"Feel what?"

"I'm still getting used to being keyed to the estate shields, but I thought I detected a breach." She turned back to them with a confused frown. "There and then gone. But if you didn't feel it…"

Kai exchanged a look with Lyr. "*Mialn*, I sensed nothing but your unease. But after the attacks last month, I don't think we should ignore what you felt. With Lyr's permission, I'll go scout the area and see if I find anything off."

After nodding his consent, Lyr watched his friend depart. He also had sensed nothing, but Arlyn was part human and had magical abilities that he did not. If his daughter had indeed detected a breach, danger might have found them once again. After all, Lyr still hadn't tracked down the mastermind behind Allafon's betrayal. Perhaps their relative peace was at an end.

᭒ᱬᱬᱬᱬ᭒

"I love you, *Laial.*"

Ralan squeezed his daughter tight, his soul complete at the feel of her arms around his neck. At six, Eri would no doubt outgrow such hugs before long. He wouldn't use his gift of foresight to verify, though he could. Heartbreak, he well knew, didn't need a preview. He tightened his hold for one more moment before settling her back on her feet. "I love you, too, Eri. Always."

"I know." She giggled before running to the door, intent on finding her new friend, Iren, the son of Arlyn's magic teacher. And since Eri shared Ralan's gift of foresight, she probably *did* know.

Ralan turned to the mirror but hesitated to activate the communication spell that would connect him to the palace. Though he'd searched through the countless strands of possibility, he could find no good future where he remained at odds with his father. He had no real reason to delay. Ralan rarely looked at possible futures relating to himself—that way led to madness—so it wasn't because he knew the meeting would go badly. Perhaps it was a matter of pride. For over three hundred years, he'd avoided all thoughts of his father. He'd sworn to never return to Moranaia, but when Eri had grown ill, unable to pull in energy on Earth, he'd broken that vow. To reconcile with his father seemed almost like a betrayal of his resolve.

Just as his fingers were about to touch the edge of the mirror, Ralan felt Lyr's presence at the edge of his shields. His hand dropped to his side as he opened the line of mental communication. *"Yes?"*

"I need you to come to my study. Teyark is here."

"Teyark?" His confusion was reflected in the pane before him. *"My brother? Did you send for him?"*

"You know I wouldn't do so without talking to you. Besides, I have enough to deal with without another prince in the mix."

Both eagerness and nerves twisted through him. Though Teyark was the only warrior of all Ralan's siblings, he was also the kindest. Growing up, his brother had often taken the time to listen to Ralan's woes, though Teyark was almost five hundred years older. Ralan's greatest regret was not confiding in his brother after the argument with their father. Would his brother be resentful about that? He worried over the question for the entire walk to Lyr's study.

It shouldn't have been a surprise, but Ralan still stopped short when he saw the number of people in the room. In addition to Lyr and Teyark, there were five guards in full armor and another male dressed in a simple but well-made tunic and pants. The usually airy room felt stuffy, and Ralan wondered how Teyark's guards could stand to keep their helmets on. He hoped Lyr had a mage nearby who could renew the cooling spell on the room.

With no sign of anger, Teyark strode forward to greet him. "Brother, I am pleased beyond telling to see you."

"And I you," Ralan answered, though he was startled by his brother's lapse in courtesy in leaving his companion without introduction.

Teyark followed his gaze back to his companion, and he gestured the other man forward with a smile. "Beloved, come meet my brother, Moranai Elaiteriorn i Ralantayan Moreln nai Moranaia. Ralan, this is Moranai Mierorn i Corath Moreln se Teyark nai Moranaia."

Despite his time away, Ralan picked through the title for the relevant information with ease. His heart lifted at the revelation. "You found your soulbonded. Congratulations!"

Teyark's eyebrow raised. "You seem surprised. Was I not supposed to?"

"I looked once a few centuries ago, but I didn't see a future then where you found him. Something must have changed to open up the possibility." Ralan grinned. "Well met, new brother. Please call me Ralan."

The other's face lightened with pleasure beneath his short, blonde hair. "As you must call me Corath. It brings me much joy to meet the brother so long mourned by my beloved."

"Teyark—" Ralan began.

His brother held up his hand and shook his head. "We can speak of it later, in private, though I will say that I'm not angry. I have come to urge you to return. Father announced your new status as heir, and the nobles at court are growing nervous at your absence."

"It's not right, me being heir. Even knowing what the future holds, I cannot be happy about taking your rightful place." Based on a prophecy by Ralan's aunt, the king had long ago decreed that the first to have a child with an outworlder would be his heir. Now that Ralan was using his talents once more, he could see why his aunt had made such an odd declaration, but it wasn't easy. "It feels biased to base this decision on who can have a child."

"That's what's bothering you?" Teyark laughed. "I've met women here and there that I fancied well enough in my thirteen hundred years. If I'd cared about being king, I could have looked for an outworld woman before you were even born."

The tension eased from Ralan's body as he considered his brother's words. If Teyark had thought this through and made his choice, then Ralan could release some of the guilt.

"Regardless, I cannot return right now." He glanced at the guards before meeting his brother's eyes once more. "It's a matter of state. I would speak with you without your *loreln*."

The bodyguard closest to Teyark, likely the leader, removed his helmet and stepped forward as if to protest but halted at Ralan's raised eyebrow. Though the guard scowled, he gestured to the others and led them out the side entrance. Lyr's study, an oval-shaped room on the edge of the estate, was lined with floor-length windows. Even though the estate was well protected, the royal bodyguards surrounded the exterior, backs to the room. Ralan had forgotten how seriously the *loreln* took their jobs.

He led the others to the seats situated beneath skylights in the center of the room and waited for them to get settled. It was finally time to reveal a little of what he'd seen. "The Sidhe are in trouble. If we don't help them, we're all doomed."

4

oomed?

D The air left Lyr's chest in a rush. When the hell had they gone from a small but serious problem to doomed? For a solid month, they'd discussed possible solutions to the energy poisoning, and not once had Ralan suggested something so dire. "By all the gods of Arneen, why are you just now telling me this?"

The seer shrugged, his expression unconcerned. "Now is the right time."

Teyark and Corath exchanged confused glances. "I've heard nothing about any problems with the Sidhe, nor has father mentioned this," Teyark said.

The censure in the eldest prince's tone caused Lyr to tense. "Your Highness, I assure you that I have not neglected my duties to the king. Until recently, I thought this a minor issue. Poisoned energy has been trickling into the Sidhe realm for some time, but it has only just begun to cause illness or madness. I've been gathering more information and planned to send a report soon."

Corath frowned. "Our world is not closely connected to Earth, unlike theirs. I fail to see how this concerns us."

"So I thought, too, except for any diplomatic complications," Lyr said. "However, Kai reports that the Veil between worlds is becoming increasingly chaotic. Just today, a colony of the Seelie Sidhe came to request our aid."

Brow furled in concentration, Teyark listened intently to the day's events, including Kai's experience on Neor, and then turned a questioning glance on his brother. "Bold of you to offer our help without consulting Father."

"Father had no problem using my talent when it suited him, at least until my prophecy involved Kien." Ralan sat with head held high, golden eyes free of worry. "If he wishes me to be heir, then he will heed me now. This problem is closer to Moranaia than you think. I can only do my best to guide us to a favorable outcome, though so many things can change the paths. When navigating the futures, timing really is everything."

"*Miaran dae fe onai!*" The curse slipped free before Lyr could pull it back. *Iron in the heart.* Though not the best manners for such a formal meeting, the sentiment was echoed in both newcomers' eyes.

Teyark smirked. "Well said, Lord Lyr. I've no doubt my father will feel the same."

"Especially when he reads my latest report, if he hasn't already." Lyr leaned forward, lowering his voice. "Whoever is responsible for the poisoned energy may have an agent here. The late Lord Allafon, Kai's supposed father, was working with someone to eliminate this House, and Kai's brother believes the two problems are related."

Teyark's brow lifted. "*Supposed* father? What has happened here?"

"More was brewing than either my father or I knew. Kai's mother wasn't Allafon's soulbonded as he'd claimed. He murdered her in part because Kai wasn't his." It was Teyark's turn to curse, but Lyr only sighed, exhausted with it all. "For five hundred years, he plotted, and none of us suspected. Not until he trapped me, Kai, and Arlyn and tried to kill us."

Corath broke the sudden silence. "But how was he connected to poisoned energy reaching the Sidhe realms?"

"He might not have been," Lyr conceded. "But the assassin he first sent warned us to stay out of Sidhe business. The pommel of his knife was engraved with the same symbol as the one on the sword used to murder my father—Allafon's work. And Kai's brother, Morenial, believed Allafon had an off-world connection."

"It seems we have more questions than answers," Teyark said.

Lyr let out another sigh. "Indeed."

୧ଓଓ

The small fragment of iron taunted Lyr from atop the silk cloth placed carefully on his desk. It was well past the twenty-fifth hour. Teyark and Corath had adjourned to their room. Kai had finally returned from a fruitless search of the estate, and Arlyn had gone to work with her magic teacher, Selia. After spending several hours making simple mistakes on the same batch of paperwork, Lyr had given up on productivity and switched to his newest obsession. Iron conversion.

Arlyn had had been the first to discover the trick and was on her way to mastering it. Like many of his kind, Lyr was allergic to the metal, and his daughter shared a milder form of the allergy. The secret seemed to be related to iron's magnetism—the polarity in the iron worked against their energy, repelling it or sometimes draining it. Arlyn could push her own energy through the metal and reverse the polarity, but so far, she was the only one among them who could reliably do the trick. Lyr couldn't do it at all.

He could feel the strain on his shields just from the tiny shard on his desk. While previous attempts to replicate Arlyn's spell had left him shaken and weak, he was determined to master iron conversion. Maybe then he could move beyond what had happened. Maybe he wouldn't feel the bite of iron at his wrists every time he heard the rattle of metal against metal. Most of all, maybe he could covert the iron flakes left in the wound on his chest so Lial could finish healing it. He was tired of hiding the problem, but he couldn't bear to confess it either.

Lyr lifted a shaking hand to hover over the shard and closed his eyes before sending his energy forth. The iron repelled his power like a dam against a flood, and he struggled to keep control. Such a small fragment, yet his magic wanted to bounce away in a thousand directions. He gritted his teeth and pushed more energy toward the iron. Bit by bit, it started to give way. Sweat began to bead his brow. So close this time. Almost…

The click of the door latch penetrated his focus, and he made the mistake of looking up. His energy fractured, the rebounding streams absorbing into the shielding he'd set around his desk for that purpose. Kai stood frozen in the doorway as Lyr released a string of profanity that would have made his soldiers proud. The closest he'd ever come to success, only to be interrupted. The glare he turned on his friend could have melted the metal that had defeated him.

"I'm sorry to interrupt. What—" Kai's eyes widened at the sight of the shard. "What the hell are you doing with iron?"

Lyr took his time wrapping the fragment back up in the silk and stuffing it in the pouch, being careful not to touch the iron. Before answering, he opened the most secure drawer to his desk, the one keyed only to himself and Arlyn. When he had the pouch put away, he turned to his friend once more.

"I've been working on the conversion trick, for all the good it has done me. I think I would have had it this time but for your interruption."

"You might try putting a sign on the door, you know." Kai advanced to the edge of the shield around Lyr's desk and waited for him to remove it. "But I *am* sorry. I forgot to ask earlier if you had spoken to Selia about the security breach."

"You need to know this now, in the middle of the night?"

Kai sighed. "Not really, but I can't sleep. Something about this whole situation disturbs me."

"Yes, well, Ralan claimed that if we don't help the Sidhe, we're doomed," Lyr said wryly as he slumped back in his chair. "Perhaps you have good reason for your concern."

"He actually said *doomed?*" Kai snorted. "Drama queen."

"What?"

"Sorry. I picked that slang up from Arlyn." Kai's eyes lit with humor despite the situation. "It seems like an extreme way to phrase it."

"Perhaps, but I can't disregard a seer of his power." Lyr tapped restless fingers across the surface of his desk. "And yes, I spoke with Selia. Neither she nor young Iren sensed a thing. If there was a breach in the estate shields, Arlyn was the only one who detected it. It could be another half-blood, but if so, how did they get here? Your brother said Allafon killed the half-bloods he'd tried to send against us."

Kai's expression sobered. "The person behind Allafon's actions must be based on Earth."

"Yes," Lyr said, suddenly weary. "How and why—two words that are rarely as simple as they should be."

⁂

Meli could almost *feel* time slow and stretch. Hours, days, years—she had no idea how long they had wandered the endless mists. Rolling gray fog surrounded them, even beneath their feet, though it held as firm as ground. Sometimes, they encountered small springs of pure water bubbling up from seemingly nowhere, but it was impossible to use them to gauge how far they might have traveled or where they had been. Strands of color floated through the gray here and there, and on some instinct, she'd followed the emerald green line that matched the haunted eyes from her dream.

But how long should she trust instinct before using the emergency beacon in her necklace? Half of their food was already gone, and one of the attendants, Berris, had started to look a little wild-eyed at the constant monotony. The other two seemed withdrawn, barely speaking to the rest of the group, and the ambassador…well, she appeared as annoyed as always.

Gods, what a fool's mission. Meli had no idea what she was doing.

For all she knew, the emerald strand led to nothing. And yet she felt drawn in a way she had only experienced in dreams. As though another part of herself lingered somewhere ahead, just waiting for her to claim it. Despite the ambassador's hostility and the furtive glances of the attendants, Meli followed that thread of feeling and prayed devoutly that it was the correct one.

"You realize that if you get me killed my family will seek redress from yours?"

Meli flinched at the sound of the elder's voice, cold with fury, and met her gaze. "I should think they would seek such from the king, since he ordered this madness."

"Perhaps." A hint of something like jealousy passed across the ambassador's face. "But my family will hold you to blame. How much longer do we have in this accursed place?"

With a shrug, Meli faced forward. The ambassador had threatened her often enough that she no longer cared what the other woman thought. Meli had asked for none of this, and she

refused to be castigated for their king's command. All that mattered now was following that green strand. "Until we arrive."

Though subtle at first, the shifting mists began to roll around
them with increasing intensity. Other strands began to swirl and
snarl around the green one, causing Meli to shift directions. Her
feet and legs ached with each endless step. Gods, how long had
passed? The way had grown harsher, the mists growing thick
around them and making each movement seem tougher. It
could have been a turn of the moon or millennia.

The withdrawn attendants began to glance around uncer-
tainly. The third hugged herself, rubbing her arms in a rhythmic,
almost frantic pattern. Meli no longer acknowledged the ambassador. She could feel the elder's presence through the spell on
her necklace. She didn't need to see the living reminder of the
pressure she faced.

ᴄᴏ⨀ᴏ

A cry of pain ripped Lyr from his troubled sleep. Gasping for
air, he jerked upright and clawed at his chest in search of the
wound. The dull ache of the healing flesh added to his panic
before memory returned. Shaky, he dropped his head to his
knees and tried to slow his breathing. Some nights, it was the
iron biting into his wrists and sapping his energy. Other times,
he relived the pain of his mother's near-death. Then, like tonight, he envisioned the iron dagger descending, only to glance
off his necklace and cut through his flesh.

The nights after he worked on the conversion spell were
usually the worst. This time, though, the dream had been different. Before the knife vision, Lyr had wandered through the
mists of the Veil, completely lost. Though he didn't possess the

gift of the guide himself, he'd traveled through often enough with Kai to learn now to find the path to anywhere he needed to go. But in the dream, the mists had writhed around him, the gray pushing and pulling him until he had no sense of time or place. Just as that panic filled him, the scene had cut to the small room where Allafon had kept them captive, the iron blade already descending.

His long hair clung to his sweat-drenched chest and back as he shifted off the bed and stumbled to the refreshing room. A pull of a plug, and water trickled over his head and down his body. Thank the gods he'd had a shower created after discovering them on his visits to Earth. He kept the stream cool like the mountain falls on an early summer day, though the spell that purified the water could have warmed it as well. With the stone stall carved to resemble a cliff face, he could almost imagine himself outside.

Lyr dried himself with a simple spell, one even non-mages could learn. He could have cleansed himself the same way, but it wouldn't have been as satisfying. The cool water usually soothed his mind and emotions, bringing him some peace, though it failed to erase his troubled thoughts this time. Besides the ache of his wound, the clinging mists wouldn't leave him. Now that his panic had faded, he thought about the dream, and...he'd swear it had felt like someone had traveled with him—someone who felt like Aimee, the soulbonded he'd lost years before.

He hadn't dreamed of his bonded in some time. Why now?

After pulling on a lounging robe, he padded over to the balcony that overlooked the massive trunk of Eradisel, one of the nine sacred trees of the nine gods of Arneen, in this case Dorenal, Goddess of the Veil. It was his right and privilege, as guardian of the tree, to consult with her whenever needed. In the two decades he'd been Myern of the estate, Lyr had become almost friends with the sacred tree, an honor he tried never to abuse. Perhaps she would know the meaning of his dream.

He placed his hand on the smooth trunk. Eradisel's energy pulsed around him, and he opened his mind to her gentle voice. *"What pains you this night, young one?"*

At almost five hundred and fifty years old, Lyr smiled to be called such. *"Besides the usual nightmares, I dreamed of the Veil. It was puzzling."*

Her energy stilled in the equivalent of a sigh. *"You know I cannot share the secrets of the Veil with you."*

"I do know. It's just…I thought I sensed Aimee, dead for years now."

"Dreams can rarely be trusted, though they are the closest you mortals come to living the Veil." A sense of peace flowed through him through their link, though her next words hurt. *"I can only say that Aimee Moore is not traveling through the mists of any time or place. You will never find her in the Veil."*

5

"Relax into the pose and clear your mind of all thought."

Sitting on a mat in the specially-shielded training room, Arlyn allowed her muscles to go soft and attempted to follow her teacher's instructions. The hour was early, a few marks until breakfast. The cold of the stone beneath her thin cloth cushion seeped into her body, numbing her lower limbs, but it did nothing for her turbulent thoughts. How was she supposed to clear her mind with everything that was going on? With a sigh, she tried her hardest, locking up each thought as it began to intrude.

"I want you to search your mind for the spell that connects you to the estate," Selia said. "Examine it and see if you can figure out what portion is the estate shielding."

Arlyn cracked one eye open to catch a glimpse of her teacher's face. "Do mages seriously do this every time they use magic?"

Selia chuckled. "Of course not. After a century or two, these things become natural."

"Right."

Though Arlyn had begun to settle into life on Moranaia, she still had difficulty thinking of time in such a broad sense. She'd known from an early age that her father was elven, but she hadn't considered what that might mean for her own lifespan. How long would it take to get used to the casual mention of centuries? According to the healer, her body used magical energy to regenerate the same as full-blooded elves, so she supposed she would have more than enough time to find out.

Arlyn scrunched both eyes closed and tried again to shove aside her stray thoughts. But dammit, the two other times she'd used her magic had been an accident. She hadn't had to *know* how to teleport Kai to safety or how to convert iron. She'd willed those things to happen...and they had. Over the last month, Selia had worked with her on pulling in and grounding energy as well as basic shielding. Now she worried so much about using her magic with intent that it was tough to remember any of her lessons.

With her hands shoved in her lap to hide their trembling, Arlyn felt for the spell that gave her access to their home. With it came a mental map of the estate, locations of all guardians on duty, and access to the magical shielding that protected the area from attack. Since the murder attempts on Kai and Allafon's betrayal the month before, her father had added spells designed to detect and alert them of anyone who didn't belong on the estate.

"I have it," Arlyn said.

"Good. Now take my hands."

Arlyn reached for her teacher, sitting on another mat in front of her. As she had learned to do over the past month, she opened her mind to Selia, just enough to form a magical connection and speak telepathically. Though the other woman wasn't keyed to the protection spell and couldn't alter it, she could watch and guide Arlyn.

"I want you to examine the shield. See if you can find some hole or anything that seems wrong. If you do, then we'll fix it."

৵৩৫

Mornings, when Lyr could manage it, were for combat training. Though his wound still pained him, he'd returned to sword work the week before. Sometimes he sparred with Kai or trained Arlyn, but after nights like the one prior, he trained alone. He could find no other catharsis like the dance of body and blade. After all the loss, it was the only time he felt complete.

Lyr shifted through the positions over and over. His magic flowed to augment his speed and senses until he could feel the whisper of the air and the movement of the grass on the practice field. As he thrust and parried, he could pretend that he fought the jumbled emotions inside him. All his anger and all his fear stood before his whirling blade, but like the wind, they evaded him. There would be no release once he stopped.

After half a mark, Lyr sheathed his blade and crossed to the fountain, a series of stone basins connected to a small spring at the edge of the field. He dunked a cloth in the lowest basin and wiped the sweat from his face before dipping a cup into the upper portion. He drank deep and then poured another cupful over his head. Though they were fast approaching early autumn, the heat still clung to the skin. The only time worse than the season of Toren for practicing was Pioren, the month or two of ice that fell before the spring. Even *he* tended to stay inside then.

Lyr stilled in surprise at the sight of Teyark approaching. Had the prince actually come to train? Of the four royal children, he was the only one who possessed combat magic similar to Lyr's, but the prince was more than experienced enough not to have to practice when he was away from home. And he hadn't been formally presented to the household, so most potential partners would avoid him out of courtesy.

Teyark smiled as he reached Lyr. "Good morn to you."

Had it been Kai greeting him, Lyr would have given a wry retort on the true quality of the morning, but he only smiled in return. "And to you, Prince Teyark."

"I was hoping you'd be out here." Teyark's gaze scanned the practice field and the handful of warriors training. "I don't see anyone else with our type of magic. I've been longing for a true challenge."

Lyr nodded, although his limbs were heavy with exhaustion and his barely healed wound burned from his first practice. There was no graceful way to dodge the sparring session without revealing his weakness. Teyark probably wouldn't hold it against him, but...Lyr had already failed once in his role as Myern. He refused to falter again.

As they proceeded to the center of the field, he wanted to curse. Training with someone as powerful as the prince was a rare opportunity, and Lyr couldn't even enjoy it in his current state. Even better, the others on the field stopped their own training to watch. Just what he needed—an audience.

Resigned, he set the spell to protect against serious injury and fell into position. His wound burned harder as he let his combat magic flow through his body unhindered. Well, *almost* unhindered. The iron flakes within the half-healed slash pulsed against his power, but he forced the discomfort from his mind. The dance of blade eclipsed all thought.

Teyark paused for a moment before springing into action, his first attack direct. Each possible counter flickered through Lyr's mind, but he was long accustomed to processing such information. He parried low and then danced to the side, cutting upward toward the other's belly. He was not surprised to find his blade parried at once, the return attack faster than the eye could process.

Back and forth they flowed across the field, neither able to gain a true advantage over the other. Still, if not for the protection spell, Lyr knew he would have quite a few cuts while the prince would have none. Teyark had trained for a good eight hundred years longer, and his power was intense.

Then Lyr faltered.

His breath hissed out in surprise as his power stuttered, then dispelled. Only training saved him from serious injury, protection spell or no. Lyr countered the next swing out of reflex even as his muscles began to shake. His free hand darted up to clutch at the burning wound on his chest, and he stumbled through a few more moves before Teyark motioned for a halt.

The prince's brow furrowed. "Lyr?"

"A moment," Lyr gasped out.

Fumbling, he sheathed his sword and bent at the waist, hands on his knees, until he could catch his breath. Gods, Lyr hoped the prince couldn't see how his whole body trembled. Bile rose up his throat, and he straightened in a vain attempt to ease the feeling. But no position could change the sick shame of yet another failure.

"I...I fear I am not as recovered as I'd thought."

Teyark relaxed, but a hint of regret flickered through his eyes. "I should have considered your recent injury."

"It was my own error." Lyr forced a small smile to his lips. "You found me here training, after all."

A movement behind Teyark caught Lyr's attention, and he blinked at the sight of Eri skipping along the trail that bordered the training field. A grin lit her face as she met his gaze. What was she doing out here? Her father, Ralan, had warned her not to approach the field during training hours unless he was with her. A six-year-old had no business playing near sparring soldiers. Yet here she was, skipping through the break in the stone fence and past a trio of shocked warriors.

"You might want to duck now," she sang into Lyr's head, her mind meeting his without seeking consent.

⁂

Arlyn's breath caught at the complex beauty of the estate's protection spell. Though she'd expected the sacred tree to provide the energy for it, the source seemed to be a spring so deep underground that she never would have known about it without searching. From there, the magic was built, layer woven deftly into layer. The techniques used to create such a thing were so far beyond her rudimentary skills that she barely understood a fraction of what she saw.

The only thing Arlyn truly recognized was her magical "key." Meshed into the inside layer, it was connected to every location and every person on the estate. She cast her senses outward to search every part of the spell but found nothing amiss. As best she could tell with her limited training, the protections hadn't been breached. The strange disturbance she'd felt yesterday must not have affected them. Perhaps she'd imagined it after all?

Arlyn began to pull her essence back into her own body as Selia had taught her. Just before she disconnected from the estate's shields, a current of energy washed over her. She shivered at the odd, cold sensation as she searched for the source of the disturbance—only to find it wasn't from the shield set to detect those who didn't belong. It had nothing to do with the protection spell at all.

Like a beacon, the spark of foreign energy glowed against her senses for a heartbeat longer before fading away. But Arlyn knew the flavor of it.

It felt like Earth.

❦

In contrast to her cheerful face, Eri's words were delivered with such force that Lyr instinctively obeyed. As he dropped to the ground, he caught a glimpse of Teyark doing the same. And just in time. The sluggish energy that Lyr had managed to gather after his magic's collapse fragmented away again just as a thud sounded overhead. He looked up to see an iron dagger imbedded in the tree behind him.

"*Clechtan*," Lyr muttered, trying to gather more energy but failing in the presence of so much iron.

Lyr pulled himself to a crouch, his boot dagger already in hand, as his soldier's shouts filled the training field. He slipped his sword from its sheath and scanned the clearing for signs of his attacker. Warriors rushed the area with blades drawn, but there was no sign of an intruder. No one out of place except for Eri, who skipped back toward the stone wall as though she didn't have a care.

"What is she doing?" Teyark muttered, his own weapons in hand.

"I'll warn her," Lyr said aloud. Then he tuned his mind to hers. *"Eri! Seek cover."*

The girl tossed a glance over her shoulder, and a hint of power sparked in her eyes. *"No need."*

Lyr's hand tightened on the hilt of his sword. She was right. Teyark's *loreln* circled the area, casting spells of revealing, but no hint of the attacker appeared. One glance at the crest engraved in the hilt of the dagger confirmed his worst fears. Whoever had attacked Kai and then disappeared over a month before was back. And this time, they couldn't have been sent by Allafon.

May iron pierce his rotten soul. Lyr tried to pull in more power to do his own search but hissed out a breath at the flare of pain in his chest. "*Miaran*," he cursed softly.

Teyark studied Lyr. "Did you see something?"

"Only my own weakness." Eri caught Lyr's gaze from where she'd settled on the low stone wall. Her expression was calm, a smile now tilting her lips. "Ralan gave no warning of any possible attack. How did she know there was a problem? My own wards detected no breach."

"She's Ralan's child, for certain." The prince gave a mock grimace. "He used to do the same sort of thing when he was young no matter how often our great-aunt scolded him for using his sight carelessly. Good to see it was merely punishment delayed."

Despite the situation, Lyr smiled. "Indeed."

6

Lyr had his servants, young elves earning coin as they
trained their respective gifts, bring an early luncheon to
the garden dining room. His stomach ached with tension, making food seem unappealing, but he knew that eating
would help restore some of the energy the iron had stripped
away. Besides, it was the most practical place to discuss the latest
attack.

Lyr had included not just his family in the meeting but also
each of his houseguests. To his right sat Arlyn and to his left
Kai. Along his daughter's side of the table were Selia, her son
Iren, and Eri. Teyark, followed by Corath, had chosen the seat
by Kai, and Ralan took the last place across from his daughter.
Lyr had kept his eyes on his plate as his mother settled into her
seat at the end of the table. His emotions were jumbled enough
without watching her struggle.

The captain of the *loreln* frowned at Lyr from his place outside the window. Whether it was from being forbidden entry once more or from their highly informal seating arrangement, he neither knew nor cared. In a court setting—indeed, in most settings—the princes would have been afforded the highest honor. Here, they sat as friends. Lyr expected such casual behavior from Ralan, but Teyark had surprised him by insisting on informality as well. They passed the trays of bread, cheese, and water fowl with an easy disregard of place.

Lyr frowned at the relative calm of the room, a sad sign of how often attacks had occurred. Perhaps he was the only one whose muscles knotted with tension. But then, they hadn't been searching for almost thirty years for the source of that crest. It had been on the pommel of the sword sticking out of his father's back and the dagger used on Kai. And now a third knife with the same. How long was this going to haunt him? Lyr forced each bite of food around the lump in his throat and waited until the others were near to finishing their meal.

"Forgive me for my haste," Lyr began. Accustomed to the speed of humans, Arlyn rolled her eyes at him and grinned. He returned a brief smile before glancing around the table. "But I can no longer delay discussing this attack."

Kai shook his head. "There isn't much to discuss. The only clue we have is the dagger."

"Actually, bonded, that isn't quite true. I haven't had a chance to tell you." Arlyn exchanged a look with her teacher. "Selia was guiding me through an exercise when the attack happened. As I examined the shields looking for the strange breach I thought I'd felt, I sensed something else. Whoever it is can somehow cloak themselves, but…once that cloak is removed, I can detect them."

Teyark lowered the bread in his hand and gave her a skeptical look. "Yet no one else felt their energy?"

"It's like a beacon. Maybe it's supposed to catch the attention of humans or other half-bloods," Arlyn said.

Lyr's heart gave a hard thump at her words. Would she be in danger now? "Do you think they know you're here and able to sense it?"

"You'd have to ask *them* that," she answered with a shrug.

Selia's brow furrowed as she met Lyr's eyes. "It was very…human, the spell. I watched how it affected Arlyn, and it seemed to identify that part of her. However, the hint of illusion I caught reminded me greatly of my own training in illusions. One of our kind is involved—possibly even a Moranaian."

Eri, who'd been whispering to Iren between bites of food, looked up and laughed. "The mystery shouldn't take much longer to solve."

"Is that so?"

"Sure, less than a month. Practically nothing."

Ralan's attention snapped to Eri, his brows lowering. Even those who knew of Eri's abilities as a seer paused to stare, though she seemed unconcerned. All at once, the feeling of being guided grew within Lyr along with anger. If the gods had taken enough interest in him to bring two seers to his table, then why couldn't the events of the last few months have been stopped? It wasn't Ralan or Eri's fault—Lyr *knew* it wasn't. But he couldn't hold back the rage that shook his body.

"I tire of this," Lyr snapped. "Your warning today was moments from being too late, and the next might not come at all. Just tell me what you know."

Ralan's chair scraped across the floor as he stood. "I'll not have you intimidate or pressure my daughter."

"And where were you today, Ralan? For a seer of some renown, you have done little but entangle us in more problems," Lyr said, turning his glare on the prince.

"I use my talents at no one's command." Ralan leaned forward, hands gripping the edge of the table. "But if you must know, I try not to examine the futures of those closest to me. Unless a vision comes to me, as did with the Neoran issue, then I do not look. What would you do if we weren't here?"

"Enough!" Lynia snapped, her narrow-eyed gaze flicking between the two. "We do not need more discord here, at this table or in this house."

Even after five hundred years, Lyr winced at his mother's rebuke. But she was right. What was wrong with him? He'd been friends with Ralan for centuries and never expected him to share prophecies before. "Forgive me, Ralan. This situation has me on edge."

The prince gave a nod and eased back into his seat, but a glint of anger still hardened his eyes. "Likewise."

Suddenly weary, Lyr forced himself to sit tall. They needed him to stay strong. To lead. And not just the people at this table—everyone under his dominion. All else had to be shoved aside. With that thought in mind, he addressed Selia. "Do you believe you could add some kind of ward to detect the magic Arlyn sensed?"

Selia gave a considering frown. "Perhaps. I'll work with her on the problem later today."

"Thank you," Lyr said. "Until then, I bid you all to be careful."

Arlyn leaned forward. "I could say the same to you. You haven't been…"

Her voice trailed off, and she bit her bottom lip. Was that worry in her eyes? His shoulders went taut. Surely, she hadn't guessed how close to the edge he was. "What is it?" Lyr asked softly.

Arlyn's lips parted, but after a quick glance around the table, she shook her head. "Just watch out for danger. Okay?"

◈◈◈

The mist flowed thick around Meli's ankles, pulling at her until each step felt like an eternity. No longer merely chaotic, the fog coiled around them like a physical force. Had the spell in her necklace not kept them all together, the others would have been lost long ago. She fought against the mist as best she could, ever following the emerald green strand.

Beside her, Pol fidgeted. He crossed his arms. Then uncrossed them. He tilted his head back to stare at the all-encompassing mists. Then turned his gaze to Meli. Every movement caught her eye, distracting her. By Freyr, was he *bored?*

Finally, he spoke. "Could you hurry this up, please? We are almost out of food."

Meli froze. She had to take a few deep breaths before she could face him without shouting. But despite his harried words, a smile lit his face. "I'm sorry if I've ruined your plans," she

* **63** *

snapped. "If I had the first clue how, I assure you we would have long ago arrived. I am not a mistwalker."

"No, you're a diviner." He felt around the pockets in his tunic before pulling out an ancient-looking leather bag. "Would you like some runes to cast?"

"You are mistaken," Meli answered, her anger fading into bewilderment. She barely glanced at the bag, not wanting to indicate acceptance of the offered pouch by her actions. This was the first time he or the other attendants had spoken to her, and she was wary of his sudden interest. "I am even less a seer than I am a mistwalker."

Couldn't he see that she was nothing? She'd failed the magic tests twice—if there'd been a skill to find, the mages would have discovered it already. It was a new level of cruelty for him to pretend otherwise.

His laughter echoed through the rolling mists until the sound seemed to surround them. "Who said you were a seer? You're a diviner of things. Finder of the lost. Revealer of paths. I suppose it's a skill not often tested for or trained among the Ljósálfar. Seems as clear as the crystals on your spires to me."

Meli shook her head in confusion. He spoke as though he were not one of her people. While it was true she didn't recognize him, she couldn't imagine that the king would send an outsider on this trip. But...an outsider wouldn't know about her disgrace. Perhaps he hadn't meant to taunt her.

She glanced at the ambassador, but the elder didn't seem surprised by Pol's words. "Who are you?" Meli asked. "If you are not one of us, why are you here?"

"The Old One thought it wise to have an outside opinion. I traveled from the land of the Dökkálfar to accompany you at her request."

One of the dark elves? With pale skin and red hair, he didn't look the part. The Dökkálfar were almost universally dark in complexion—skin, hair, eyes—with few variations. In fact, she would have welcomed one of her swarthy kindred. She could never understand why humans equated the reliable and resourceful dark elves with evil. They were stoic and unconcerned with realms beyond their own, but they rarely sought to do harm.

Though tempted, Meli decided not to challenge his claim. If one of them was not who they claimed, well…the three attendants were the ambassador's problem. Meli's purpose was to find the land of Moranai and nothing more. "Sorry, Pol of the Dökkálfar, but I know nothing of divining."

He thrust the bag toward her. "You will once you take these runes."

"I thank you, but I cannot—"

"Do you want to be stuck here forever? Take them and get us out of these damn mists. This journey has lost all sense of fun."

Sense of fun? Though she doubted, Meli found herself reaching for the bag. Still warm from his hand, the smooth leather pouch was heavier than she expected. She untied the strings and poured the stones into her palm. Nine flat, oval river stones, eerily similar in all but the carvings. But the designs weren't typical for runes. Glowing lines swirled on each side, never settling into any discernable pattern.

Her eyes shot back to his face. "What...?"

"Just cast them. You'll see."

Meli crossed to their supply cart, the only place with a flat enough surface. Although they walked on solid-seeming ground, she doubted it was a good idea to cast the stones on the rolling gray nothingness beneath their feet. She cleared a spot on the cart, and then after one more hesitant glance at the others, she shook and dropped the runes. The clatter of stone hitting wood resounded, making Berris jump and moan. But Meli had no time to spare for the crazed elf. Her attention was trapped on the flare of light spearing upward from the stones.

After a moment, the light settled into glowing shapes unlike any runes Meli had ever seen. They'd landed in a rough circle with one rune in the middle, and each stone bore a swirled line in differing shades. Only the green rune on the center stone had anything in common with the emerald line she followed through the mists. But other than the matching color, the lines meant nothing, and frustration clawed through her.

Pol was clearly mistaken, Meli scoffed to herself. Then the symbols on each rune began to weave into something else entirely. She felt her mind dodging through and around the colored strands of energy that permeated the Veil. They were meaningless to her, a power she could only follow but not touch, but the magic of the runes traced the length of the emerald path.

When the trail locked in her mind's eye, Meli studied it, careful to memorize every facet in case the vision faded. Then she tried to release the magic—but it refused to let her go. She spun, her feet moving along the path of their own volition. What was happening? Why couldn't she stop herself?

Hard fingers bit into her shoulders, pulling her to a stop. "Control it," Pol said in a commanding tone.

With his words, the runes' hold snapped, and Meli sucked in a breath. "I'm sorry."

"You'll learn," Pol stated, shrugging.

Trembling, Meli gathered the runes. The set patterns had returned to ever-swirling lines, and the light had faded. She touched the surface with a hesitant finger and found only smooth stone. Whatever magic had almost swept her up had been imbued within the rocks themselves, not carved. Her hand hovered for a moment before she scooped the runes carefully into their pouch. They were too far beyond her knowledge for comfort.

Meli pulled the drawstring closed and held the bag out to Pol. "Thank you for loaning me such unique rune stones."

His smile lit his golden eyes until they seemed to dance. "I didn't loan them to you, little elf. They have always been yours."

With the path still glowing in her mind, Meli decided not to waste time arguing. She tucked the pouch into a compartment on her belt and gestured for the others to follow. For once, she knew exactly where to go.

ତ⊙ଓ

Lyr strode down his favorite path through the woods, his footsteps guided more by habit than intent.

It was beyond foolish to take his daily walk with another assassin on the loose. At the least, he shouldn't have ducked the bodyguards who trailed him every time he left the estate—the same three who'd been unable to detect or deflect the danger just hours before. But for the moment, Lyr didn't care, a thought that crept in more every day. Maybe if he walked fast enough, he could outmaneuver his frustration and discontent.

His hands curled into fists at the helpless feeling that washed through him, the same sick emotion that had plagued him for nearly thirty years. He kept telling himself that it would pass. After five hundred and forty-nine years of life, he knew that all things shifted and changed, even among the slow-paced elves. Yet here he was, his father's murder still unsolved, the person behind their recent troubles unknown, and his soulbonded forever lost to the world. Despite his training and his power, he could fix nothing.

And now he had to worry about the Neorans.

Lyr was halfway to the portal when the alarm set into the estate shielding resounded through his mind. Muscles tensing, he paused to examine the spell. Five people had come through the gate unauthorized, and not guided by someone connected to Braelyn. The guides who escorted travelers possessed medallions to let their charges through, so it had to be a true incursion.

He only wore his boot knife, but time was more of the essence than his safety. *Clechtan,* but he was a warrior in his prime. These were his lands, and he knew them better than any intruder could. He didn't need bodyguards with him just to check the gate. It would only take a few moments to creep close, and the land guards shouldn't be too far away.

Lyr brought his own personal shields to their highest state and darted off the trail. The forest here had minimal undergrowth, much of the excess cleared to prevent fire, so remaining undetected would take some caution. Still, he knew the best routes. He wove through the trees as he flung his senses wide, but he detected only the intruders and the guards perched in the trees surrounding the portal area. The *Tayianeln* were taking no chances after their previous failures and had rushed extra guards to the portal. Though they awaited his command, they would not be caught unprepared again.

Lyr slipped behind a log bench designed to look like a natural part of the forest. It was the largest and most distant of the three scattered around the clearing near the portal, perfect for crouching behind. Unsure if the interlopers would have the kind of magic capable of detecting him, he sent out several false energy signatures around the edges of the clearing. Finally satisfied, he looked up to examine the newcomers.

Four females and a male. An older elf in long robes stood closest to his hiding place, and the two females nearest her seemed to be servants of some kind. His gaze moved to the flame-haired male, and Lyr's breath caught. Power swirled around the newcomer, but it was unlike anything Lyr had seen before. Not quite like Eradisel, but...

Ralan's voice broke into his mind without warning or apology. *"Do not attack, and stay wary of the male. He is not what he seems."*

Lyr's eyes narrowed on the group. The elder's white robes were richly embroidered. More elaborate than the others in her group. And although the male's power was undeniable, none of them were armed beyond ceremonial knives. More diplomats? There was one more who could have been some type of guide. She stood apart from the others, and tension hitched her delicate shoulders so high he could see it from across the clearing.

The older one barked a single word Lyr didn't recognize, and the slender woman pivoted, her long robes swirling around her ankles. The cloth was of good quality, but the robes were simpler than the elder's and cinched by a leather belt. She took a step forward, and a pendant on a thin chain glinted between her breasts. Was the amulet mere decoration, or was it some kind of weapon?

Perhaps he'd been reckless to leave the estate without his sword after all. Lyr eased forward, his focus on the metallic glimmer. She shifted again, falling into shadow, and the source of the flash came clear. A large crystal encased in silver mesh. If this female was an assassin, he'd eat moss off the back of the bench.

Then she spoke, and his attention darted back to her face. Though she hadn't noticed him, he fell into her light blue eyes. A shudder went through his whole body.

They had never met, but he knew her.

Lyr's hands gripped the bark of the log bench until lichen crumbled beneath his fingers. It was not possible. Aimee had died four Earth years before, and his daughter had witnessed it. Arlyn wouldn't have mistaken her own mother's death. Besides, the woman before him had pale blond hair, so unlike the vibrant red Arlyn had inherited from her mother. He could see that they weren't the same with his own eyes, yet he could feel the connection between their souls.

It matched the one he'd shared but never completed with Aimee. As much as this stranger's energy differed, her spirit was the same.

This woman was his *aenac*—his soulbonded.

Impossible.

He had never heard of an elf finding another soulbonded after losing the first. Since the souls of bonded pairs connected, the death of one would take a bit of the person left behind, leaving a piece that could never reconnect. Still, his soul sang for the female across the clearing. No matter how much he tried to deny it.

Suddenly, he understood how Kai had panicked and given Arlyn the binding necklace on their first meeting. Lyr wanted to run forward and do the same before he lost yet another soulbonded, and it took all his willpower to resist. Even if the entire group was set to kill him, they were *not* walking back through the portal. Not until he'd spoken to her.

With a mental command to the *Tayianeln* hiding above him in the trees, Lyr prepared to reveal his presence. Feeling Kai's approach, he established a quick connection between them. *"Do not attack. Stand down and let me handle this. One of these women feels like Aimee."*

7

"**G**irl!"

Meli spun so fast that she almost tripped on her own robes. Beyond tired of the ambassador's attitude, her eyes narrowed on the elder. Was this hostility born of some political slight or because of the rumors about Meli's pending exile? Meli neither knew nor cared the reason. Her fear and nerves had been buffed away by the rolling mists, and she refused to accept continued mistreatment.

"I thank you, Ambassador Teronver, to address me by my name. Ameliar, if you've forgotten."

The elder's fists clenched, and even Berris maintained enough sense to back away. "You are nothing, girl. I will speak to you as I please. You deserve no respect after bringing us to this wilderness. Everyone knew the king was mad, and this proves it."

Not that we needed this as evidence, Meli snickered to herself. "And how, exactly, do you know this isn't our destination?"

"You think we could find aid from such a place? I doubt any from this savage land could manage more than the great mages of Alfheim." Expression pinched, Teronver gestured at the empty clearing. "Not a building in sight. I demand you take us home."

Meli shook her head, prepared to argue, but was interrupted by Pol's soft laugh. Following his gaze, her breath caught. A male elf stood alone at the far end of the clearing. She barely registered his dark brown hair and handsome face. She was too caught up in his eyes. The same shape and color as the ones that had haunted her dreams for as long as she could remember. Even when the ambassador grasped her arm, she could not look away.

It was him.

Teronver's fingernails bit into Meli's arm, but her focus didn't stray from the newcomer. He advanced with slow, fluid steps, his stance similar to the warriors who had practiced in the fields near her home. She had little doubt that he was prepared to fight if they proved hostile, and her chest tightened with the first hint of fear she'd had since stepping through the gate. Berris was the closest they had to a warrior, and she was rocking from side to side behind the ambassador. Wonderful.

Despite Teronver's position at the head of their group, the stranger stopped before Meli and bowed slightly. *"Mor gher Ayanel."*

She shivered at the smooth timbre of his voice. She could swear she'd heard it in her dreams, but she had no idea what he'd said. "I beg your pardon, but I do not understand."

His brow scrunched into a frown, and he spoke again, the cadence of his words a little different. At the helpless shake of her head, he tried several more times, seeming to be searching for a language she understood. None of her group had considered that these people wouldn't speak their language. A foolish oversight.

"I need to speak to Freyr about your isolation," Pol muttered as much to himself as to her. "This shouldn't hurt. Much."

"What—"

Without warning, Pol raised both arms, his palms pointed at each of them. The sudden burst of power caught her by surprise, but the stunned expression of the stranger eclipsed her own. Just before darkness consumed her, she saw his face tighten with pain. Then she knew nothing.

ॐ

Lyr groaned as awareness returned. His muddled brain tried to process why a stick was digging into his back and who was yelling above him. Then he remembered the blast of energy from the flame-haired male, and his eyes shot open to greet the additional agony of light. A shift from above provided shadow, blessed relief, until he realized it was Arlyn standing over him with an arrow nocked in her bow.

When had she arrived? He blinked against the ache in his head and rolled to his feet.

The land guards ringed him and Arlyn, Kai at the forefront. Now that Lyr's head was beginning to clear, he could tell that his friend had merely been raising his voice. The foreign mage, on the other hand, bent over laughing as the others in his group stared in obvious confusion. Lyr rubbed at his temples and pushed past Kai.

When the man finally straightened, his eyes still twinkled with humor. "Now we've found the fun."

With some surprise, Lyr realized that he understood the words. He himself knew spells to transfer language, but this was the first time he'd had one forced on him without consent. He located the woman he'd tried to speak to, but she appeared more shocked than hurt. Had Lyr's pain come from the spell being forced through his shields? The stranger had managed the feat with alarming ease. Ralan was right—the man was not at all what he seemed.

"I bid you good day," Lyr began, trying to match the tone and cadence of the stranger's words. Unsure of the parameters of the spell, he struggled to find the proper pattern. "I am Callian Myern i Lyrnis Dianore nai Braelyn, which you might translate to Lord Lyrnis, Duke of Braelyn. Our House offers you welcome to Moranaia, provided you come here in the spirit of peace."

Lyr didn't glance at the elaborately dressed woman who was likely their leader. For that one moment, he cared nothing for protocol. Instead, he waited for the younger elf to puzzle through his words. Since all but the male still glanced between them with confused expressions, the spell must have only been for the two of them. He hardly minded the excuse to exclude the others.

"I…yes, we come in the spirit of peace. So this *is* Moranaia?" She glanced nervously at Kai, who stood with blade drawn, before meeting Lyr's eyes once more. "We come from Alfheim seeking aid."

Alfheim? He struggled to hide his surprise at *that* revelation. The Ljósálfar were famously insular, most not even acknowledging their relation to the other fae races. From what he'd heard, they counted themselves too close to the gods to seek help from anyone else. "Could I have the pleasure of your name?"

"Ameliar Liosevore, but most call me Meli. Really, though, you need to speak with Ambassador Teronver. I just brought us here."

At the sound of her name, the elder barked another sharp, foreign word and dug her fingers into Meli's arm once more. Meli tugged, but the woman only gripped harder, giving a small shake as she spoke again.

Lyr's eyes went cold, though his blood burned with anger. "If she does not release you at once, she may return from whence she came."

Meli snapped out a short phrase in her native tongue, and the ambassador let go. Rubbing at her arm, Meli approached, and the guards around Lyr shifted restlessly. He lifted his hand. "Stand down." To Kai, Lyr sent, *"They are seeking aid for Alfheim."*

Without a word, Kai sheathed his blade and stepped back beside Arlyn. After looking between the two of them, Arlyn put away her own weapons. *"Alfheim?"* Kai asked. *"No wonder I can't understand them. Arrogant bastards have avoided us for millennia."*

Lyr almost smiled at his friend's blunt but accurate statement. Before he could answer, Meli addressed him, though she
glanced uneasily at the circle of guards who still protected him.
"Is there some place we may stay while petitioning for aid? If
you have some small bit of land we might camp on, we would
be grateful. Especially if there is hunting."

He wanted to demand that she stay in his home, close
enough for him to see, but prudence warred with desire. They
knew little about this group, and their arrival was suspiciously
close to the latest attack on the estate. For all he knew, the connection he felt to her was a ruse. Until he knew for sure, it was
best he choose where they stayed very carefully.

಄ಅ

An increasing sense of urgency ripped at Kien's insides. Another failed assassin had returned, this one half human and half
Dökkálfar. How had Beckett been detected? The cloak he wore
was designed to slip through Moranaian shielding, and he was
skilled enough with iron to work magic around and even
through it. But somehow they had still known.

Worse, his brother Ralan's disappearance from the human
world made it clear that he had returned to Moranaia with his
daughter. Kien's entire purpose in setting up the energy poisoning—killing the girl and possibly Ralan—was now moot. It was
only a matter of time until Ralan became king. Their father
stood little chance of survival now.

There is no future in which you will be king. Resign yourself.

Damned seers. First, Kien's great aunt had tried to manipu-
late him into believing he could never rule. Then, she'd proph-
esied that the first of the king's children to have a child with an

outworld female would be the next in line. As Teyark rarely fancied women, that left Ralan as the most likely candidate.

Another fucking seer.

Why could no one else understand that a seer should not rule? Kien would never blindly trust those who glanced into the future and worked to alter it. Such power led to evil. Hadn't his aunt conspired to promote another of her kind to the throne? Too bad for her. Kien would make his own future.

He'd have to focus more energy on capturing the portal. After his exile, it had been spelled to prevent his return, but at least two of his troop of half-bloods could reverse the spell if they could only take control of the portal for long enough. The energy poisoning could wait. There would be grumbling, but Kien didn't mind a little dismemberment if he needed to be convincing. The atrocities a seer would bring about as king could not be allowed.

∽◉◡

Lyr finally decided to place the newcomers in the guest tower built around one of the trees between the barracks and his study. Their intentions might prove sinister, but he couldn't deny hospitality to visiting diplomats. Besides, if they were connected to the attacks, it would be best to keep them close.

Close and under constant surveillance.

He led the group up the stairs circling the guard tower until they connected to the covered walkway that linked to the guest suite entrance. Lyr could just spot the guard in the branches that hung over his study, ready to report any suspicious activity. A necessary precaution of late.

With the estate built around and sometimes on trees, their guest rooms were scattered enough that the group's placement wouldn't seem to be a slight. In fact, having a guest tower to themselves might appease the elder diplomat's obvious sense of superiority, and it would be easier for Lial to heal the two attendants most affected by the crossing. Lyr worried most about the small, pale female still hugging herself and moaning. If Lial couldn't help her, they would have to send for a full-fledged mind healer.

Lyr showed them the latch to the door, carved like the tower to match the bark of the tree, and then ushered them inside. The room curved gently around the trunk of the tree, each living section divided by steps as the structure spiraled around. Downward and to the right was a small table for taking meals, while upward and to the left was a sitting and relaxation area. Above that was a library as well as six separate sleeping rooms.

Careful to maintain a polite expression, he gestured to the room. "This is the only entrance, and a guard will be stationed at the walkway to ensure your safety."

All but Ameliar and Pol stared at him blankly, the rest still unable to understand. Ameliar looked back down the walkway with a frown. "A guard for our safety? Do you mean that we are prisoners?"

"Of course not." *Only very well-watched.* "We've had some difficulty of late, and I would see you protected. In addition, the guard can provide you an escort so you don't get lost. Braelyn can be a difficult estate to navigate."

The glint in her eyes told him that she saw through his efforts at diplomacy, but she offered no protest. Considering their sudden appearance, the security was not unreasonable. Even one so obviously young would understand that. She merely nodded and turned to explain to the others while Pol stood grinning.

Lyr couldn't imagine how this one had been included in the group. His bright hair burned like a beacon amid his pale, blond companions, but his buoyant demeanor stood out the most. How was he unfazed by the Veil when the others were clearly exhausted? Lyr would have to ensure his guards watched Pol the most.

As Meli explained the situation to her companions, the ambassador's face pinched tight. She barked a few words at Meli that he couldn't understand. The young woman's entire body tensed. Her answering words were low, but it sounded like she might be defending herself from blame. Why the elder treated Meli with such malice was not yet known to him, but protective urges filled him like a living thing. Despite his uncertainty of the truth of their bond, the draw to her was unmistakable.

He'd need to be on guard against that.

"Lady Ameliar, please assure your leader that these are among the best accommodations on the estate. We favor smaller dwellings that fit into the environment. Not even the king's palace rises like the stone spires of Alfheim's fame."

"Lady? No, no—I am not a lady. Just Meli." Her fingers plucked at the pouch hanging from her belt. "You mention our stone spires. Have you visited Alfheim? You seem…familiar."

Mistrust was difficult to maintain as he looked into her confused eyes, blue like the pale flowers that dotted the fields in the spring. She spoke with such hesitation and revealed her nerves so readily that it was obvious she had no experience dealing with these types of situations. "I have only read about your land in our histories. Have you traveled on Earth?"

"Oh, no. I have never left Alfheim. Until now, at least. I just finished my schooling."

Lyr nodded, his suspicions confirmed. Elves appeared young for centuries, but mannerisms often exposed the youngest among them. Meli was likely no more than thirty, an unusual choice for a diplomatic party—but too old to be Aimee reborn. "Perhaps later we can discuss this odd recognition. First, I must verify my schedule and determine when I will be available to receive the ambassador's petition. Please convey to her that I will send a message soon with this information."

Meli inclined her head. "Of course, my lord."

Though his every instinct screamed at him to stay with her—or better yet, take her away with him—Lyr forced himself to nod and turn away. Forced his feet to move him toward his ever-present duty to his people.

8

Lyr meant to head to his study once he'd descended to the ground, but he found himself in the garden instead. His steps slowed as guilt welled up. He had a great deal of work to do, and he'd told Meli that he would arrange a meeting. But Lial would check on the newcomers soon, anyway, so Lyr could afford a few moments' peace before consulting his schedule. At least what passed for peace these days.

Resolved to take what time he could, Lyr sped up to a fast walk. He darted along a small path that wound down by the stream meandering across the back of the estate. At first, a low stone wall separated the trail from the water, but it was more decorative than a true barrier. Built by his grandmother, if he remembered correctly. The stone was so worn by the millennia that only magic maintained its current state.

He followed the stream until the sound of children's laughter blended with the gentle gurgling. To the right, where the trees opened into a meadow, Eri and Iren chased one another around the soft green grass. His heart gave a little lurch. While neither child resembled Arlyn, he still ached to see their unfettered joy. Had Arlyn once looked so happy and carefree during the years he'd missed? The lost time cut into his soul.

His daughter might have forgiven him for not returning to check on Aimee, but he didn't think he'd ever forgive himself.

"They've become so close in such a short time. Is that normal for elven children?"

Lyr actually jumped when Arlyn interrupted his musings, so caught off guard was he by her sudden appearance. Few could sneak up on him, intentionally or not. "I think children everywhere are much the same. They know few constraints, unlike their elders."

"So true." Arlyn smiled at the two a moment longer. "I'm sorry to bother you when you're so lost in thought, but I was looking over the reports you wanted me to handle when the mirror in your study chimed."

He turned back towards the manor, though it was the last place he wanted to be. "*Clechtan.*"

"Is this a bad thing?"

Seeing the steps Arlyn had to take to keep up, he slowed. "Probably. That mirror is my connection to a few other realms of elves and fae. I'm guessing it's yet another group wanting something from me."

"Why didn't the group that just arrived contact you in advance if there's a way to? It seems rude to just show up."

"I don't have a link to the Ljósálfar. They split from Earth long before we did, and they believe themselves to be near godhood. Even if they deigned to acknowledge their relation to our kind, they certainly cared nothing for keeping contact. Nobody that I know of has heard from them in the millennia since we left Earth."

"Near godhood?" Arlyn asked, surprise in her voice. "The one you spoke to didn't come across like that. I couldn't understand her, but her hesitation was obvious. She looked like she wanted to sink into the ground."

"She is quite young. Younger than you, perhaps. It is odd indeed for someone of her age to be in an expedition like this." Wanting to watch his daughter's expression, Lyr halted her with a gentle hand on her shoulder. "I don't suppose you noticed anything different about her? Maybe something familiar?"

Arlyn's mouth pursed. "Now that you mention it, yes. I'm sure I've never met her, though."

Chest squeezing, he looked away. "Arlyn, I…I feel a soulbond link with her."

The only sound for a long moment was the distant giggling of the children. When Lyr dared to meet his daughter's eyes, he was alarmed by the tears gathered there. Was she upset that he might have found someone besides her mother? Then, she stunned him by launching herself into his arms, a laugh slipping out as she hugged him. When she pulled back, her face shone with joy.

"I thought you said that you wouldn't get another chance. Gods, how wonderful!"

"Slow down, Arlyn," Lyr said, though he couldn't help but smile at her unexpected enthusiasm. "Such happiness is still far from certain. For one thing, I *haven't* heard of anyone gaining another bonded after losing the first. There are a few rare bondings with three or four partners, but that isn't the same. I'm not certain I should trust this feeling."

Arlyn shook her head. "The soulbond is sort of hard to mistake."

"I've learned to take nothing for granted." He sobered at the thought, and the smile slipped from his face. "There's no guarantee that she'll have any interest in me, and bonding isn't required. There's hardly a penalty for not joining, save losing something rare. As I am not as impetuous as Kai, I refuse to bond first and ask later. Though I must admit that the method is tempting."

Grinning, Arlyn gave him a teasing shove. "Hey!"

The casual affection caught at him, pinching his heart in a different way than his earlier grief. He might have missed her childhood, but he had the chance to get close to her now. Now and for centuries to come. "You can tell him I said so."

"You know I will," Arlyn answered with a laugh. "But let's go. The mirror won't answer itself. Better go see about this latest crisis."

They entered into the back hallway, and Lyr's mood soured further at the sight of the door to the library. The same library where his mother had fallen, taking his traitorous captain with her. Even after a month, he could not bear to go in. The healer had already moved her—saved her—by the time Lyr had made it back to the estate, but he could still picture her crumpled on the stone floor. The room was a perpetual reminder of how she'd suffered for his lack of attention. Only the gods knew how long it would be before he could reenter it without his stomach lurching.

Guessing his feelings, Arlyn squeezed his arm as they passed, the gesture warming him. But he merely sped up, still unwilling to release the depth of his pain. He couldn't burden her with that, not when she and the others needed him to be strong. If he recovered quickly enough, they would never know his weakness.

Arlyn stopped him just before they entered his study. "I'm working with Selia on the wards, so I can't stay. I was wondering, though…if a priest of Arneen can sever a soulbond, could they also help you with your questions about this potential bond? Maybe *they* have record of this happening before."

"An excellent idea." He tossed a look over his shoulder as he opened the door. "Most of the priests here take care of Eradisel, so their training is centered on the sacred tree. But there is an enclave not far from here. When we have finished with the Neor and now our new guests, I will have to see what I can find out."

Then she left Lyr to the task he dreaded.

In front of the tall windows behind his desk sat a large mirror on a delicate *peresten* frame. Because of the way it reflected the windows on the opposite side, most visitors didn't notice it— Arlyn had almost knocked it over once. Yet it was one of the most important items in the room. The first Myern of Braelyn had traveled back and forth between Earth and the other races of elves and fae to set up links, allowing the Moranaians to communicate with their once-close kin. Over the forty thousand years since, each Myern had added more links as needed. One little mirror connected so much.

Lyr stepped up to his reflection in the glass and frowned for a moment at the dark circles beneath his eyes, a sure sign that his energy was running low. His body and his energy stores no longer seemed to fully regenerate since the injury. If he didn't speak with Lial about it soon, the healer was going to kill him. But the communication he was about to initiate was of more immediate urgency. Any weakness would be noted, and he could not allow that. With a wave and another expenditure of energy, he cloaked himself in a simple glamour. It would do for a mirror conference.

He ran his fingers down the cool metal frame, the swirls reminiscent of the Veil. Lyr found the spell he needed, hooked his own energy into it, and pulled back. The mirror flickered with images as he sought the most recent attempt at communication. When he settled on the cold face of Meren, Seelie lord and general pain in the ass, Lyr groaned aloud. Kai's last mission to the Seelie court had been to negotiate with this particular Sidhe, and it had not gone well.

Many of those the human myths referred to as Sidhe lived under the rule of the original Tuatha de Danann or among the courts of the Seelie and Unseelie with other types of fae. The Sidhe hills of the Tuatha were scattered and insular, but the courts were large and active. Yet no matter where they lived, the Sidhe were bound by the oath of their ancestors—they were to stay underground while the humans ruled the surface, the price of a war they'd lost. Magic had forged a world for them in the underrealm, beneath the earth and a dimension barely removed. Over time, most of them had come to prefer it.

Meren, however, was more than eager to return to surface Earth to find the solution to the poisoned energies. He'd first approached Lyr over a year before for aid since the Moranaians' departure from Earth had happened prior to the oath that had formed the underhills. Meren had hoped that Lyr's scouts, able to work more openly, might discover something on the surface that would force the Sidhe to break their ancient oath. Based on the assassination attempts Kai had faced while visiting the Seelie court, at least some of the other Sidhe were against the idea.

With a sigh, Lyr reactivated the linking spell and prepared for a formal discussion. The surface of the mirror turned bright blue, the waiting pattern for the Sidhe lord. Lyr expected a long delay, but the blue background faded almost instantly to reveal Meren's pinched face, the visible tension a surprise. Though the pale-haired Sidhe was a thousand years older than Lyr, he didn't look it. Only a slight weariness around the eyes gave some clue.

"I bid good day to you, Callian Myern i Lyrnis Dianore nai Braelyn, eighteenth in line to the throne of Moranaia and Chief Ambassador to the Seelie court of Queen Lera. Thank you for your quick response. I do hope all is well for home and kin."

Lyr knew better than to fall for that bit of bait. Lord Meren cared less for Lyr's well-being and more for any weakness that could be exposed. "Good day to you, too, Lord Meren of the Seelie court. All here reside in good health and peace, a state I wish for your own House. To what do I owe the pleasure of our speaking?"

The Sidhe lord went straight to the point. "The queen received word that one of our colonies, Neor, has fallen. Queen Lera is quite distressed to hear that her subordinate came to you instead of our court."

"*Queen* Lera? I thought Tatianella was your queen."

Meren's nostril's flared. "Her mother is...indisposed. Queen Tatianella has stepped down temporarily."

The reason for the lord's obvious tension became clear. Something major was happening in the Seelie court, and Lyr would wager it had to do with the energy poisoning. "I am grieved to hear that. As to your previous question, we have indeed been contacted by a representative of the Neoran queen."

Lord Meren glanced to the side for a moment as though listening to another. When he turned back, his eyes were filled with regret, though Lyr had no doubt the emotion was feigned. "I am afraid I must insist that you stay out of this matter. This is an internal affair of the Seelie, and we will handle it as we see fit."

"And I am afraid that I cannot do that." Lyr shifted, standing taller. The memory of the exhausted, despairing messenger flashed through his mind. "My own prince, the current heir to the throne, has ordered me to give aid."

"What?" Meren's brow furrowed with anger. "How dare you do so without contacting our court at once!"

Lyr allowed his expression to curl into cool disdain. "Oh, no, Lord Meren. How dare *you?* You contacted *us* to deal with your problem a year ago, yet repeated attempts at negotiation resulted only in attacks on my diplomat's life. The mists of the Veil grow more turbulent as you refuse to settle on a solution. I will not allow an entire city to fall into violence and chaos because your court cannot reach accord."

"No matter our previous discussions, you should not interfere in our sovereign business."

Feeling his energy begin to wane, Lyr brought the discussion to a rapid close. "From my understanding, the queen of Neor is largely autonomous and has the right to work with other nations. Regardless, we have already promised aid, so aid we will give. If Queen Lera would like you to pursue a treaty with us, then I will send Ayal Kaienan once more."

Though his face had reddened with anger, Meren's tone was level. "I must, of course, consult with the queen about this matter. I will contact you again in a few days' time."

Their conversation ended even more abruptly than it had begun. Lyr disconnected his energy from the mirror, releasing it to its default state, and stripped off the glamour he'd used to hide his fatigue. His face was pale and almost gaunt beneath his dark brown hair. He needed to rest, to regenerate the energy he never seemed to keep hold of, but after the chaos of this day, he wasn't sure if he could get his mind to rest.

Lyr stumbled to a nearby chair and sank into its embrace. By all the gods of Arneen, why were the Sidhe delaying? Why call repeatedly for negotiations but then shrug them aside? The Neorans were proof enough of the poison's danger, and he had his suspicions about Queen Tatianella being "indisposed." How could they watch their people sicken for the sake of politics? It defied all sense.

Lyr rested his head against the chair's soft back as he considered all of the possibilities. He didn't even realize when he drifted off to sleep.

∽☙☙

The burning glow of Caolte's hair led Naomh across Knocknarea. Their midnight rides were more difficult now, as modern life crept ever closer to the ancient site. Where once they had traveled freely between twilight and dawn, they now only dared the darkest night. They could, and did, have fun with the humans from time to time, but too much would bring unwanted scrutiny. They preferred to be legends on the wind. Only a single time had the two allowed a human to immortalize their names, but Caolte had formed a surprising fondness for the lad. Naomh had not—but then, the damned poet had turned *him* into a woman.

Their horses' hooves sped over the slope of the hill, never quite making contact. The humans could never say the Sidhe broke their word—never did their feet touch land. As Caolte approached the Cairn of the Old One, he slowed, both of them glancing below. Despite the late hour, an array of lights glowed from the city by the waters. Not so many years before, only a few small buildings stood in darkness, but human expansion and technology had changed things. Why did so many of his kind want to return to this...this oddness?

Caolte rounded to the other side, this one overlooking darkened fields much closer to times past, before pulling his horse to a stop. His eyes scanned the top of the hill before turning to Naomh. "She is not here."

After centuries, Naomh understood exactly what his brother did not say. She was never here. For well over five hundred years, they had returned to the place he had first met Elerie. Hundreds of years of wishing that he had insisted she stay after their last trip to his underhill home. They'd never bonded in the way of her people, but he had felt their connection in his soul. She had sworn to return to him as soon as she completed her business, a task surely finished by now.

Naomh knew very well that she wasn't likely to return. But he had given his word to come for her, waiting every month on the dark of the moon by the old cairn. They might prevaricate or evade, but a Sidhe always kept their word. He would ride these hills each month so long as he was able. So long as his fool brother didn't ruin it all by breaking the treaty. A return to the surface would no doubt lead to war, and their kind would be hunted every time they appeared.

"You needn't come with me, you know," Naomh said. "I am well able to make this journey on my own."

Caolte glared, his hair sparking with frustration. "Millennia we have made this journey, brother, and so it will continue."

With a shake of his head, Naomh turned his horse to follow the hill back down. Though the two were only half-brothers, he was closer to Caolte than he ever could be to Meren. Naomh glanced over his shoulder with a smile. "Come away. There is still mischief to be had."

9

Lyr rubbed a hand across his face, trying to block the light shining across his eyes.

Wait, light? He jerked upright. His chair faced east, and it was too late in the day for... Then his gaze caught on the mirror, where the low-slung sun reflected from behind him. He must have slept for a couple of hours. And if his senses weren't mistaken, he wasn't alone.

Squinting, he inspected the room to find the presence he'd detected. It didn't take long. The shock from the beam of light faded quickly, and Lyr's vision adjusted enough to make out Lial sitting in the shadows across from him. How long had the other been there? He was unsettled to think that he had slept through the healer's arrival.

"How long were you going to let this go on before you came to me?" Lial asked.

Lyr ran a hand through his hair to settle it from his unexpected nap. "I suppose it would do no good to deny it since you found me sleeping in the middle of the day like a child."

"Not unless you single-handedly defended the estate from an army while I was otherwise occupied. I can think of little else that would drain your energy so thoroughly." Lial tapped his lip with his index finger. "Kai told me you've been acting strange, and I realized that I couldn't let this go on any longer. If I have to call in a mind healer, I will."

"I haven't lost my mind, but I will grant that I am not well. Nightmares of being captured, of Mother's injury, even of losing Aimee—they keep me from rest." Lyr rubbed reflexively at the wound on his chest. "Beyond that, my injury never seems to fully heal."

"*Miaran,* Lyr, why didn't you call for me?" Lial leapt to his feet and strode to Lyr with an expression that had shifted from irritated to truly angry. "Move your tunic out of the way, or I'll do it for you."

Lyr's eyebrow rose. "You might have been born to the royal family, but you are under my command now."

"In matters such as these, the healer obeys no one but the gift."

Taking him at his word, Lyr untied the laces at the top of his tunic and parted it to reveal the scar that trailed over his heart, the flesh barely knit even after a month. Lial held his hand above the wound and closed his eyes. In less than a heartbeat, a blue glow flowed over the injury. The healer's energy tingled through Lyr, but it didn't cause pain. After a moment, he relaxed and closed his own eyes until he felt the sensation fade.

Lyr looked up to find Lial glaring at the wound as though it had committed some grave offense. "You see why I didn't tell you?"

"I should have insisted on looking deeper when you first returned." Lial shoved back, a hint of hurt beneath his glare. "Why would you hide this from me? Iron in the wound, Lyr? You knew it for a lie when you said it was healing well."

"What was there to be done?" Lyr asked. *Clechtan,* but he hadn't meant to cause insult. "When my daughter had flakes in her arm, you said they'd have to work their way out on their own."

"Don't tell me that was all of your reasoning," Lial bit out.

With a long sigh, Lyr slumped against his seat. "Fine. *Fine.*" He threw up his hands. "I thought I could handle it. *Should* handle it. I'd been told that Arlyn had converted the iron while I was unconscious, but the effect started to fade. I'd been able to work magic despite that—until today. But I wanted to convert it again myself. Then you could heal it faster."

"Iron in the heart," Lial cursed, then let out a short bark of laughter. "An apt phrase, that. Damned Dianore pride." With a huff, he pulled his small leather roll of tools from a pouch at his waist. "Anything foreign trapped beneath the skin can become a problem, Lyr. I need to break through the skin and remove the metal since it won't come out on its own."

Lyr grimaced. "Here? You plan to cut me open in the middle of my study?"

"Unless you agree to come with me to my work room." Face hard with resolve, Lial took out a scalpel. "These chairs are spelled to resist staining, after all."

Lyr eyed the sharp blade in the healer's hand. "You wouldn't."

"Do not test me, Lyrnis Dianore," Lial snapped. "I am almost angry enough to forget the numbing spell."

"Very well," Lyr answered through clenched teeth. Before Lial could carry through with his threat, Lyr jerked to his feet and started for the door. He'd rather not bloody his favorite room—cleaning spells or no.

⚬⊚⚬

The healer's work room was at the base of one of the towers that surrounded the central building. But Lyr couldn't enjoy the walk despite the lovely view of the valley to his left. Curse it all, he *hated* the sensation of a wound being stitched. Not to mention the blood. With a shudder, he focused on Lial's back and tried not to think about what was coming.

Lial opened the door to his work room and crossed toward the back staircase without pause, the sharp, spicy scent of herbs flowing out behind him. Lyr let the comforting smell surround him and ease some of his nerves as he followed the healer in. Although Lial could and often did use healing magic to fix a wide variety of injuries, he was cautious and stingy with his personal reserves. When possible, he used a combination of magical and mundane methods. Many Moranaian healers scorned the mixture, preferring to rely on magic alone.

Thankfully, Lial didn't care what others thought. The healer's methods were one of the main reasons Lyr's father had requested he join their House. The previous Myern had spent decades trying to find a solution for iron allergies, so having someone available who could stitch up an iron-inflicted wound had been invaluable. Lyr found it equally so.

As Lial darted upstairs, Lyr paused just beyond the threshold. The left side of the room held a long workbench filled with jars of herbs and reference books, all arranged neatly. A stone bench stretched across the back wall, separated from the bed on the right by the spiral staircase leading into the healer's personal chambers.

Lyr traced the skin over his heart and eyed the exit, but Lial stepped down the stairs before he could sneak out. The healer's clothing was now a deep rust red. The bloody color raised bumps on Lyr's arms despite centuries of being patched up during training exercises gone wrong. Not even time made the experience pleasant.

"I suggest you remove any clothing you don't wish to get stained."

With a sigh of resignation, Lyr disrobed and hung his clothes on hooks near the stone bench before stretching out on the cool surface. "Do you not have a spell that could remove the fragments without cutting me open?"

Lial smirked as he pulled a small table full of tools over to the bench. "Certainly, though I wager you would not like the feel of hundreds of iron flakes ripping through flesh any better."

"You're enjoying this a bit much for a healer," Lyr grumbled.

"Consider it a form of 'I told you so.'" Lial perched on a wooden stool and focused on the wound. "All options would have been easier when the injury was newer. But if you'd rather I rip the iron through…?"

"Cutting it is, then." Sitting up for a bolster to be placed behind his neck, Lyr draped his long hair over the edge of the leather cushion. "What else will you do?"

"Once you're freely bleeding, I'll use a spell to pull the fragments out with the blood. Then, I'll close the wound with magic since there will be no iron to interfere with healing."

With a frown, Lyr rubbed his thumb along his pendant. The engravings and the nick that had saved his life blurred together in ridges too difficult to discern. An oddly comforting pattern. Reluctantly, he pushed it out of the way as well.

"I thought injuries inflicted by iron could never be healed with magic," Lyr said as Lial bound his hands to the table.

"That's usually caused by remnants of iron that are later pushed out during the natural healing process. Once the flakes are expelled through the skin, magic is possible. Besides, this iron doesn't seem to interfere with my powers, likely thanks to your daughter. Fortunately for you, since I can extract the pieces magically." Lial picked up a sharp scalpel made of purest *peresten*, a metal mined only on Moranaia. "Now, do you prefer to be unconscious or awake and numbed?"

Lyr sighed, his face twisted in a grimace. "Awake and numbed. As difficult as things have been lately, I dare not be unaware. And I'll need to be alert when negotiating with Lord Loren for mages."

Healing energy flowed from Lial's hand, and all feeling dulled before disappearing entirely from his chest. Lyr let out an involuntary shudder and gasped out a breath. Had the healer not bound him, he would have grabbed at his chest to make sure it was still there. He could barely even detect his own heartbeat or the movement of his lungs.

"Relax. The feeling is disconcerting, but your organs are functioning properly."

With a nod, Lyr squeezed his eyes shut and tried to block out the world.

Not an easy feat. Over the *plop* of a dripping water clock and the occasional muttered curse from Lial, the squishy sound of Lyr's flesh shifting beneath scalpel and magic seemed to fill the room. Nausea crept up the back of Lyr's throat, and he began to concentrate on the surprisingly soothing sensation of blood trickling down his side and into the deep channels carved into the sides of the bench. With his eyes closed, he could pretend it was water.

"Are you feeling pain?"

"No." Lyr cracked his eyes open and shook his head at the healer. "I've been healed many times over the centuries from various practice sessions gone awry, but none have been as bad as this. I can only be grateful that I was unconscious the first time this injury was treated."

Three thousand, one hundred and twenty drops of the water clock later, Lial held both hands over the wound and slipped into a full healing trance. A few heartbeats longer, and the skin knit together. Though Lyr was still numb, the spell faded enough for sensation to slip through. Lyr gritted his teeth against the odd feel of muscle and flesh seaming together.

Lial finally pulled away and slumped, leaning his elbow on the edge of the bench. When Lyr glanced down, nothing remained on his chest but the faintest scar, a sure sign of iron since elves rarely scarred otherwise.

"How do you feel?" the healer asked, his voice soft with weariness.

Lyr flexed his arms and twisted his torso. For the first time in over a month, he felt physically like himself, except for the lingering exhaustion. "Foolish for not having seen to this sooner." He studied Lial's face. "How about you? You're not usually so worn down after a healing."

The healer heaved himself up and grabbed a pitcher of water. "I attended to a difficult birth before your nap. Mother and child are well, but it took a fair amount of energy."

"Coric and Fena's firstborn?" Lyr asked, accepting the pitcher.

"The same. I was coming by to tell you that Coric would need extra time away from his duties to ensure Fena's recovery." Lial gestured at Lyr's chest. "Now clean off."

He poured the water over his chest and scrubbed with an offered cloth. As the water and remaining blood flowed down the side of the table to a basin at the end, the door opened to admit Lial's assistant, Elan, who darted to the basin to empty every drop into a stout stone jar. He even used a cleansing spell to ensure that nothing was left behind.

Elan set a spell in the top to seal it and presented the container to Lyr with a salute. "I have collected every particle, Myern, as Healer Lial requested."

Lyr shot a questioning glance at Lial, who shrugged. "Kai told me that Allafon attempted a blood magic spell before he was stopped, so I thought you might want to see to the disposal of your blood yourself."

Was he serious? Lyr wondered, brows raising. "What in the name of Arneen am I supposed to do with this?"

Lial huffed out a breath and put down the scalpel he was cleaning. "Do you want me to come over and transmute it?"

"Well, I certainly don't want a jar of my own blood as room décor."

A surprised laugh slipped from Elan before Lial glared his assistant to silence. The healer stomped over, grabbed the jar, and muttered a few sharp words as he cast his energy into the container. After a moment, he opened it to show it empty. "I forget the deficiencies of others. If only everyone could be as talented as healers."

The pallor beneath Lial's smirk revealed the true reason the healer had wanted Lyr to take care of the matter. *Clechtan,* but he shouldn't have let him do the spell. Lyr almost apologized for giving the healer trouble, but experience told him the other would rather he not mention it. "You never told me what happened with the Ljósálfar."

"The two most afflicted will require further treatment, but I believe they will recover without a mind healer. The others were perfectly healthy." Lial looked up from rearranging his tools. "At least I assume Pol is healthy. He alone refused to be examined."

"Refused? And you let him?"

The healer folded up the leather pouch and tied it with a sharp tug. "You know as well as I that he is not one of the Ljósálfar. Until I know what he is, I choose prudence."

"That, at least, is something I can try to solve." Lyr donned his clothes, not even bothering to tie the laces of his tunic. "After a shower. Thank you, Lial, truly. Try to rest."

"Ah, but that's the paradox. The healer rarely gets his own rest."

∾ᘏᘐ

Meli's fingers gripped the balcony railing as she gazed at the valley below. The sun had just set behind her, casting the forest that covered the hills in twilight shadow. Trees. Everywhere, trees. The last time she had stood at such height, she had been on her own balcony overlooking the white stone buildings of Alfheim and the rolling plains beyond. Not this wildness. The City of Light was orderly, small trees and gardens carefully placed, animals tame. Even the forests that bordered the plains were gentler than this.

But unlike the last time she had gripped a balustrade, Meli found herself more excited than afraid. Oh, the dread of the wild still filled her, but it was buried beneath an unexpected thread of anticipation. She missed the comfort of her home and the love of her parents, yet honesty forced her to admit that her soul did not belong there. She'd always been a person disjointed, split between the staid safety of Alfheim and the strange images of her dreams.

None of the dread could overcome the thrill of meeting those green eyes. But the confusion that knotted her belly came not from the male, at least not alone. After Pol had cast the spell of understanding that knocked Meli unconscious, she'd wakened as a red-haired girl burst from the trees with her bow nocked. A girl with eyes just as green—and just as familiar. Strange images had flickered through Meli's mind at the sight of her. Odd, square rooms, moving machines, and a laughing child who looked like a miniature of the woman before her.

Meli had yet to speak with the girl, but from Lord Lyrnis's words, she thought he might feel a connection, too. Though she had asked if he'd ever been to Alfheim, she knew he hadn't. The arrival of any outworlder would have caused enough commotion that all but the littlest of babes would hear of it. Still, she was uncertain what to make of his response. Speak of it later? Perhaps their "odd recognition," as he'd called it, was commonplace for him. She knew nothing of the Moranaians but what she'd seen this day.

"Spectacular, is it not?"

Meli spun at the sound of Pol's voice, and his amused gaze met her frowning one. "Provided one likes trees," she said. "And darkness. How do these people function without light crystals?"

Pol laughed. "Spoken like a true Ljósálfar."

"What do you mean by that?" Her glance turned into a glare. "I'm not like the ambassador, scorning these Moranaians when I know so little. I'm certain they have their own ways."

Holding up his hands in mock defeat, Pol chuckled again. "I only referred to your love of light. It *is* why you're called the light elves, after all."

"Oh." With a sigh, she faced the darkening valley. "It's the wildness I have trouble with. Part of me wants to explore, but anything could be out there. I cannot even see a break in the trees. But maybe tomorrow I'll venture into the gardens we passed through."

The corner of Pol's mouth quirked up. "A shame. The wildness is the best part."

They stood in silence for several moments as Meli pondered the odd elf—or something—beside her. "I am surprised you're not out there already, then. Did you need to speak to me?"

"Lady Ameliar—and do not argue with me, for a lady you are whether you know it or not—I am here mostly *for* you. The others are irrelevant."

Meli chose to let the "lady" go in favor of his other words. "I don't know who you are or where you really came from, and I do appreciate your help in the mists. But how can you possibly be here for me? My part in this is over. I needn't even guide the group back if the Moranaians can find someone who better knows the way."

"I may feign carelessness, play the necessary villain, or spur others to needed anger, but I am never mistaken."

"Then I suppose you see more in me than I do in myself."

"Oh, yes." The grin he gave her seemed to light his eyes with little flames. "Just play with your runes. See the sights. You'll figure it out in time."

Frustration drove her back to the tower even if it risked another encounter with Teronver. At the door, two globes now glowed from alcoves carved into the walls, and when Meli entered, she noticed more of them filling the room with soft light. They blended with the rest of the room so well that they looked like simple decorations during the day. It seemed that these elves had some alternative to the light crystals, after all. As the door closed behind Pol, she wandered over to the table to find a generous amount of food, apparently delivered without her noticing.

Like survivors of some disaster, Berris and Orena gathered together on the far side of the table to eat, each lift of their spoons slow but fairly steady. Although their faces were drawn, the glint of barely contained insanity had disappeared. Meli stacked her own plate with the simplest fare—a pale meat, dark, nutty bread, and a firm chunk of yellow cheese—and sat across from the other two, but they didn't look up. She didn't mind. As long as the ambassador stayed upstairs, Meli was content.

Just as she savored the last tangy bite of cheese, a soft knock sounded on the door. Even Berris and Orena glanced up, faces lighting a little with curiosity, as Pol let their visitor in. Meli's breath caught as she waited to see if Lord Lyrnis had returned, but the male who entered was a stranger, his short blond hair and earth-toned tunic and pants drawing little attention. Assuming she would need to translate, Meli hurried to greet him. When she stopped, smiling, before him, he tapped his chest once and spoke, but the words were unintelligible.

Meli frowned at Pol before turning back to their visitor. "I am sorry, but I don't understand."

The blond elf shook his head and held out a folded piece of paper. Meli reached out to take it, but as she opened the note to read the text inside, annoyance swept through her. Eyes narrowing, she rounded on Pol. "Could you not have allowed me to understand the written language? Or anyone else besides our host?"

"Thanks be to me that I decided to come on this trip," Pol muttered, snatching the paper from her. "It's a message from Lord Lyrnis. 'Honored visitors, Chosen of Alfheim: It is my fervent hope that your accommodations have brought you ease after your long journey through the Veil. I have set your reception for tomorrow at the fifth hour so that my House might accord you highest honors. If your task requires greater urgency, please send word through my messenger.'"

"The fifth hour?" Meli frowned. "That's so early."

Pol shrugged. "If it makes the ambassador feel important, who cares?"

10

Lyr cursed under his breath all the way to the stream on the far side of the garden. Over an hour of discussions with Loren, Selia's father and baron of a small estate along the Taian branch, and still Lyr had no mages to send to Neor. With their new-found family connection and the size and relative unimportance of House Baran, it should have been an easy negotiation. However, Loren wasn't pleased that Selia had discovered his lost half-blood child, Arlyn's grandfather, and the baron had made each conversation since as difficult as possible.

If negotiations didn't progress soon, Lyr would be forced to move farther up the Taian branch, but that would have its own complications. Of course, he could always have Ralan intercede. The prince certainly wanted them to help Neor, but Lyr hesitated to involve the seer more than he needed to. His feelings of being manipulated warred with centuries of friendship. He would rather have that friendship than knowledge of the future.

A splash drew his attention to the far end of the stream, and he turned to meet the startled gaze of Meli, robes pulled up to her knees as she walked through the water. Lyr's breath hitched, and he fought to contain the lust that hardened his entire body with unexpected swiftness at the sight of the damp cloth clinging to her curves. They both stood frozen for a moment before she seemed to shake herself and step out of the water.

"Lord Lyrnis, I…" she began, trailing off as she met his eyes. "Have I broken some rule? The guard who directed me to the gardens said nothing against swimming. The heat here is just so overwhelming."

He took in the long sleeves and the yards of dripping fabric settling around her bare feet. Despite being fairly thin—and clingy— her robes did look as though they'd be stifling outside the spell-cooled rooms of the tower. "Was it cool when you left Alfheim?"

Her gentle smile softened the worry lines from her face. "Always. Never really hot or cold, just…perfect."

"No seasons?"

"The leaves might change and fall, then return once more, but the temperature barely varies." Meli shook her head. "I read of seasons during my studies with the ancient tomes. Legend says that Alfheim was placed into the branches of the Great Tree as a realm of infinite beauty. Even extremes of weather wouldn't dare mar it."

Lyr trained his eyes on her face and resolved to keep them there. "It's little wonder that the Ljósálfar rarely leave, then. Things must be dire indeed to seek our aid."

Her pale skin reddened. "It's terrible of us, I suppose, to come here after so long in isolation. I'm afraid you will have a difficult time with Ambassador Teronver. She would rather us all die than rely on someone outside our own people, so set is she on tradition. Of course, it is that very tradition that required her to obey the king and undertake this journey."

"I see." Nodding, Lyr gestured for her to walk with him along the path. "I'll keep that in mind during our meeting."

"One not as early as I'd thought, thankfully."

He chuckled. "Forgive me. I didn't think to have the messenger explain the water clocks and how we count time. How did you find out?"

"The ambassador was not pleased by the early hour, so Pol went to find a guard."

By the time they reached the other end of the formal gardens, Lyr still hadn't broached the topic that most needed discussion. But finally, he stopped her with a gentle tug on her arm. Then he jerked his hand away as the shock of the contact stole his breath. For several heartbeats, they stared at one another, heedless of any who watched.

"You said we would speak later. About our connection." Her gaze dropped to his chin. "Perhaps this is common for your people, but it is not for mine. I have no reason to feel like I know you."

"Like our souls are pieces long parted?" he asked, his voice going rough.

Her eyes darted up to his. "Yes. Exactly thus."

Lyr studied her face, lined with confusion and a hint of fear, and swallowed hard. "Do you not have soulbonds, then?"

Meli's brow scrunched. "Do you mean like soul companions?"

"A soulbonded is one whose soul can bond with another's, given energy and intent. We exchange necklaces and words, though words alone suffice. It solidifies the connection so our souls would forever be fully bound." Lyr stopped himself from reaching for her hand, not wanting to startle her. "What are soul companions?"

"Those whose souls sing together as one. But they are not bonded the way you say." She bit her lower lip. "Their spirits aren't merged as far as I know."

"Your people are ancient, perhaps more so than ours," Lyr said. "Could you have lost the method to bond? Even without joining souls, the bonded feel a close connection."

"I don't know. I studied little of such things, never thinking—" Her eyes widened like a startled *daeri* in the forest. "I didn't expect to find a companion. But I don't understand any of it."

Everything within him seemed to still. "Don't understand what? That our souls are a match?"

Her chest heaved with her gasping breaths, and she gave a helpless shake of her head. "That I've seen your eyes in my dreams from infancy."

"What?" he sputtered, his heartbeat suddenly loud in his ears.

A tear slid down her cheek as her body began to tremble. "Everyone said it was my imagination. A delusion. Or…other, less complimentary things. Yet here you are, alive. Real."

"Ameliar. Meli." Lyr grasped her shoulders and squeezed. Then he pulled her into his arms when she continued to shake. "Stop. Please, stop."

"I have never met you. I know I haven't." She sucked in an unsteady breath before pulling back to face him. "There's something wrong with me."

He grimaced. "I am sorry if I've made you feel as such."

"No." She stepped away, smoothing her hands down her robe though he could see no wrinkle. "It's not you. I have never been—it is no matter. Please forgive me for my outburst."

"There's nothing to forgive."

"But there is." More tears welled in her eyes. "You seem very nice, but I don't think I can do this. This place. The bond. It's too much. I just—"

With a choked sound, she covered her mouth with her fist and fled. Lyr could only stand and watch, his spirit broken on the stone path beneath his feet.

᪥

The dragging weight of Lyr's formal robe fit his mood as well as it did his body. Embroidered in silver and studded with countless black stones, it took effort even with his strength to pull the length of it behind him. The tunic and pants revealed by the open front were a deep charcoal gray, while the circlet around his brow was silver and jet. Though it verged on mourning, his hands had reached for the somber attire anyway.

He opened the door to his study with his head high and his face carefully blank. With a nod to Arlyn and Kai, Lyr went straight to his desk to look over his notes before the formal reception. He'd spent much of the previous night reading what little information he had of Alfheim, and his notes were even more sparse. He could find no dealings between their nations since before the Moranaians had left Earth. Whatever happened, he would have to trust his instincts.

A glance at the water clock told him it was almost time. He tucked his papers into a drawer and crossed to his daughter and her bonded. Kai stood at the window, and his robe, embroidered to match his favorite scene, mirrored the valley beyond the glass almost exactly. The sight surprised a sharp laugh from Lyr. As the two turned confused looks his way, Lyr couldn't hold back another chuckle. He still ached from his earlier meeting with Meli, but he found his body relaxing by slow degrees.

"Come. It is almost time."

Arlyn's eyebrows raised. "And that's funny?"

"No." Lyr grinned. "Look at Kai's robe."

She shifted, glancing at Kai's robe and then back out the window. Her confusion turned to mirth, and even Kai shook with laughter when she pointed out the match. It was a minor thing to find so amusing, but it was a welcome relief. As Kai and Arlyn followed him from the study, all three moved less stiffly. By the time they reached the reception hall, Lyr had even managed to lose some of his tension. The negotiations with Alfheim concerned him little, despite the potential complications. But speaking with Meli again so soon after their emotional exchange—could he keep control when all he wanted was to sweep her away to continue their discussion? Lyr shoved that question down and tried to maintain his sense of calm.

He'd lost one bonded already. He'd just have to learn to live without another.

The dais was set at the far end of the room, just before the glass doors overlooking the gardens. At midday, entering was like stepping into the forest on a bright summer day. Interspersed between the tall windows and doors that ringed the room, columns carved to resemble tree trunks stretched to the ceiling and split into branches. Bright blue, a perfect match for the sky, peeked from between artificial leaves. The immense space was a worthy work of art.

Ralan and Eri stood to one side of the dais, and Teyark and Corath were on the other. Lyr's lips quirked at the sight of Ralan and his daughter. They had only returned from Earth less than a month before, and Ralan had spent centuries away. Yet both of them wore robes cut to the current Moranaian style and embroidered with countless tiny leaves. Apparently, the prince's latest occupation as a fashion designer had served him well.

With a long-practiced flourish, Lyr took his place in the center and settled his robe behind him. But as Arlyn struggled to twirl the end of her silken robe around with equal grace, sadness washed through him, squeezing his heart. She muttered a curse in English and scowled at Kai, not seeming to notice Lyr's shift in mood. Nor did Kai, who merely chuckled and rushed to help her.

By Arneen, she should have been raised here. Then she wouldn't have to struggle with something as simple as dealing with formal robes.

But Lyr didn't have time to linger on the regret. Just as Kai returned to his place at Lyr's left hand, the princes' *loreln* along with Lyr's own guards filed in to circle the room. There would be no others to fill the vast space, save their guests. None to distract him from the exchange ahead.

Lyr fixed a neutral expression on his face and gave Koranel the mental signal to bring in their visitors. His heart twisted when he spotted Meli walking in with the others. Through dint of will, Lyr forced his gaze away from her and turned his attention to the ambassador. Coolly regal, she stared straight at the dais, though her eyes never met his, and her mouth was pinched with little lines that revealed her displeasure.

Meli hadn't been joking about the ambassador's attitude. He should have asked Meli for more information but had been too distracted by talk of their bond. *Clechtan*. So much for fulfilling his duty as Myern.

When the group reached the dais, Koranel tapped his chest twice and inclined his head. "Myern Lyrnis and Honored Witnesses, I present to you the delegation from the Royal House of Alfheim. May peace and reason reign between you."

Lyr doubted the traditional phrase would come to pass if the ambassador's sour expression was any indication. Perhaps she was part of the royal family herself, a princess unhappy with her task. "The House of Dianore bids welcome to the Royal Delegation of Alfheim. Honor, peace, and happiness upon you this day."

He hid his satisfaction at the ambassador's growing scowl. She couldn't understand him, of course. He left it to her to recall that she would need Meli's help and could see by the darkening of her eyes when she did. Her nostrils flared as she snapped a terse, commanding word over her shoulder. Meli bowed her head and stepped around the ambassador's attendants to stand beside the elder.

"Thank you for your words of welcome, Myern Lyrnis," Meli answered clearly, though her gaze was directed at the inlaid wooden floor. "Allow me to present the ambassador from Alfheim, Lady Teronver Aniore."

Apparently understanding that she had been introduced, Lady Teronver stepped forward and spoke directly to Lyr, not even bothering to acknowledge Meli. The younger elf frowned and then met his eyes. "Milady bids me to tell you this: 'We have come on a journey of some importance, although I deeply fear that you will be unable to aid in our quest.'" She paused and shook her head. "I hope another's words translate as clearly as my own."

She kept her tone calm and her manner humble, but Lyr could practically feel the thread of anger beneath her words. Not at him—the shift in tone when Meli said "milady" told him more than she likely guessed. "If not, I suspect your other companion can lend aid."

Laughter burned in the red-haired male's eyes, but he said not a word. If anything, it was Meli who tensed and sent a frustrated look back at him. "Let us hope not, milord."

Lyr stifled a chuckle. After the pain the man's spell had caused them both, Lyr could hardly blame her. "I would like to know why Lady Teronver feels that we are unable to help. It seems a poor show of faith to declare defeat before naming the beginning."

He waited as the two spoke, the delay made enjoyable by watching Meli try to control her temper. She intrigued him. On the surface, she appeared shy, but hints of boldness sometimes peeked through. She was an ember held at bay, needing only a bit of kindling to flare into her true self. But only she could provide that type of tinder, that final spark. Lyr found himself hoping he'd be there when she did.

Meli's expression had darkened considerably by the time she turned to him once more. "Before I continue, please understand that these are the words of Lady Teronver."

Lyr's eyebrows raised. "It has not escaped my notice that the two of you seem to disagree."

"All the more reason to clarify." Meli straightened, her chin lifting high. She took a deep breath before continuing her message. "'I, Lady Ambassador to the king of Alfheim, have come on a mission of great importance. Poison threatens the City of Light, and the situation requires swift action. Who knows how much time has passed as we...'" She paused as though searching for words, but her flared nostrils and lowered brows gave her emotions away. "'As we stumbled through the wretched fog at the hands of our inept guide.'"

He wanted to applaud, but he merely inclined his head as though accepting her words. "You have more forbearance than I do to repeat that, milady."

"I doubt it, but I'm certain the rest of her statement will give us the proof." A small smile softened her expression, but she still stood straight and tense as she continued to translate for Lady Teronver. "'Though I thank you for the hospitality you have shown, I fear that your resources will not be significant enough to aid us. Alfheim is a great and glorious city, and saving it will be no simple matter. If you have betters, I ask you to send us to them instead.'"

Silence filled the hall after the echo of her words faded. Years of discipline kept Lyr's hands relaxed by his side, but the level of insult so casually and expertly delivered trapped the air in his throat. Oh, on the surface, the ambassador's words seemed polite enough. But as with many races of fae, the undercurrents held the true meaning. She had judged them wanting in a mere day's time.

"Are you accustomed to misjudging size, Lady Ambassador?" Lyr gave a cold smile, frostier than the northern mountains during the season of ice. "I assure you that the resources of my estate are ample."

Meli bit down on her bottom lip and her eyes sparkled with mirth. At least for a moment. When she turned to translate, her face grew strained once more. "Milady bids me tell you that since you have not seen the greatness of Alfheim, you cannot possibly comprehend what is needed."

"Is she serious?" At Meli's nod, his mouth pinched into a hard line. He discarded his first two possible replies before he found some semblance of diplomacy. "Don't translate that. Please inform Lady Teronver that I will search at once for a guide to escort her and her attendants back to Alfheim so that she may seek aid from a more worthy source. I have neither the time nor the inclination to negotiate through her prejudice." He paused, heart suddenly pounding. "To you alone, I say that you are welcome here if you wish to stay."

"I will consider it, but—" Her gaze darted to the floor as her face paled. "First I must tell the ambassador your decision."

As Meli spoke in hushed tones with the increasingly-agitated emissary, Ralan looked over at Lyr and cleared his throat as if to speak. With a sidelong glance at his friend, Lyr shook his head. "I don't want to hear it. I listened when it involved the Neorans, but I will not deal with this woman."

Ralan chuckled. "No prophecy here. I thought you might tell us what she said."

"Shouldn't you know already?"

"There are many possible futures," Ralan answered with a shrug. "I can hardly memorize them all. I rarely hear actual words, anyway."

Lyr made note of that bit of information before answering the question. By the time he finished, his fellow Moranaians stood with cold expressions, fury buried beneath centuries of politeness. Only Arlyn, so new to such politics, seemed confused, though Lyr doubted those outside the family would guess. Her intent gaze rested on the arguing pair from Alfheim as though searching for the cause of the disagreement.

Voice growing shrill, Lady Teronver suddenly gripped Meli's arm and shook her with each forceful word. Lyr strode forward, hand raised for his guards. "Enough!"

Though the elder could not have understood him, his advance flanked by two guards was clear. She released Meli and stepped back just as Lyr stopped before them. "Am I to assume, Lady Ameliar, that the ambassador does not approve of my words?"

"She blames me. Said I must have mistranslated." Meli turned pleading eyes his way. "Perhaps I did err in small ways, but I assure you that I reported her words in good faith. What I said was what she meant."

Lyr had no doubt that the ambassador's words had been accurately translated, but the fury flowing from Lady Teronver made it clear that she wouldn't accept such a judgment. He glanced to their smirking companion, Pol, who merely nodded as though confirming Lyr's suspicions. Pressing *that* one would likely do more harm than good, and in this he needed to tread carefully. Though he could dismiss the ambassador for impertinence, he would leave her no reason for complaint to her king. Well, no valid reason.

"*Laial,*" Arlyn murmured, her tentative call bringing him around in surprise. "You have a spell to transfer languages, don't you? I mean, I'm assuming you had some way to extract all of the Earth languages you know, so the transfer can go both ways. You gave me Moranaian."

By Arneen, she was correct. Why hadn't he thought of that at once? After Pol's spell, his mind had been muddled and... Had the iron-cursed *drec* tampered with his thoughts? Lyr glowered at the man but received only a slight nod and smirk in return. If not for Ralan's warning about Pol the day before, Lyr would challenge him at once. *Clechtan.* This would take consideration. *Later.*

He turned back to the delegation. "My daughter has reminded me of a spell that can transfer or extract languages. If you would allow me to use it, then I can speak to Lady Teronver in her own tongue." He paused, letting his eyes go hard. "Otherwise, my earlier decision stands."

11

A mere quarter-mark later, Lyr sank into a chair in his study and glanced at Meli in the seat beside him. She had already rejected him just this morning. How would she react to the language spell, which was an intimate thing? Though no thoughts or memories would be exchanged, he would know her very words. Her favorite phrases and expressions. His knowledge of her tongue would be forever shaped by her inner voice.

And for her, it would be the same for Moranaian.

"Are you certain that you're willing to do this?"

Light from above caressed the frown lines creasing her face. "No. But it needs to be done."

Lyr quirked an eyebrow. "Do you always do what needs to be done?"

"Unfortunately." Her mouth twisted, caught between a grimace and a smile. "Why else would I have gone on this mad mission?"

"I suppose that is for you to say."

She held his gaze, a show of spirit that he was gratified to see. "Perhaps someday even I will know the answer."

His emotions twisted by the awkward exchange, Lyr looked away. Meli had no interest in their bond, a position she'd made clear by her emphasis on duty. If not for their meeting in the garden, he would never have guessed the depth of the draw she felt for him. He stilled against the sudden pain of it, his chest burning as though Lial had cut him open once more. As if a thousand tiny shards of iron burrowed through his flesh. The gods, it seemed, had decided that he didn't deserve a second chance after all.

"So," Meli began, the word sounding strangled. She cleared her throat as her fingers curved around the arm of her chair. "What do I need to do for this spell? I'm sure the ambassador is pacing the reception room now, cursing every moment of delay."

He smiled and shook his head. "I had the others in your group escorted back to your tower. I will not rush this, lest I make a mistake. We will reconvene this evening."

Lyr didn't tell her that it would hurt or that they would need time to process the transfer. He *could* not, for the knowledge would cause her to fight against the spell. It would be hard enough for him to complete, knowing full well the cost, but he'd gone through the process countless times and had built a certain resistance to the pain. Instead, he sent a mental call to Lial to be prepared and then moved his chair up to hers until their knees almost touched.

He found the place within his mind that held the spell and triggered it as he pulled in energy from the world around him. He gathered the power into his left palm, the light of the spell pulsing blue, and sketched a series of symbols with his right hand. As he had done with Arlyn just a month before, he turned his hand to place the ball on Meli's forehead, pushing the energy through. But this time he would pull forth her language before giving his own.

There were no words to trigger this part—Lyr's language held no sway over hers. As he touched a finger to her forehead, he hummed a deep, resounding tone that streamed the essence of her language into a second ball of energy in his left palm. Meli's breath caught, and she trembled beneath his finger. Only a handful of heartbeats, but he knew from experience that it felt much longer. When he pulled away, she shuddered and shook her head.

He forced himself to relax as he cupped the spell in both hands. Meli watched him, and if she saw his pain, she might tense during the next portion. With a slow and steady exhale, Lyr lowered his shields and pressed the ball of energy to his own forehead. But despite his best efforts, his breath hitched as the power slammed into him, her language pouring in so fast he didn't try to grasp at the words. His mind shrieked with the new channels being built.

All he could do was allow it even as his vision grayed around the edges.

When Lyr could focus once more, his lungs burned with the breath he needed to take. He fought to stay steady, to keep from pulling in gasping lungfuls. A frown gathered between Meli's eyes, and he feared he hadn't hidden the pain as well as he should have. Alfheimir had been one of the most challenging languages he'd learned so far—he had the headache to prove it.

"I am not sure of this. You understand me now, right? It's well?" she asked.

Lyr puzzled through her words, her language not yet fully integrated into his mind. Language was a tricky thing, a social construct that took time to fine tune. "Mostly, I think."

"Isn't that sufficient?"

He could have explained that she needed to understand what his own people said to avoid any diplomatic confusion. He could have told her that he wanted to hear his words on her lips. He could have said many things, but none of them would have eased the worry lighting her eyes. If he tried to do the final portion of the spell now, it would fail. Possibly permanently. She needed a distraction.

Lyr leaned forward and pressed his lips gently to her forehead before she could protest, the simple contact like the sting of iron on flesh. But powerful. So powerful. As she sucked in a breath, he whispered the final words against her skin. "*Laeial by maliar na Moranaia dae gher.* I imbue the Moranaian language into you."

Meli cried out as the power flowed through her, and she pushed at him blindly before grasping her head. He released her, knowing she would be angry at him for the kiss but unable to regret it. After a moment, Lyr reached out once more, caressing her arms in a comforting rhythm as he waited for her to pass out as Arlyn had. But in this, she surprised him. After several long moments, she looked up and glared.

And turned his own favorite curse word against him.

⁂

"*Clechtan!*" Meli shouted as she leapt to her feet, the chair behind her scraping the floor. The word tasted strange on her tongue, the literal meaning warring with her innate understanding of it as an expletive. Something about an unpleasant afterlife? *What?*

Her head hurt as though a frost giant crushed it between his fingers. *Except frost would be soothing.* Hoping to ease the pain, Meli tried to relax the scowl she levelled at Lyr and steady her breathing. *In and out. In and out.* She closed her eyes against the afternoon light spearing through the regrettably large number of windows. Nothing helped. In her mind, she practiced every swear word of her new vocabulary.

She didn't even look when the door opened. If it was a person of ill-intent, she would welcome them, so long as they ended her misery. Meli hadn't felt pain like this since failing the mage test, and that had shredded every personal shield her meager magic could scramble together. Still, when Lyr grabbed her arm to steady her, she jerked away and bit back a moan at the jolt in her head. Her eyes snapped open so she could glare at him once more.

A chuckle caught her attention, and she turned to see an auburn-haired Moranaian approaching. He shook his head at Lyr even as he smiled at her. "Still charming the ladies, I see."

"Enough, Lial." With a scowl, Lyr gestured to Meli. "Just heal her headache and leave off needling me."

"Not yours?"

Lyr walked to the window, his gaze focused on the garden beyond. "I can manage."

Meli's frown deepened even as she returned to her seat. Did he think her weaker than he? Although part of her wanted to prove otherwise, she was no fool. She closed her eyes and let the sweet relief of the healer's magic wash through her. Her muscles relaxed as the pain faded, and her previously jumbled thoughts clarified. He had kissed her, and with no warning or permission. All for the sake of a *spell.*

The soothing energy faded, and the healer moved away. She gave herself a few more moments before she glanced up, only to see the healer's hands spilling blue-colored energy into Lyr's head. Good. Now she could yell at him without feeling guilty about his headache. The thrill of that kiss, that unwelcome brush of his lips, shot through her once more as if to mock her. Instead, it raised her ire.

After a quick, muttered exchange with Lyr, the healer departed, taking a bit of Meli's courage with him. Lyr's direct gaze, focused completely on her, eroded it further. "You should not have done that," she snapped.

He could have prevaricated or evaded, but he surprised her. "The kiss? You are correct, and I offer my sincerest apologies."

Meli's anger deflated to a shadow of itself, though she tried to sustain it. "To do such a thing without consent, all for a spell—"

"There you are wrong." Lyr took a step forward, his shoulders drawing up tightly as he straightened. "I shouldn't have done it without your permission, simple though it was. And it is true that I needed to distract you so you didn't block the spell. But I assure you that I kissed you only because I wanted to."

"Oh, I…" Meli cleared her throat to cover her uncertainty. "This should be nothing. I mean, it was my forehead. The same way you might kiss a child."

His mouth quirked into a wry smile. "Was it?"

Had she thought of frost giants earlier? Meli felt certain she would burst into flame from the strength of her blush. "Nothing can come of this. I cannot—"

"What?" he demanded when she cut herself off. "Consider an attraction to a Moranaian?"

Meli bit her lip and tried to hold back her tears. Trembling, she stood. "I apologize if I've given that impression. It is *my* weakness. You would do better to seek a match elsewhere."

His brows rose. "I don't understand, Meli. I haven't tried to force you into completing our bond."

"I know." She huffed out a breath, no longer certain if she was annoyed with herself or with him. "Just…forget this happened. I'd better get back to the others."

Lyr's gaze was intense as he stared into hers, but he only nodded. "Of course."

⚬ ⚬

Head tipped back and eyes closed, Lyr rested in the chair he kept next to Eradisel. He'd left his long coat on a display stand and tossed his circlet onto a side table before settling himself into the cushions and propping up his feet. He didn't have long before he had to meet with the ambassador again, but his mind needed a break. Just after Meli's departure, Loren had contacted him for yet another negotiation. Perhaps Lyr's formal attire had been impressive—the requested mages would be arriving in two days' time.

Though they exchanged no words, Eradisel soothed him with her energy, the gentle warmth easing the tension that had knotted his muscles since speaking with Meli. But it didn't take away his troubles. So much pain and so much loss. When he'd first seen Meli by the portal and recognized the connection between them, a secret well of hope had formed. But based on her reaction to him, he should probably fill the damn hole with sand and fire the whole thing into glass. Even a simple kiss on her forehead was distasteful to her.

By Arneen, he had too much to do to let himself linger on it. Aside from the meeting, he still had to transfer Alfheimir to Kai and Arlyn. With a groan, he pulled himself from the comfort of his chair and sent a wordless thanks to Eradisel. As he dragged on his long, heavy vest, Lyr reminded himself that a potential soulbond was no guarantee of happiness.

How very well he knew.

⤜⦾⤏

"Let's dispense with formality, shall we?"

Lyr stood before the desk in his study, no longer willing to grant the ambassador the honor of a full reception. The shift hadn't gone unnoticed. Ambassador Teronver lifted her chin and glanced at Arlyn and Kai, who were flanking him. A flicker of ire flitted through her eyes as she noticed the absence of the others, though she hadn't known their rank. A smaller number of people hearing her petition was rebuke enough.

"If you wish, my lord."

"I will give you one chance to present your request to me."
His gaze bored into hers. "Do not ruin it."

The lady inclined her head, but there was no sign of defer-
ence in her expression. "I come from Alfheim, City of Light and
Air, home of the Ljósálfar since time immemorial. My king
sends us forth to find aid for the blight that is spreading ever
closer to our home. Our most wise and aged seer picked us herself and bid us come to those of the land of Moranai."

Lyr was accustomed to formal language, but he still wanted
to roll his eyes. Hadn't they just agreed to dispense with it?
"What is the nature of the blight?"

"We are uncertain." Her spine stiffened, and she lifted her
chin higher. "Our mages are powerful beyond measure, yet they
know only that the energy is poisoned. The source is from outside our realm."

"Have any become ill?"

The lady's tinkling laugh filled the room. "Ill? The Ljósálfar
do not sicken. *Others* might suffer such affliction, but we are well
beyond that."

"I am not speaking of human illnesses, Lady Teronver." Stifling a sigh, Lyr searched for more patience. "Our ancient cousins, the Sidhe, are also afflicted with poisoned energy, and they
have suffered madness and death. We all need energy to survive—even the Ljósálfar, I presume."

"We have not noted signs of madness." The ambassador
paused, her gaze cutting to Meli for a moment. "Though perhaps we should verify that it is not causing…weaknesses in our
children."

Meli's gasp at the insinuation sparked his already tenuous temper, but Lyr shoved that feeling down, too. "If you are not concerned about illness and your own mages are beyond compare, why have you come to us?"

Lady Teronver's hands twisted together as her face went blank. "My king assured me that we needed aid, and the Ancient One sent us here. I thought we would find a greater civilization, full of power, but—" She choked off her own words, her mouth pinching into a white line. "It is no matter. I will do as my king bid."

Why had Alfheim's most ancient seer picked this elf above others to represent their people? He could hardly stand to speak with her, much less negotiate. Nothing he offered would satisfy Lady Teronver. "What sort of aid did your king wish you to obtain?"

"Mages, of course, and earth-healers if you have them. None venture into the blighted lands, but there is little left beyond Alfheim proper. The poison has overtaken the distant forests and is seeping into our fields, disrupting some of our food production spells. Our city must be shielded and the land purified."

They'd let it affect their food supply before seeking help? The Ljósálfar truly had grown reclusive beyond all measure. "My House is more known for warriors and scouts than mages and healers, but Moranaia is much larger than you have assumed. There are other Houses I can contact for what you need. It will, however, take some time."

"Time?" Lady Teronver flicked a disdainful glance around Lyr's simple study. "How long could it possibly take to contact your...outliers?"

This time, he did allow a small smile to slip free. "Milady, there are almost thirty million people in our land at last count. Finding the right person is rarely an easy task."

"Thirty million…" The ambassador looked to the window. "But where…?"

"You would do well not to judge us by your own ideals. Although there are some, particularly those of the plains, who build large cities, many prefer to live in harmony with the forest."

Her mouth tightened at the rebuke. "As you say."

"Indeed." Lyr merely nodded, ignoring her peevish tone. "I'll begin consulting with our mage branch at once. You are welcome to remain so long as you can avoid causing offense, and I will arrange another meeting as soon as I have more information."

He waved a hand in dismissal, but she simply stood, staring. "But this is for Alfheim. City of Light. Its well-being is of vital importance. How soon might I know more?"

"I heard nothing in your report to indicate urgency." He gestured for one of his guards to step forward. "I hope to have some news for you in three days' time, though it may be four. There are other matters of importance that I must attend to."

"But—"

"It is my job to work with any Earth-originating fae culture, and others have petitioned for aid before you," Lyr snapped. "However, I will proceed as quickly as possible. If I am unable to gain cooperation from the mage branch in a timely manner, I will send a missive to the king."

Her eyes narrowed. "Our people deserve precedence."

"Good day, Lady Ambassador," Lyr replied, implacable.

She glared at him but said nothing more before marching from the room. The others followed, Meli's gaze lingering for a moment before she, too, rushed away.

ৎ৩৫

As the light faded beyond her window, Meli paced the confines of her room. Food had been delivered below, but she hadn't gone down to collect a plate. She was too upset to eat. Besides, her bedroom floor swayed with every gust of wind, making her stomach lurch with more than just nerves. How did the Moranaians get used to this?

If she took Lord Lyr up on his offer, she might just find out.

Meli shook her head, and this time, it was her heart that clenched. She still couldn't believe he'd said she could stay. Casually, like it was a simple thing. Didn't he see that she'd be a terrible match for him? He was powerful. Confident. Assertive. Everything she was not. It had to be due to the bond he sensed between them. If he knew *her*, he'd let her go without a thought.

She'd already hurt him with her cowardice. But then, he didn't know the cost he'd pay if he joined with her. When she returned to Alfheim, she would be forced to choose her future path, and her lack of talent would confirm her place in obscurity. The Ljósálfar had little patience for imperfection, and she was the embodiment of it. In her own land, she would be deemed unmarriageable—unlikely to have children. She could hardly bring that stigma to a man who seemed as honorable as Lyr.

And if she didn't return to Alfheim at all? It would only confirm the rumors of her weakness—rumors her high-ranking family hadn't been able to entirely stifle. A wasted attempt, Freyr bless them. Meli brushed away a wayward tear at the thought of her parents and her brother, though she saw the latter rarely. Either way, they would suffer shame.

Too bad she couldn't just disappear into the mists.

12

Lyr leaned against a column and stared out the observation tower window. With both moons nearing full, he hadn't bothered with a mage light, and the night wrapped around him like the gods' own peace. So high above the estate, bathed in the moonlight pouring in the windows, Lyr could almost forget the turmoil that awaited him below. Almost.

In the morning, he'd have to draft a formal report to the king. After the arrival of both the Neoran diplomat and the Ljósálfar, matters were clearly escalating. The energy poisoning problem had to be addressed, and Lyr would get much more done with the king's full awareness and backing. By Arneen, it might *take* a royal command to get one of the rare earth-healers to travel off-world.

Unless he could gain the fairies' cooperation. Lyr frowned into the distance, though the fairy pond was hidden by the trees.

They weren't technically under Moranaian rule, having been offered asylum millennia before. But when they'd fled Earth...Lyr let out a groan. The Ljósálfar had denied them entry to Alfheim.

The fairies would not offer aid.

Sensing Kai's energy at the base of the tower, Lyr pushed aside his worried thoughts. Or at least tried. No telling what dark news his friend might bring. Maybe a flood? A war between Houses? An invading army of dragons? Lyr's lips twitched at the last thought. If the dragons broke their truce after close to forty thousand years, his current troubles would be nothing.

"I knew I'd find you here."

Lyr turned at the sound of Kai's voice. "Is all well?"

"For once, yes. No new disaster." Kai jostled the basket in his hand, catching Lyr's attention. "After today, I thought you could use a break."

They settled on the cushioned benches that curved around the room. While Kai opened the wine and pulled out glasses, Lyr put the plate of sweet cakes between them. He understood what his friend did not say. They'd been friends for over five hundred years, and before Arlyn's arrival, they'd spent time together much more often. This lull was a fine excuse to do so.

Lyr took a glass of dark red wine, one of the few types that could intoxicate one of their kind, and cradled it in his hand. Getting drunk was a difficult and intentional process for elves, since they had to purposefully stop their own regenerative magic to avoid purging the alcohol before it could take effect. Even still, there were few brews that affected them at all. When he was able to indulge in such wine, he savored it.

"So what do you think about the *lovely* ambassador?"

"As Arlyn says, she's a snobby bitch," Kai said, tipping his glass in mock salute.

Lyr chuckled. "She actually said that?"

"Once she could hear the woman for herself. And she's right. From what I've heard, the Ljósálfar have always been…difficult."

"There was little information about them in my books. At least…" Lyr took a sip of wine. "At least in the books in my study."

"Still can't brave the library?"

His sigh rippled the liquid in his glass. "Not yet. Most of the relevant books *should* be in my study, but I could be wrong. Would you mind checking for me? I just—I just can't enter."

Kai nodded. "I don't mind. You'll go in when you're ready."

"I hate this weakness." Lyr lifted a slice of sweet cake from the plate, but he only stared at it. "*Laiala* lived. There's no reason for this."

"Some traumas take time." Kai leaned forward, his fingers going white around his wine glass. "I still wake with nightmares from my own attack, you know. Or of killing fath—Allafon. His bloody head has rolled across that dungeon floor in more dreams than I care to count."

Lyr grimaced at his friend's words, though he himself had been unconscious by the time Allafon had been beheaded. "*Miaran*, Kai. Have you spoken to Lial?"

Kai lifted a brow. "Have you?"

"Point taken." Lyr took a long drink of wine and let it burn through his blood.

For several moments, they ate in silence—but an easy one. Lyr shoved back the dark thoughts their conversation had brought forward and waited until some of the tension had eased from Kai's expression before speaking again. "I don't suppose you know any earth-healers?"

"Hmm," Kai hummed around his latest bite of cake. Brows furrowing in thought, he took a long drink of wine and gave a quick nod. "I believe Oria has one, if she's still alive. If father—Allafon—didn't murder her. Moren would know."

Lyr winced at the strain that returned to his friend's voice. He still hadn't asked if Kai was relieved to know that Allafon hadn't been his real father, but he didn't want to press. He knew what it was like to have others poking at such things. "Would you mind going out to the fairy pond in the morning? If they're unwilling to help, head over to Oria to speak with your brother."

"As you request, milord," Kai said, grinning.

Lyr rolled his eyes and downed the last of his wine. "For that, you can clean up this mess. *I'm* going to get some sleep."

Kai's laugh followed Lyr from the room, but it was a hollow sound. The tension in it dragged at Lyr with every step down. *Clechtan.* He should have seen Allafon's darkness sooner. His *father* should have seen. Had House Dianore done their duty, Kai's mother would be alive. And Kai wouldn't have had to kill the person he'd thought was his father.

One more thing to place at Lyr's feet.

⁂

Sunlight barely wove through the tree trunks, and Lyr's feet left prints in the morning dew as he walked to the village. He had woken to a message from the tavern keeper, an unusual enough occurrence to cause alarm. That his actual presence was requested had him hastening to respond. According to Merrith, morning would be the least busy time.

Lyr cut down the stone path that circled the pond in the center of the village and curved back toward the tavern. Light globes suspended on delicate wooden poles lit the way, the only sign of life in the otherwise dim courtyard. A few lights flickered from the homes built into the trees above the shops, but most windows, save the tavern's, were dark. Of all those in Telerdai whom Lyr knew, Merrith slept the least. Rarely was The Middle Ground shuttered.

The main room was quiet when he entered, and the worn wooden tables were all empty. Merrith, his long blond hair tied back with a piece of string, stood at the back cleaning glasses. Against the long mirror behind him, a line of bottles gleamed, though not many. Most people came to eat the midday or evening meals, not merely to drink.

With a nod, Merrith set down the glass he held and waited for Lyr to approach. "Good morn, Myern. Forgive me for calling you here at such an early hour."

"I was already stirring when I received your message. I hope all is well?"

They chatted for several moments, the tavern keeper updating Lyr on business and general village gossip. After politeness was satisfied, Merrith pulled a freshly-cleaned cup from the counter and poured a drink. "But I know you did not come here at dawn for an update on my sales. I have a fine juice just in from the north, where the ereth berries are harvested early.

Please sit and have a glass, if it pleases you, while I share the true reason for my message."

Lyr took a seat at the bar and lifted the drink to his lips. The tart hit first, as usual, followed by a rush of sweetness that blended perfectly. "*Erethai* juice is always pleasing."

"Certainly more so than my news." Merrith poured one for himself and took a sip, his gaze sober over the glass. "There have been rumors swirling through the village."

"Aren't there always?"

Merrith shook his head. "Not the typical. Word is that there was another attack, one like your previous trouble. In that instance, I paid little more heed than usual. Up until I heard that Allafon had rebelled, I found the rumors overblown. This time, I've been inclined to listen. Listen and watch."

"Indeed?" Lyr savored another sip of the juice. "I assume you've seen or heard something I need to know?"

The glass clanked on the counter as the tavern keeper set it down and leaned toward Lyr. "A stranger came in last night around the twenty-sixth hour. We get travelers now and then, but this one was different. Despite the heat, he wore a heavy cloak. He asked for a good deal of fresh bread and a hot meal in broken Moranaian."

Lyr's fingers tightened around his nearly empty cup. "You think it's the assassin?"

"I can't be certain," Merrith answered, a frown curving his lips down. "He deflected all questions I asked about where he was going or where he'd come from, but with the medallions given to travelers having our language spell, I can't imagine anyone but an intruder speaking that way."

"Were there any other clues?" Lyr ground out. His vision narrowed on his white fingers as anger poured through him, and he forced his hands away from the glass before he broke it.

Concern pinched Merrith's eyes. "I heard him mutter something about the lack of streams on the east side of the valley as I slipped into the back. He might not have realized I could hear him, but it could also—"

Lyr shoved away from the bar, toppling the stool behind him. He barely registered the crash as he spun toward the door. The *drec* had dared to enter *Lyr's own village* for fucking supplies. Did the assassin think he couldn't be stopped? If so, he had no idea of Lyr's true power—now that he was healed. It was time to stop cowering. Out of reflex, he gripped the hilt of his sword as he pushed through the door.

"Myern!"

He paused to look at Merrith. "Send a message to Kai and tell him to follow."

"You shouldn't go alone. This could be a trap," the tavern keeper said.

"Maybe." A slow, humorless grin twisted Lyr's lips. "But once I find him, he won't live to regret what he catches."

ↁↂ

Hands clasped, Kai and Arlyn walked along a path on the back edge of the gardens. To the left, the trail leading to the portal stretched into the distance. Another, smaller path forked off to the right, and in easy silence, they took it. Arlyn smiled. Their mission might be important, but the day glowed with promise. There weren't even lingering clouds from the storm that had blown through a few hours before dawn. The relentless heat of summer had also dimmed a bit.

"Fairies, huh?" Arlyn asked, giving Kai's hand a quick squeeze.

His brow furrowed. "I told you about them, didn't I? You saw my glass sculpture."

"Yes, and it is beautiful." Her smile widened at the memory. He'd been unpacking some of the glass figures he'd created, a complete surprise to her. Her brash bonded, a patient artist. "But I don't remember if you said much about the fairies themselves. Just that most creatures like them remained in dimensions closer to Earth."

"That's right." With a gentle tug, he brought them both to a stop. "But most of the ones who are here aren't really citizens of Moranaia. They have their own leaders and laws."

Arlyn frowned. "And my father just lets them stay?"

"In return for asylum and the use of the land, they guard that segment of the border. And they help the Myern when necessary." Smiling, Kai ran a finger along her cheek. "Nervous?"

"A little."

"Just be sure to stop at the perimeter and wait for permission to enter."

Arlyn pulled them into motion again, her pace faster this time. With a chuckle, Kai followed her eager steps. What could she say? It wasn't every day a person got to see a myth. Then her lips twisted up. *She* was half-myth herself. *Ah, perspective.*

As they approached the end of the path, the trees thinned to reveal the gleaming water beyond. A fine mist rose in lazy tendrils from the surface despite the growing heat of the day. Arlyn halted just before the end of the trail, but there wasn't a living creature in sight. Were they in the right place?

Then three fairies darted above the surface to hover over the mist, and all she could do was stare.

All three were about a foot in height and pale-skinned. The female in the center had dark blue hair that flowed around her gauzy dress like water, and the other two, both male, wore shades of green and orange. All three stared in silence, their faces inscrutable, before the female in the center shook her head.

The fairy's lips moved, but the voice seemed to come from all around them. "Not yet. You will have need of us, but not now. Return only then."

Before the echoes of the strange voice had faded, the fairies were gone. The mist floated above the still water as though it were never disturbed, and no sound was left but that of the forest. A trickle of dread skipped through her as she turned to Kai. "What did she mean by that?"

The worry in his eyes rebounded through their bond. "I don't know, but it didn't sound good." He sighed. "Well, onward to Oria, I suppose. Maybe we'll have better luck with Moren."

13

The sun had already risen over the tops of the trees as Lyr climbed up the eastern slope of the valley. His fury burned hot, but his steps fell silently. Though the chances were small that he'd catch the assassin sleeping, it was possible if he moved carefully. Merrith had said the man spoke in broken Moranaian, a clear sign of an outworlder, so the assassin might not have adjusted to their thirty-hour days.

The fiend could only have come through the portal.

Kai's brother, Moren, had claimed that their father had followed the orders of another, one he'd been unable to uncover. But from another plane? There were plenty of worlds that could be reached through the Veil, but few of them were inhabited. It could be no coincidence that this was occurring at the same time as the energy poisoning affecting so many realms. If Lyr could find the source, then perhaps he could solve all their problems.

There were few good places to camp on this particular hill, the lack of water only one of the problems. The forest here was largely untouched, the ancient trees and undergrowth allowed to run wild. Though the inhabited lands appeared uncultivated to some, they were carefully maintained as such. Not here. The homes of Telerdai stretched to the north across the base of the valley instead. If the assassin was hoping to be undiscovered, he had chosen a good location.

After an hour of climbing rocks and giant tree roots, Lyr stopped to rest. Sweat poured from his back onto the boulder he'd found to lean against. Though the season of Toren was nearing a close, it was as hot as the solstice at noon. He longed to strip off his tunic, but he could leave nothing traceable behind. He'd even dissipate every droplet of sweat from the rock with a spell before he moved on.

He might feel numb most days, but he had no wish to die, either.

Lyr was methodical in his search, but by midday, he'd found no sign of anything save the *daeri* that grazed the hillside in herds. He peered down into the valley below, the village all but invisible from this height if he hadn't known where to look. He settled in the lee of two massive trees for another rest and tried to ignore his stomach's rumbling. His rage might have settled into simple anger after the long search, but it had only left room for other sensations. Like hunger.

Where was Kai? He and Arlyn should have returned some time ago from Oria, but so far, Lyr had not detected his friend. Not even Kai could have tracked him through these woods. Lyr knew every rock and tree from his boyhood years of exploring them. Did the delay spell more unpleasant news, or had Merrith's message gone awry? Either way, it looked like he was on his own.

With a sigh, Lyr shoved away from the tree. There were few favorable places left for the intruder to hide, and one in particular stood out—the hidden grove. As he turned to head toward the clearing near the summit, he palmed a knife in his left hand and made sure his sword was loose in its scabbard. He might not be able to feel the assassin with his usual senses, but he would do his best to be prepared.

♰

Kai walked through the portal and stepped to the side so Arlyn could follow. He had enjoyed seeing his brother, a relationship finally possible between them with their father dead, but the day had otherwise been a waste. The earth-healer he'd remembered from his childhood had died six years before—and not of natural causes. Another attrition caused by Allafon.

Arlyn laid a hand on his arm. "Are you okay?"

"Yes, I'm just..." Kai ordered his muscles to relax, but they seemed disinclined to listen. "We lost a day trying to find out what happened to the healer just to hear of her murder. Let's just say I'm relieved to not really be of Allafon's blood."

She sighed. "I hate having to tell *laial*. He was so hoping that this part, at least, could be solved easily. I'm worried about him."

"As am I."

Dreading the coming discussion, Kai trudged toward the study in silence. It was an hour or so before the evening meal, and the halls were empty. Kai had no idea where Ralan might be, but he hoped it was with Lyr. Who knew if the prince had foreseen this news? Kai would rather report it only once.

But when they entered the study, it was empty. He glanced at Arlyn in concern. "Did he say he was going out? He told me to report to him here."

"No." She rushed toward the desk as though she'd somehow missed seeing him. "This is the time of day that he typically reviews estate accounts. Could he be training? Checking on Grandmother?"

Kai searched along the mental link, his key to the estate, and was further alarmed to find no sign of his friend. His energy was completely absent from Braelyn. "He's not here."

"Yeah, I know."

"No, search along the estate key. He's completely gone."

His mental conversation with Ralan was even less productive. The prince hadn't seen Lyr all day, and if he knew why, he refused to say. Kai's chest tightened. His friend clung to habit tightly, any deviation fairly unusual. Could the assassin have come without anyone the wiser? Just as he turned to search his friend's room, Koranel entered.

"Lord Kai, is all well?"

"Have you seen the Myern?"

Though he looked taken aback by the abrupt question, Koranel shook his head. "I have not. But I do have a message for you."

Kai grabbed the paper from his hand with unseemly haste, caring little for what the other thought. He broke the seal so quickly that the paper tore, forcing him to slow down. But when he finally read what was inside, he cursed. He cursed long and hard.

"What is it?" Arlyn asked, even as she reached for the paper.

"It's from Merrith, the tavern keeper. He spoke to Lyr just after I left this morning. There was a suspicious person at the tavern looking for supplies last night, and Lyr went after him. Alone. He wanted me to follow when I returned."

"Damn," she muttered in English before scanning the paper as though he'd missed some detail. "Damn, damn, damn."

"That was hours ago now. I have to head out at once."

"I'm going with you." Arlyn grabbed his arm. "But before you rush off, might I recommend we get our weapons?"

Kai grinned despite himself. "I knew there was a reason we bonded."

ം⊙⊘

It was almost evening before Lyr reached the summit. The large clearing a half mark behind him had been empty, leaving only a few small pockets near the top of the hill to search. It was beginning to seem that the stranger's words to Merrith had been a diversion at best or a trap at worst. But the search was nevertheless gratifying, something more active than the endless negotiations in his study.

Lyr slowed as he approached the next clearing. This one was difficult to reach, the entrance hidden between two downed trees the size of a house. The walls of the clearing were bound in boulders taller than a man. As a child, he'd pretended it was a fort. But it was a lonely fort, his invaders all invisible. There had been few other children near his age even in a relatively large settlement. The cost of longevity was often loneliness.

Vines draped over the small opening between the disinte-
grating tree trunks, but he knew better than to enter there. It
was the most obvious point, the one most likely to be guarded.
Instead, he followed the edge of the tree trunk on the right. The
wood had long crumbled into the suggestion of a tree, the wood
near to compacted earth by now. As a child, it had been fresh,
the trees only fallen a few years before. But when he climbed
over the heavy trunk, he found that the secondary entrance between two of the back boulders was still there.

Lyr flattened himself against the cold stone and peeked into
the gap. Flowers twisted gently in the evening breeze, the only
sign of movement. But something felt...off. The insects still
buzzed and the birds still called, but their songs sounded tentative. Like they, too, were unsure of the safety of the place.
Soundlessly, he pulled his sword free and readied his knife in his
other hand.

Though he cast his energy in a wide search, he found nothing. He slipped between the boulders and crept closer to the
clearing. Nothing but swaying flowers in the center. But as he
neared the edge of the stones, a mound near the far edge took
shape. The remains of a camp fire? Lyr stilled everything—his
body, his energy. This had to be it.

Without warning, the intruder appeared, his cloak falling
free. Lyr caught a glimpse of dusky skin and black hair before
the other strode forward, sword in hand. The steel blade of the
man's weapon wasn't much better for Lyr than cold iron, but at
least it wouldn't shred his shields or drain his power so long as
it didn't make contact.

If it did make contact, well, he'd be prepared this time for the loss of power.

Lyr sprang into motion, his quick, sharp movements designed to mask his intentions as he met his attacker in the center. Metal connected with enough force that a lesser warrior might have lost his grip. Lyr merely pushed the other's blade aside and slammed the pommel of his knife into the assassin's exposed shoulder. With a hissed breath, the man danced back.

"Who sent you?" Lyr asked in English.

His opponent laughed as he recovered, spinning into another blow. "Do you think I'm stupid?"

"Choosing this clearing? No." Lyr smiled as he parried. Then he ducked into an opening and cracked his foot into the other's knee. "But one can hope."

Whoever the man was, he had a talent for fighting. Though he stumbled back, almost dropping from the kick, he managed to dodge Lyr's return blows. Perhaps a hint of combat magic? He spared a moment's attention for a quick scan and smiled again at the result. The assassin *did* have the ability, but he lacked control over the magic. Perfect.

"You might stand a chance if you'd been properly trained," Lyr said as he pushed his opponent back and ducked in to slice at his waist.

"I *have* been trained," the assassin ground out, spinning just in time to avoid a wound.

"Not fully, I'm afraid." Lyr feigned a look of sympathy. "Who taught you?"

The other man only grinned. "Not stupid, remember?"

The hair on his arms rose when he sensed an object hurtling toward his back, and he shifted to avoid it. A costly move. His opponent slipped beneath his guard and sliced a line across his right rib, the contact with the metal sapping Lyr's magic until little remained. He cursed and darted back. Turning himself to face both threats, he watched the cloak fall off another. Two of them. Foolish, foolish, *foolish* of him not to consider the possibility.

"Ready to give?" the first assassin asked with another laugh.

Though blood flowed freely from his side, Lyr's eyebrow rose. "For this scratch?"

Lyr swung into action, going on the offensive despite his missing magic. He might have been caught by surprise by the loss of power during his practice session with Teyark, but he'd prepared himself for the possibility in the interim. Magic was, after all, only a bonus. And he *would* fight—he'd never let himself be captured again.

For a while, the second man merely watched the renewed battle, his stare unrelenting. In fact, he seemed to hold no weapon. No scabbard or bow. If he was a mage, he was a useless one. Another frown pinched Lyr's brow. He could sense that they weren't entirely human. Didn't they realize the steel had rendered his magic useless? A mage would strike with impunity.

His opponent grinned. "Come now, is this all? I hope my own bastard father has more power than this."

"Power isn't everything," Lyr responded.

The assassin snorted, his expression twisted into disdain. It was all the distraction Lyr needed. He shoved his sword forward faster than thought. The blade pierced the man's stomach and twisted through, severing the spine. The assassin's dark eyes widened, and the air whooshed from his lungs. Lyr heaved his arm back, jerking the sword free, as the man fell into a heap.

Out of the corner of Lyr's eye, he caught the quick shift of cloth as the other man hid once more. *Miaran.* He cast his senses out as best he could with his magic so reduced, but he didn't have the skill to break the spell imbued in the cloak. He shifted restlessly, ready for the slightest hint of attack. Then the first man let out a groan, and Lyr glanced down.

The assassin's dusky skin had gone gray—half-Dökkálfar?— and his hands pressed uselessly against his open wound as he writhed in pain. He should finish him off now, granting some mercy. Not even an assassin deserved to waste away in the slow, miserable death that kind of wound would bring.

Lyr sheathed his knife and crouched down, balancing his sword with both hands for a quick, precise blow. He paused to scan the clearing. Still empty. A shudder rippling through him at the necessity, he took a deep breath and prepared to plunge his sword into the assassin's heart.

A presence flared to life behind Lyr, shrieking through his shaky combat senses. His magic tracked the motion as the second man struck, plunging his knife around to slip into the soft spot beneath Lyr's left lung. Lyr twisted to the side, but he didn't have time to completely dodge the blow. The blade sliced into his abdomen and then slashed up his chest until it tangled with his pendant.

Letting his cry of pain turn into a bellow of rage, Lyr slammed his elbow into the assassin's stomach. Before he could bring his sword around, the man retreated with a breathless chuckle. Lyr tried to turn so he could trace the assassin's movement, but the world pitched around him as his magic drained away.

The knife must have been iron.

Lyr toppled over. Great Gods, the agony... His body convulsed as the iron burned through him. He lifted his free hand to the wound and hissed as his fingers found the dagger tangled in his necklace. Trembling, he grabbed the hilt and pulled it free, then used his last bit of strength to toss it away.

A thunk against flesh and a cry of pain gave some satisfaction amidst the pain.

"Fucking elves." A voice muttered from above. "Now I have to haul Beckett back before he bleeds out. Should've brought a damn healer."

Lyr shifted to his back, looking for the source of the voice, but his vision grew hazy as the iron drained his energy. Light. A shifting blur. Then even that cut off, and soft fabric brushed against his flesh as it settled around him. He lifted his hand to pull the cloth from his face, but he was too weak to shift the flimsy barrier.

"Be a good elf and stay here to die, okay? You're invisible now. You'll be bones before they find you." Then a muffled chuckle. "My best kill yet."

The cloak. *Miaran.* His whole body chilled as he realized the stranger was right. No one had been able to detect the assassins under these cloaks. Lyr's people would never find him. His eyes slipped closed, and the ground grew sticky with his blood. With each gasping breath, his chest burned as the flakes of iron left behind by the knife dug deeper.

One last chance. With the last of his strength, he shoved his magic against the iron, trying to convert it with Arlyn's spell. A fine time to realize how much he wanted to live. If this failed, well... He might not have been captured, but he wouldn't have an easy death.

So much for mercy.

14

Meli shook the runes yet again and let them drop onto the stone bench beside her. When nothing happened, she groaned. The swirling lines refused to settle into a solid pattern, even when she asked to find easy things, like the stream on the other side of the garden. So much for showing her paths. Over the two hours since Pol had needled her into working with them, she had stuffed the runes back into their bag more than once and resolved to leave them there.

Maybe it was because she was searching for things that weren't lost. She was a stranger here with few belongings—nothing of her own to find and no one who needed help. Sighing, Meli swept the runes into her hand and ran her thumb along a smooth surface. Could the runes' first success have been some trick of the mists? Pol could have been mistaken—or he might have manipulated the entire situation. He could have controlled the runes without her knowing.

Or maybe she was too distracted. Part of her—the most foolish part—wanted to see Lyr, despite all the reasons to avoid him. Not that he'd want to see *her*. The look in his eyes when she'd told him a match between them wouldn't work…Meli shuddered at the memory. Had she ever seen such despair?

"Let me do this on my own."

Meli's head jerked up at the querulous words, and she blinked hard at the sight of an elven woman leaning heavily on a white, wooden staff. Though she visibly trembled, the woman shot a dark look at the elf walking beside her. The healer, if Meli wasn't mistaken. As she stared, he steadied the woman again, earning another glare.

"If you fall, you could undo—"

"You said my spinal column was fully healed and my muscles only need strengthening," the woman said, her brows lifting. "So let me strengthen them."

Meli couldn't hold back a gasp. What could have injured an *elf* so gravely? The Ljósálfar could be hurt, of course, but she couldn't recall seeing one of her own people so nearly crippled. She clutched the runes against her stomach and tried to look small. Maybe they'd pass by without noticing her. Surely, the woman would not be pleased to have a stranger see her weakness.

Unfortunately, Meli didn't have the power to make herself invisible. Her movement must have caught the woman's eye, for she paused to look at Meli before hobbling a few more slow steps closer. "Good day to you," the lady said with a smile. "Please forgive my interruption."

Meli frowned in confusion. "I'm afraid I don't understand. How could you be interrupting me?"

"A guest's comfort is paramount here," the woman answered. The healer moved between them, though he kept giving the lady worried glances. From the words Meli had overheard, he was probably afraid the woman would topple. "If not introduced to the household, guests are given their privacy."

"Oh," Meli said. No wonder the gardens always appeared empty. "I should probably return to the tower. I don't want to deny anyone the use of the gardens just because I'm here."

The woman smiled as she hobbled a little closer. "There's no need for that. You've met Lial, correct?"

"I…" Meli glanced at the man again. "I think so. If I'm not mistaken, you're the healer who examined us after we arrived. And you healed my headache."

"I see I'm memorable," he muttered, then chuckled at her wince. "Ah, forgive my ill humor and allow me to introduce you. This is Lady Lynia Dianore, Lord Lyrnis's mother."

Meli's cheeks cooled as the blood rushed from her face— probably to join her stomach at her feet. Lyr's *mother?* What had he told her? Did she know that Meli had rejected her son? *Freyr help me.* "I'm…my name is Ameliar Liosevore," she choked out. "But please call me Meli."

If Lyr had said anything, Lady Lynia gave no sign, her expression just as pleasant as it had been a moment ago. "It is a true pleasure to meet one of the Ljósálfar. I'd pay my weight in gold to have accurate books on your history and culture."

"You're a scholar?" Meli asked, relaxing a bit.

"Oh, yes. I—" The lady's words cut off, and she swayed on her feet. The healer darted forward to steady her. "Lial...something..."

For a long moment, Meli's head spun, and she lifted a hand to her forehead. Bile rose up the back of her throat along with a sick sense of dread. *What...?* She shook her head to clear it as the healer lowered Lady Lynia onto the bench beside her. Lial knelt, taking the lady's hands in his own.

"What is it?"

"Lyr." Face ashen, Lynia stared at the healer. "I thought I caught pain from him. Now...now I can't detect him."

Meli felt her eyes go wide. Had she sensed Lyr's pain, too? It would explain the sense of apprehension. "You think he's dead?" she whispered.

"No," the lady answered. Her worried eyes pinned Meli's. "I would have felt that. It may not be the same for the Ljósálfar, but we Moranaians share a link with our children. He's in trouble." Lynia turned back to the healer. "We have to find him."

Lial didn't look at Meli as he swept the lady into his arms and started up the path, but his voice echoed back as he hastened away. "I'll take you to the study and call for Kai. If there's a trail, we'll find it."

If there's a trail... Meli's chest squeezed, and she forced herself to release her breath. Then take another gasp of air. Could she do it? *Breathe out.* Could she use the runes to find Lyr? *Breathe in.*

She'd just spent hours failing. Surely the Moranaians had people more skilled than she. But the memory of Lady Lynia's stark, desperate fear caught at Meli, and her hand tightened around the runes.

Too bad they couldn't show her the best way forward.

She yelped as light flared from between her fingers and her hand began to tingle. Trembling, Meli dropped the stones onto the bench once more. The light settled to a soft glow, and she gasped. The emerald green line she'd followed through the mists speared from the center stone. It took a few more moments for the other shapes to settle, their energies weaving around the green before they too shot into the distance.

And suddenly she knew. The light she'd followed through the Veil hadn't been to Moranaia. It led to Lyr.

As did this light.

She gathered the stones back into their pouch and jumped to her feet. The magic carried her beyond what was currently visible—beyond the estate and into the valley she'd admired her first evening here. Her mind's eye rushed from the valley floor up to a small, hidden glade, where the glow ceased. She couldn't see Lyr, but she sensed he was there. And the path to him didn't move.

I should find the others. But she didn't. Meli's entire body shook with the urge to follow that green line, and she found her feet propelling her forward. Though she had no weapon, though she knew it was foolish, she gave herself over to the power. She passed through Lyr's home without escort, her feet and instincts taking her into a side door and all the way to the front entrance.

She couldn't speak to the puzzled bodyguard who trailed her as she stepped out the front door. She could do nothing but follow where the magic led.

ৎৡ৫

"You can't sense him anywhere?"

Arlyn tried to keep her voice calm, but panic set in with the darkness. The barest hint of twilight remained, leaving the rising first moon to guide them. Thank goodness Kai was familiar with the terrain. The rocks and ancient trees were a maze she never could have navigated on her own.

"Nothing." Kai's voice caught. "It's like he never passed through here."

Just a few weeks before, she hadn't even met her father. Now the thought of never seeing him again terrified her. "Could he be hiding himself magically?"

Kai stopped to lean against a boulder. "Possibly, but he's expecting me to follow. He should have left some sign. Some way for me to contact him."

"Maybe the tavern keeper was wrong about the direction."

"Arlyn, I…" He squeezed her hand, his eyes somber. "I just don't know."

She understood what he didn't want to say. That chances were good that her father had been captured—or killed. Arlyn gripped her bow tight. It would be next to useless in the dark, especially against an assailant they couldn't see. But her bow was as much comfort as defense, and she was still barely passable with a sword.

Her shoulders straightened with resolve. "We have to keep trying."

"I never said we wouldn't." Kai scowled, his frustration pouring through their soulbond. "I can't believe he left by himself. What the hell was he thinking? It's the kind of thing…well, it's something I would have done."

"Would have?" she asked with a lift of her eyebrow.

"Before you," he murmured, and his expression softened for a moment before he pushed himself away from the stone.

They climbed to the next clearing, this one as depressingly empty as the one before. They searched every bit of ground they could find, but they saw no signs of passage. No footprints—not even a bruised leaf. Arlyn bit her lip as she watched Kai examine a small pile of moss-covered rocks. How were they ever going to find her father?

Kai stiffened as a rustling sound broke the peaceful silence. He gave a quick signal, and they darted behind a giant tree, its huge roots providing extra shelter. Carefully, they peered over the side, and Arlyn was grateful for her elven eyesight. Though the forest had darkened with shadows, she could still discern the difference between trees, rocks, and trails.

As though nature held its breath with them, the noises around them stilled—all but the shifting of the brush. Someone was coming, and the newcomer was not being subtle. Beside her, Kai drew his knife, and Arlyn nocked an arrow in her bow in case she found a clear shot. Unlikely in the gloom, but better than doing nothing.

When Lady Ameliar stumbled into the clearing, Arlyn's mouth dropped open in surprise. It could be no accident that the elf had appeared here, so far away from the estate. Were the Ljósálfar involved with whatever had happened to her father?

Her heart ached with the realization that her father's potential bonded could be a traitor.

Or perhaps Ameliar was drawn to Lyr through the soulbond.

Resolved to find out, Arlyn stood. "Lady Ameliar!"

Kai tried to tug her back down, but she pulled free. The blond elf barely turned, her eyes unfocused. "Meli. By Freyr, why won't any of you call me Meli?"

Though he huffed out a sigh, Kai followed Arlyn as she approached the dazed woman. He fussed at her through their mental link, but she ignored him as she grabbed Meli's arm. "What are you doing out here?"

"Can't you see the green line?" Meli whispered. "I must follow it."

Arlyn gave Kai a worried glance. "I'm sorry, but I don't."

"I think it goes to Lyr." Meli lifted the bag she gripped in her right hand. A soft light pulsed through the seams. "I've been following and following, but he still isn't here. Close, though. Much closer."

"Alive?" Arlyn couldn't help but ask.

Meli shook her head as though trying to clear it. "I'm not sure, but I think so. I think..."

Arlyn let her go, and the woman lurched forward, not sparing them another glance. After sharing a nod with Kai, they turned as one to follow Meli—their only hint at Lyr's location.

Their only hope.

15

This was nothing like the mists. Meli's heart pounded as she fought to gain a measure of control over magic that had taken over her world. She'd managed to surface enough to speak to the red-haired girl—her daughter?—and the girl's mate, but that hadn't lasted for long.

Her daughter? Meli shook her head and gasped for breath. What was she thinking? This power had muddled her mind. Too much for her. *Arlyn.* The girl was Lyr's child, not Meli's.

She heard rustling behind her, but she couldn't make herself turn to discover the cause. The green line of power drew her ever harder. *Over that rock and around that tree. Climb the downed trunk.* Meli caught the sound of a thump and a muttered curse from Arlyn's mate as they followed her beneath a fallen branch. She could spare nothing more than a sympathetic wince as the magic carried her forward.

By the time she reached the summit, the moon's light filtered through the branches to give the forest a silvery glow. She stumbled to a halt, staring at the spot where the green path disappeared into a dark opening between two huge mounds. Had this been part of her initial vision? Everything looked different at night. But though her feet slowed and her mouth grew dry, Meli couldn't help but approach the place.

She yelped when a hand wrapped around her arm.

"I am sorry for startling you, Lady Meli," Arlyn's mate whispered. "There's a hidden clearing there. Let me go first to ensure your safety."

Meli fought against the draw of the runes, but she managed to allow him to dart ahead before she followed. Her hand clutched the pouch as she slipped between the two mounds and into a moonlit clearing—this one far from undisturbed. The scent of crushed flowers filled the air, and she followed the green line to a seemingly empty spot near the far side.

She heard Arlyn's despairing voice behind her. "There's nothing here."

When the path of power ended, Meli sank to her knees and fumbled along the ground. Her hands didn't find the grass her eyes saw—they sank into fabric-covered flesh. "Here. Here."

She pulled at the cloth, frantic. When it was removed, Meli could finally see him. Lyr's face glowed white under the moon, and his eyes were closed. The girl cried out behind her and rushed to his side, but Meli barely paid heed. Blood, black as the night, coated his light tunic, the moon's gleam giving it a sick sheen.

It's too late. For the barest moment, her heart seemed to stop.

Then she heard him groan, so low she almost missed it, and she could breathe again. She tossed her head to clear it of the last traces of magic and then looked up at the others. "What do we do?"

"Maybe Arlyn can teleport us. She did it when I was attacked a few weeks back." The male looked over at the girl. "Do you think you can?"

"I can try." Arlyn placed her hand on her father's shoulder as her mate grabbed her hand. "Meli, hold on to my arm."

Meli reached across Lyr and gripped the girl's arm, perplexed but willing to try. Her magic was so slight that she knew little of how it worked. Arlyn's eyes closed, and her brow pinched in concentration. Moments ticked by as they waited, until finally the girl jerked her hand free in frustration.

"It won't work. I'm willing us back as hard as I can, just like when you were hurt, but nothing," Arlyn said in a quivery voice. "I need Selia."

The male sank down next to his mate. "I'll see if I can stabilize him. I have enough healing talent for that."

Meli stared at the glow that sprang from his hands as he hovered them over Lyr, but she could see little difference when the light faded. She squinted against the sudden dark, searching for some sign of improvement. "Did you heal him?"

Arlyn's mate shook his head. "I only had enough power to stop the bleeding. I think there's iron in the wound. We'll have to get him to Lial."

"Is he well enough to move, Kai?" Arlyn asked.

Kai merely nodded and bent to lift Lyr, the move effortless. Meli studied the crushed grass to see the large pool of blood reflecting the moonlight. Lyr had been invisible under that cloak. Without her power, he wouldn't have had much longer to live. He might have never been found.

A shiver going through her, Meli followed the others as best she could. She was fit and strong, but her speed was no match for Kai, clearly accustomed to this clime. As she stumbled on another rock, her footing less sure without the magic to guide her, another hand gripped her arm. Even Kai and Arlyn paused at her startled scream.

"At peace, milady."

Her pulse calmed at the sight of the guard who often trailed her, the one she'd tried to talk to at the estate. Kai stared for a moment and then nodded at the pale-haired male who held her before turning to go. "You followed me this far?" Meli asked.

"As my Myern commanded. I can carry you down if it would not cause you discomfort. I train in these woods and can make greater speed."

The idea *did* cause her discomfort—but not as much as falling behind in the ancient forest. Without the glow of power to guide her, she would get lost quickly in the darkness. "Very well."

۞

When Kai swung through the doors of The Middle Ground, the place was empty, a few of the tables pushed together next to the anxious healer. Thank all the gods Lial had come this far. With each step of their eternal descent, Lyr had grown weaker, his breathing shallower and his skin cooler. Kai might have thought his friend dead without benefit of the healing magic.

Kai stretched Lyr out as gently as possible and stepped back. "I got much of the bleeding stopped, but with the iron in the wound, I'm not sure why I could work on it at all."

"Let's see." Lial placed his hands over the gash now visible across Lyr's chest and stomach and released his power. His look of concentration changed into a frown as the glow faded. "You're right but…not. I believe he tried to convert it. Ayala, could you finish what he started so I might better heal him?"

With a nod, Arlyn held her hands over her father, her power pulsing around them for several moments. As soon as she finished, Lial nudged her aside, and the blue glow of his magic lit the room. Then his assistant stepped forward with a needle and thread and began to sew the wound in Lyr's stomach.

"I told him not to do this," Merrith muttered as they stood aside to give the healer room.

"When I spoke to him last night, he wasn't himself. He said he hated his weakness." Kai's hands clenched at the memory. "But I thought his mood had eased by the time we parted."

Merrith's brows rose. "He acted much more careless than usual. I told him to wait for guards, but he would not."

"He *did* send for Kai," Arlyn said, her expression tightening as she glanced at her father. "If we hadn't been delayed, the outcome might have been different."

Kai took her hand and gave it a squeeze. "Maybe. But he's not usually so reckless. And he just found another soulbonded. Why would he—" His gaze fell on Meli, and his words choked off at her pained expression. Had something happened between her and Lyr? "Well, he hasn't been himself."

Meli let out a gasp as pain speared her heart. Had Lyr almost gotten himself killed because she'd rejected him? Surely not. He'd only met her a few days before, and there was nothing about her to create that sort of response. But the weight of grief shading his eyes even when he smiled and the hollow, hopeless look he'd given her as he'd spoken with the ambassador? Meli's hands twisted together. No, her rejection certainly hadn't helped his mood.

She found herself standing above his head. The healer and his assistant blocked her view of the wound, but the pallor of Lyr's face shook her. Meli didn't know him, not really. But she *did*. She ached with the need to see his eyes open again. Would they have the answers she sought? As she'd wandered up the hillside to find him, she hadn't been herself. Emotions had tangled within her—a mix of love and fear that made no sense in such a short time.

Giving in to the urge, Meli stroked her hand through the spill of his dark brown hair. Just before she'd cast the runes, she'd wished to find the best way forward. They had lead her straight to Lyr.

It doesn't mean we're meant to be together. Then she sighed as the truth of that caught in her heart. Lyr was a powerful lord. He would never want the liability of mating with an Unfavorable One. However he was supposed to help her move forward, it wouldn't involve love.

৩৩৩

Fingers aching from her grip on her walking staff, Lynia heaved herself to her feet and bit back a groan at the quick movement. *Torture.* Each drip of the clock had been torture as the others had searched for Lyr. All Lynia had been able to do was sit—sit and ache, inside and out. As his energy had been born and nurtured in her womb, so they were connected, and she knew when he felt true distress. His pain resounded in her own bones. Had it been this agonizing for him when she lay dying on the library floor? Gods, she hoped not.

But the agony of waiting was nothing compared to the heart-stopping burn in her chest as the door opened and Elan, Lial's assistant, entered with Lyr magically suspended on a carry-board behind him. Lynia cried out when she saw the angry, newly sewn gash across her son's chest and stomach. What had led him to be so reckless? She shoved a hand across her mouth as the horror of it washed over her. Not her son. *Please, Gods, not Lyr.*

Lial entered behind the carry-board and then paused in the threshold to order the others to remain outside. His pallor alarmed her almost as much as Lyr's. How much energy had the healer expended already? But he didn't waver as he shut the door firmly behind him and helped Elan settle Lyr in the bed. That cursed bed. She'd spent more hours healing there than she wanted to count.

By the time she made her fumbling way over, Lial had settled into a chair and entered another healing trance, his magic surrounding Lyr. Lynia sank down next to her son and rested her brow against his. Not even the shrieking pain in her back could stop her as she gave him what energy she could. Whatever he needed.

"Lynia," Lial said, his voice rough with exhaustion. "Lyni, stop."

She didn't bother opening her eyes. "I won't let him die."

"He won't." She felt the soft pressure of Lial's hand around her wrist. "I healed the worst of it in the village. This is just for strength. For a faster recovery."

Lynia tilted her head so she could meet the healer's eyes. "If I can give him my strength—"

"Stop," Lial whispered. "This isn't your fault. You know he wouldn't want you to do this."

"I should have talked to him." She let out a hiss of pain as she straightened, but she pushed the agony of movement aside. After all these weeks, it had become a near-constant companion, anyway. "I knew he was upset about what happened, but I thought he needed time. I should have forced the issue."

Lial cupped her cheek, and a hint of his power flowed from his fingers to soothe her aching muscles. "As should I. I'm his healer."

"And I'm his mother," Lynia said, swatting his hand away. "Save your power for him."

The healer stiffened. Pain and anger shifted in his gaze, and she worried that he'd taken her action as a personal rejection. But before she could reassure Lial, he turned back to Lyr and fell into another healing trance without saying a word. *Clechtan.* Lynia pressed her fist against her chest and bit back a sigh. She really hadn't meant that the way he'd seemed to take it, though in truth, she wasn't certain *what* she wanted to do about Lial.

He might be in love with her, but she had no idea how she felt. Lyr's father, Telien, had been her world. Her soulbonded. How could she consider another, even after twenty-two years? Was the draw she felt toward the healer worth the risk of pain?

Of another loss? Lynia's shoulders slumped. A month since she'd guessed Lial's feelings and she still had no idea what to do.

Elan moved away from Lyr's other side and placed a hand on her shoulder. "Allow me to get you a chair, Lady Lynia. Lial is certain to slip me an unpleasant potion if I let you injure yourself further."

She snorted at that, knowing as well as Elan that the healer's threats were mostly bluff. *Mostly*, of course, being the key, since one never quite knew with Lial. To spare Elan's stomach—and her own back—she allowed him to help her to her feet and settled herself into the chair he brought. Then waited. And waited.

By the time Lial pulled away again, dawn chased the edges of the sky. Lynia swayed in her seat with pain and exhaustion, but she'd refused Elan's suggestion to seek her bed. Not until she heard from the healer himself that Lyr would be okay. She'd seen the gash on her son's chest ease into a deep, red scar, but that wasn't enough. She needed the words more than breath.

"He'll truly live?" she whispered when Lial looked up.

The healer nodded. "He will be weak, but yes."

Lynia sagged with the relief of it, and tears welled in her eyes. "Thank you. And I'm sorry for earlier. I—"

"Don't," Lial snapped. Then he ran a hand across his face and gave a weary smile. "Forgive my ill humor. I am exhausted beyond telling." He stood, swaying for a moment as he stared down at her. "You were bonded, Lynia. I understand. I always have."

Her heart lurched as he stumbled away and then climbed the stairs to his room. What could she say? Part of her wanted to call him back, but the other part wanted to run. She struggled to her feet with a wry grimace. Running wasn't in *her* immediate future. Wincing, she waved off Elan and waited for the agony in her back to ease before hobbling across the room.

Lynia slipped into the quiet of morning's twilight. Then she let out a muffled yelp as a hand closed around her arm. She spun around, almost falling with the movement, only to meet Lial's eyes.

"What...?" She frowned at him. "I thought you were sleeping. Go rest before you collapse from lack of energy."

His lips tipped up in a smirk. "And let you get hurt stumbling back to the house? I'd just have to use more magic healing you."

"Fine," she muttered, though she let him tuck her arm in his.

She really didn't know what she was going to do about him.

16

L ight glared into his eyes, and Lyr threw his arm across his face to block the glow. Where was he? The afterlife? A pleasant place, if so. He was cradled on some soft surface, warmth bathing his face. The scent of herbs flowed around him, and he relaxed into the feeling it brought. But the smell tickled his memory, and when the truth hit, he groaned.

The healer's workroom.

With a sigh, he moved his arm and opened his eyes, squinting against the burst of light. Almost immediately, his face fell into shadow, and he blinked against the sudden shift. A person stood above him. Was it... "Aimee?"

The figure jerked back with a gasp. "No."

Lyr rubbed his face and struggled to a sitting position, a more difficult task than it should have been. When his eyes finally focused, he found himself looking at Meli. He winced.

"Forgive me. No doubt it was the feel of the bond that confused me."

Her smile was slight and somehow sad. "I should find it an honor to be mistaken for someone so loved."

What could he say to that? Lyr would never forget Aimee—would never want to—but he didn't want to hurt Meli, either. With a helpless shrug, he shook his head. "I'm sorry. I don't know what—"

"Lyrnis Dianore!"

He flinched, his senses so dull he hadn't even noticed the healer's presence. Behind Meli, Lial rushed over from his workbench, and Lyr's gaze caught on the table where his last wound had been healed. At least he wasn't there again. "You sound like my father, Lial."

The healer scowled down at him. "If he were here, I imagine he'd sound much worse."

"Why am I…"

Before he finished the question, the memories rushed back. The battle in the clearing. His injury. Blood pooling beneath him in the dark. A quiver passed through him at the thought of that hopeless dark. He'd tried to convert the iron in his wound so he could gather the energy to escape, but he'd passed out before he could succeed. How had they found him?

"Why are you alive? Here? Foolish?" Lial snapped, eyes flashing.

Lyr had never seen the healer so angry—a feat considering Lial's general surliness. Lyr sat up as straight as his wavering muscles could manage and swallowed back embarrassment at his weakness. A few paces away, Meli stared at him with wide eyes. Did she think less of him now that she'd seen him at his worst? She'd rejected him with less cause.

"Do you have some explanation for this?" Lial demanded.

Lyr's brows rose. "Watch your tone."

"When you watch your suicidal decisions." Lial pushed him back down, taking no care to be gentle. "Do you know what it's like to heal someone so close to death? You were a few breaths away, my friend."

That close? Lyr's body went cold at the thought, and the tension that had begun to build at the healer's anger slipped away. How could he begrudge another's worry for him? "I'm sorry. Truly. I should have waited for Kai. But all I could see was a quick resolution to this mess. I thought I could take the assassin unaware and find the source of it all." His gaze slid from Lial's. "Besides, I'm no longer indispensable. Kai is more than capable of helping Arlyn with estate—"

"You thought to leave an inexperienced girl from Earth in charge of negotiations between the Sidhe and the Ljósálfar?" Lial barked. Then—worse—his voice fell soft and frigid. "That's almost cruel."

The truth of that stole Lyr's breath. Had he died the night before, poor Arlyn would have been left with an even greater mess. None of the other fae races would be inclined to deal with an heir so newly established, much less a half-blood one. The Ljósálfar could fall to their own pride, but people like the Neorans relied on his help. Arlyn was far from ready to take over.

"You're right," Lyr whispered. "I am foolish beyond compare."

"Now that you've regained some sense, let me see how you're healing."

Lyr closed his eyes and let the energy pour through him. His body was so heavy with exhaustion that sitting up had sapped him, but he couldn't relax. Not with Meli lingering by the window, her attention focused on him. He shifted uncomfortably and tried to think about something else. There was a great deal he needed to get done. For one thing, the mages for Neor would be arriving today.

At least he hoped it was today. How long had he been unconscious?

"Aside from lingering weakness caused by blood loss, you're remarkably well," Lial said as the blue glow faded from his hands. "I guess you should have kept that jar as decoration after all. I certainly could have used it last night."

Lyr bit out a laugh at the reminder of his last healing. "I'll keep that in mind next time."

"It had better be a few centuries from now," Lial muttered. He looked over his shoulder at Meli. "If not for Lady Ameliar, you'd not have that chance."

"Meli?"

She stood in front of the window, washed in light. Her blond hair gleamed as white as her robe, the cloth made nearly transparent by the glow. Without thought, his body hardened. If she were wearing one of the thin summer dresses favored by Moranaian women, the sight would have been even more spectacular. Perhaps he should speak with Telia, the head seamstress. That long-sleeved robe was surely stifling Meli, and—

"Lyr." Lial snapped his fingers. "Mind hearing the tale?"

The healer's smirk brought a flush to Lyr's face. He hadn't been caught so brashly appraising a female since he was thirty years of age. "Yes, of course."

"Kai and Arlyn were wandering the hillside and having no luck finding where you'd gone when Lady Ameliar appeared out of nowhere. She said something about a green line and knowing how to find you. Certain enough, she led them right to you. You were completely invisible to the eye."

The lady in question turned from the window—a shame, that—and walked over. "It wasn't me. It was the runes."

Both men looked at the pouch she tugged from her belt. The word was familiar to Lyr, but he had no true understanding of what she meant. "Runes?"

She opened the pouch and poured the contents into her hand. The nine smooth stones were beautiful, but they hardly provided an explanation. "These. See the patterns? Somehow when I ask a question, they show me an answer, a path. I followed them through the mists, too."

Lyr frowned and shook his head. "They appear blank."

"Blank? But..." Meli gave them a scowl of her own. "I suppose Pol enchanted them for me, then. I thought the others saw the patterns in the mists."

"If the runes came from him, there's no telling *what* anyone else saw," Lyr said wryly.

She blushed, an interesting contrast to her pale hair. "I should not have taken them, but he insisted. It seemed even less wise to refuse."

"Indeed."

They settled into a sudden, awkward silence, the healer smirking at them both. Lyr sat up once more and was about to turn so he could stand, but at the smooth slide of cloth against flesh, he glanced down. He was completely naked under the blanket. He shot Lial a look that had the healer chuckling.

"The wound went down to your stomach, assuredly easier to treat without clothes. Rest easy, though—I waited until we'd brought you back from the village to strip you." Lial walked to the staircase leading up to his quarters. "I'll see if I can find something to fit you so you don't scandalize the lady. You never know about the Ljósálfar."

This time Meli's flush was one of anger. "My people are not so prudish as that, nor am I some innocent maiden, despite my age. Do you take me for a human miss from times long past?"

"Forgive me, milady." Lial shrugged. "If it's no bother to her, then come. It will be easier to find something with you there to try it on."

Lyr was too tired to do anything but take her at her word, and he needed to get back to work before the mages arrived, if they hadn't already. Recovery time was a luxury he didn't have. Though his every muscle protested against it, he shifted his feet to the floor and paused, gathering his energy. With a deep exhale, he pushed himself to standing and then wavered there for a shocked moment. Gods, he was weak. But he wouldn't let himself crumple in front of Meli.

Closing his eyes, Lyr pulled in energy from around him, and the gentle support of Eradisel flowed through, strengthening him. He straightened and then opened his eyes to find Meli staring. She'd flushed red, but she couldn't seem to tear her heated gaze from his body. A groan slipped free as he began to harden again. He cut his eyes away and sought control before he embarrassed them both.

Where was his reserve?

Lyr gritted his teeth and staggered to the staircase. Her gaze burned into him as he shuffled forward, and a spark of pride lit beneath his embarrassment. At least she could no longer deny her attraction to him. Whatever held her back, it certainly wasn't that. A slow smile slid across his lips as he reached the stairs. She *did* feel the same pull.

He turned back to her at a sudden thought. "Meli? Why were you using the runes to look for me?"

Meli picked at the sleeve of her robe. "I—I wasn't. Not at first. I was practicing in the garden when your mother sensed you missing. It just happened. I just had to go."

Lyr nodded, though he suspected there was more that she hadn't told him. "Then I thank you."

☙⊛❧

When Lyr finally disappeared up the staircase, Meli found her breath once more. She only had herself to blame for falling for the healer's needling. Although it was true she was no innocent and nudity was not taboo in Alfheim, her heart could have done without the sight of Lyr naked. By Freyr, he was gorgeous. Every warrior inch of him. She tried to block the image from her mind, but it was probably burned there forever.

Meli's fight for control wasn't won within herself but by Arlyn's arrival. Her eyes went directly to the bed and widened when she found it empty. "Lial said my father was awake," Arlyn said. "Where is he? Is he okay?"

"He is well." Meli gestured toward the staircase and hoped devoutly that her red cheeks weren't too noticeable. "He went up with the healer to find some clothes."

"Ah, yes. I didn't think about that." Arlyn peered at Meli and then grinned. "Wait, was he naked? I'm definitely glad I missed that."

Meli sighed and cursed her pale coloring. "I imagine so."

It was confounding how familiar Arlyn seemed. Memories from the night before flashed through Meli's mind, especially the one where she'd almost called the other woman her daughter. Could whatever bond she might have with Lyr cause that kind of confusion?

Arlyn's smile faded, replaced by a considering frown. "Have you ever been to Earth?"

"No." Meli twisted her hands together. "I'm only twenty-five, just at the age of traveling."

"Father was right. You *are* younger than me." Arlyn stared at her for so long that Meli's stomach pitched with worry. "Yet you still seem...familiar."

Should Meli tell the girl—woman—that she seemed familiar as well? That Meli felt like she knew both Arlyn and Lyr? It was nothing but the truth, but truth often came with its own consequences. Still, she deserved to know.

"I feel the same," Meli admitted.

Arlyn's forehead furrowed. "Interesting. I wonder what it could mean?"

Before Meli could reply, Lyr and the healer returned. Both Lyr's borrowed tunic and pants were a bit snug, and her body heated at the memory of what the cloth hid. Ah, curse it. Mortified, she spun toward the door before they could see her blush. She had no desire to face the healer's mocking smirk once more.

"Meli?" Lyr called, and she looked over her shoulder to see him swaying on his feet.

"The others must be looking for me." She smiled. "Besides, I'm sure you wish to talk to—to your daughter."

She fled before he could stop her. Had she almost said *our daughter?*

ℰ

"Do you need to sit?" Arlyn asked softly.

Pulling his gaze from the door where Meli had stood, Lyr shook his head. He had no idea why Meli had run away, but she'd been right. He did need to speak with Arlyn. His daughter deserved no less than his full attention. "I'll be well enough for a moment."

Her brow quirked. "You're swaying."

"I'll live," Lyr said with a smile, though his body had tensed. Why hadn't she yelled at him yet? "And…I'm sorry. As Lial rightly reminded me, I would have left you with quite a lot of trouble to deal with. You must be angry. If you need to—"

Arlyn threw her arms around his neck, cutting of his words and knocking him a step back. "I'm not. I'm just glad you're alive. I thought I'd never see you again."

"You almost didn't," Lyr whispered into her hair as he gathered her close.

They stood like that for a while, squeezing each other tight. Lyr's throat clogged with all the words he couldn't say. He had a lifetime to apologize for, and it would never be enough. Now he'd done this. How had she forgiven him so easily? *Clechtan,* but it was time for him to stop living in the past. Time to be the father Arlyn deserved.

When she pulled away, they smiled at each other, and something within Lyr eased. He tugged at a lock of her beautiful hair, so like her mother's. "I suppose this means you have truly accepted me."

Arlyn laughed. "Somewhere along the way, I guess I have. But I need to work on my fierceness."

"You…what?" he asked with a frown.

"Don't you remember the first time I helped you with paperwork?" Mischief glinted in her eyes. "I seem to recall saying that if you ever grew suicidal, I'd kill you."

Lyr let out a chuckle. "Ah, yes. Though I swear I wasn't *trying* to get myself killed."

"Tell that to your mother," Lial said, his voice slicing through their moment of humor. "She was up until dawn sitting with you. Her injury pained her so much she could hardly walk back to her room."

The slice of iron through flesh was nothing to the agony of that thought. Lyr's shoulders slumped. Of course she blamed herself. Wouldn't he do the same if Arlyn had done something like this? "I'll go speak with her. The meeting with the mages can wait."

Lial shook his head. "She's only been asleep for an hour or two. Let her rest."

Lyr sucked in a breath. It would be beyond difficult to focus on estate business knowing how he'd hurt his mother. "You have a healing-link to monitor her?"

"Of course," Lial snapped.

"Let me know when she wakes." Lyr swayed again and then pulled in more energy to augment his waning strength. At least walking around injured for over a month had taught him how to ignore physical weakness. "I'll push aside any other business for her."

The world would just have to get by on its own for a while.

17

As soon as Meli opened the door to the tower, fingers wrapped around her arm and tugged, and she let out a yelp in fright. What *was* it with people grabbing her lately? Scowling, she jerked her arm free and straightened. As expected, the ambassador stood with mouth pinched and hand stretched out as though to reach for Meli again.

"You have no right to touch me," Meli bit out.

"Well, well." Lady Teronver sneered, though she dropped her hand. "Bold for one who disappeared without a word and stayed gone all through the night. Dare I ask where you have been?"

Meli tilted her chin up. *No one* needed to know that she'd lingered outside the healer's tower until dawn, unable to pull herself away until she could check on Lyr herself. "No, you do not."

The ambassador gaped. "You insolent—I will see you re-turned to Alfheim as soon as I can arrange it."

"I wish you good fortune in getting the Myern to agree to such a thing."

Teronver eased closer, expression suddenly sly. "So that's where you were. Earning favor on your back, no—"

At the crack of Meli's hand against the ambassador's cheek, everyone in the room stilled. Berris, the attendant assigned to be Teronver's guardian, stood by the dining table with Orena, both trying to stifle a grin. *Possible allies after all?* Before Meli could explore the thought, the ambassador stepped back, a ball of energy growing in her hand.

Meli drew her stinging palm against her chest and tried to pull up her meager magical shields. Teronver was no true mage, but just about any spell would be enough to harm Meli. It didn't matter. By Freyr, she refused to cower any longer. She had done no harm to this woman, and if there was enmity, it wasn't Meli's doing. Disparaging another's sexuality was a grave insult, and she would not back down.

"Go ahead," Meli said, her eyes narrowed. "The others will be certain to report your slur to my parents."

The elder merely shrugged. "My family is powerful enough to weather it."

The hum of magic filled the air, and Meli braced for the blow. But as Teronver raised her hand to cast her spell, Pol stepped from behind Meli to grasp the ambassador's arm. The ball of energy winked out instantly. "Enough, hag."

"You!" The lady tugged, but Pol hardly budged. "You forget your place, and it is beyond foolish to ally with this one."

"There is only one fool here, and it's not me." A spark of fire seemed to light his eyes as he grinned. "Probably."

When Teronver pulled on her arm again, he released her. "I will send you back with the girl."

"You think so?" he asked smoothly, and something in his tone made Meli shiver.

Pol stepped close to the elder and leaned forward to whisper in her ear. Had she heard him mention Hel? She couldn't be sure, but whatever his words, the ambassador grew paler than Meli had ever seen her. The woman actually trembled where she stood. When he backed away, she nodded and then turned to rush up the stairs.

Silence fell, and Meli exchanged looks of awe with the other two girls. Whoever Pol truly was, she was no longer certain she wanted to know. Then he turned his grin on her, power still flashing like fire in his eyes, and she amended that thought. She absolutely *did not* want to know.

"Thank you," Meli said

He bowed before her with a flourish. "My pleasure. I take it you found purpose in your lessons yesterday?"

"You knew," she whispered. "Why didn't you warn me? Or him?"

His smile never wavered. "It was not for me to do. Didn't you want to explore those woods?"

"Not like that." The memory of the darkness, the fear, the compulsion—Meli shuddered. "Never like that."

ఌఄ

Lyr propped himself upright with one trembling arm and stared into the long mirror on his dressing chamber wall. Gods, but the gash had been a deep one. The line of his wound, well knit but still dark pink, stretched from just above his heart almost to his belly button. After a moment's hesitation, he touched the healing injury with his free hand and winced at the dull pain that throbbed in his chest.

No wonder Lial had argued against Lyr returning to work.

Yet with the Neorans in such need, Lyr had no choice but to return to his duties. This was beyond the petty feud between House Anar and House Nari or the bickering of travelers in the tavern. He could spare a day or two away from *those* types of reports. The lives of thousands of Sidhe? Lyr wouldn't rest abed while others went insane or died—not if he could do something to help.

Just meet with the mages and see the details set for the mission to Neor, Lyr chanted to himself as he shuffled over to his clothing shelves. *Just that, then rest.*

It took longer than Lyr would ever admit to get dressed, though he wore only a fine tunic and a matching pair of pants. His gaze fell on the heavy, embroidered overcoat he would normally put on next, and he snorted. Not even *he* would try to feign that level of strength. If the Taian mages were offended by his lack of formality, well…a small insult would be better than the indignity of collapsing at their feet.

By the time he placed a small, silver circlet across his brow and returned to his bedroom, Lyr's body felt heavier than his entire estate. Though he eyed the bed, he knew better than to risk that—he'd surely sleep the day away. Instead, he dropped into the seat next to Eradisel. His breath came in short gasps

and his hands shook where they rested on the chair. How was
he going to do this?

"You need aid," the sacred tree whispered into his mind.

Lyr slumped as he looked at Eradisel. *"You have given a great
deal already, and that much I didn't deserve. I forgot my most important
duties to race away after—"* His breath caught. *"The assassins. I forgot
the assassins."*

"Ease yourself," She said. *"They have passed through the portal to
the Veil."*

"Passed through..." he said aloud, smacking his forehead
with his palm. *Why* hadn't he thought to ask Eradisel, living link
to the Goddess of Portals and the Veil, if She could sense the
assassins? *"You can see through the cloaks they wear?"*

"Sometimes." Vague, indecipherable images flickered through
with the words. *"Like rain on the wind. Here but not."*

His brow furrowed. He'd grown adept at communicating
with the tree, but there were times She couldn't put her thoughts
into a form he could understand. *"Rain on the wind?"*

*"Hints of moisture wrap around the leaves, but the source remains out
of touch."*

"Ah." Lyr smiled as the confusion cleared. She meant the
humidity of an approaching storm. *"You get hints of their presence
but nothing clear?"*

He sensed her affirmation—the touch of energy She used as
a nod. *"Until they entered the Veil. They revealed themselves on the way
to the Earth-portal."*

His breath hissed out at that, and he levered himself to his
feet. So the source of their trouble *did* hail from Earth. *"Thank
you, my friend."*

"Be well," Eradisel whispered.

Her words were not an idle benediction. Strength poured into Lyr, and he stood straighter, no longer in danger of toppling under his own weight. Maybe, just maybe, he could do this.

⁕⁘

Groaning at the sight of the new stack of papers waiting on his desk, Lyr sank into his seat. He didn't have the time or energy to read about crop yields, especially since he had competent people in charge of those estates. A long sigh escaped, and he shifted the reports to the side. They'd have to wait.

He let his eyes slip closed as he pulled in more energy from the world around him. The simple walk from his bedroom had burned off much of what Eradisel had given him, and his healing wound ached at the slightest movement. Maybe he should nap on a cushion of unfinished paperwork. He snorted at the thought. Wouldn't that be a sight?

A knock sounded on the door. Lyr had just managed to straighten before it opened and Kai strode through. "I can't believe you just—"

"At peace," Lyr interrupted with a lift of his hand. "I know what I did was foolish. For what it's worth, you were right."

Kai's brow furrowed. "About?"

"Remember when I yelled at you for trying to go after your attacker while you were still healing?" At his friend's nod, Lyr continued. "You told me I wouldn't handle being injured any better than you. Consider me humbled."

After a long pause, Kai let out a sharp laugh. "I hadn't meant to curse you."

"I know," Lyr answered, grinning. Then he shifted forward, and the pain that sizzled along his chest made him wince. "I just hope I recover quickly. I have no doubt that other assassins will be sent soon."

"Did you find out more about them, then?"

"Only that they truly are from Earth," Lyr answered, his fingers tapping an angry beat on the surface of his desk.

Kai's brows rose. "You know this for certain?"

Lyr's thoughts flashed back to the clearing. *I hope my own bastard father has more power than this,* the man had said in clear English. So much for half-bloods being rare. Lyr's stomach dropped. *He* hadn't known about Arlyn. How many other races of fae had left lovers behind on Earth without checking for children?

Silence fell as Lyr's fingers froze. "Gods," he whispered.

"Lyr?" Kai took a quick step closer. "If you *aren't* certain, there's no—"

"It's not that. Eradisel Herself confirmed they were from Earth." Lyr's nostrils flared. Why would half-bloods journey to Moranaia to attack him? How would they know the way? "At least one of the two was half-Dökkálfar."

"*Dökkálfar?*" Kai's eyes widened. "I didn't think their kind traveled to Earth very often. You think they'd be careless enough to leave children behind?"

Lyr stiffened, his throat convulsing around a sudden lump. Careless. Lyr had certainly been that with Aimee. "We both know that once can be more than enough."

"Fuck it all," Kai muttered with a frown. "You know I wasn't thinking about you."

"I *do* know." And he did. With a deep sigh, Lyr pushed a few stray strands of hair from his face and forced himself to relax. "But it'll take a few centuries to truly forgive myself, no matter how inadvertent my actions."

Kai opened his mouth as if to answer, but they both froze at the mental ping the estate shield emitted to signify gate or portal activity. Lyr's heart gave a quick jolt even as he scanned the magical link. Ah, the transportation gate that eased travel between estates in Moranaia. The Taian mages had emerged into the portal room.

With a groan, Lyr heaved himself to his feet. His head spun, and he had to grip the edge of his desk until he was certain he'd remain standing. "The mages are here," he murmured.

"Are you sure you can do this?" Kai's eyes narrowed on Lyr. "You look unwell."

Lyr let out a laugh. "That's because I *am* unwell. But the only other person who wouldn't cause offense for this type of meeting is Arlyn, since she's my heir, and I'm not putting her through that. Though…" He frowned. "I suppose I should have included her."

"She's working with Selia, anyway. They're examining the cloak you were left under."

At the memory, Lyr's hands tightened on the desk until his palms burned. "If I ever find the man who did that…"

Kai gave a sharp nod, his eyes full of anger. "Death would be too kind."

For a moment, Lyr let the rage pour through him. His vision went red, and his breath came in shallow gasps. *Iron pierce the person responsible for all of this!* Killing Allafon had only been the beginning. "Too kind, indeed," he ground out.

Three quick knocks sounded on the door, and Lyr stiffened. The mages. He forced his breathing to slow. *In. Out. In. Out.* He made himself let go of the desk and straighten before glancing at Kai. One of his brows was quirked, but he didn't say a word as Lyr rounded the desk and settled into place in front of it.

"You should stay for this," Lyr said, "since you're leading the mission."

Nodding, Kai crossed to stand beside him. "Ready when you are."

Lyr locked his legs to hide their shaking and pulled in more energy to augment his strength. Then he gave the command to enter, and Kera led the five mages into the room. Though none were as dark as Kera with her Dökkálfar heritage, all of them had duskier skin like Selia, a mark not just of ancestry but of life on the plains. Their thin linen robes swirled around them in shades of blue or green as they walked to the center of the room.

One woman stepped forward, her knot of dark hair bobbing as she nodded her head and tapped her fist against her chest in salute. "Blessings of the Nine Gods upon you, Myern. I am Taian ia'Kelore ai'Flerin ay'mornia Maean i Ilera Erasan nai Fiorn, sent at your request by Lord Loren."

"Blessings upon you, Ilera. I am Callian Myern i Lyrnis Dianore nai Braelyn." He smiled and introduced Kai by title. "Please be welcome in my home."

"It is an honor to be included in this mission," Ilera said.

As she introduced the other mages, Lyr inclined his head to each in turn. "I thank you for your aid," he said. "I have arranged for you to stay in the garden tower, if that is acceptable."

Eyes going wide, Ilera's gaze slid to the window before darting back to him. "In...in the trees?"

"No." He almost grinned, but he held it back in case she took offense. There were few trees on the plains of Fiorn and none large enough to hold structures. After meeting Selia, he'd thought the stories of plains elves being terrified of heights was an exaggeration. Apparently not. "The tower is tall, but it's made of solid stone."

Ilera gave a shaky chuckle. "Forgive me, Myern. I am certain your tree homes are just as safe as those on the ground."

Lyr could tell by the way she bit her lip and kept glancing out the window that she was decidedly not certain, but he let the comment pass. "Taysonal Kaienan will lead the mission tomorrow morning, provided you are prepared."

After a quick look at the other mages, Ilera nodded. "We will be ready."

"I'll meet with you in your tower before dinner to discuss the details," Kai said.

Only a few more words of pleasantry later, Kera escorted the mages from the room. As the door closed behind them, Lyr lowered himself to perch on the edge of his desk. His arms shook as he held himself upright. "Gods, I'm tired."

Kai grinned, though concern shadowed his gaze. "You look like the humans' hell."

"I feel worse." Lyr glanced at the water clock. He could spare a little time to rest—but not much. "Could you take care of things while I get some sleep?"

"*You* are asking for help?" Kai asked, brows lifted.

Lyr rolled his eyes. "Just shut up and do it."

Kai's laughter followed Lyr all the way out into the hall.

∽∾

By the time Lyr reached the top of the stairs, his wound throbbed with each heaving breath. He paused to lean against the wall, and his hand drifted to his chest. Gods, how he wanted to scratch at the unrelenting tingle-pain of it. Fighting against the urge, he jerked his hand away. Who knew what Lial would do if Lyr broke his injury open by scratching it?

An unpleasant potion in his drink, for sure.

Lyr shoved away from the wall and started the long trek down the hall. Though he wavered on his feet like a scout walking along a wobbly tree branch, he managed to make it almost to his room before his mother's door opened. Lial stepped out and then paused to give Lyr a scowl.

"You'd better be headed to sleep," the healer grumbled.

Lyr gave a frown of his own. "You were supposed to tell me when my mother woke."

"I wanted to check her spine for further injury first," Lial answered, shrugging. Then his eyes narrowed. "It looks like you need another healing session, anyway."

"Later." Lyr waved a hand as he brushed past the healer. He tossed a look over his shoulder. "Go rest. You have energy stores of your own to restore, and there are certain to be more attacks. You can shout at me later."

Lial's brow rose. "I *never* shout." He paused, his lips sliding up in a grin. "I simply show my concern loudly."

The healer slipped from the room, and Lynia's laughter caught Lyr's attention. His own chuckle strangled in his throat at the sight of his mother, her face almost as pale as the white pillows propped behind her. But he couldn't rush forward as he wanted, not without revealing the depth of his weakness.

His head pounded with the effort of pulling in more energy, a sure sign of his low reserves, but Lyr managed to gather enough to walk to his mother's bed without swaying. Not that it helped. Her laughter faded, and her face pinched with concern as he reached her side. With a huff of effort, she swung her legs over the edge of the bed.

"*Laiala*—"

"If *you* treat me like an invalid, I will scream." Her gaze pinned his. "I am still your mother, and I am *not* weak."

Lyr grimaced. "I know that. But you're pale, and Lial seemed concerned about your back. I'd rather—"

"Lyrnis!" She grabbed his hand, and he helped her balance out of reflex as she levered herself to standing. "Stop. I'm healing." Her other hand cupped his cheek. "Stop all of it. The guilt. Blaming yourself. Worrying over me. My injury hurts less than knowing what those things led you to yesterday."

His breath caught, and he forced it loose. "I didn't go out there because of you. Not specifically. I thought...I thought I could make up for my failure."

"By all the gods," his mother snapped, her hands falling to her sides, "the failure was not yours. Telien started all of this. Your father was more concerned with his magical research than in checking on the branches under his command. Allafon never, *never* should have grown so dark and cruel without Telien noticing. He was Myern for millennia. You've only held the title for twenty-two years."

Lyr's fists clenched. "Long enough to do my own checking."

"Why would you?" His mother's mouth pinched as she shook her head. "Think. Kai was born and raised on that estate. By the time he was born, Allafon had masked his deeds so thoroughly that *Kai* didn't even know." Then her expression softened. "You are not responsible for the world."

His gaze slid to the side. "Maybe someday I'll believe that."

"So long as you don't scare me like this again," she whispered.

The anguish in her voice caught at him. After a quick glance at her worried face, Lyr pulled her into a hug. Pain jolted him at the contact, but he shoved it aside and dropped his forehead to her hair. "I'm sorry, *Laiala*. I'll try. But I am a warrior."

She pulled back, her brows rising. "One who has better sense than to venture out alone."

A chuckled slipped free, and he winced at the ache that came with the movement. "Usually."

"Use that sense and go get some sleep." His mother shifted to the side, grabbing her walking stick from its place by the bed. "I'm going to make my way to the library for some research."

Lyr tensed. "You've been to the library?"

A hard gleam entered her eyes as she met his gaze. "I refuse to let one moment ruin millennia of good memories. It is difficult, but some things must be faced. Avoidance only brings more pain in the end."

Speechless, Lyr stared at her with wide eyes as she made her way to the door. *Laiala* was right. He'd tried so hard to shunt his feelings to the side so he could avoid dealing with them, but they'd built into a mountain that had fallen, burying him. All that time, she'd been resolutely rebuilding her life. He rubbed the back of his neck. *Gods.*

"I love you, *Laiala.*"

His voice was soft, but she heard. Smiling, she glanced over her shoulder. "I love you, too. Always."

Lyr's muscles loosened with a sudden sense of relief. His mother was right—enough avoiding. Then he shook his head, chuckling, as he headed toward the door. Did finally getting some sleep count as avoiding?

18

Meli shifted on the stone bench and lifted her hair away from the back of her neck. *Should have braided it,* she grumbled to herself. Why didn't the Morana-ians do something about the oppressive heat? Their buildings were magic-cooled. Couldn't they surround their lands with a similar shield as the Ljósálfar did? It would make staying here more pleasant.

Not that Meli would be able to stay once she announced that she'd no longer work with the ambassador. A shame, consider-ing how drawn she was to this world. Meli closed her eyes as the peace of the garden filled her. The gentle rustle of countless leaves swaying together above, the gurgle of the nearby stream, the woodsy tang of the forest wafting around her—they melded, a balm soaking through to her soul. More home than Alfheim had ever been.

But Meli refused to be silent and complacent any longer. Lady Teronver had gone too far with her insults. Meli would share her body with whomever she chose, as was her right, and the ambassador went beyond all politeness to question that. It was never acceptable to deride another's sexual choices.

Then again, hadn't Meli allowed the woman's abuse from the beginning? It didn't make it right, but she should have stood up for herself sooner. Freyr knew she'd always struggled to stand up for herself. Maybe it was time to learn how.

"Are you unwell?"

Meli jumped, letting out a yelp, as Lyr's voice sounded from behind her. Hand over her pounding heart, she spun to face him. "Gods!"

"I'm sorry," he said, brows pinching in concern. "I called your name from farther down the path. It wasn't my intention to startle you."

She forced her breathing to slow, though her heart maintained its frantic beat. But not out of fear. She took in the loose tunic and pants he wore, and the memory of their last encounter flashed through her. Would she ever be able to look at him without thinking of him naked? Her skin heated in a blush. Probably not.

Lyr's frown deepened as he sat beside her. "Is it the heat? You're flushed."

She let out a choked laugh and shook her head. "The temperature doesn't help, but, truly, I am well. I'm only surprised I didn't hear you. Shouldn't you be resting?"

"I slept a couple of marks and had another healing session." He smiled, and Meli had to admit he looked better than he had that morning. More color. More...vitality. "It's almost time for dinner. I was on my way to the dining room when I sensed your discord."

Meli stifled a groan. Had she been broadcasting her confusion to him? "I'm sorry I bothered you. But I needed to speak with you, in any case."

His eyes focused on hers, and she froze, her attention caught like a dragon in the thrall of flawless emeralds. Too bad she couldn't keep him.

"Dare I ask why?" he finally asked.

"It's not..." Meli swallowed against the lump in her throat. "It's not about the bond."

Lyr slumped, and all at once, he looked tired. Resigned. "What is it, then?"

Chin lifting, she straightened. "I will no longer work with the ambassador."

"I don't blame you," he said, another frown pinching his brows. "But is there a specific reason?" His shoulders went taut as he leaned closer. "Did she threaten you?"

Again, she froze. But this time, *he* seemed more the dragon, ready to rend. Instinctively, she wrapped her hand around his tense forearm to soothe. "Yes, but Pol handled that. She offered me grave offense. Grave enough that I can bear her no longer."

Lyr glanced down, and the muscles beneath her hand loosened as he relaxed. But only a little. "Might I ask what she said?"

Meli bit her lip. "I stayed near the healer's place last night, hoping to find out how you fared. After everything, I..." She paused and took a deep breath. "I couldn't leave. But when I returned to the tower this morning, Lady Teronver claimed I'd used my body to gain your favor."

Lyr jerked to his feet, breaking her hold. "I will see her gone before the sun sets."

"No!" Rising, Meli grabbed at him again as he took a step forward. Her fingers curved around his wrist, stopping him. "Don't doom Alfheim because of me. The ambassador's role here is more important."

For a moment, he simply stood there, head bowed, and a hint of his anger washed over her. Meli's heart jumped. How could she feel so much from him when they weren't actually bound in the way of his people? Then he turned, and she knew she'd only sensed the barest hint of his emotions. The pain and fury of ages swirled in his eyes.

"I care more for you than a city too long awash in its own self-importance," Lyr bit out.

Meli threw up her hands. "Why? You barely know me. I mean nothing to you beyond our potential bond."

Lyr stepped closer. "But I want to know you," he said. He brushed his fingers down her cheek, and she trembled. "I want to know why you hesitate so often even though you're brave. I want to know why I can feel your desire for me even as you turn away."

"I'm not brave," Meli whispered. Her hands fluttered at her side, uncertain where they wished to be. *No, not true,* she admitted. They'd rather be on him. "Or I wouldn't turn away."

He reached for her. Paused. "May I?"

Meli took a long, wavering breath. Then raised her wayward hands to his shoulders and nodded. His strong arms gathered around her, pulling her close despite his wound, and his sigh ruffled her hair as he settled his cheek against the strands. Then he flinched as she shifted closer, and she stilled.

"You're hurt," she said. "I shouldn't—"

"It's worth this slight ache to hold you." Lyr slipped his hand into her hair and tipped her head back. "I want to kiss you again. But *not* on the forehead this time."

Her hands tightened on his shoulders, and her heart throbbed a frantic beat in her ears. Did she dare let herself get closer, more attached? A quiver traced down her spine at his heated gaze. What other chance would she have? Lyr might be forced to send her home when he learned about her disgrace. By Freyr, they deserved at least one moment for themselves. Meli gave a shaky nod, and he captured her lips with his own.

Nothing could have prepared her for the feel of his mouth on hers. *Nothing.* The burn that flared through every muscle and bone. The singing of her soul. The belonging. She gasped, and Lyr took the kiss deeper, his tongue tangling with hers in a delicious dance. *Ah, gods.* Meli ran her hands down his side and snaked them around his back to pull herself tight against him. Anything to get closer.

Lyr's quick hiss of pain brought her back to reality. With a groan, Meli jerked away. "We can't."

"If you're still concerned about—"

"No!" At his raised brows, she grimaced. "Well, I don't want to cause you pain, but that's not…I wasn't…" Meli huffed. Could she ever just say what she meant without fumbling the words? She stiffened her spine and forced her gaze to stay firm on his. "We can't let ourselves get this close."

He flinched as though she'd struck him. "This wasn't an attempt to pressure you."

"I know. I didn't think…" Meli closed her eyes and let the words tumble free. "I return to ruin when I go home. I failed every test posed to Alfheim's children, every chance to have a place there. My family saved me. Because of their influence, I was given a little more time to find some talent that might benefit our people. I am almost out of that time." Her shoulders twitched with an involuntary shudder. "I'll be banished from regular society—unmarriageable."

His hand cupped her cheek, and she opened her eyes to his intense gaze. "They would *banish* you?"

"I have no magic," Meli blurted. "I can't shield in the way of my people. Can't summon the elements or light a candle. I've no skill for crafting, and I can fight only well enough for basic self-defense. Magic is fundamental to life. A Ljósálfr so imperfect could never be accepted."

"But you aren't powerless." His eyes narrowed on her face. "What of the runes?"

Meli grasped the rune pouch at her waist, and the barest tingle danced along her fingers before fading away. She glanced down, but there was no sign of magic coming from the bag. "I've only had these since the mists," she answered, letting the pouch drop back to dangle from her belt. "But this new power wouldn't be enough. The Ljósálfar are traditional beyond all comprehension. Those who do not fit are considered Unfavorable, their place tenuous."

"Meli." At her questioning look, his lips curved up. "You aren't in Alfheim."

ഐൟ

Her mouth fell open, and the color drained from her face. "You can't...you can't just dismiss this."

"I didn't intend to." Lyr's smile never wavered, though the fear in her eyes bit at him. "You expect me to judge you by the standards of another world. We are not so inflexible here, nor so foolish. Everyone has value. *You* have value."

Meli stepped back, breaking his light hold. "Not in Alfheim." She bit her bottom lip, and a hint of her pain drifted over him, settling in his heart. "This might be a different world, but to ally with me would make negotiations with Alfheim impossible. Even if I never return there."

His eyes narrowed. "Why would you consider going back? Why do you care?"

"My family. They've shown me nothing but love, and I'll not leave them to the poison," Meli answered softly. "My people haven't always been so afraid, you know. We even reached some accord with the humans. But Alfheim is maintained by magic. It's life. When that started to fade among some, the Ljósálfar pulled away. Tried to regroup."

"They disavowed us long before that day," Lyr said.

"You moved away from the nine known worlds," she answered, shrugging. "At least that's my guess. Tradition is almost as sacred as magic. That's why I can't consider a bond with you if I hope to save Alfheim. Accepting my status would forever lessen you in their eyes."

Anger surged, and Lyr clenched his fists in a vain attempt to repress it. "*They* came to *me*." Meli's eyes widened, and he sucked in a deep breath, searching for calm. "If they wish my aid, then they will meet my terms. I will work with none but you."

"You can't do that," Meli said, eyes going wide.

"Oh, I can." Satisfaction flashed through him, and he lifted a brow. "I am eighteenth in line to the throne of Moranaia and cousin to the king himself. It is my duty to deal with all of our kindred from Earth, though we left long before the Sidhe were defeated by the humans. Your family can come here if the situation becomes dire. The rest will negotiate on my terms or fend for themselves."

Her hand flew to her throat. "You'd leave Alfheim to its doom?"

"No," Lyr answered, taking a step closer. "Your king would. If he's unwilling to make amends for the discord Lady Teronver has caused, then he is responsible. I'll not take the blame for his blind inflexibility."

"But he follows the Ancient One." Meli's forehead furrowed. "She advised him in this."

A smooth, amused voice cut through the sudden silence. "My sister's words have no doubt changed."

Lyr stiffened, and his hand fell to the knife at his belt as he spun. Pol leaned against a tree, a smirk on his face and his legs and arms loosely crossed as though he'd been enjoying a play. Lyr's eyes narrowed. "Your sister?"

Pol shrugged. "When she claims me."

"Who *are* you?" Meli whispered from behind Lyr, her robes rustling as she stepped close to his side. His heart leapt as she slipped her hand into his. "You couldn't possibly be as old as that."

"Some connections aren't formed by blood." A flame seemed to light his eyes for a moment before he shrugged again. "Then again, some are."

Meli's grip tightened on Lyr's hand. "You truly aren't Ljósálfar."

"I am not." Pol's grin widened. "The better to see how much the Ljósálfar need to change. They have grown stagnant behind their walls."

"Alfheim has no walls," Meli said, confusion ringing in her tone.

"Doesn't it?" Pol's harsh chuckle cut across the garden. "You should know better than anyone the truth of *that*." His head tilted as though he was listening to something, and he straightened. "It's time for dinner. Stop being idiots."

With an absent wave, Pol strode away. Gone as suddenly as he'd appeared. Lyr's nostrils flared as he stared at the spot where the other had been. That one bore more watching. *Way* more watching.

❧

The steady hum of voices blended into background noise as Lyr's gaze drifted to Meli once more. She, on the other hand, stared at her plate of food as she perched on her seat next to Eri. She'd argued against joining them for dinner at all, but the thought of avoiding another meal with the ambassador had swayed her. Lyr's lips curved up when she stuttered out a thank you as his mother passed the platter of summer greens. How could someone brave enough to lead four people into the Veil on nothing but the word of a seer shrink from the slightest social situation?

"Care to share?"

Lyr jolted at his daughter's whispered questioned and snapped his attention away from Meli. Heat crept up his neck at the smirk Arlyn gave him. "Share what?"

"Whatever you found amusing about Selia's homeland." Laughter danced in his daughter's eyes. "Our topic of conversation? Though more bread would be nice, too."

Biting back a groan, Lyr reached for the basket on his left and caught a matching smirk from Ralan. *Miaran.* Had *everyone* noticed Lyr's distraction? But next to Ralan, Teyark and Corath focused across the table at Selia as she spoke of a recent wildfire that had threatened a village on the southern plains. Kai, at Arlyn's right, also focused on Selia. Eri and Iren smiled at each other, no doubt passing mental messages since they weren't seated together. Meli hadn't glanced up from her plate. But his mother lifted an amused brow, and Lyr knew he'd been caught.

Some host he was.

Lyr passed the basket to Arlyn and forced his attention to Selia in time to hear the last of her words. "Thankfully, the mages contained the flames before anything important burned."

"A blessing, indeed," Teyark said with a nod.

Selia smiled at the prince and then turned to catch Lyr's eye. "However, there are more important things to discuss than a crisis already passed, are there not?"

"A guest's words are always paramount," Lyr answered smoothly. At Selia's raised brows, he chuckled. "But politeness aside, yes. Thank you, Lady Selia."

"Kai told me the Sacred Tree confirmed that the assassins came from Earth." Arlyn leaned forward, her expression filled with concern. "Did they follow me? I mean, why would people from Earth be trying to kill you?"

Lyr shrugged. "I couldn't say. But the one who stabbed me spoke fluent English."

"So do you, Kai, and Ralan," Arlyn said. "And most of the people on this estate are at least passable."

"That's true. Yet according to Merrith, the man who came in for supplies spoke very little of our language, and those few words were poorly accented as though learned naturally and not by spell."

Selia lowered the bread she'd been about to eat. "Wouldn't that mean he was *not* Moranaian?"

"Someone would have taught him our language," his mother said, shaking her head. "I still haven't found record of an exile to Earth capable of doing all these things. The information has to be somewhere. The energy poisoning. The cloaks. Those are specific types of magic."

Silence fell, the earlier ease of the meal gone. Even Meli appeared upset, her teeth worrying her lip as she glanced around the table. Lyr pushed his plate away and rubbed a hand across his face. "The timing of all this is suspicious. I just don't understand why. Or who."

"Kien," Ralan ground out.

Lyr's gaze snapped to Ralan's face. The prince's jaw clenched tight and his nostrils flared in fury. *Not good.* "Suspected or Seen?"

"Both, for one led to the other." Ralan's eyes closed, and he paused, a few deep breaths hissing into the silence. When he looked up, only a hint of anger remained in his gaze. "We all know my brother has long been mad."

"And you're just now telling us?" Lyr snapped.

Ralan grimaced. "I just *now* found the thread."

"Do you…" Meli's words trailed off, and her face reddened as everyone's attention shifted to her. But she straightened in her seat and held her head high. "Do you believe these attacks are related to the poison creeping into Alfheim?"

Lyr rubbed an absent hand across his aching chest and fought against the urge to slump. "It's possible."

"It is certain," Ralan said in a voice gone cold with power. "If the future threads are not adjusted, then—"

"*Laial!*" Eri snapped. She spun toward her father, and the spark of something *more* in her eyes ran a chill down Lyr's spine.

Blinking rapidly, Ralan shook his head and then ran a hand through his hair. "Sorry."

The room went silent once more, all eyes on the two seers. Then Eri relaxed and turned back to her plate as though nothing had happened. With a grin, she shrugged. "You never know about the future. Sometimes the telling can break it."

Ralan gave a terse nod, though a hint of red crept into his face. "I went too long without using my power. My control is…not what it should be. But I suggest you focus on the cloak. Much can be learned from the spells imbued within."

"Lady Selia, would you be willing to help?" Lyr asked.

Selia's brow furrowed as she considered the question. "I did an initial examination, but I dare not delve too deeply alone. I'm not a magical artisan. I can recognize the techniques but cannot use them myself."

"Might I offer assistance?"

Lyr turned at the sudden question from Corath, who smiled at the surprised glances he received. "You are an artisan?" Lyr asked.

"I was born and trained on the Rieren branch," the prince answered. "I am a master level mage with metal. The spells imbued in the cloak should be similar enough."

Selia's eyes lit. "It's our good fortune that you're here. Your help would be more than welcome."

As the mages discussed the best way to move forward, Lyr settled back against his seat. It was something resembling progress, at least. He lifted his weary gaze to Meli and smiled when he noticed her staring. She glanced away, but not before he caught the hint of interest in her eyes. Maybe progress in more way than one.

The conversation drew to a halt as plans were settled. Biting back a sigh, Lyr heaved himself to his feet. A wave of weakness hit him, turning his knees to liquid, and he leaned his weight as subtly as possible against the table. He could only hope no one would notice. "If that is all, let us part to our tasks."

"I hope your task is sleep," Arlyn muttered, ruining his hope. "We'll alert you if we discover something pressing."

Resigned, he pushed away from the table. "See that you do."

19

Kien stared down at Beckett's mangled corpse and smirked. Foolish of them to return. But, hey, his gain. His previous trophies impaled around the camp had been picked clean by birds, so it all worked out in the end. Grin widening, he hacked down with the axe, severing the head. He bent, wrapping his hand in the man's tangled hair, and quivered at the sensuous feel of the warm, slick blood that slid across his fingers.

Swinging the head like a pendulum, Kien glanced at Patrick, a half-Sidhe he'd found in Ireland the year before. "Find a free spike for this."

The young man paled, but he grabbed the knot of hair Kien offered and strode for the far side of the clearing. Right past Nicholas, tied spread-eagle between two trees, his cries finally silenced by unconsciousness. The satisfaction from Beckett's death washed away under a wave of rage, and Kien bared his teeth. Nicholas would suffer the most for his stupidity. The cruelty of leaving Lyrnis Dianore to die alone couldn't be faulted, but the idiot should have finished the job.

There was a time and place for torture.

Patrick shuffled back into view, and his face went even whiter at the sight of Kien's rage. Kien smiled again. What was it the great rulers here said? Better to be feared than loved? He gestured the half-Sidhe closer. "Come clean up this mess."

Gulping, the boy bent to pick up a severed arm. Still stooped, he glanced up with wide eyes. "Milord, some of the others are concerned about Beckett's death—"

"Do they not have what it takes to rule over Earth, then?" Kien asked, his tone frigid.

Patrick's body shook with the strength of his trembling. "They do, milord. Truly. I think we're—they're—worried about this latest failure. It just seems…"

Kien's eyes narrowed, and he took a step forward. "You think it wrong I did not grant mercy, I suppose. Tell me, Patrick. Can a group of failures overcome the humans once the fae are gone? This is war, and war is only won by the strong. You'll never rule Earth if you're soft."

The boy straightened, his hand gripping the severed arm like a club. Color flooded his face, and his eyes lit with renewed eagerness. "You're right. I'll talk to the others. I guess they just worry about your focus on Mere…Moreh…"

"Moranaia." Kien handed him the second arm to go with the first. "Once I rule there, we will have much more power. With my kingdom your ally, you will take over this world with ease."

Patrick scuttled off to do Kien's bidding, his steps jaunty once more. Perhaps it was the human blood that weakened the idiots. For the fools actually believed him.

∾◐℘

Arlyn shivered as she stepped into the shielded workroom, but not because of the spell-cooled air. Why had Selia asked her to help examine the cloak? Arlyn had barely begun to learn the basics, and this task was vital. Her eyes fastened on the fabric spread across a table in the middle of the room. Hard to believe the simple brown bundle had caused so much trouble.

After a long, steadying breath, Arlyn approached the table, Selia and Corath filing in behind her. Had the man who'd stabbed Kai worn this cloak? One of her father's attackers certainly had, and if not for Meli, Lyr would have been lost beneath its spell. Arlyn closed her eyes against the rush of anger and tried to center herself. To block out the memories of what it had wrought.

"Are you well, Ayala?" Corath asked, his quiet voice ringing loud in the shielded room.

Arlyn jerked in surprise and then let out a shaky laugh. Wincing, she glanced at the prince. "I'm sorry. I didn't expect to be so angry at fabric."

A slow smile stretched across his face, lighting his eyes. "I did. But I'm an artisan-mage. I've seen my fair share of tumultuous emotions wrought by imbued spells." The humor faded from his gaze, and he glanced away. "All too many of them unpleasant."

Though she wondered at the sudden pain shadowing his expression, Arlyn merely nodded. Corath might be friendly, but he was a stranger—and a prince. She had no right to delve.

"So what am I supposed to do?" Arlyn asked. "I don't want to mess this up."

"You're the only one who sensed when the power of the cloak wavered before the attack in the practice field," Selia said, crossing to the other side of the table. "I know you have no experience with this, but I hope you'll be able to detect something we can't."

Arlyn rolled her shoulders back and nodded. "I'm willing to try."

After Corath took his place between them, Selia lifted her hand and let it drift along the cloth, just sort of touching. Her brow furrowed, and the hair on Arlyn's arms tingled as energy built in the room. But nothing else happened. At least, nothing Arlyn could detect. Then Selia let her fingertips brush fabric. She jerked back at once, a yelp escaping, and shook her fingers.

"Well, then," Selia muttered. "This is going to be a fun piece of work. Had I rushed in, that trap might have done true harm."

"Trap?" Arlyn's throat tightened in concern. "Great."

Selia glared down at the cloak as though her anger could force out all its secrets. "I sensed different types of spell work. I'd swear there was more than one person involved."

"Shall we link together and examine this further?" Corath asked.

"I'm not sure I should be included at this stage, Your Highness," Arlyn answered. "If there are traps, I could inadvertently trigger them."

"Call me Corath, please," he said with a wince. "I was not born to a noble House and never considered the possibility of a title until I met Teyark. Becoming a prince was one of the downsides to accepting the bond." Corath ran his hand through his hair and gave a sheepish smile. "More to the point, there might be traps only you can detect. We'll deal with what comes."

At Selia's nod of agreement, Arlyn shrugged. She closed her eyes as they joined hands, forming a ring around the table. After a moment, she sensed Selia's mental nudge and opened a link. Then she gasped at the odd echo of Corath's presence. Like a conference call in her head, their dual thoughts sounded together until it was difficult to tell one speaker from another. Dizziness hit, and Arlyn pulled back from the connection just enough to dull the waves of sensation.

"*Sorry,*" Arlyn sent along the link.

"*All is well,*" Selia replied. "*Now watch. Alert us if you detect anything.*"

Arlyn did her best to follow them as they explored the magic of the cloak, but much of it was a blurred mess to her. From the frustration she caught along the link, maybe a mess to them, too. Disparate layers of spells stacked haphazardly, some a different "flavor" than she'd come to expect from Moranaian magic. None of them were similar to the energy she'd detected when the cloak wavered.

Though she hadn't been an active participant, Arlyn's brow was beaded with sweat by the time Selia and Corath pulled away from the cloak. She opened her eyes as the others dropped their link and then pulled her hand away to wipe her forehead. Selia leaned against the table, her gaze fastened on the cloak, and

Corath stood with folded arms, his fingers tapping a soft beat as he frowned. Had it been that bad?

"What is it?" Arlyn asked around the sudden lump in her throat.

Corath's narrowed eyes met hers. "There was Sidhe magic involved in this. And not just from one caster."

"The spell nullifying the estate wards was the oldest," Selia said, though she didn't glance up. "A fancy bit of earth magic, that. But the invisibility? A Moranaian enchantment for certain."

Arlyn straightened. "You mean they're working together? We're supposed to be negotiating with the Sidhe."

"Then I'd say the Sidhe have at least one traitor," Corath answered, anger ringing in his tone.

Damn. Arlyn glared down at the cloak and wished she dared set it on fire. Yet more bad news to drop at her father's feet. Tomorrow. Tonight, they'd all get some rest.

∽◎↺

Sunlight gleamed across the altar placed next to the Sacred Tree as Lyr knelt for the morning dedication. First and always, he lit a candle for Dorenal, Goddess of portals and the Veil, the mother of Eradisel. Next came the candle for Ayanel, God of Summer, though that honor would soon pass to Leres with the change in seasons. But today, he also lit the candle for Meyanen, God of love and relationships. He certainly needed divine aid to untangle his relationship with Meli.

As usual, Lyr heard no actual words in answer. Instead, a sense of peace flowed through him, and the tension knotting his shoulders eased. He let his hands drop into his lap as he soaked up the moment of respite. He was no priest, nor did he expect to ever be, but his prayers always brought him more in tune with the world.

Too bad he didn't have time to linger.

With a soft groan, Lyr stood, wavering a moment as he found his balance. Sleep and another healing session had helped, but his chest still ached and his reserves were too low. He ground his teeth together against a wave of weakness and strode from the room, headed for his study. Today would be a fierce one, Kai's mission to Neor the worst of it, and he couldn't afford more time away. May the Nine Gods grant him strength.

It was early yet when Lyr reached the study, but Kai already sprawled in his favorite chair, his face turned toward the sun rising over the valley. Lyr drew up short at the sight of him without Arlyn, as they often met the day together. "Something wrong?"

"No. I tried to rouse Arlyn, but last night's work exhausted her." Kai closed his eyes and sighed. "I needed time to think, in any case. I worry about the trip we take this day."

Lyr settled into the chair next to him so he could enjoy the view of the valley lighting beyond the window. "Have you had a bad feeling?"

"Nothing like that. But this is not going to be easy."

"I've little doubt of that." Lyr let out his own sigh. "I still can't decide if Arlyn would be better served staying or going."

"Staying. And not just because I fear for her."

Lyr's eyebrow rose. "What, then?"

"When we visited the fairy pond, they didn't grant us entry." Kai opened his eyes to meet Lyr's. "They told us to return later, when we knew we had need. Their message was a mystery. But it occurs to me that the fairies are strong in earth-healing. Arlyn should try to work with them while I'm gone."

Lyr's mouth twisted. "You think she will accept that?"

"I don't know. I'm not giving this as an excuse or a way to shield her. We need an earth-healer, and soon."

"I'll speak with her about it when she wakes. She's supposed to tell me what happened with the cloak this morning anyway." Lyr looked over at the water clock. "Not long until the mages arrive for our meeting. Do you think the five of them will be sufficient?"

"They'll have to be." Kai shrugged. "There's no telling the state of the place or how much time has passed in their realm. I hope we find people alive to help."

"As do I." Lyr stood, then bit back a groan at the twinge of pain. "I suppose we'll see."

The door clicked open, and Arlyn shuffled through, her bleary gaze focusing on Kai. Lyr smirked as his friend rose, lifted a cup from a side table, and carried it to Arlyn. She'd once tried to transmute tea into coffee before Lyr had told her she didn't possess that type of magic. Good thing they had this particular tea, the herbs selected by Lial to energize. A gentle, minty smell wafted through the room as Kai used a simple spell to heat the blend.

Arlyn downed half the cup before she glanced at Lyr. She shoved a few stray strands of hair from her face and grimaced. "Sorry. You know how I am when I haven't had enough sleep."

Lyr chuckled. "Indeed."

"Was working on the cloak that rough?" Kai asked, his brow furrowing. "I tried to wake you, but you mumbled a curse at me and pulled the blanket over your head."

Humor lit Arlyn's eyes, and Lyr couldn't help but smile as she gave Kai a playful shove. "I guess you didn't try the right method."

A wicked grin crossed Kai's face. Lyr shook his head at the two and turned toward his desk. Even paperwork was more appealing than watching them flirt. Then his gaze landed on the top report as he settled into his chair, and Lyr sighed. The seal of Lady Alarele. He wished the sons of House Nari and House Anar would form a mating alliance and get it over with. Why they didn't recognize the source of their tension was beyond him.

"That bad?" Arlyn asked, and Lyr glanced up to find her standing on the other side of his desk. Kai had returned to his seat, though he still smirked.

Lyr tapped a finger on the stack of papers. "Another pointless conflict in an ongoing feud."

Arlyn frowned. "Could it be related to our other troubles?"

"I doubt it." Lyr skimmed a few lines of the report and then smiled. "Aren Nari's insult to Rereth Anar's tunic isn't likely to cause a multi-dimensional incident." A laugh slipped free. "But don't try to tell them that. They'd never believe it."

"Too bad everything can't be that simple," Arlyn said, rolling her eyes. Then her humor faded, replaced by a worried grimace. "Like the cloak."

His scalp prickled at the word. *The cloak.* Gods, how he hated that thing. "What did you find?"

"More than one person worked on it. At least one Sidhe."

"Sidhe?" he asked, his voice turning cool as fury washed through him. "The Sidhe worked on a cloak to breach our defenses even as they asked for our aid? Who else, then?" His fists clenched at a new thought. "The Ljósálfar?"

Shaking her head, Arlyn leaned forward. "No. Nothing like that. Lady Meli's people weren't involved, best we could tell."

"Kien?" Lyr ground out.

"Selia and Corath believe so," Arlyn answered. "A Moranaian for sure."

"Perhaps if we discover our traitor among the Sidhe, they'll lead us to Kien." Lyr's gaze slid to the mirror beside his desk as he did a quick mental calculation. "It's too early to call on Lord Meren to discuss the Sidhe's involvement. That will have to wait until after Kai leaves for Neor."

His daughter's restless shifting caught Lyr's attention, and he returned his focus to her face. "Speaking of which…" Arlyn began, then caught her lip between her teeth.

Lyr stilled. "You want to go."

"What?" She laughed, and Lyr's sudden tension eased. "No. I'm not trained enough for a mission like that. I wanted to ask about approaching the fairies again. But based on how they acted before, I was afraid I'd done something wrong."

"Doubtful. They're a mysterious bunch and prone to whims." His brows lowered in thought. Would the fairies be willing to help the Ljósálfar by sending an earth-healer if petitioned directly? "Perhaps you should take Meli with you. She can present a formal case for their aid."

"And I can quiz her about her intentions toward my father," Arlyn said.

Lyr rubbed a hand across the back of his neck. "Arlyn—"

"You should see your face," she interrupted, chuckling.

Never one to pass up a jest, Kai broke his silence with his own deep laugh. "Red isn't a bad color for you."

Lyr's eyes narrowed on his friend. "Red will be an excellent color on you next time we're at the practice field. It'll even be worth Lial's grumbling when he heals you."

"Sure." Kai only grinned. "If you can keep from getting wounded for a couple of days, we can spar."

At the knock on the door, Lyr straightened. The mages. Soon, they'd learn how the Neorans fared. He shook off a sense of foreboding even as he called for them to enter. Whatever news the day held, at least it would soon be over. He hoped.

20

Thirty guards, five mages, three healers, and ten *sonal*, including Kai. Lyr studied the group as he and Arlyn followed behind them. Would it be enough? They'd been ordered to return if the opposing numbers were too great, but that was no guarantee. Lyr's very blood hummed with the worry of a leader forced to send his people into danger, the feeling made worse by fear for his friend. And not only for the sake of that friendship but also for the risk to Arlyn if Kai was lost.

The pain of a severed bond was immense and immortal.

Children's laughter greeted them as they entered the clearing in front of the portal. In the last couple of days, a few more of the surrounding trees had been removed in case greater numbers needed to cross through the Veil, and Eri and Iren took full advantage. Though Iren was six years older, he left his young dignity behind for the little girl, playing games of tag or teaching her bits of magic. However, their presence here at this exact moment was suspect. Were they playing at something greater?

"Eri. Iren," Lyr called as he and Arlyn came fully into the clearing.

With renewed laughter, the children ran up, their faces innocent. Lyr knew them well enough to doubt those expressions. Eri merely grinned. "Yes, Myern?"

"I have no doubt your parents told you of our mission this day. This is no place for children."

Iren's brows pinched. "But Eri said—"

The girl in question grabbed his hand. "Don't blame Iren. I'm just here for Lady Arlyn."

"Me?" Arlyn glanced around the clearing as though searching for the reason. "Why me?"

"I know you're tempted to step through with him." Eri's expression sobered. "Don't."

"But...I..."

Eri released Iren to tug Arlyn's arm. "You must stay for your work here. There are other wars for you to fight, but they are not this day."

Arlyn paled, and Lyr felt the blood drain from his own face. Eri's eyes glowed with power, her words suddenly resounding. There was no denying that she was not speaking as herself alone. Other wars? And Arlyn fighting in them? He both needed to know and absolutely did not wish to.

Lyr swallowed hard against the lump in his throat. "Is there anything you'd like to tell us?"

"No." Eri giggled, a little girl once more. "Don't worry so much. It makes you look older than your years."

Kai coughed into his hand, and the others pretended to examine the trees around them. Perhaps they hoped that intruders might descend upon them to distract Lyr from Eri's words. Instead of anger, though, Lyr found himself laughing. He loved having children around. They knew little of the politeness that grew more and more ingrained as they aged, leaving cold formality in adulthood.

"Go on, then, and escort her back. I'm sure Iren can guard you well."

Iren rolled his eyes, though he chuckled. "Like she needs my help."

"True enough." Lyr shared a smile with the boy. "More than true enough."

✧✦✧

Only the barest glow greeted Kai's group as they stepped through the portal. Kai squinted against the shift from the relative brightness of the Veil. What had happened to the lights lining the cave walls? Had the Neorans depleted the energy reserves of their city in this war of insanity? He paused with the others until his eyes adjusted and then gave the signal to move forward.

Kai called for a halt again at the cave's mouth. Full night had fallen, and the magic-created moon was a mere crescent. This time, no mage lightning cracked above. No cries or shouts met his ears. He heard nothing but the eerie creaking of the broken metal lanterns swaying on their poles by the entrance.

Heart pounding in his ears, Kai examined the area. Were the Neorans hiding, resting—dead? The danger had been obvious before and thus easier to avoid. Darkness and silence bore the potential for ambush at every turn. Based on the change in the moon's phase, a couple of weeks had passed in this dimension, if not more. If Kai or the other two scouts had been detected on their last visit, the Neorans would have had plenty of time to prepare for their return.

He glanced over his shoulder. *"Mage Ilera, can you shield us from attack?"*

Ilera gestured to the female on her right, whose hands began to move in an elaborate pattern even as her eyes closed. Kai rarely witnessed the greater magics, the ones that took more than thought and energy. Almost all Moranaians could do basic things, like protect themselves or light fires, but mages spent decades constructing combat enchantments for quick use. Her hands flew through the patterns too fast for him to follow, and the shield formed around them before he had time to analyze.

A necessity during war.

"We will take turns holding this shield so our power might last longer," Ilera explained. *"It leaves the rest of us free to react to any threats."*

Kai directed the group to follow the road. He tensed in reflex as they moved out into the open, a strategy he never would have taken without the mages. Time, however, was not on their side. The mages had brought energy crystals to augment their power, but those wouldn't last forever. The group had until the energy crystals and their own reserves ran out to explore all of Neor and save whomever they could. Stealth cost moments they did not have.

As they advanced, the warriors fell into formation around the healers and mages while the sonal ranged in front. Maybe he should have left the scouts, since there was little to explore beneath a mage shield, but something told him he might need them. If there were any chance part of the group might need to break away, he would be prepared for it.

They heard nothing but their own footsteps as they followed the long road all the way to the first set of buildings. The same could not be said of smell. As the stench of death reached them, Kai gagged. Something had gone wrong. Horribly, horribly wrong. The smell was so strong he began to doubt any were left alive. None among thousands.

Kai led the group between the first two buildings and then halted, his eyes going wide. Bodies were *everywhere*, revealed by the wavering blue glow of the energy shield, and it didn't look like they'd been fighting each other. Some were scorched or run through. Some had the handles of knives sticking from their chests. People slumped against walls, vacant eyes still pinched with lines of terror, mouths open in silent screams. Entrails were strewn across the ground.

No small force could have swept through the Neorans like this.

With a quick command, he had the mages cast light globes to hover above. Greater illumination was…not helpful to his composure. Vomit burned up the back of Kai's throat, but he pushed it down. One of the mages retched, and even the scouts and warriors had gone pale. Only the healers had any color, but they'd long trained to detach from such sights. Kai just hoped there would be some left to heal.

He forced his gaze away from the blood and entrails scattered around the street. He had to lock away the horror of the scene so he could function. The army that had poured through the city must have been great, great enough to smash even the resistance of the maddened. Many had obviously been killed while trying to run. If any of the attacking force remained here, Kai's group was in danger. He couldn't afford to stand here being ill.

He broke the party into five groups, a mage with each to shield them. A risk, but the buildings had to be searched as quickly as possible. By rights, he should return to Moranaia for additional soldiers, but he wouldn't leave survivors behind. If that army happened to return...Kai shuddered. He'd have to make sure they were gone before that happened. As the others dispersed, circling the city to start at different points and move inward, he gestured his own group forward.

Neor was organized almost ruthlessly, the sections divided by use or need. The street they traveled was lined with businesses almost to the center where the palace rose, an entryway designed with visitors in mind. Through shops and inns they searched, many thankfully abandoned when the healthy had initially left the city, and found bodies left where they'd tried to hide. By the time Kai's group was halfway down the road, two survivors had been found, both near to death.

Warriors carried the injured on doors yanked from empty buildings while the healer tried to work as he walked. It was a struggle to drag the wounded into each building, but Kai dared not leave anyone outside without the protection of Ilera's shield. As he ducked into a tavern at the sound of a low moan, he directed the warriors to wait with the injured beside a narrow staircase. Then he tightened his grip on his knife and scanned the room.

The groaning sounded again, leading him to a table in the corner. At first, he thought he was mistaken. All three occupants, two women and a male, were slumped across the table. The youngest stared at him with sightless eyes from amid the food on her plate, her long brown hair tangled in the mess, and the blond male was much the same.

But the elder, her gray hair marking her age, rocked her head slightly and let out another moan. The healer rushed forward to shift her upright, revealing the black stain of mage fire that covered half of her body. The main blast must have hit the younger two the hardest, the effects weakened enough by the end for the older one to survive. Frowning, Kai eased closer. That burn had the tinge of Sidhe magic.

The elder's eyes shot open. "The cries. The cries."

As though her words summoned the sound, an indignant shriek split the night from the room above. A baby?

Though leaving the shield was a risk, Kai abandoned the woman to the healer and rushed up the stairs, not certain he wanted to see what he might find. He followed the cry to a room along the hall, hesitating only a moment before he pushed open the cracked door. And sagged in relief at what he found.

A baby sat up in her crib, her dark hair tangled with sweat as she screamed. A small boy stood beside her, trying his best to shush her cries. At the creak of the door, the boy, no more than seven, positioned his body in front of the baby even as tears leaked from his eyes. There was no sign of a struggle here.

Though their faces pinched with terror, both were unmarked by the slightest hint of injury.

"I mean no harm," Kai whispered, kneeling in the doorway. The boy's eyes widened, and he shook his head. Of course, the child didn't speak Moranaian. Kai switched to Neoran, thankful he'd learned the language during his training. "I mean no harm."

"So said the others," the child said.

"I come from Moranaia. Your queen asked for our help."

The baby had stilled, her angry cries replaced by a smile. Her brother gave her a startled look. "She likes you. The others…they didn't kill us, but we heard the screams."

So even the butchers had stopped somewhere. Kai made note of that detail. "What are you doing here? I can hardly believe that the queen left children behind."

"Father hid us." Fresh tears slid down the boy's cheeks. "Mother got sick, but he thought he could save her. I don't know where they are now."

"How old are you? Both of you?"

"I'm six." The boy paused to think. "Neris is nine moons, I think."

Kai stood slowly, trying not to alarm the children. "Do you know how long you've been here?"

The boy shrugged. "A day, maybe. I fed Neris whatever I could find for her. But she keeps crying for milk. There's none good of that."

"I have warriors, mages, and healers below, all ready to take you to a safe place." Kai took a deep breath. "Will you come?"

He held that breath as he waited for the boy to deliberate. And let out a long sigh of relief when he nodded.

꧁ꕥ꧂

The little girl called Eri skipped down the path ahead of them, happy now that she'd gotten her way. Grinning, Meli shook her head. She'd initially protested when Lyr had found her in the garden and asked her to go with Arlyn to the fairy pond. What help would she be in a meeting with fairies? But then the little girl had danced into the clearing, her eyes lit with something otherworldly, and insisted Meli should go. She'd opened her mouth to argue when Lyr leaned over to whisper that the child was a seer. The wise heeded those with the sight.

Even when it led to an insane journey through the Veil to another world.

"She's a little uncanny, isn't she?" Arlyn asked.

Nodding, Meli glanced at Arlyn. "Absolutely. I have never seen one so young with such a gift. Is that something common here?"

"I don't think it's common anywhere," she answered with a smile, though her face looked pale and drawn beneath the forced humor. "I have the greatest sympathy for her poor father."

Meli's brow creased to see Arlyn rubbing her stomach. "Are you unwell?"

"It's Kai," the girl muttered, her steps slowing. "Whatever is happening on Neor must be bad. He tries to shield me, but sometimes I catch hints of what he's feeling. It's making me nauseous."

"Should we do this later?"

Arlyn sighed. "No, we might as—"

"Keep going," Eri called from just ahead. "You'll feel better in the fairy circle."

With a soft laugh, Arlyn picked up her pace. "See? Uncanny."

Only a moment later, they reached the pond. Eri stood at the edge of the clearing, and Arlyn and Meli stopped beside the child, one on each side. Meli had no reason to feel nervous, but the mist creeping in slow tendrils over the water had her heart pounding. She'd never met fairies, as the Ljósálfar of old had considered them too inferior to allow into Alfheim. An easy distinction to attain, she was coming to find. So when the small, winged form darted up and hovered over the rolling fog, Meli jumped.

"This time you are welcome, every one."

As the voice rang around them, the figure grew until she was a bit larger than Eri. Blue and gold wings flapped incessantly, holding the fairy above the water. Blue hair flowed down like water to tangle with a gauzy dress. Meli stared, her mouth falling open. No one, not even Eri, spoke.

"Come on, then," the fairy said.

The voice broke their group free from the moment's enchantment. Together, they walked up to the edge of the pond and stopped again. The fairy's face held no discernable expression as she tracked their movements, making Meli shiver. Had coming here been a mistake? Surely, Lyr wouldn't send his daughter and young Eri so casually into possible danger.

From the corner of her eye, Meli saw Arlyn incline her head. "We thank you for your welcome."

"Perhaps now." The fairy gave an inscrutable smile. "A seer and a pair of blood-souls. Strange grouping to seek me this day."

Meli and Arlyn exchanged puzzled glances. "Blood-souls?"

"You'll figure it out when you need," the fairy answered.

Though Meli wanted to know more, her stomach pitched at the coldness in the fairy's expression. *She* certainly wasn't going to ask for details.

The fairy's blue eyes focused on Arlyn. "I know what brings you, but will you state it?"

"Dark, poisoned energy spreads to the realms most connected to Earth," Arlyn answered. "Even Alfheim has been affected."

"Alfheim?" The fairy chuckled, and the leaves on the trees rippled with the liquid sound. "I care as much for them as they do us. You'll not find a fairy willing to do aught on their behalf."

Arlyn's mouth hardened into a line. "But you said you know why we're here. You told me to come back when we had need."

"So I did," she snapped.

Water rippled beneath the fairy's feet, expanding in circles around her until little waves lapped onto the shore of the pond. A cool tendril of water flowed up to soak into Meli's soft shoes. By Freyr, the fairy had every right to dislike the Ljósálfar, considering the ancients had barred her kind from Alfheim. But Meli had to try.

Bracing herself, Meli stepped forward and let the cold water wrap around her feet. "I can only beg forgiveness on behalf of my ancestors for their inexcusable rudeness."

"There you speak truth. Inexcusable." The fairy drifted closer, a spark of anger lighting her eyes. "Do you know what the humans wanted to do to us before we left? No, for your ancestors closed us out with no hope. If not for the Myern of this estate, we would be worse than dead. For Moranaia we will move, and only that."

"I am my father's heir," Arlyn said. "He is the one who sent us."

The fairy waved a hand in dismissal. "For diplomacy. We go not for diplomacy but for heart. By blood we are bound and by blood we offer aid."

Meli's chest tightened. Did the fairy want a blood connection to Alfheim? If she meant a marriage between the fairies and the Ljósálfar, it was a doomed request. The king would never agree. "Please forgive us for bothering you. I regret that we have brought bad memories to mind this day."

Resigned, Meli motioned for their group to leave. Arlyn caught Eri's hand, but the child only smiled and refused to move.

Then the fairy alighted on the bank, and thick grass sprinkled with flowers rose beneath her feet where there had been mud. Blue-gold eyes caught Meli's gaze. "Do not despair. You hold the answer in your soul."

"Mine?" Meli's breath caught. "Even though I'm from Alfheim?"

"Are you, really?" The fairy's slow smile made her face glow. "I am Niesanelalli, Nia to your kind. Return again when you know."

With another laugh, Nia seemed to shrink into herself until she had returned to her original size. She waved in farewell and then disappeared into the mists as suddenly as she'd appeared. Meli stared at the spot with wide eyes.

Eri grasped Meli's hand. "Aren't you glad I brought you?"

Meli exchanged another glance with Arlyn as the child pulled them away. Gladness was certainly not the emotion at the forefront of her mind. Nia's riddles caught at something within her, a part she didn't want to acknowledge. Was her allegiance, her heart, still with Alfheim? Had they ever been? She loved her family, but she'd never really belonged with them. Maybe she could make a place here.

The fairy's question played through her mind over and over with each step.

Are you, really?

21

Lyr leaned against the window frame and stared into the garden, waiting to catch sight of the group Kera was escorting from the tower. Getting rid of the ambassador would be one of the few highlights of the day, if only Meli and Arlyn would return in time for the meeting he'd scheduled. He glanced at the water clock. What was taking so long?

Movement caught Lyr's eye, and he ducked back as Kera came into view. With the midday sun casting dappled light against the windows, the ambassador's group wouldn't see him spying if he kept back. His lips curved up. A fine advantage, considering the uneasy looks he spied the ambassador giving the forest around her. Her two female retainers trailed her with heads bent close in conversation, narrowed eyes on their leader's back.

Only Pol appeared at ease, but that was nothing new.

As Kera led the group out of sight, Lyr took his place in front of his desk and sent a quick call to Arlyn. *"Are you still with the fairies?"*

"We're almost back." She paused, and a hint of annoyance flowed through. *"Not that the trip did any good."*

His brow creased. *"They wouldn't see you?"*

"One fairy did. You weren't joking about them being weird."

"I'm guessing they aren't sending an earth-healer." Lyr let out a curse. *"Well, you can tell me more later. I'm meeting with the ambassador soon. Could you bring Meli to my study?"*

"Ohhh, are you finally going to tell the ambassador off?" Arlyn asked, interest slipping into her mental tone.

Lyr leaned against his desk, arms crossed. *"Tell off?"*

"Scold? Yell at? Rebuke?" Arlyn clarified. *"If so, I'll move faster. I'd love to hear it."*

As he sent an amused assent, a knock sounded on the door. Lyr dropped his arms to his sides and settled a neutral expression on his face before beckoning Kera to enter. She smiled as she led them in, but the humor faded as she took her place by the windows to act as guard. Ignoring Kera, the ambassador halted with a scowl in the center of the room.

"Thank you for your prompt arrival," Lyr said.

The lady's annoyed expression never wavered. "Have you news, milord?"

"None that concerns you," he answered calmly.

"I..." Her brow creased. "I am afraid I do not understand."

"Indeed?" Lyr stared into Lady Teronver's eyes until she dropped her gaze. "I regret to inform you that I must refuse your services as ambassador. You will be sent back to Alfheim tomorrow morning."

The color washed from her face, and true fear entered her eyes. "You cannot. Please."

His brows rose. "What did you expect? You have insulted me and our land at every meeting, and any cooperation has been grudging at best. I find it difficult to believe that you are Alfheim's finest."

"I am." The lady seemed to sway on her feet before straightening her spine. "Or was. My last few tasks did not go well. You send me back to failure and doom. I cannot shame my family again."

Lyr wanted to laugh. *This* was how she behaved when facing such a threat? "Yet you seem to have done your best to ruin this chance."

Lady Teronver's eyes sparked with temper once more. "The king himself brought me dishonor when he assigned Ameliar Liosevore to my group. The Liosevore family should be thrown from Alfheim for shielding her from her final test."

He began to understand a little then. "I take it your families don't get along?"

"One does not get along with such as those." She glanced around the room, her nostrils flaring. "Where is the useless girl? I've no doubt she has filled your mind with her tales."

"You would do well not to speak ill of Lady Ameliar." He narrowed his eyes on the woman's face. "In any case, she did not force your behavior. You acted foolishly of your own accord."

The ambassador's chin lifted. "Perhaps it is indeed best that we depart, as you will not listen to reason. We will seek aid from a superior people, and the girl will have her punishment upon our return. The king, if not Freyr himself, will know of how she has twisted these negotiations."

A cough from the doorway caught the attention of all. As Meli and Arlyn entered, Lyr's heart jumped at the conflicted feelings inside him—hope versus reason. He knew Meli did not feel prepared to take the ambassador's place, and he had no idea how she might react to the lady's dismissal. But when she halted next to Lady Teronver, Meli appeared calm.

Her voice rang out clearly in the silence. "I will not be returning to Alfheim."

Everything within Lyr froze at her words. Had she decided to stay on Moranaia? Go to another world entirely? As she spun to face Lady Teronver, Meli's face pinched in anger. *No hint that it has anything to do with me.* His toes curled against the urge to step forward and demand answers. *Cursed protocol.* But he had to dismiss Teronver properly. There could be no doubts about that.

The ambassador's face reddened as she turned on Meli. "This journey is mine to command, and I will take you back with me to face your fate. Perhaps the king will finally accept the truth about the Liosevore family."

"You may command the mission, but you have no dominion over me." Meli finally glanced at Lyr, and the spark of uncertainty that drifted along their fragile bond stole his breath. "My talents, even untrained, have found acceptance here, as have I.

If the Myern will allow, I would like to stay on Moranaia. I have no home on Alfheim."

All the reactions he had to repress burned in his gut, but Lyr would never let Lady Teronver see how important this was to him. "Moranaia welcomes one of your unique power. It is a long-standing tradition to accept those among the fae races who wish to depart their ancestral homes."

She inclined her head. "Then I thank you."

The ambassador sneered, all attempt at diplomacy gone. "Alfheim will not treat with one who harbors the dishonored."

"As you'll soon find," Pol called from behind her.

Lyr expected Lady Teronver to rage at the man, but her mouth snapped closed. If he had thought her pale before, he'd been wrong. Curious. He peered at Pol, who only grinned. *Definitely not a mere attendant.*

"If your king wants our help, he may work through Lady Ameliar," Lyr said. "Or perhaps with me directly. When my guide takes you through, he can attune a mirror for communication."

For a moment, the ambassador only stared. "Directly? That…that is possible?"

"Oh, yes." Lyr smiled in satisfaction. "Something your people would have long enjoyed if not for your arrogance."

There was little else Lady Teronver could say after that. Though the spell to connect mirrors with Alfheim would cost more energy than Lyr wanted to use, it was the best option if he wished to clear up any possible misunderstandings. And if they refused to believe? Alfheim would just have to fend for itself.

∽◉〜

By the time he led his now-expanded group through the portal once more, Kai was weary and sick to his soul. Out of the thousands who had remained on Neor after the others had retreated, they carried thirty-two survivors, nineteen of them children. Shivering children with hollow, haunted eyes. Yet their only injuries were small scrapes and bruises earned during the search for food and shelter.

The same could not be said of the adults. Of those thirteen, only three could walk. The rest were carried on improvised litters—doors, boards, sometimes only sheets. The four Moranaian healers moved between the ill as quickly as possible, fighting to keep one stable before returning to work again on the next. Lial and his apprentices would have their hands full for certain.

Muscles trembling with fatigue, Kai leaned against a tree to catch his breath. It had been no small feat, bringing such a large group so quickly through the Veil. But worth it. He watched the strain leave the Neorans' faces as they drew in the clean Moranaian energy, and the youngest of the children let out little squeals. Even the unconscious seemed to relax into their litters, their breathing steadier. Almost as though the magic here counteracted the poison.

His mind flashed back to when Ralan and Eri had returned from Earth. The energy there had sickened Eri particularly, and Ralan had worn himself down trying to purify enough for her to stay alive. As soon as they had stepped through, both had filled with vitality. The girl had gone from near death to running through gardens within a day.

The poison seeping into other realms was clearly no accident. But although the Veil became more turbulent and dark each day, nothing touched the energy of Moranaia. If Kien was to blame, he hadn't directed his magic to his birth world. A curious omission. Neor, Alfheim, the Seelie courts, Earth—none of those should have been a target for an exile seeking revenge. There had to be something else Kien wanted with Moranaia, and Kai had the sinking feeling that the dark prince planned to return.

Shoving aside that thought as he pushed away from the tree, Kai strode to the center of the group. After a quick discussion with the healers, he led them along a path in the opposite direction from the estate. Lyr had been concerned that the survivors might bring back contaminated injury, so Selia had helped shield a small camp nearby where they could be checked without risk to others. His steps were leaden with the weight of all he'd done and seen, and though he craved sleep, he wanted a shower even more.

He was smeared with more dirt, blood, and...other things than he really wanted to consider.

One of the *sonal* with a longer mental range had called ahead to Braelyn, and Lial waited inside the camp with six apprentice healers and several volunteers from Lyr's household staff. Kai stepped back as Lial took command, directing the most gravely injured to pallets circled together in the center of the clearing. Two of Lial's apprentices rushed to the supply tent on the right as the healer called out orders.

A male and a female that Kai didn't recognize gathered the older children into a small group to feed them bread and fruit while others held the three babies too young for solid food. More volunteers rushed to supply bottles to the infants and set a line of pallets to the left, away from those being healed of serious injury.

Kai shared a smile with the boy he'd saved before glancing back at the healer. But Lial merely shook his head and pointed toward the estate. "Go. Report to Lyr."

Recounting the horrors he'd seen was a task he would rather avoid, but Kai set out for home. Gods, was it only midday here? He'd been on Neor for more marks than he wanted to consider. Thank Arneen it wasn't too far of a walk back to Braelyn. He would give his report. After that, he could shower. Then find Arlyn and hold her until he could finally sleep.

❧

After the request for aid sent by one of his other *sonal*, Lyr had already guessed that Kai's report wasn't going to be good. But the sight of his friend told more than any words. Of the two of them, Kai was usually the most cheerful, but today his face was more grim than after he'd beheaded Allafon, the man he'd thought his father. Blood coated his clothes and even speckled his face. At least none of it seemed to be his.

"Do you have the book?" Kai asked as he strode across the room.

Taken aback by the abrupt question, Lyr raised a brow. "The one where I keep reports?"

"Yes." Kai stopped in front of his desk. "I want to get this out while I can. Please."

Lyr snapped his mouth closed around the retort he usually would have given at his friend's rudeness. Kai's eyes were haunted with a dull horror Lyr had never seen there before.

With a quick nod, he opened the small, leather-bound book and activated the spell that recorded everything said.

"*Taysonal*, what news do you bring to the stewards of Moranaia?"

Kai took a breath at the traditional question. "Neor has fallen. Completely, and not at the hands of its own people. Most of the ones remaining were massacred."

"Massacred?" Lyr leaned forward in his seat at the unexpected words. "They were fighting amongst themselves the first time you went there. Are you saying someone else was to blame?"

"An army went through. Very quickly. Some of the Neorans had built hasty barricades, but many were cut down by blade or mage fire while running or hiding. It was a systematic slaughter." Kai's hands shook as he gestured, and the color seeped from his face. "Bodies torn open, parts flung...you don't need that record."

"Gods of Arneen," Lyr whispered.

Kai glanced at the floor for a long moment before speaking again. "But beyond all I saw, there were survivors. Thirty-two, nineteen among them children."

Lyr's chest tightened. So few left out of thousands. "Children? Why were there children?"

"A couple of them were ill, but most were hidden by their parents. Their eyes..."

Lyr wanted to take pity on his friend and save the rest for later, but he had to know. "Could you tell who was responsible? Did the survivors know?"

"Oh, yes. It was the Sidhe." Kai's hands fisted at his sides as his furious gaze lifted to Lyr's. "The Seelie court sent an army through their own colony."

Anger shoved into Lyr's gut like a blow, and he pushed himself away from the desk to pace the room. Too bad there were no Sidhe available to throttle with his own hands. "Seelie? How certain are you?"

"The three adult survivors able to talk all agreed, and some of the older children could identify them. They specifically left the children alive, knowing this. I think they wanted us to find out."

"They cannot possibly expect aid from me after this," Lyr said through gritted teeth.

Kai snorted. "I wouldn't be so sure. They feel it is their right."

"To exterminate their own people?" Lyr wanted to slam his fist into something. Anything. He paused by the window, hands gripped behind his back to keep from smashing the glass. "Cold bastards."

"Always have been, though they hide it better than the Unseelie."

Lyr flicked a glance at Kai and then strode back over to the book. Something in his friend's gaze said there was more to tell that didn't need to go in the official record. Not yet. "Is that all you have to report?"

"I'll send you my written account soon."

"Then I thank you, *Taysonal*, for the news you have brought." With the formal words, he closed the spell and the book. His fingers tapped across the leather as he stared at his friend. "Was there more you wanted to say outside of the report? I assume your thoughts on the Unseelie did not belong there."

"You assume right," Kai said with a sharp nod. "We can discuss it at length later, but…I'm concerned. It's not like the Unseelie to be absent during so much upheaval. Surely, they are equally affected, but we've heard nothing from them. According to the survivors, an army of Seelie Sidhe swept through, but some of the murders reminded me of Unseelie work."

Lyr's fingers stilled. "You didn't think that belonged in your report?"

"I have no proof." Kai shrugged. "Only a feeling. Nothing substantial enough to include."

"I'll not have you recount your reasons now. You need rest." Lyr ran a hand across his face. "I'll have to speak to Lord Meren to gauge his level of involvement, though it's almost certain with a Seelie army involved. Later, once I've calmed."

"Good luck."

Lyr wasn't sure if his friend wished him luck for the discussion or the calm, but it hardly mattered. He desperately needed both.

ൟ

Meli paced the garden, relief and fear driving her feet in a restless beat. She'd done it. Actually cut ties with Alfheim. Maybe the fairy had infected her with some madness, for what was said could not be undone, not to the Ljósálfar. *But I'm free,* she thought, her muscles going lax with the joy of it.

Then Meli stiffened as worry rolled back in. Lyr might have welcomed her, but he had his own interests in that regard. If she decided not to bond, would she have to leave here, too? No. He was too honorable for that. But that didn't mean she would find a place to belong. The rest of his people might not feel the same about her presence.

And what about her family? They were from an ancient line, one of the first noble families after the establishment of Alfheim. That status protected them from many things, but their social standing would be shaken considerably by Meli's refusal to return. And her brother would surely suffer scorn from his fellow warriors. Could she convince them to leave Alfheim behind if the situation grew too terrible? With a sigh, she sank down on a log by the side of the trail. She would just have to try.

"Good choice," Pol said from behind her.

Meli gasped in surprise and turned to glare at Pol. "It's rude to sneak up on people."

"But it's my specialty." His familiar smirk lit his face. "I like you, Ameliar Liosevore. Few dare give me that look."

Sensing the potential for danger, she stilled. "Perhaps I wouldn't, either, if I knew who you really were."

He nodded. "Probably true."

She doubted this day, or perhaps any day, would be the day he confessed that. "Escaping the ambassador?" she asked, changing the subject.

"She does not concern me." The light of flame flickered in his eyes. "Don't worry about her once she returns. She will be dealt with swiftly. There was always the chance it might be different, but she performed as expected."

Did she dare ask what he meant? Meli straightened her spine. "You've never been an attendant, have you?"

His grin widened. "Attentive, yes. Attendant, no. Maybe I'll tell you more one day."

"Well." Meli hesitated, not wanting to risk his ire. "If not to explain your place here, why did you seek me out?"

"You're freaking out."

Brows quirked, she leaned back against the bench. "What?"

Pol shook his head. "Sorry. Too much time on Earth. You're panicking."

On Earth? She refused to analyze that right now. "I exiled myself, though I had no plan to. It was the right decision, but...I'll never see my home again. My parents will be heartbroken."

"If they're lucky, they'll find themselves here."

The breath left her lungs. "You think Alfheim can't be saved?"

"Not if they remain in isolation. Poor Freyr has no idea." Pol stood and gave a flourishing bow. "Be at ease, Lady Meli. I haven't led *you* astray."

Meli stared after him as he strode away. Pol spoke so casually of Freyr, God and High King of Alfheim, that he could only be someone of great power himself. Maybe even a god. But who would dare intrude in Freyr's domain? As she thought through the list of possible deities, she blanched. Surely, she had not just argued with *Him*.

22

Hours had passed, but Lyr's stomach still roiled with fury and disgust. He commanded a third of the Moranaian army, but he couldn't imagine unleashing them on a portion of his own populace for anything short of unprecedented treachery. And to order them to massacre the ill? He swallowed down bile. It was a betrayal of all things decent.

In a single day, he could discharge much of the trouble brought to him from the other realms. Whether Meren was responsible or not, the Sidhe had broken all faith, and the Ljósálfar insulted him at every turn. Lyr was well within his rights to leave them both to their own fates.

Except for one thing: Kien.

Kien, who had not even been exiled to Earth. If he had, Lyr's scouts would have kept up with his every move. The prince should not have escaped the world the king had sent him to.

Now he, and all his actions, became Lyr's problem.

Giving up on calm, he strode to the mirror and activated the spell that would connect him to the Seelie lord. He expected to wait or to have to leave a message, but Meren appeared almost at once. As if he'd been waiting. "Good day to you, Myern Lyrnis."

The Sidhe smiled, and Lyr clenched his hands behind his back where Meren couldn't see. "It is certainly not good for the Neorans."

"Am I to understand that you did not stay out of our business as I said you should?" Meren asked, a smirk playing at the edges of his lips.

"I told you I would follow the order of my own prince," Lyr answered. His throat stung with the effort of keeping his voice calm. "You were to return word to me of any decision reached by your queen."

Lord Meren's chin lifted. "Queen Lera determined that our sovereign business was none of your affair, so we took care of it ourselves. Of course, you are welcome to send a diplomat if you wish to settle the matter with the queen yourself."

Lyr ground his teeth at Meren's confession. He would not negotiate with butchers. "I think not."

The smile dropped. "Then why have you called me?"

"An artifact was discovered on an assassin here." Lyr paused to tamp down his own emotions. "When examined, Sidhe magic was found."

This time, the Seelie lord's surprise did not appear feigned. "I know of none who have ventured to your land for any reason, much less a nefarious one. You must be mistaken."

"I assure you that I am not." Lyr's hands itched to wrap around Meren's neck. "Considering your cruel actions to your own colony, I hardly believe your claims of innocence."

Meren shook his head. "In this, I offer no subterfuge."

In this. Interesting choice of words. "Your reassurances are meaningless. We will no longer negotiate with the Seelie court, at least and until restitution is made to the Neoran people and House Dianore."

To Lyr's surprise, the Sidhe merely shrugged. "The queen tires of hiding in the dark. We will send our own people to the surface. I am sure we will have no need of you in the future."

"So be it." Lyr allowed a hint of fury to flash in his eyes. "And if any assassins are proved to be sent by your command, I'll consider it a declaration of war against Moranaia. Take control of your people."

Without another word, Lyr severed the connection in one final insult. At least now, Lyr had no need to consider Sidhe sensibilities. Once the Neorans were healed, he could send his own scouts more widely across Earth to seek the source of the problem. The Seelie could go mad in their own hills.

His temper heightened by the encounter, Lyr strode from his study and down the hall to the garden. The king wouldn't be happy that Lyr had threatened war, but it wasn't *entirely* outside of his authority as General. Especially considering Ralan's command to help the Neorans. *Clechtan,* but this would be a tricky report to write.

Lyr slowed at the sight of Kera entering through the outer door. Her brows rose, no doubt at the anger he didn't bother to hide, but no sign of concern creased her forehead. "Myern," she said. "I was headed to your study to find you."

Grimacing, Lyr crossed his arms. As second-in-command to his captain, Kera might bear bad news indeed. "Did something happen?"

"No," she answered. "Nothing like that. You asked me to keep an eye on our visitors, Lady Ameliar in particular. I thought I should mention..." Kera hesitated, and Lyr's stomach dropped at her uncharacteristic show of nerves. "Earlier, during the meeting? You didn't arrange for the lady to have her own quarters. She has been pacing the gardens all this time, probably avoiding that foul ambassador."

"Thank you for reminding me, Kera," he answered automatically, though he wanted to curse again at his own lack of thought. "Would you mind having the room beneath Prince Teyark's prepared? I will check on Lady Meli."

"I can do that." Kera smiled. "She was on the path to the guest suite a moment ago."

After thanking her again, Lyr slipped out the door and headed right. This time, he had no waves of distress to follow— a promising sign—but he managed to catch a hint of Meli's energy near the base of the nearby guard tower. If he hurried, he could catch her before she entered the guest suite. She needed to know she'd have a place away from the ambassador's ill humor.

And Lyr needed to be with her.

∽↺∾

Caolte pushed into his brother's room, slamming the door against the wall. "What are you playing at, Meren?"

"It is good to see you, too, brother." Meren looked over his shoulder, his long pale hair rippling with the motion. "I hope all is well."

Caolte halted in the center of the room. He dared come no closer lest his temper erupt in full flame. If his spy had been correct, Naomh's plan would be ruined. "Tell me, does the queen know of your murderous deeds?"

Meren laughed. "Queen Lera can hardly hold up her own court robes. She was not prepared for her mother to fall ill."

"Your oath—"

"Was to Queen Tatianella." Meren's satisfied expression sparked Caolte's growing fury. "Lera has not been wise enough to demand another."

"I was speaking of your oath to Naomh. You gave your word to work with the Moranaians for a solution."

Meren turned back to the window with a shrug. "I decided he was wrong. Look out there, Caolte. Why should we stare at a spell-cast sky, barred from feeling the light of the sun? The humans have long forgotten our oath. Even if they hadn't, they are nothing compared to us."

"The Sidhe keep their promises, even through time." Caolte's fingers dug into his palms. "If our father—"

"Do you think I care what he would have done?" Meren's voice cut, smooth and calm, through his brother's words. "He betrayed my own mother with some half-Unseelie spawn."

Although centuries had passed, the shame of it still burned. It wasn't because Caolte's mother had been a half-blood from the Unseelie court. No, in that one mistake, his father had broken his word to his wife, Meren's and Naomh's mother, for a few nights' pleasure.

"That is a point long settled and useless to debate," Naomh bit out. "If you wanted free of the underhill, you need not have run an army through Neor."

Meren waved a hand. "They were no longer Sidhe. Any who succumb should be eliminated, for they no longer belong to our kind."

"Even Queen Tatianella?" Caolte smiled as his brother paled. "Perhaps I should alert her guard."

"The royal family is ever above reproach."

Caolte's smile broadened. "Funny how that works."

"Be gone," Meren said, the calmness leaving his demeanor. "Don't try to implicate me merely because I didn't follow Naomh's directives. I had grown tired of working with the Moranaians concerning a matter we should deal with ourselves."

If there had been a way to damn his brother in that moment, Caolte would have done it. But Meren had the ear of Queen Lera. Aggression on his part would cost more than it gained. Naomh was going to be furious, his plans for the future now fractured. They'd hoped the Moranaians would cure the poison Kien had assured him would keep the Seelie underground for centuries more. A poison that never should have seeped beneath the surface. Now Naomh and Caolte would have to find their own way to solve the problem.

Caolte turned, tossing words over his shoulder like the flames he'd rather cast. "Break your word to us again, and you'll regret it."

෩

Meli stopped at the base of the stairs that curved around the guard tower to meet the walkway above. This was not going to be pleasant, but she'd lingered in the garden long enough. Lady Teronver held grudges almost as closely as the Elder Gods, and Meli had no doubt the woman already had some form of revenge in mind. It might be nothing more than angry words—for the moment. But if Pol wasn't there, the lady might dare another spell.

Only one way to know for certain.

Shoving her shoulders back in resolve, Meli took a step forward. Then paused again, a tingle in her spine as she sensed Lyr's energy approaching. Even without a formal bond, the link between them strengthened. She'd almost returned to his study several times that afternoon at the hints of anger and distress she'd sensed from him.

But Meli had caught a glimpse of Kai, grim and blood-splattered, as he'd crossed through the garden. Something serious had happened, but she had no idea what it might be. She would bring no comfort if she made matters worse by interrupting. So instead, she'd continued her pacing. Useless pacing.

"Meli?"

She spun at the uncertain tone of Lyr's voice, and her heart thumped at the shadows darkening his eyes. "Is something wrong?"

"No. At least nothing urgent," he answered as he moved closer. "I wasn't able to speak with you after the meeting earlier. With everything happening right now, Kera had to remind me to arrange a room for you."

Meli's brow quirked. "Don't I have one?"

"Something more permanent, since you're now a citizen here." Lyr tucked a strand of her hair behind her ear, and heat flushed her skin where his fingers touched. "Another guest suite until I can find you a home you like, but one reserved for Moranaians."

A new worry struck. "How will I pay for this? I'm not certain what I'll do here. I used to help my father find what he needed for spell research, but I doubt that type of work would earn much. There was nothing important I could train for in Alfheim without magic."

Lyr smiled. "There are many who would pay a Diviner to find things. My mother is a scholar, and I've no doubt there are days she would love that skill."

"But that would earn enough for lodging?" Meli asked, doubt tinging her tone.

"Such basics are provided to all who contribute to society, though anything more is on your own merit," he answered. "You're given time to get established after formally settling here."

"That's it?" Her stomach fluttered in an odd dance of hope and doubt. "It's that easy to become a full citizen?"

"Moranaia was formed by those who left Earth as the humans grew in number. Over millennia, we have welcomed plenty of our kindred who wished to do the same. Citizenship is at the lord or lady of an estate's discretion." Some of his earlier sadness faded as he leaned closer, a grin curving his lips. "I was dubious about you, but I decided I'd give you a chance."

Her lips parted on a chuckle. "Thanks."

"Once I present you formally, it will be official."

"Formally?" she whispered, aghast. "How formal?"

His brows creased together. "It's a joyous event, not an unpleasant one. Everyone on the estate is called together to be introduced to new residents. But with matters between Alfheim unresolved and concerns of state paramount, I may be forced to do something simple."

"Thank Freyr," Meli responded, her breath rushing out as the tension in her stomach eased. At his quizzical expression, she smiled. "I'm sorry if that sounded rude. I hate formal meetings. They haven't always been pleasant for me on Alfheim."

Lyr reached out, twining his fingers loosely with hers. "I hope you'll find your place here." His gaze lowered to their joined hands. "Bonded to me or not."

Her palms dampened even as her mouth went dry. She'd already dared much that day. Could she dare more? Meli gathered her resolve and leaned closer. "I don't know what I'll do about the bond." His worried gaze flicked up. "But I don't have to consider Alfheim now. I have only myself to please, and it would please me to get to know you better."

"Me as well," Lyr answered, his expression softening as he relaxed. "I'll have to arrange time for us alone. Even if the rest of the world has to wait."

Joy, like sunshine, chased away the shadows in her heart, and she smiled up at him. "Then let's fetch my things. The sooner I can get away from the ambassador, the better."

Bolstered, Meli rushed up the stairs, Lyr close behind. But her steps slowed as they crossed the walkway. Could she stand up for herself if confronted? Meli's hand trembled as she opened the tower door, but if Lyr noticed, he didn't comment as he followed her in. She hadn't told him the ambassador had threatened her with magic in addition to words, or he no doubt would have insisted on entering first. She refused to bring him more worries. Such a foolish, pointless conflict with assassins on the loose and worlds being poisoned.

The front room was blessedly empty, and only Berris and Orena sat at the table in the dining area. Meli sagged in relief. Perhaps she could avoid a conflict with Lady Teronver after all. They'd all be better off that way.

Berris and Orena exchanged glances and then rose. Orena gave a slight nod, and Berris approached.

"She is in her room," Berris said.

Meli's eyes widened at the other woman's kind tone. "I hope you two didn't bear the brunt of her anger."

"No more than usual." Berris shrugged, though her gaze kept flitting to the staircase. "I would stay here to guard you, Lady Ameliar, if not for my oath of service to the ambassador. She has let your family's feud go too far."

For a moment, Meli couldn't breathe. Couldn't think. She lifted a hand to her flushed face and fought for words. "You would stay here for me? I am practically an Unfavorable One."

Orena rounded the table and strode to Berris's side. "We have seen many truths beyond the sheltered walls of Alfheim. The world, or maybe the universe, is not what we have ever been told. I agree with Berris but am also bound."

"But I..." Meli stared at them with wide eyes. "I almost got you lost in the mists."

Berris smiled. "And then you saved us. You found a power you never would have known in Alfheim. I've thought much of that since my recovery. One wonders how many *unfavorable* people have simply never had the chance to find their true talents."

A creak echoed down the staircase, and the Ljósálfar went silent, their postures suddenly tense. Lady Teronver descended a moment later, but the elder barely spared them a glance before heading to the table. Meli frowned until she noticed Pol following close behind the ambassador. He caught Meli's eye and winked. She couldn't help but return his wicked grin.

As the ambassador glared down at the platters of food, Lyr broke the silence. "Thank you for your service, ladies," he said, his measuring gaze moving between Berris and Orena. "I will see that you, at least, are mentioned favorably in my formal letter."

A gasp sounded, and Lady Teronver spun to face them. "Letter?"

"I wouldn't rely on *you* to recount my words truthfully," Lyr answered with a wry smile.

The lady's face whitened. "You—"

Pol wrapped a hand around the ambassador's wrist, though his eyes sparkled with humor. "I will make certain it is delivered."

Lady Teronver's mouth pinched shut, and she snatched up a small loaf of bread from the table before marching back to the stairs. She paused a few steps up to glance over her shoulder. "Berris. Orena. Prepare more food and bring it at once. You will ensure my safety this last night in this wretched land."

Meli's mouth twitched with humor as the attendants scrambled to obey. Whatever hold Pol had over the ambassador was a welcome one. Once Berris and Orena had disappeared with enough food for a royal feast, Meli nodded gratefully to Pol. He gave his favorite flourishing bow and gestured toward the stairs.

"Better go before her boldness overrides her sense."

As Meli climbed the stairs with Lyr, she catalogued her possessions. Aside from the runes she carried at her belt, she had one small bag of clothing and a few necessities. She pushed open the door and crossed to a small dresser, grabbing her bag from the top as she opened the top drawer.

The gleam of pale metal caught Meli's eye as she slid her hairbrush and some hair pins into the sack. Her fingers hovered over the delicate silver chain for a moment before she lifted it, the weight of the mesh-encased crystal pulling the strand straight. Staring at the gently swaying crystal, she nibbled at her lip.

"Is something wrong with your necklace?" Lyr asked.

With a quick shake of her head, Meli faced him. "This held the spell that kept our group and our supplies together as we crossed through the mists. It's an expensive artifact, and I'm not sure I should keep it."

"May I?" Wordlessly, she dropped it into Lyr's hand. His brow creased in concentration for a long moment, and Meli caught a hint of his magic before he glanced at her. "Are you certain?"

"What do you mean?" Frowning, she took the necklace back. Then she closed her eyes and concentrated on the resonating hum of the spell that had wrapped around them in the mists. Nothing. "It's gone. The whole spell. I felt it from the moment Lady Vionafer placed it around my neck."

"Even after you passed through the portal?"

"I…" Meli paused, considering. Had the High Mage created a temporary spell designed to fade at the end of the mission? Had something gone wrong with the magic? "I couldn't say, truthfully. So much happened after we arrived that I hardly thought of it. I took it off before bed and forgot about it completely."

Lyr touched a finger to the pendant. "I'd say it's yours. It feels attuned to you, much like the necklaces we wear. A great symbol of your heritage."

Meli hesitated. Then she lifted the chain over her head with a shrug. "I don't know what will happen if I keep it when the Lady Mage wanted it back, but she gave no clear direction."

"Ask Pol. He seems to know much he shouldn't," Lyr said, smiling wryly.

She chuckled. "More than *I* want to know for certain."

23

Lyr strolled with Meli along the garden trail, their hands clasped loosely. Despite all that loomed, he allowed himself to enjoy this one perfect moment. He'd be hearing from Lial about the Neorans and debating his next move soon enough. Much better to focus on the late afternoon light gleaming gold through the trees and glinting in Meli's pale hair. Clear and beautiful—a glow of hope. He snorted softly at the thought, earning a questioning glance from his potential bonded.

No way he was sharing *that* bit of fancy. "What do you think of my home?" Lyr asked instead. "I read that Alfheim is mostly stone. Having towers and rooms built around the trees must be quite different."

"Yes," Meli said, nodding. "The City of Light. Full of huge edifices made of white stone. Spires top most buildings, and the crystals at the peak channel sunlight through every room. We have gardens, but they're carefully maintained to keep out anything wild or disordered." She tilted her head back, and her expression softened as she glanced up at the canopy. "I think your home is glorious. Everything is more in harmony despite being closer to nature."

"If only that were the case of late," Lyr said, but he didn't let it ruin his mood as Meli turned her smile his way. "I'll have to see that it is so again."

She squeezed his hand. "All things cycle. A lesson I never believed before arriving here."

All things cycle. So true but so easy to forget. Lyr had lived enough centuries to experience that endless reality. The lows of life always circled around to the greatest heights. Good and evil fought perpetually, neither winning against the other for long. All things ended to begin again. And through it all, hope persisted, an unwavering light.

Even things sundered could be rejoined.

"I didn't mean to upset you," Meli said.

Lyr blinked, and his eyes focused on Meli once more. "You didn't. That was a reminder I dearly needed."

Her brows rose. "You were frowning."

"I'm sorry," he said, his mouth softening into a smile. "I hadn't realized. Truly, your words were helpful. It's all relative, isn't it? If I fail to stop Kien, someone else will. Evil never succeeds for long."

Meli shrugged, but her lips tilted up. "So we can hope."

They fell into a companionable silence, the swishing leaves and chirping birds flowing around them. Then they rounded a bend in the path, and Selia came into sight. As the mage smiled and waved, rushing their way, Meli slowed. Her hand grew damp in his, and when Lyr glanced her way, he noticed her expression had gone blank.

"Meli?" he asked.

She shook her head, her eyes pleading with him to drop the issue. "It's nothing."

Had something happened between the two? Lyr's brow furrowed. "Will you tell me later?"

Meli bit at her lower lip, her gaze flicking to Selia and back. Finally, she nodded. But the smile that crossed her face was a weak shadow.

Lyr had no time to offer comfort before Selia halted before them. If there had been a disagreement, it hadn't affected the mage, who smiled at both of them with cheerful ease. "Lord Lyr, I was about to come find you."

"I hope nothing else has gone wrong," Lyr said, wincing.

"Not that I've heard." Selia lifted a bundle of cloth she'd had tucked beneath her arm. "Corath and I created a new cloak based on the spells set in the other, and I wanted to see if you would test it. It's designed to muffle the energy signature of anyone wearing it."

Lyr eyed the fabric. Green, not brown, and made with summer weight cloth. Not the same as the one he'd been trapped beneath. "To what purpose?"

"I asked myself how the assassin found you out of all the people on the estate." She unbundled the cloak and shook it out. "They must have some way to target your energy."

His eyes skimmed the leaves embroidered along the hem as he considered her words. "I stood with my father when Kien was taken through the portal, but we had little contact otherwise. It's hard to imagine he had the time or would take the effort to memorize my energy and use it centuries later."

"I could be wrong." Selia held out the cloak. "But I made this, just in case."

Lyr accepted the cloak and then swirled the fabric around his shoulders. "How do you want me to test it?"

Selia's gaze sharpened on him for a moment before she nodded. "It's dulling your energy signature already, but when you raise the hood, it should stifle you completely. I'd like to test how well it works at a greater distance."

"I should have time after I show Meli her new room."

"Did I hear correctly, then?" Smiling, Selia glanced at Meli. "You have decided to stay?"

Meli's hand convulsed around Lyr's. "Yes, Lady Mage."

Lady Mage? Lyr wondered. Then it hit him. Magic was prized in Alfheim, and Meli had been destined for banishment for her lack. She had no way of knowing that Selia was kind. He'd told Meli that magic wasn't required, but that didn't mean she'd believed him. Instincts didn't fade overnight.

Selia's brow wrinkled, and her smile faded. "Are you unwell, Lady Meli? I hope I did not cause offense by being so forward."

"No," Meli said. Though her grip tightened, her expression was resolute when Lyr glanced at her. Meli's chin lifted, a less severe echo of the ambassador's pride. "But I wish to start off well here. With truth. I have little magic, a flaw many mages detest. If that is so for you, I would rather know now."

Selia stared for a moment. Then her eyes narrowed and her lips pursed. "What do you mean, no magic? Who told you that?"

"My teachers on Alfheim," Meli answered. Lyr winced in sympathy at the pain he sensed from her at the admission. "The mage tests almost killed me. When they tried to channel energy into me—"

"Into?" Selia's face flushed red. "You aren't an energy crystal. You might not be able to hold much, but that doesn't mean…" Her eyes slipped closed, and she took a few deep breaths before looking up again. "Forgive me. I know little about magic among the Ljósálfar. But I do know it takes power to use the runes. It's your mages' lack for not recognizing that fact."

At first, Meli stood frozen. But then a slow smile curved her lips. "Thank you."

"It is only the truth." Selia took a step back, the anger easing from her face, and glanced at Lyr. "And you're certain you're willing to test the cloak?"

"I don't mind," Lyr answered. "I've missed hiking the woods. I'll let you know when I go out so you can monitor the spell from here."

Selia smiled. "Of course. I'll be in my room."

∽◉∾

Meli placed her bag next to the door and examined the rounded tower room. Across from where they'd entered, a bed rested beneath one of the windows, and a desk was under yet another to her right. To her left, a straight wall broke the semi-circle, a door the only thing taking up the space. The chamber was sparse but beautiful, the walls carved to look like the trunk of a tree.

Lyr gestured to the door on the left. "There is a place for your clothing as well as a washroom beyond. If you would like more furniture, it can easily be provided."

It was so different from the square stone walls of her bedroom in Alfheim. Instead of the white wash of light from energy crystals above, a soft golden glow emanated from globes set into wall sconces that looked like tree branches. "It's lovely."

"I had hoped you would like it."

They stood awkwardly, neither willing to move. Meli's insides still twisted from the mage's words, and now her chest tightened with the need to keep Lyr with her. Without even realizing, she had begun to grow closer to him, taking his hand at times without conscious intent. She might have a lot to think about, but she wanted him with her while she did it.

"You're going for a hike?" At his nod, her heart pounded and her breath stilled. Her last experience in the forest at night had been less than pleasant, and she could see the twilight fading beyond the windows. But with him? It would be worth this moment of bravery. "Do you mind if I go with you? I'd love to see a true forest. Well, so long as I needn't save you again."

Lyr laughed, and the shadows he'd held in his eyes faded away. "These days, I can make no guarantees. But I'll do my best. I'd love for you to join me."

They walked hand in hand again as they retraced their steps in the growing dark. But this time, they went beyond the base of the guest tower and continued north. Meli looked to the east where the valley fell away to the village nestled below. Thank

Freyr Lyr hadn't planned to go that way, for the memory of stumbling through the dark was still strong.

At the edge of the gardens, he paused. "Can you speak telepathically?"

"Of course," she answered, brow quirked. "Is that not common here?"

"It is, but I know little of the Ljósálfar."

Her expression cleared. "It's a talent held by most of my kind. One of many traits we likely share."

"Indeed." With a smile, he gestured to the forest beyond. "It is less wild here than the area where you found me. This side of the valley is more maintained and in some places, inhabited. I would rather not alert anyone to our presence by speaking aloud."

Meli nodded and sent a gentle mental nudge his way to make sure they could connect. The intimacy of the brief contact made her shiver. *"Very well."*

"Let me contact Selia," he sent. At her nod, his gaze went vacant for a moment. Then he lifted the hood and led her to the forest.

The ground here was soft with moss, the path level. If there had once been boulders the size of the ones on the other side of the valley, they had long ago been cleared. The trees, however, were just as large, and their canopy distilled the light of the rising moon to a dim glimmer. From Lyr's sure steps, she assumed his people shared another fae trait—excellent eyesight. He moved as surely as in daylight, and his confidence helped her relax and enjoy the scenery.

They followed along the ridge top, the valley stretching to their right. Lights winked through the treetops in places below, revealing the houses that would go unseen during the day. She saw no sign of any homes where they walked, but she felt peace rather than isolation. The steady drone of insects sounded through the humid air in a soothing cadence.

Lyr stopped when the valley opened up to a wide plain below. The trees thinned there, and moonlight glimmered across patches of clear land. Farms? *"Do you mind climbing?"* he asked.

Her gaze shot from the view to his face and then down to her robes. *"Climbing?"*

"There is an observation tower in that tree," Lyr answered, gesturing to a broad trunk beside them. *"Rain is coming, and it's a nice place to rest."*

Meli looked to the sky but saw little beyond a few stray clouds passing over the moons. Still, the wind had picked up, and the earth smelled somewhat…wet. A life lived in controlled Alfheim gave her little experience with natural weather. *"I'll see if I can manage."*

She unbuckled her belt and pulled off her overrobe, chuckling to see that she had Lyr's undivided attention. She let out a sigh at the caress of the breeze around her legs and arms. Her clothes were better suited to her cool homeland, not the heat of Moranaia, but the thin, short underdress was perfect. She would have to get some of the light dresses the ladies here wore.

"Perhaps this was a bad plan," he murmured. Then grinned. "Or a very good one."

With an answering laugh, she followed him to the base of the tree and up the rungs shaped into the side. "Did you cut into the bark to make these?"

Lyr peered down at her. "Mages formed the way so the tree would not be harmed."

Of course they did. Meli was coming to realize that Moranaians took their trees quite seriously.

They ducked into a shelter tucked between three massive limbs. Lyr scooted to the side, his legs stretched before him, as Meli settled next to him. Though she was out of breath, the view she earned was more than worth it. She could see beyond the patch of fields to more hills in the distance. At the base of one, the moonlight glimmered silver, revealing a lake.

Lyr sighed, a content sound, and leaned back on his hands. The shelter was just large enough to hold them and maybe one other person, and they were so far up in the trees they could have been alone in the world. Perhaps she should have been alarmed, since she barely knew him, but he had no reason to hurt her. He could have sent her back to Alfheim if he'd wanted to do that.

"Worth the climb?" Lyr asked, his voice resounding pleasantly in the small space.

She smiled over at him. "Absolutely."

The first drops of rain pattered against the roof and dipped the leaves outside the shelter. But Meli was more curious about him. "Do you like it here? Do you like your place as lord?"

"I do. Mostly." Lyr leaned forward, his expression turning serious. "Though I would rather not be Myern, for it meant my father's early death."

"How terrible. I'm sorry I mentioned it."

Lyr took her hand. "Don't be. I wanted us to get to know one another. He was murdered over twenty years ago, the reason I rushed back from Earth without Arlyn's mother. I never knew I left a daughter behind."

"Arlyn told me a little of the story." Meli nudged him, trying to lighten the mood. "This has not been a good half-century for you."

"No," he answered, though with a laugh. "But overall worth it."

They leaned against one another in companionable silence as the rain pounded out a symphony. "Would you tell me more about the bond?" Meli finally asked. "What is it? How is it formed?"

"You told me you have soul companions." Lyr's forehead wrinkled in thought. "I suppose it is a formal linking of that. First, there's an exchange of pendants. There are words that can activate them before given, but intent can also work. Finally, there is physical union."

Horrified, Meli pulled back to look at him. "You have to wait until soulbonding for physical intimacy in this world?"

"Gods, no," Lyr choked out around his laughter. "We'd be mad, for soulbonds are not very common. But it does act to solidify a bonding once the process has begun."

"Thank goodness," she breathed.

One side of his mouth quirked up. "I'd assumed the Ljósálfar were much stricter about such things."

"Yes and no." Meli grimaced, trying to find the words to explain. "We may join with whomever we wish. But that act of joining is no small thing. Our bodies are our dominion, so it is considered an honor to share that body. It is why Lady Teronver's insult was a grave one."

"I'll be glad to see the back of her."

She nudged him again. "As will I."

The feel of his skin pressed to hers, even in that innocent contact, caused her heart to race. Meli had never understood soul companions until she'd touched him. "So are males in charge of bonding?"

"Not really. Either of a couple might begin the process." She could hear the smile enter his voice. "Though it's usually whoever rushes to it first. Soulbonds are rare and valued—and they've been known to make fools of many. When Kai first met Arlyn, he was so afraid he would lose her that he began the bond without her even knowing. He's fortunate that she forgave him."

"How were you able to resist doing the same?" she asked, careful to keep her voice measured. To keep him from hearing how much the answer meant to her.

Lyr pulled his leg up and rested his arm on his knee, his gaze shifting to the distant valley below. "I suppose restraint is my curse."

Meli stilled. "Curse?"

"I did not bond with Aimee." His eyes met hers. "She was human, or so I thought, though she ended up having more than a bit of elven blood. I wanted to wait until I'd talked to Kai about bringing her through the Veil. I didn't want to harm her, and humans struggle crossing through the mists since time is so much in flux."

For a moment, the cold mists of the Veil flowed around her again, and she winced. "Wise."

"Was it?" His face twisted with pain. "I had to rush away, not knowing I would be unable to return. Both Aimee and Arlyn suffered for it."

What could she say? Had he bonded with his first love, it would have left Meli in an awkward place. Her stomach lurched at the thought of what might have happened had she arrived to find Lyr already bonded. But to say so would be to wish his pain. "I'm sorry."

"All is as it should be." Lyr tucked a lock of her hair behind her ear, his expression softening. "Only on days like today do I think of the past. It doesn't seem real to me that you're here. I never thought to have another chance at a bond. I didn't know it was possible."

The words stabbed at her. "And here I am, uncertain if I even want it."

He nodded, averting his gaze. His sudden isolation tore at her as surely as his pained story. What was it that drew her to him? She felt like she had always known him, like he had whispered words of love even in her dreams. There was an entire history between them that she didn't comprehend. A pull that went beyond any she had ever known.

The wind picked up through the trees, gusting droplets of rain through the small opening where they'd entered. So high off the ground, the air was cooler here, and as her thin gown grew damp, her teeth chattered with the cold. Meli wanted to laugh. All day, she'd been sweltering in the heat, and now she wanted nothing more than her hated robe.

She rubbed at her arms to warm them, and Lyr glanced over at the movement, a frown pulling his brows together. "Cold?"

"Unbelievably, yes."

He lifted the edge of his cloak invitingly. "Come, bundle up. We can admire the view while the rain passes. It shouldn't be too much longer."

How could she resist an invitation like that?

Meli slid the short distance between them and under his arm. Almost instantly, she warmed, in no small part because of the male beside her. He radiated heat, life, and something…some energy that meshed so perfectly with her own. She sighed and settled into him, home for the first time in memory.

He turned his face toward hers, so close their breaths merged. "Meli? I'd like to kiss you again."

24

Lyr expected Meli to hesitate as she had before, but she didn't. Instead, she closed the distance and brushed her lips against his. Just the barest touch, but his body hardened. Burned. He slid his hand from her shoulder and down her side, and she trembled. Then she pressed against his side and kissed him once more.

Her sweet taste filled him, pulsing through him like blood. Lyr's fingers tightened on her hip as desire exploded within him, the restraint he'd mentioned before gone. His free hand dove into her hair as Meli opened her mouth fully to his. And the feel of her breasts against him... *Gods*. A groan escaped as he plundered.

She twisted to straddle him, and her arms wrapped around his neck. His hands wandered up her spine and then down her waist until he gripped her hips. If she kept moving against him, he would lose all control. Lyr bent his head to trail his mouth along her throat, and her panting gasps echoed in the tiny shelter.

All fear of offending her faded from Lyr's mind, but he hesitated before his palms slid up to cup her breasts. Meli caught his gaze as her lips curved into a smile. "Stop worrying. I offer permission."

Lyr needed nothing more. Their lips met again, volatile, as he lowered her to the floor of the shelter. She gripped the edges of his cloak for a moment before her own hands started to roam. As his fingers teased at the bottom of her short robe, she began to tug at his tunic. *Clechtan,* but he was going to go mad.

Lyr sat up, searching for the cloak's clasp. He wanted to shed his clothes, the better to be close to her. As close as she would let him get. He fumbled with the metal closure for a moment and then sighed with relief when it fell free. He shrugged the cloak off, the tunic following, before returning to Meli once more. Her mouth was better than any wine.

"LYR!"

The contact blasted through his mind, the pain instant and searing. He jerked upright with a strangled cry and then rolled to his back. Blindly, he shoved his fingers against his temples. He hardly noticed Meli's hand on his shoulder as he struggled to control the agony. "What's wrong?"

"Lial. Mind blast," Lyr whispered.

He had no idea what she thought of his explanation, for the healer's next words brought a fresh wave of pain. *"WHERE ARE YOU?"*

"For the love of all the gods, TONE IT DOWN," Lyr sent back with force of his own, letting the full scope of his agony filter through.

There was a moment's silence before shocked regret flowed through the link. *"Forgive me, Lyr. I didn't mean to cause you pain. I've been searching for you for over an hour."*

With the healer's words, a bit of soothing flowed in. Not much, but it was enough to help Lyr think. *"I've been on a hike. Lady Selia is having me test a new cloak."*

"Did the damn thing wipe you out of existence?"

"What?" Lyr sent back.

He let his eyes slit open, though he continued to rub his temples, and relaxed when no new pain resulted. Meli's face glowed pale in the dim moonlight as she leaned over him, and he struggled to form an explanation. "Lial contacted me telepathically. And rather forcefully."

Her breath hissed out in a relieved sigh, and Lyr's gaze shifted to her mouth. He wanted to return to kissing her, but the healer's voice broke through again. *"You disappeared. Gone from the estate key. Gone from our senses. If Kai had better range, you'd be hearing worse."*

Though he wanted to kill Lial in that moment, he had to smile at the assessment. *"I've no doubt. You can assure him that I am well. I might have been more than well if not for your untimely interruption."*

"Ah…my apologies." The healer hesitated. *"But there is much unresolved with the Neorans. You wanted my report when I could get away."*

Lyr bit back the string of curses that flowed through his mind. Work. Ever work. *"I will return as soon as possible. At least Selia can rest assured that her cloak does a fine job of muffling my energy."*

"That it does."

Sighing, Lyr rubbed a hand across his face. Remnants of pain pulsed between his temples, and his good humor was gone. "Forgive me, Meli. Lial has news to report, and I fear the estate, or at least Kai, is in an uproar. The cloak worked better than expected. They thought I'd disappeared until I shrugged it off."

Her eyes widened. Then she surprised him with a laugh. "Too bad we didn't keep them waiting longer."

"You're certain you aren't offended? I moved faster than I'd meant."

Meli rolled her eyes. "I gave you permission."

"True. I suppose I am uncertain of such things since I don't know your customs." Bemused, he pulled his tunic back on and shrugged into the cloak, though he kept the hood lowered. "Maybe you could tell me more about Alfheim."

She moved to the door and then twisted, lowering herself down the rungs one careful step at a time. "Certainly."

It took longer to descend the trunk than it had to climb it, as it was slippery after the rain. Lyr worried that he should have gone first, as Meli did not seem familiar with climbing trees in any weather, but she moved down steadily. When he dropped down beside her, she was already reaching for the heavy robe she usually wore.

"Ah, Freyr," she muttered, holding the cloth away from her body. "The whole thing is soaked. I should have thought to take it up with me."

Lyr eyed the thin cloth of her underdress and could find no reason to agree. Still, it would be rude of him not to offer aid. "I can dry it. Here."

It was a short spell, one learned when he'd first started camping as a boy. Within a moment, he held out a perfectly dried gown. Meli took it almost hesitantly, stared at it, and then draped it over her shoulder. "Thank you. I think I'll wait until we get closer to wear it. It's so much hotter down here."

Lyr grinned. He wasn't going to argue with that. Taking her hand once more, Lyr led her back the way they'd come. The air was thick with moisture from the rain, the smell of wet earth strong, but he hardly paid it attention. He listened to her voice as she described the world of her birth, the words painting images in his mind. How could they bear cold stone over the life of the forest?

It pained him that she had struggled in her life there, though her family was loving. He'd always known the Ljósálfar were fairly inflexible and that they considered the other fae races lacking. He hadn't realized that some of their own people were treated the same. On Moranaia, whatever talent one possessed was welcome if it brought greater good. But Alfheim required one fit into a smaller mold.

"Does everyone have to be a mage?" Lyr asked.

"No." Meli grimaced. "Those with fighting skills can become warriors or guardians. Some do well at a trade, like making furniture or growing food—all magically assisted. There are those like the ambassador who are skilled with words. The least talented are often assistants, using their meager skills as best they can. And the untalented, like me—"

Lyr halted, unable to resist caressing her cheek. "You are not untalented."

Her eyes went soft, but she shook her head. "To the Ljósál-far, I am. I'd be the lowest of servants if I returned."

"Remind me that I don't need a war," Lyr bit out. "Not in the middle of this."

Meli merely laughed. Then she grabbed his wrist and tugged him forward. "I thought restraint was your curse. Perhaps it is honor."

"The last turn of the moon would strain the greatest discipline," he muttered.

She gave a teasing grin. "So it would."

ᚱᚧᚥ

After escorting Meli to the base of her tower, Lyr strode toward his study where he sensed the others waiting. It was interesting that Kai, Arlyn, and Lial couldn't detect him through the estate key, for he could still access it with no difficulties. Selia's spell must have been a powerful one considering she herself didn't have the key. Well, formally at least. She *had* worked with both him and Arlyn on strengthening Braelyn's ancient defenses.

As soon as the door opened, Kai shot to his feet. "That was a cruel trick."

Lyr stopped short, surprised. "What are you talking about?"

"After a day filled with corpses, it was no small matter to think you dead."

Understanding washed over him. Though Lyr was several years older, Kai had grown protective ever since Lyr had lost Aimee. But then, it was always wise to watch someone in power who had lost a soulbond. "It was no trick, but I'm sorry nonetheless. I had no idea the cloak would have such an effect. I did tell Selia when I left."

"I haven't seen her." Kai sank into his seat and ran a hand through his hair. "Arlyn said she didn't think you were dead, but…"

Lyr winced. After his friend's earlier report, he could imagine what Kai had visualized. "I should have told you. I decided to show Meli the forest and gave leaving no thought. I've roamed at will for centuries, after all."

"Perhaps." Lial pushed away from where he'd been leaning on the front of the desk. "But you also gave no thought to the current crisis."

Though Lyr should have been embarrassed by the reprimand, he wasn't. He refused to regret the time he'd taken with Meli. "If I'd known mental communication couldn't get through, I'd have warned you. Meli could speak with me, so I assumed others could also."

"I thought I could sense you somewhat, too," Arlyn spoke up from the chair next to Kai. "Not clearly, but enough not to panic. Even as you stand before me, it's just a hint."

He was still wearing the cloak. Lyr unclasped it—an easier task in the clear light—and draped it across a chair before stepping away. "Now?"

"Much better," Arlyn answered, relaxing. Lial and Kai nodded.

Lyr dropped into the seat behind his desk. "Though it certainly has its uses, I'll have to see if Selia can adjust the spell. Those keyed into the estate should be able to speak to me at the least. But why didn't you contact me, Arlyn?"

She lifted her hands. "I tried, but every time I almost reached you, you seemed to flicker out of range. I'm still learning how to connect."

"We'll work on it." Lyr rubbed his temples where a faint ache from the healer's mental blast still resided. "I'd certainly rather Lial not contact me again for some time."

"I sent my call wide and quick," Lial said as he walked around the desk. Though often biting in his humor, Lial was a healer to his core. True regret haunted his eyes at the pain he'd caused. "I gave little thought to my own strength."

The healer reached out, his energy sparking to life before Lyr could protest. A few breaths, and the pain was gone. "You should save your strength for the Neorans."

Shrugging, Lial stepped back. "I'll be heading to my room to rest after this, as there isn't much more I can do for them tonight. There was no sign of the poisoned energy in any of the survivors, and their physical injuries are stable."

"Wait." Lyr shook his head. "The poison is just...gone?"

"As though the Veil washed them clean," Lial answered. "But their minds are in terrible shape. Magical pathways blown open or bleeding. Other, more mundane sections of the brain in tatters. It's no wonder so many are insane."

"Can you heal them?"

Lial nodded. "It will be a slow process, but I believe so. Ralan's pathways were similar after his contact with the poison on Earth, and I repaired that damage."

The door clicked open, and Selia entered, Lynia shuffling in behind. Lyr froze, reminded of the others' cloak-induced panic, but his mother's face held nothing but concentration. He eased back in his seat as she smiled up at him. "I was speaking to Selia when you disappeared. She explained what happened," his mother clarified before he could ask.

Lyr flicked a glance at the healer. "I'm surprised that Lial didn't check with you if he thought I'd been injured. It seems that would have saved us all some grief."

"I…" A flush crept up Lial's neck, and he rubbed a hand across the telling color. "I have endeavored not to disturb Lady Lynia of late."

In the sudden silence, Selia stepped forward. "I'm afraid it's my fault. Or, rather, Iren's. Even at eleven years, he is difficult to get to bed. I'd intended to warn the others after Lynia, but he distracted me."

"I was much the same at that age," Lyr said, smiling. "I was too distracted to notify everyone, myself."

Lial flicked an inscrutable glance at Lynia and then straightened. "If there's nothing else, I'll go get some rest. We all should."

With a nod, Lyr slumped back against his seat. "Excellent advice."

Too bad Lyr had too much work to take it.

25

D awn light sifted through the trees and gleamed against the white robes of the Ljósálfar as they stood in the clearing before the portal. But this time, Meli waited with Lyr, Arlyn, and Kai. As a dark-haired Moranaian female gave the Ljósálfar instructions on the crossing, Meli's gaze darted around the space, and she frowned. Hadn't this clearing been smaller when they arrived?

With a tentative mental brush, she got Lyr's attention. *"Have I lost my senses, or are there fewer trees?"*

"Kai believed there would be more survivors on his last mission, so we broadened the space." Lyr's fingers twined with hers. *"Would you like to say something to the group before they depart?"*

"I'd like to speak to Pol." Meli peered at the group. Only the white-robed women were present. *"But where is he?"*

A movement caught her eye a moment before Pol strode into the clearing, customary smirk twisting his lips. "Wondering about me?"

"I wanted to thank you," she said. "I'm not certain why you helped me, but you have my appreciation."

"Alfheim has grown more stagnant than is wise, and you and your mate will surely bring about needed change. Getting the jump on Freyr by solving this? That's more than reward enough." Pol leaned close, and his voice dropped to the barest whisper. "I count you and Lyr as friends, by the way. And my friends call me Loki."

With a laugh, he ran past the Ljósálfar and darted through the portal. Meli stared after him, a hard lump forming in her throat. By all the gods, she had argued with *Loki*. And lived. He'd called her a friend. Her mouth worked, but no sound came out.

Beside her, Lyr shook his head. "I knew he was no Ljósálfar, but I hadn't guessed he was a god."

The others stood by the portal gate, expressions caught in various levels of surprise as they stared after Pol. Then an odd gleam entered the ambassador's eyes, and her lips curved up. She gestured to Berris and Orena, and they proceeded to the arch behind the Moranaian guide. At the last moment, Lady Teronver spun around, and her grin widened.

"Meli. I almost forgot."

A tingle of apprehension swept through Meli. "Forgot what?"

The spell slammed into her, quick and deadly. Her meager shields shredded in an instant. As Meli began to fall, her vision faded to black.

∽⊙∾

Lyr's breath rushed out, and he almost doubled over at the odd, icy pain that swept in along his connection to Meli. He gasped as the feeling faded, replaced by an emptiness more terrifying than the pain. Heart pounding, he spun to see Arlyn lowering Meli's still form to the grass. Fury rose, choking him, and Lyr pulled his knife from its sheath.

When he glanced toward the portal, his eyes widened to see Berris holding Lady Teronver immobile, the warrior's own knife pressed to the ambassador's neck. Lyr took a step forward, his grip tightening on the hilt of his blade. But neither he nor Berris had a chance to act. Color draining from her face, Teronver went still.

"Pol," she gasped out. Then her eyes rolled back, and she whispered one last word. "Hel."

The ambassador's body went limp. Berris lowered her to the ground, and Orena knelt to search Teronver for signs of life. Face pale, Berris glanced up. "Dead. Just…gone."

Lyr's chest squeezed tight, the ache almost as bad as a wound. He dropped to his knees beside Meli, his fingers going to her neck. Though the restriction in his chest eased at the feel of her steady pulse, he could tell something was seriously wrong. Her skin was cool, her breathing a bare wisp. He gripped her hands, willing her to wake. Even the connection between them seemed lessened. Muted.

"Father?"

His gaze flicked to Arlyn, who knelt on Meli's other side. "She is alive, but only barely."

"Where's Lial?"

Lyr searched the clearing before his dazed mind recalled the healer's location—with the Neorans in their camp. He lifted Meli's limp body in his arms and then glanced at Kai and the *sonal* ringing the Ljósálfar. "Detain them while I seek care for Lady Meli. Respectfully, as they are not yet prisoners."

Without another word, he set off at a run for the Neoran camp, a couple of guards falling in behind. A blessedly short distance, for his fear seemed to grow with every footfall. He sent a mental call to the healer to be prepared moments before he broke through the magical barrier surrounding the camp.

The glow of power was just fading from his hands as Lial pulled away from a woman asleep on a small cot. "I'm doing a healing. What…" The healer's eyes grew large as he saw Meli, and he rushed over to an empty cot. "Here. What happened?"

"I don't know." Lyr stretched her out gently and sank down beside her. "The ambassador turned back at the gate and cast some spell. Meli collapsed."

Lial wasted no time, the blue glow lighting from his hands as he held them over Meli's head. The power spread as it flowed around her entire body. But when it faded, she still didn't wake. "Her body is fine. There is no physical damage," Lial said.

"Then why is she unconscious?"

"I'm…" The healer glared. "I'm not sure. I think something is holding her spirit removed from her body. But I know of nothing that can do that."

Lyr's heart pounded. His connection to her was growing gradually but alarmingly weaker. "Can you fix it?"

Lial shook his head, his scowl deepening. "No. I don't even know what it is. Perhaps Ralan can reach her. Or maybe Lady Selia can identify the spell used."

With a quick thanks to the healer, Lyr bundled Meli in his arms once more and began the race back to the estate. He'd never counted the length of the walk before, but every moment that passed seemed an eternity. He sent a frantic call to Ralan and Selia to meet him in his bedroom, not caring if they found the request strange. But then, the seer should know what was happening. He seemed to know everything else.

If no one else could fix what was wrong, perhaps the energy of Eradisel would help. Lyr darted through the halls and up the stairs in a blinding rush. And prayed to whichever god would listen as he placed Meli on his bed. Her pale blond hair stretched across his pillow as he'd dreamed it would, but nothing else was similar. Instead of desire, he was filled with soul-deep fear.

Ralan entered first, the shock on his face in no way comforting. "What happened?"

"You mean you don't know?" Lyr sat on the bed next to Meli. "Or are you being predictably vague?"

Eyes flashing, the prince came to a halt in the middle of the room. "I don't deserve that. When I last looked at the strands of the futures, I saw no sign of harm to her. I truly do not know."

"Sorry." Lyr forced a few deep breaths through his clenched teeth. "My anger isn't for you. The ambassador cast some spell at Meli, and Lial can't help."

Before Ralan could ask for more details, Selia knocked on the door, and Lyr called for her to enter. She rushed in, her brow puckered in confusion. "Selia. I will explain to you both."

Lyr recounted the scene by the portal, trying to examine each detail. But no new observation came to mind. When he was finished, Selia and Ralan looked perplexed. Selia shifted to the side of the bed to stand next to Meli, her eyes meeting his. The concern he saw only heightened his fear.

"I'll see if I can find the spell to blame."

Unlike with the healer, Lyr saw no sign of Selia's power. But he sensed it, a gentle buzzing that stood his arm hairs on end. Lyr stilled out of instinct, not wanting to disturb her work in any way. Only when her power faded and she opened her eyes did he realize that he'd been holding his breath.

Selia's eyes sparked with rage. "I found it. A nasty piece, built of magics from ages long past, even for our kind. It's a death curse, designed to sever the soul from the body. But it wasn't completed."

He thought back to the scene in the clearing. "Berris must have stopped her. Or Pol. Can you reverse it?"

"I'm not sure. This isn't something I know much about." Selia frowned down at Meli. "You might try bonding with her so her spirit doesn't slip away."

Bonding? Lyr recoiled at the suggestion, nausea rising. "I cannot do such a thing without her permission. Especially since she has said she is unsure of the bond."

"Kai did it," Ralan said from the foot of the bed. "Arlyn forgave him."

"Arlyn was conscious and had the choice to reject the necklace." Bile almost choked him. "It's not the same."

Selia's shoulder's drooped, and she nodded. "You're right. I'll see what I can do before we consider it. Consent should be given, most especially for a bond. I'll need a seat, for this is likely to take some time."

Wordlessly, Ralan pulled a chair over. Selia sank into it and closed her eyes. As the energy built once more, there was nothing for Lyr to do but wait. *"Can you see what happens from this?"* he sent to Ralan.

"Somewhat." Ralan sat gingerly on the end of the bed, his gaze on Meli. *"There are so many possible futures that it's hard to untangle. I don't understand it. None of this was possible yesterday. I saw the ambassador leave. What could have spurred her to this?"*

"Nothing happened when Meli and I gathered her things that would warrant this. And Lady Teronver had no chance to see her again, because Meli and I went for a hike..." Lyr's breath hitched. *"Could she have seen us leave? She already blamed Meli for the failure of her mission. Perhaps seeing us together tipped her over the edge."*

Ralan shrugged. *"She can hardly tell us. Things are unlikely to go well with Alfheim after this. Though the gods in play can change the future possibilities widely."*

They watched the mage work in silence for a moment before Ralan spoke to him again. *"Why did you call for me?"*

"You are the strongest in mind-magic I know. Lial said you might be able to reach her."

Ralan went silent, his golden eyes distant. Searching the futures? Lyr didn't want to know. Then the prince blinked and nodded. *"If I work with Selia, it will help."*

The seer's eyes closed, and his mind blocked to communication. Time dripped, and tension mounted. Lyr wanted to enfold Meli in his arms or at least hold her hand, but he was afraid to touch her. Or to even move. With no understanding of what Selia and Ralan were doing, he could interfere. Lyr clenched his hands together to keep from touching her.

When Meli's eyes shot open, he almost jumped. Selia and Ralan hadn't moved, and energy swirled the same as before. Her pale gaze met his with confusion. "Lyr? Where am I?"

"My room."

"Moranaia?" She glanced around in surprise. "This isn't the world I left."

Even his breath stilled. What did she mean? "You recall me but not the journey here?"

"No, I…" Her eyes widened. "Did Arlyn find you?"

His chest began to burn, and he pulled in a gasp of air. "You were with her in the clearing. I don't understand."

Her hands gripped the blanket beneath her. "There's more to me now, as I knew there'd be. I'm pulled to her. To you. We are."

As abruptly as she'd spoken, her eyes slid closed and her body went limp. But Lyr found himself so tense he might snap at a touch. The way she'd looked at him, the way she'd spoken— for a moment, Aimee had stared at him through Meli's eyes. How was it possible? Did time vary so widely on Alfheim that she'd grown to adulthood, reborn, in just a few Earth years?

Yet so much made sense. Because they hadn't bonded in her first life, her soul could have returned whole, never blended with his. It explained his second chance. It explained his dreams of

Aimee roaming through the Veil. He glanced at Eradisel, re-membering the tree's assurance that Aimee was not there. Did She know?

Lyr's gaze returned to Meli's still form as his emotions tum-bled within him. Aimee reborn. But she wasn't Aimee. She was Meli, and he liked her as she was. How could he possibly sepa-rate the two now? In a strange sense, he wanted them both. No, that wasn't quite true. He'd come to love Meli's quiet serenity, though he hoped she'd get past her self-doubt. But that in itself seemed a betrayal of his first love.

Before anything, any consideration, they had to save her. Uncaring now, he reached out and took her hand. If she could wake without disturbing Selia and Ralan, then surely that would have no effect.

When her eyes opened again, everything within him froze. But the gaze that met his was somehow different than the first time she'd awakened. "I'm alive? She didn't kill me?"

"Who?" he asked hesitantly, uncertain who was speaking.

"Teronver. That spell…" Meli's voice trailed off, and her eyes seemed to go heavy before she forced them open. "Who is the male who kept calling to me?"

His muscles eased with something like relief, though the feeling made no sense. "Ralan. Do you remember waking be-fore?"

Her face scrunched. "Before? I…There is something, but…"

"Don't worry about it." Lyr squeezed her hand. "How do you feel?"

"I think I'm slipping back again."

Before he could answer, she pulled her hand free and reached for the pendant around her neck. Meli struggled to pull the netting loose from her hair, but in a moment, it was in her hand. "Take this."

"Don't give up." His heart seized. "We will keep trying."

She gripped the chain tighter. "No, take it. And save me."

When light flared from the necklace, he understood what she meant. Bonding required only intent. "I'll not trap you this way. It's not right."

She laughed softly even as her hand trembled. "I offer it to you. Freely. As I wish it. If there is a trap, it's my own design."

Lyr wavered, the restraint he'd held for decades crumbling around him. She didn't even know about Aimee, about her rebirth. How could she think clearly right now? And yet his hand reached out, brushing against hers as it wrapped around the chain. When she came to herself, she might hate him. They might face a priest of Arneen to have the bond severed. But as magic flowed between them, he couldn't find the strength to care.

26

When Meli opened her eyes again, the world was no longer a swirling haze. She blinked against the light spilling across her face until her vision adjusted. Then she blinked again. Above, the ceiling was carved to look like branches stretching from a large tree, so well-done she'd thought she was in the forest. *Where...?*

Then memories flooded in. A voice had whispered in her head, commanding her to stay. It had shown her visions of Lyr's panicked face as he sat beside her on the bed. Was she in Lyr's bedroom, then? It seemed most likely.

She could sense Lyr in the chair beside her without turning her head to look. Their bond was stronger, an actual link now. Meli didn't regret it, though he probably believed she would. Or he would think she hadn't understood what she was doing. But even ill, Meli had known. She'd lost her fear of the soulbond the night before.

Meli never would have given Lyr her permission, for the kiss or anything that had followed, if her spirit didn't sing with his. Not without knowing him much longer. She'd spent a great deal of time staring at her own ceiling last night, trying to make a decision. And she'd decided she wanted him.

She let out a soft breath and shifted, pleased to find she was merely achy. Lyr sat forward at once. "Meli?"

Worried about the odd timbre of his voice, she levered herself to her side and leaned her weight on her trembling arm. "What's wrong?"

"You should lie back down." Lyr's chair screeched against the wood floor as he shot to his feet, and his face twisted with concern. But Meli also detected a hint of fear through their tenuous bond. "Once the bonding had begun, Selia was able to break the spell, but you're still weak. We had to stop your very soul from leaving your body."

At Meli's shiver, Lyr rushed to pull a blanket from the end of the bed. She settled back against the pillows and let him gather it around her, though her shudder hadn't been from the cold. "I've only heard of such things in hushed whispers," she said. "Plenty think that spell is a myth. I suppose I can clarify things in that regard."

"Provided Alfheim will speak with us once the ambassador's body is delivered." Lyr settled on the bed beside her, but he didn't quite meet her eyes. "Meli...I'm sorry."

She knew what he was apologizing for, and it wasn't her injury. "I'd decided before this."

His gaze darted to hers. "But I thought—"

"I wanted to wait until Lady Teronver left to tell you. This only hastened things." Meli reached out, resting her hand against his forearm. "Is that what's bothering you?"

Lyr's brows drew down. "Do you recall the first time you woke?"

"First time? No, I…"

But then she did. Her eyes closed against a wave of dizziness as the memory hit. She'd been drifting, that faint voice trying to hold her close, when her consciousness had split along a fissure long unnoticed. The images that had always teased at her mind—of Lyr, of Arlyn, of strange people and places—had so-lidified into memories of a life she'd never lived.

She'd pulled almost frantically at herself as that other piece had drifted away. As part of her being had panicked in the dark void, the other had spoken to Lyr. And when that fragment of her spirit returned, she'd felt whole for the first time ever. It must have been from a past life, a version of herself that hadn't been ready to settle into a new existence, causing memories to haunt Meli's current life. There were legends of such things, but she'd never known of anyone who'd gone through it.

What had the fairy said? Blood-souls with Arlyn. Meli's mus-cles clenched as the meaning of the term became clear. Though the vague images she'd always seen had faded again, that final rejoining had given her the truth. She had been Arlyn's mother in her previous life. They'd been connected then by both soul and blood, now only the former. Arlyn's mother—and Lyr's first love.

"By Freyr…" Meli whispered, stunned.

How would Lyr handle the news? She might share a soul with Aimee, but she was *not* the same person. Being reborn among the Ljósálfar and growing up in Alfheim had left their own marks. Her spirit had shifted and expanded, her past self only a vague dream. Would he expect her to be like his previous bonded once he realized?

Gulping, she met his eyes. "What did I say when I woke?"

He shifted closer, and his hand took hers. "You seemed confused. You asked if Arlyn had found me. You were...not quite yourself."

"That's an understatement," she muttered.

"So you remember?" Lyr asked, his words carefully measured.

Meli squeezed his hand in case he withdrew it once he heard. "I don't remember what was said. I only have impressions. For a moment, I was divided. Lyr, I—I think it was my past self. I think I was your first bonded in another life. But I don't understand how."

Instead of appearing shocked, he merely nodded. "So I gathered from what you said. How differently does time pass on Alfheim?"

"Much faster." Meli stared, confused by his apparent calm. So he already knew? Though she detected a hint of worry through their link, he was less upset than she would have expected. "In ancient times, a Ljósálfr might bring a human back for a few years. Almost no time had passed on Earth when they'd returned them."

He lifted a brow. "Humans in Alfheim?"

"As lovers, usually." Meli's face reddened, though her people no longer did such a thing.

"Ah." Lyr nodded again. "The Sidhe do the same."

Meli canted her head. "You don't do that here?"

"No humans have been allowed on Moranaia in recent memory, but no one has asked to bring one, either. The Veil crossing is much rougher between Earth and Moranaia, sometimes even for a trained guide." With a sigh, Lyr glance down at their joined hands. "It's why I didn't try to rush Aimee through when..."

Meli couldn't hold in a helpless snort. "I suppose I wouldn't be here otherwise."

"True." The pain she'd expected finally flowed from him across their bond, and when he looked up, his eyes were shadowed with it. "She—you, I suppose—must have known. She sent my pendant with Arlyn and said I'd need it again. Twice, it has stopped a blade, and so I believed that was her intent. But maybe not. When you—she—spoke earlier, she said 'There's more to me now, as I knew there'd be.'"

What a tangled mess. Meli shifted restlessly beneath her blanket. "I don't know what to make of this."

"Nor do I." Lyr released her hand to rub his face. "Meli, I don't want you trapped in this bond. Could your link with Aimee have influenced your choice? If you decide that is so, our priests can sever a soulbond, but—"

"Stop." Though her body ached, she pulled herself upright. "I told you I'd decided before the ambassador's attack. I'd thought to give us more time, but I knew what I wanted. I may seem weak, but when I make a decision, I follow through."

His face went blank. "I didn't say you were weak."

"I know it." Meli's shoulders slumped as exhaustion swept through her. Her energy was low enough without having to deal with such an important conversation. "Just as I know this past life makes everything more complicated. Still, I'll not do something irrevocable out of your misplaced nobility. I am grateful you told me of the choice, but I'm resolved."

"I'm sorry." He huffed, though he smiled with it. "Again."

"I suppose I can't blame you. I was hardly encouraging when I first learned of the bond." Meli dropped back against the pillows. "The night you were injured and I found you in the clearing, I'd hoped the runes would show me the best way forward. They led me to you."

His eyes flashed with a maelstrom of emotions, so mixed she couldn't tell one from another even with their bond. "I've been sitting here thinking over it all. Trying to decide if I should give my own pendant to you or wait."

She swallowed hard. "I'd force you no more than you would me."

Lyr peered at her as he wrapped his hand around his necklace. After a long moment, he pulled it from his neck and held it between them. "*i Tayah ay nac-mor kehy ler ehy anan taen.*"

As the pendant flared with power, she reached out to take it. And marveled as their connection grew even stronger when her fingers tangled in the chain. Energy hummed around them as she settled the pendant around her neck.

For the first time, she no longer felt lost. She was found.

❧

For a moment, Lyr couldn't remember how to breathe. He'd believed he would never say the words that would bind him to another. Even after meeting Meli, he'd had little hope. But as she placed the pendant around her neck, he couldn't deny how the bond wove stronger between them.

Was it foolish to follow impulse? Even as he struggled to accept Aimee's rebirth, he longed for this bond with Meli more than anything. Maybe even more than when he'd met Aimee, a thought that sent guilt burning through his blood. He should have waited until he'd reconciled the past with the present to give her his pendant. But for once, he'd released all doubt and followed the lead of his friend. Like Kai, he'd acted on instinct. *Please don't let it be a mistake.*

The light of the spell faded, though the pendant glowed for a moment longer. Meli traced a finger across the carvings. "It's dented," she whispered.

"As am I," Lyr answered without thinking. But it was true. "I've my own scars."

Meli's lips curved into a soft smile. "They've made you who you are, just as my past has made me."

"Something we both must learn to face," Lyr said. Then he chuckled. "That sounded more dire than I'd intended. But we do have much to learn about one another."

Her eyes sparkled with humor. "Maybe when I've recovered, you can show me some of those dents."

❧

The dining room was empty when Lyr escorted Meli in, save for one of his helpers placing a tray of food at Lyr's usual place. With a nod of thanks, he helped Meli into a chair and then served them both some bread, meat, and cheese. He'd wanted her to rest longer, but she'd refused. Lyr examined her face for signs of strain, though he could feel through their bond that she was well. His bonded was more stubborn than her acquaintances would ever believe.

They were partway through when Kai and Arlyn entered. His daughter paused to peer at Lyr and Meli, her gaze falling on their switched necklaces, before her face lit up. "Thank goodness."

Lyr's fingers tightened around the cup he'd just lifted. If he was uncertain about what he'd learned of Meli, he couldn't imagine how Arlyn would take it. But she needed to know. "Have you eaten? Or are you searching for me?"

"The second," Arlyn said as she took the seat on his other side. Kai regarded Lyr quizzically before sitting next to Arlyn. "I thought I sensed you here. Ralan told us what happened, but I wanted to see for myself how you'd fared. Both of you."

"I am better than I should be. Far better," Meli said. Then patches of red bloomed on her cheeks. "But we learned…"

Arlyn glanced between them, a frown gathering. "What's wrong?"

"There is little to do but say it." Lyr set his cup down with a thump. "When we were trying to bring her back, we learned…Meli's soul…she was once your mother. In her previous life, she was Aimee."

Silence consumed the room. Arlyn's mouth had dropped with shock, but she quickly snapped it closed. She tossed her head, and a dry chuckle slipped free. "That's impossible. It's only been a few years since Mom died."

"Time flows swifter on Alfheim," Lyr answered, his chest constricting with concern.

"She's twenty-five. She's grown. I feel some connection, it's true, but…" Arlyn shot to her feet. "She is *not* my mother."

"You are correct. I am not," Meli whispered. Sorrow haunted the gaze she lifted to Arlyn. "And yet, I've always had odd memories. Impressions. A red-haired girl with her hair in two strange tails. Buildings of metal, and stone, and glass. And that girl dancing in a blue dress in front of an odd wooden house in the woods. I used to dream of green eyes."

Arlyn paled. "It's impossible."

"I thought so, too," Lyr said. "But it's true."

"I can't just…" Arlyn lifted a shaking hand and then dropped it. "I need to think about this."

For a moment, she stared at them. Finally, Arlyn turned and strode from the room, a helpless, choked sound echoing behind her. Lyr pushed away from the table to follow, but Kai shook his head.

"I'll go to her. She needs a little time." Kai stood and headed after her, but he turned at the door. "There's a lot we have to do. Talk to Ralan about it."

Though none of this was his fault, Lyr ached nonetheless. His eyes met Meli's saddened ones, and they both released a sigh. They weren't the only people who would have trouble adjusting. But he understood. Oh, how well he understood.

৩৯৫

Meli had been tired after lunch, so Lyr had escorted her to her room. He'd thought then to check on Arlyn, but she'd told him she needed to be alone. Though she hadn't seemed angry during their brief communication, he couldn't help but worry, their relationship still tenuous enough that he feared damaging it. He didn't want to intrude if it would make the situation worse. So he was left with work when he'd rather be anywhere else.

It was rare that Lyr resented his place as Myern, but today, he did. Instead of exploring his new bond with Meli, he was stuck at his mirror preparing for two unpleasant communications. Lyr had sent a formal letter and a spelled crystal through the Veil to Alfheim before lunch, and if the soft, golden glow around the frame of his mirror was any indication, someone had attuned it to one on the other side. First, he'd contact Alfheim. Then the Neoran queen.

Lyr sucked in a breath. Time to find out how Alfheim would react to Lady Teronver's death.

After pulling in a bit of extra energy, he activated the spell that would open the new link. The drag on his power was instant, the distance vaster than any he'd ever tried. But when an image flickered to life, the drain slowed and evened. The Ljósálfr female appraising him from the other side must be strong to contribute so much power.

"I bid you greeting. I am Callian Myern i Lyrnis Dianore nai Braelyn of Moranaia. Have I reached Alfheim?"

One golden-brown eyebrow rose. "You have indeed. I must say, you speak our language well for one so far removed."

"It is not by merit of memory but by grace of spell," Lyr answered.

"A spell unknown to me." A look of consideration entered the woman's gray eyes. "I am Lady Vionafer, High Mage of Alfheim. I am no diplomat, but then, you seem to still possess the one we sent."

Lyr held back a sigh. "I trust you received my letter? Lady Teronver was killed in an attack against Lady Ameliar."

"I did." The mage's brows drew together. "Why did someone attack them?"

"You misunderstand." His teeth ground together in anger at the memory. "Just before she stepped into the portal, the ambassador tried to kill Lady Ameliar. My own mage said it was a death spell. A soul-rending. Had she not been stopped before it was finished, Ameliar could not have been saved."

Lady Vionafer paled. "Soul-rending? That's a closely held secret well beyond her training. I thought only a few..." she said, trailing off. Her mouth formed a thin line as she composed herself. "You have my deepest apologies. I must report this news to the king. While I understand she was being sent back in disgrace, she was the king's cousin. I do not know how this will be received."

"Please know that Moranaia bears Alfheim no malice. Though my interactions with the lady ambassador were...unpleasant, the others in her party represented Alfheim well. I will be sending Berris and Orena through with a guide this afternoon with all honor."

"I also understand that Ameliar has decided to stay?"

"Indeed," he answered. The mage's expression had grown inscrutable. Lyr hoped it didn't bode ill. "Her talents are more than welcome here."

A small smile slipped across Lady Vionafer's face. "As I suspected might be the case. She is well?"

Lyr heard the click of the door opening, but he didn't turn. He detected Ralan's presence without the need to look. "Recovering, thankfully."

"I must apologize on behalf of Alfheim for the actions of Lady Teronver." The mage's mouth turned down once more. "I will send word of the king's reaction once I have delivered this latest news. It may be some time before he is willing to open negotiations once more."

"Understandable, though I would remind him that it was he who sought our aid."

"Of course." She inclined her head. "May fortune and blessings shine upon you until we speak again."

When the mirror faded to his own reflection, Lyr finally turned to face Ralan. His friend looked surprised, brows still lifted. Lyr gestured him forward. "Are you just going to stand there?"

Ralan frowned for a moment before shaking his head. "Sorry. Who was that?"

"The High Mage of Alfheim. More pleasant than I expected, honestly."

"I can't see her," the prince murmured.

"Then how did you know—"

"Her futures." Ralan's expression grew puzzled. "When she answered the mirror, the lines of the futures that concern Alfheim became muffled. Where she is, I cannot see."

Despite his unease with seers and their predictions, that news caused Lyr's heart to race. "That can't be good."

"I'm not sure. It's never happened before, but after centuries of blocking my talent while on Earth, I'm out of practice."

Lyr wanted to accept the reassurance, but the worry in Ralan's eyes negated it. However, he knew well enough that the prince would say no more on the subject until he was ready. "Did you need something?"

"Before you contact the Neoran queen…" Ralan sighed, his gaze going to the view beyond the window before returning to Lyr. "Someone is going to have to go to Earth, and soon. I can't see events there as well as I can things here, but I can tell that Kien has changed camps for the final time. If he finishes this portion of his plan, we fail."

"You want to attack Kien?"

"Not directly. I think we should send Kai and Arlyn to his previous camp. If they disrupt the spell there, the entire thing will begin to crumple." Ralan's jaw clenched, his eyes suddenly alive with fury. "I'll take care of Kien myself when the time comes."

Breath hissing in, Lyr strode over to the prince. "You want me to send my daughter and my best friend into danger on nothing but your sight? You just told me you were out of practice. *Miaran*, Ralan, but you are not a god."

The seer stepped close, and his voice lowered to a whisper. "No. But Megelien is."

27

"It's like losing her again."

Arlyn lay curled against Kai, his hand running soothingly through her hair. The tears had caught her by surprise, almost as much as the news that had caused them. She wasn't a woman prone to crying, but even she had her limits. The thought of her mother being so close and yet not there at all was one of them.

"I'm sorry, *mialn*," he murmured against her forehead. "I cannot imagine learning such a thing."

She pulled back to look into his eyes. "Can't you? Finding out Allafon wasn't your father was painful. I sensed it from you. I still do, at times."

He stilled, and his lips turned up. "I should've known I couldn't hide it. But it's not quite the same. I have no desire to encounter him again, in this life or another one. Unless I get to kill him again for murdering my mother."

"A fine pair we are." She dropped her head back on his shoulder. "Only one good parent between us, and he was late to the job."

"You aren't angry at Lyr?"

She frowned, considering. "No, not now. And certainly not about Meli."

Kai's hand ran through her hair once more. "Then why wouldn't you see him?"

"I needed time." Arlyn sighed. "To process. To feel. I've never given much thought to reincarnation. Meli may have memories of her past life, but she isn't the same. I don't know what to think about it or her."

"Lyr probably feels conflicted, too."

She nodded against his chest. "I'm sure."

They lay together quietly for a few moments, sharing comfort. Then Kai groaned, the sound vibrating against her ear. "I don't suppose you're ready to see Lyr now?"

"I guess I can. Why?" Arlyn sat up and looked into Kai's frustrated gaze. "What's wrong?"

"He just contacted me and said he needs to speak to us." Kai tugged his long hair behind him and tied it back with a bit of leather. "Something about a mission."

Her mouth fell open. "He wants to send me on an actual mission?"

"I guess we'll find out soon enough."

Arlyn heaved herself to her feet. What could have happened now? "Should we go to his study?"

"No," Kai answered. "He'll be here any moment."

Heart pounding, Arlyn walked to the window, though she didn't care about the view. When the knock came, she shoved her shoulders back to brace herself. She'd told Kai the truth when she'd said she wasn't angry, but her emotions were jumbled. Would Lyr be awkward around her? Upset? As Kai opened the door, she spun and met her father's eyes.

Lyr entered with hesitant steps and stopped in the center of the room. "Are you well?"

Her feelings solidified into one thing—love—and she found herself closing the distance between them. Peace filled her as her arms wrapped around his waist and his closed around her. Despite all of the upheaval she had gone through leaving Earth to find him, she had no regrets. Meeting her father had been worth it.

Arlyn pulled away to smile up at him. "I'm sorry if you thought I was angry with you."

"I bonded with Meli even though my mind is conflicted. Even though I knew yours would be."

"You didn't need my permission." Arlyn chuckled, and she glanced at Kai. "I understand the insanity of the bond."

Lyr rubbed at the back of his neck. "What does it say of our life that bonding is the least of the insanity?"

"Kai said you needed to speak to us about some kind of mission." Her smile fell. "I get the feeling I'm not going to like it."

"None of us are going to like it, least of all me."

Arlyn gestured to a chair. "Do you want to sit?"

"I don't think I can." His shoulders sagged, a sign of weariness she'd seen all too often from him of late. "Ralan said that Kien's spell must be stopped now."

Kai flushed, his hands clenching and loosening as though he sought the hilt of his sword. "Does it involve retribution for the Neorans?"

"Not directly," Lyr answered. "I spoke with their queen a few moments ago. I have never in my life seen a ruler openly weep until this day. At least I can send her the children, as they have all been healed, and then the others in a few days' time."

Kai nodded, though Arlyn could sense his pain. "So little. Hardly enough."

"Unfortunately," her father said. "But if we can disrupt Kien's spell, perhaps the effects can be reversed. If nothing else, maybe we can clear their home of the poison."

Arlyn took her bonded's hand. "What do we need to do?"

⚮

As Lyr climbed the stairs to Meli's room, he wanted to smash his fist into a wall. Or Ralan's face. It didn't matter that the prince wasn't to blame for his brother's actions. He was to blame for the way he manipulated them all, never telling more than the barest details but expecting his orders to be obeyed. It was bad enough when he'd done it to Lyr. But now Arlyn was involved.

Though it was unreasonable, Lyr had never wanted her to step back through the portal to Earth. Now she would be doing just that. Aside from the danger of finding the camp, dealing with the poison, and possibly encountering Kien himself, there was the chance she would want to stay. He well remembered the excitement of Earth; the humans surrounded themselves with technology more creative than any magic. Would a visit awaken a longing for her former home? She'd only lived on Moranaia for a month, after all.

As Kai and Arlyn gathered supplies for the journey, Lyr was left adrift to worry. He'd wanted to go himself, unwilling to remain behind through one more mission, but Ralan had commanded he stay. Stay and wait for word, like a civilian hoping for a beloved warrior's return. The mission was set. Even now, the prince spoke with Selia about the type of spell Arlyn would carry.

Lyr hesitated outside of Meli's door, unsure if he should disturb her. His emotions were turbulent, fury at Ralan and fear for his daughter mixing with his uncertainty about the bond. Meli needed rest, and in his current state, he could provide only upset. He would check on her when he was under better control. If she were truly ill, he would sense it along their growing bond.

Before he could force his feet to move, the door opened. Meli stared at him with sleepy eyes. Then a small smile curved her lips. "If you're going to wake me with your concern, at least come in and tell me what's wrong."

Guilt blended with everything else. He should have tried to shield his emotions before they could pass along the bond. "I'm sorry. I'd just thought better of disturbing you and was about to go. I'll come back."

"No." She huffed out a breath. "I was only dozing, easing out of my nap. I want to know what happened."

His body hardened at the sight of her. Her blond hair tangled around her waist, and she wore only the underdress he'd seen in the observation tower. The late afternoon light streaming through the windows left little to his imagination. Lyr swallowed, struggling with himself a moment before forcing his gaze back to her eyes. Eyes that laughed at him.

"I'm not sure—"

Meli grabbed his hand and pulled, cutting off his words. "I've seen Moranaian women wearing less than this. Surely you aren't scandalized."

That surprised a laugh out of him. "No. But the others don't affect me the way you do."

True pleasure lit her face then as she closed the door. "A fine compliment, considering their beauty. Now, are you going to tell me what's wrong? Is Arlyn still upset?"

"Confused and hurting, but not angry," he reassured her. "Though I hate to see her in pain, it isn't that. Ralan commanded me to send her and Kai to Earth. Not suggested. Then I watched a queen sob as if the world had ended. And for her, I suppose it has."

Meli took his hand again, this time for comfort. "That's a great deal to handle after this morning."

"Exactly." His anger began to dissolve at her quiet commiseration. "I'd thrash Ralan if he hadn't disappeared. He was with us this morning. He saw what we went through...and now this. It's too much."

She wrapped her arms around his waist, much as Arlyn had earlier, but the feeling this time was completely different. As she rested her cheek on his chest, he closed his own arms around her and let himself be. Meli was a haven, her serenity a balm to his rawness. In that moment, he forgot about Aimee and the echoes of the past. He held Meli and no one else.

ↄ๏ϲ

Meli tipped her face up to study Lyr. His eyes were closed, and the turmoil that had surrounded him was ebbing. Her chest ached for him. And maybe a little *because* of him. She could sense how he worried over her past life. It should have bothered her, that life, but she was at peace with the memories for the first time ever. Her soul felt…settled. She'd never realized how split she had always been until Aimee's remnants had merged during the spell.

What did bother her was the others' reactions to the revelation. Meli had no desire to be bound to a male who forever saw another woman, one he'd loved, and she feared that Arlyn would always avoid her. While she couldn't blame her, it would make life awkward and unpleasant for them all. Could they accept Meli beyond what they knew of her soul's past? The dread caught at her breath and held it.

Lyr's eyes opened, meeting hers. "What is it?"

She exhaled in one long gust of air. "I'm not her."

"Wh—" he began and then stilled. The turmoil began to build in him once more, spilling into their bond. "I didn't think you were."

"Are you certain? I know it is difficult."

His arms tightened. "It is. But I don't see her when I'm with you. Somehow, I don't."

"But our souls—"

· **325** ·

"Are similar, yes." His lips twisted. "But there isn't really an 'our' anymore. Your spirit is richer, more vibrant. Your current life has had its own impact. Just as beautiful but not the same. So, no, I don't mistake you for her."

Warmth flowed through her at his words, at his expression, and she relaxed in his arms. Her worry wasn't completely gone, for she knew the transition would not always be so easy. But in this moment, she believed him. Perhaps her decision to bond would one day prove foolish. She couldn't find it in her to care.

Meli released his waist to run her hands up his chest. As she linked her arms behind his neck, she lifted herself to kiss him. Their lips brushed, light and hesitant, before he captured her mouth. He pulled her closer, supporting her weight. Then he devoured her. A fire seemed to light within them both, and she ceased to think.

Hands turning frantic, they pulled at clothing, mouths parting only when necessary. She wanted to touch every inch of his flesh. Nothing had ever felt as wonderful as his skin. When they finally pressed together with nothing between them, she moaned. Complete and yet so empty. She trembled with the tension consuming her.

Meli hardly noticed when he lifted her and carried her to the bed. Lyr lowered her to the mattress, his mouth barely leaving hers as she fell beneath him. She'd dreamed of this, but imagination hadn't captured how he would affect her in real life. The bond between them hummed, the connection so intense it heightened every touch.

Neither had patience for gentle caresses. The link tightening between them was too strong, too consuming. Meli opened to him, her body beyond ready, and her breaths came in sharp pants as he entered her. Energy gathered even as passion rose, even as she burned with it. They moved together for a seeming eternity before the tension released and they both cried out.

As the energy settled and their breathing eased, Lyr turned to his side and pulled her close. Meli rested her head on his shoulder, her mind empty of everything but the bond that had grown strong between them. The touch of his body and his soul were so familiar, as though she had always been missing them. Their unity brought peace.

For the first time, Meli could sense Lyr's emotions clearly. How could he be so calm at his core? Not just the temporary relief of their joining, but an ease she had never sensed from him before. Her gaze caressed his face, relaxed as she'd never seen it. The ever-present worry lines had disappeared.

She blinked, and his eyes met hers. His smile began there. "Thank you."

Meli pulled back a little. "I didn't offer myself as a gift to soothe you."

"That's not what I meant." His arms tightened. "For...being. For accepting." His sigh ruffled her hair. "I can't seem to find the words to explain."

Her confusion cleared. He referred to the same joy she experienced in being bonded. It would have been easy for either of them to run from it, considering the past. Yet here they lay. "I think I know."

Meli's hands tangled in his long brown hair. The first time she'd done so, he had been near death. Now he was life. But then he heaved another sigh, and she felt the worry begin to creep into him again. "Stop stressing."

His laugh jostled her. "At this point, I'm not sure I can. At least I no longer want to thrash Ralan."

"Isn't it a prince's job to command?"

"Yes. And logically, I know it." He caressed her side with gentle fingers. "But it's difficult to think of him that way. He lived on Earth for three centuries and was nothing but my friend. There were times, during my trips to Earth, that we simply explored the world. The easiest way to poke at him was to *treat* him like a prince."

Meli chuckled. "A contradiction."

"The embodiment." Though he smiled, his hand stilled. His expression grew thoughtful. "Maybe I haven't forgiven him. He failed to see my mother's attack in time to save her from grave injury. I didn't blame him, and yet…"

"You wonder," she answered. "Every time he acts as a seer."

Lyr sat up, pulling her with him. He didn't seem to notice the arm he curved around her waist. "That's it. He didn't see Lady Teronver's attack, either. How can I send Kai and Arlyn on a dangerous mission on his word? What if…I don't even want to consider it."

Meli pressed herself against him, offering comfort. She knew well enough the trouble seers could cause, having been sent into the mists by one herself. Then again, that hadn't turned out so bad. "Talk to him."

Lyr's mouth quirked. "I'll just get vague nonsense."

"If he's your friend," she began, meeting his eyes, "then talk to him."

෮෨෬

Once again, Lyr stood before a door, uncertain if he wanted to enter. His body might be lax, but his mind was in turmoil once more. He had returned to his room to shower, a luxury he hadn't installed in the guest rooms yet, and soaked up the comforting warmth of Eradisel. When Meli slipped in some time later, her bag of meager belongings in hand, she had simply smiled and left him to his thoughts as she headed into the dressing chamber.

At least she'd agreed to the move without hesitation.

He had skipped dinner as he puzzled over his mixed emotions. For the first time in over a month—maybe longer—he felt like himself. The anger that had simmered after his mother's injury had dulled, eased by the truth he hadn't been able to acknowledge until Meli's words. Though the fault was ultimately with Allafon, Lyr blamed himself for not being there. And Ralan for not seeing.

Being captured, being chained—it had been Lyr's first true failure. He should have recognized Allafon's insanity and cruelty long before. Instead, his lapse had put his entire family at risk. If Arlyn hadn't learned the trick of converting iron, they'd all be dead. As it was, his mother had paid.

Now he stood in front of Ralan's door, ready to apologize. Lyr knew how much the prince mourned his failure to stop Lynia's attack. He knew but hadn't been able to accept. With a sigh, he raised his hand to knock, but the door opened before he had the chance. Instead of his friend, Eri gazed up at him with solemn eyes.

"Hello," she said.

"Might I speak with your father, Eri?"

She shook her head. "He's not here."

"Not..." For the first time, Lyr thought to search along the estate key for the prince. His stomach tightened when he found no trace. "He's gone?"

"Yep." The little girl practically glared at him. "He decided to return to court early. He wanted to give you time to calm down. Should've Looked before bothering with that."

Returned to court? Lyr stared at her as comprehension trickled in. Ralan had ordered Lyr's family into danger and then left. He'd said his gift might be a bit rusty and then *left?* "I can't believe he did this."

Eri rolled her eyes. "I told him to Look, but he didn't want to. Don't worry, though. I'm here to help."

The statement was in no way comforting.

28

Even after several centuries, the stone palace at the heart of Moranaia felt like home. And yet it didn't. As Ralan emerged from the portal room into the large formal entryway, memories washed over him no matter how he tried to shove them aside. Listening to his father as he told the tales behind the ancient carvings on each wall. Sliding down the banister of the grand staircase on a dare by Kien. Storming down the small steps at the far end, rage and hurt consuming him.

He halted, Teyark and Corath stopping beside him. The few milling about the room froze at the sight of the princes. "Thank you for coming with me," Ralan murmured.

Teyark snorted. "You didn't phrase it as a request. Myern Lyrnis may never forgive my rudeness in leaving without a word."

"He'll blame me." Ralan rolled his eyes at his brother, pleased to be able to do so. Their comradery was slowly returning. "Besides, you've never hesitated to tell me no in the past. Truth be told, you wouldn't miss this encounter."

His brother grinned. "Fair enough."

Beyond the windows, the sky was dark, the mountains beyond barely illuminated by the moon. The palace sat on a flat ridge at the base of the Great Range, mountains so tall that some had never been scaled, with the foothills rolling away to the north. Lyr's estate nestled a day's ride away where the hills began to drop into the plains. Millennia before, Ralan's ancestors had emerged through the portal where Braelyn now stood, but their queen had not been content to rest there. She'd left it in the hands of one of her sons and headed south until she reached the mountains.

Here, the forest was sparser, leaving room for larger buildings. Ralan had been in castles on Earth that tripled the size of the Moranaian palace, but in his mind, none could compare. As he started toward the large doors at the far end of the entry, his gaze caressed the carvings, a scene of their arrival on this world, immortalized in the stone. He'd told Lyr he planned to find his own home, but being in the palace, he was no longer certain he needed to.

The circlet on Ralan's brow constricted, a reminder of a rank he hadn't wanted—one he'd told his father he would never accept. Unlike the long vest he wore, created by the seamstress at Braelyn from an image he had placed in her mind, the copper band was ancient. For much of his life, Ralan had seen his brother wear it at important functions. A symbol of the heir. But Teyark had presented it to him.

Ralan paused to take a deep breath. He'd sworn never to return, but he should have known the future was never so certain. *No point in delaying.* Steeling himself, he pushed open the doors. Gods, it was just the same. The great room beyond had been transformed for the evening feast with the king's family and court, though during the day, the tables were removed. Those seeking formal audience with the king had to do so standing. Ralan took a few steps forward before the noise of dinner abruptly halted. It hadn't taken long for their entry to be noted.

Alianar's golden eyes, a gift he'd passed to all of his children, widened, and his glass slipped from his fingers to shatter on the table. More shattered glass and a woman's cry turned Ralan's attention to the end of the table. Enielle, his mother, leapt to her feet, tears already streaming, and raced toward them.

"Perhaps we should have waited until after dinner," Teyark murmured.

Then Ralan was caught, stunned, in his mother's embrace. "*Laiala.*"

"I thought I'd never see you again!" she cried.

"I—"

"Hush. I need to look at you." She placed both hands on his cheeks, searching his face for signs of injury. "The gods have answered my prayers. Ah, Ralan, you must not go away again, especially not without word."

Ralan could only stare at her. She hadn't shown him such affection since his boyhood. He'd thought she cared little for him, but the tears in her eyes were real. They cut at him in a place he'd never realized was raw. What else hadn't he seen about her? "I cannot promise to remain, at least in the palace, but I will not leave you so abruptly again."

She opened her mouth, probably to argue, but the king's voice cut across the silent room. "Moranai Elaiteriorn i Ralantayan Moreln nai Moranaia—welcome home. We have long missed our son and now heir."

Ralan's lips curved up. His father had not wasted the opportunity to confirm him as heir before they could argue over the matter, though the circlet announced it without words. The king would leave nothing to chance. "Perhaps we might speak in private?"

⚬৯৹

Ralan followed his parents to the king's personal antechamber, Teyark and Corath trailing behind. When they entered, Teyark settled beside his bonded near the window, his expression clearer than any mental message: *This explanation is on you.* Ralan gave his brother a mock salute as he took a seat across from the king. He didn't want to be here, either, so he could hardly blame Teyark.

Damned shifting futures.

"You must be wondering about my sudden arrival," Ralan began, holding back a snicker at *that* understatement. "Unfortunately, there is serious trouble. And it's all caused by Kien."

"*Kien?* How could he be to blame?" the king demanded.

Ralan's heart pounded. The question brought back the worst memories, ones of their parting. Ralan's visions concerning Kien had already torn their relationship apart once. "Believe me or not. I do not care."

The king scowled. "It's impossible."

Like a punch to the gut, the words forced the air from Ra-lan's lungs. When he'd first returned to Moranaia and contacted his father, the king had acted regretful. *So much for that.* Ralan stood, ready to leave the small reception room as he had the great hall centuries before. "I should have known better than to come here."

"Ralan, wait." Alianar jerked to his feet and took a step to-ward his son. "Not because of you. Not…not like last time. You were right about Kien. But he wasn't exiled to Earth. He was banished to a small colony of outcasts."

"Then he escaped," Ralan bit out.

His mother let out a soft cry. "It's my fault. I must have done something wrong."

A surprising softness crossed Alianar's face. Were his par-ents on the verge of another marriage alliance? He'd thought his father wanted no more children. "Enielle, you are not to blame."

Eyes downcast, she didn't answer. Ralan let out a sigh. "He's right, *Laiala*. But it doesn't matter who is to blame," he said. "Kien is on Earth, and he's creating havoc. His poisoned energy is spreading across multiple magical realms, causing madness and sparking betrayal."

Ralan returned to his seat, waiting for his father to do the same before going into more detail. By the time he had finished recounting recent events, the hour had grown late. Noise from the diners in the adjoining great hall faded into nothing as dis-appointed courtiers sought their beds. He wondered how many lingered in the hall like statues, hoping their patience would re-ward them with the sight of Ralan storming from the room or with news about the state of accession. This time, they were destined be disappointed.

"So this is why you have returned," the king finally said, his eyes full of grief. "I suppose it is enough."

"To forget the past, to forgive…" Ralan glanced away. "It will take some time."

The silence was heavy, though not as strained as expected. Then the king leaned forward, and his shift in demeanor had Ralan bracing for something unpleasant. "You didn't bring her."

He should've known. Ralan's breath hissed out in a rush. "I will not bring Eri until I know it is safe. She is too important to risk."

"You wound me to imply I would hurt a child." Alianar pounded a fist on the arm of his chair, but the terrible heat of his temper was surprisingly absent. Only hurt. "Even through your bitterness, you must know that. I'll not ask her to use her talents. In fact, I will no longer ask you. Give what information you will, for I will not force it."

Ralan's eyes widened. Before his departure, he'd worked closely with his father. The monarch always had a seer to advise him if possible. "But it is customary—"

"I no longer care for custom." Alianar waved a hand. "I've been three centuries without a seer, and Moranaia still stands. I was blind to what my demands did to you, and I will not fall into that again. Even less would I order such from a child."

The mention of his daughter brought tension to Ralan's muscles once more. "I don't fear you. Not anymore. Once, but…" A helpless laugh escaped. "Eri is a law unto herself. The futures are too fragile to bring her to our seat of power. There'd be chaos, and we don't need that kind of distraction. If we don't act quickly and well, even Moranaia could fall."

⊷⊗⊷

Eri skipped through the grass, morning dew darkening her slippers, as Lyr stood before the portal to see Kai and Arlyn off. Beside him, Meli squeezed his hand in reassurance while he sought inside himself for what he wanted to say. His daughter had come to mean so much in only a month. Fear for her choked the words in his throat.

Both Kai and Arlyn hefted packs full of supplies and then exchanged a worried glance. Lyr's daughter turned to him. "We'll be okay. I'm experienced in the woods, and the abandoned camp should be fairly safe. It's a national park."

Lyr let go of Meli and enfolded Arlyn in a hug, ignoring the jabs of weaponry and the awkward bulk of her pack. "Come back."

"Ralan's vision said Kien would not return." She squeezed once and then pulled away. "It should be a quick mission, since Ralan told us what we're looking for. I have the crystal holding the counter spell safe in my pack, ready to go."

"I know. But it's your first time going back to Earth. I…" He gripped her shoulders. "Just come back. I love you."

"I love you, too," Arlyn replied, her expression softening. "We'll return soon. Try not to worry so much, okay? Moranaia is my home now. And I don't think Ralan would send us into danger."

Lyr bit back a curse at the thought of the prince. "I suppose we'll see."

Then he watched as part of his heart disappeared through the gate.

ᏋᏮᏋ

Arlyn's breath hitched for a moment as the cool, swirling gray of the Veil wrapped around her again. On her last trip through, she'd walked for…days? Years? She shuddered to consider how easily she could have been trapped here. Then Kai's hand wrapped around hers, and he sent reassurance along their bond. She exhaled slowly before sending back her gratitude.

"Thanks."

"You will not wander this time. Let me show you."

Merged with him, the strands of color she had barely glimpsed before flared to life. Kai's energy expanded, seeming to wrap around a strand of palest blue. He latched on, and the world tilted askew as they hurdled across fathomless space. Though the mists caught at them, they stumbled through the portal into woods as familiar to her as her breath.

His hand still squeezed hers. "The Veil has grown rough these past days, but not too bad. Next time, you can try it."

"Me?"

He shrugged. "You've some *sonal* talents to train, if you've forgotten."

Arlyn reddened, not wanting to admit that she had. Her focus had been on her lessons with Selia. "Why did we come out here? Is it the only portal?"

"It's the main one." He studied the clearing. "Any others are connected through this one. Normally, I would have found their separate strands when we grew near, but I thought you might want to see your home. Your first one."

Did she? Arlyn had made peace with leaving Earth behind. She'd told her few friends and neighbors that she was moving across country. Automatic payments were deducted from her bank account for the caretaking service that maintained the yard around her house. Unsure of how her journey to Moranaia would go, she'd been hesitant to sell or rent her family home, bought by her grandfather when he moved from Ireland.

"After three years in Earth time, I suppose I should at least check on it." She started down the trail. "But quickly."

The old farmhouse, somewhat out of place in the forested hills, stood in the middle of a large clearing just as she remembered it. The white wooden siding was faded, but the lawn was well-kept. At least nothing had gone wrong with the payments. On the far side of the clearing, the apple trees her grandmother had tried to cultivate grew wild. She'd always laughed about them, saying she'd wanted some reason to live in a farmhouse.

Arlyn had been afraid she might feel some draw or regret, but she didn't. Only the glow of pleasant memories. Another lifetime, removed but well-remembered. Her father's house was the home of her heart. She squeezed Kai's hand, realizing what it had cost him to bring her here. Even with their bond, he worried that she would want to stay.

"Looks like it's being well-maintained. I wonder if I should sell it."

He relaxed. "Do you need to? It would be useful to own the land the portal is on. Are there laws that say you must live here?"

"No." She frowned as she tugged Kai back toward the gate. "Though when too many Earth years have passed for me to look so young, I'll have to figure something out."

SUNDERED

"That's easy enough. There are a few Moranaians who live here, and I'm sure Ralan knows how to handle that sort of thing."

Their trip through the portal was faster this time, so much so that she barely saw the strands he grasped. They emerged into a more mountainous area, the forest here wilder. Untouched. The lack of human inhabitants was a sense she couldn't describe, but she knew it to be true.

At least the portal opened onto a fairly flat area. They were cupped in a large valley that stretched ahead of them until it ended at the foot of another mountain. If Kien's base was down there, they wouldn't have to do too much climbing.

Arlyn glanced at Kai. "Did Ralan say how far away the camp is?"

"Not to me. I'd hoped he told you." He peered up at the sun, midway across the sky. "It would be nice if we could make it before dark."

They crept through the forest, searching for any sign of life. Kai held his sword unsheathed, and Arlyn had taken out her bow. Tourists rarely hiked this deep in the Smoky Mountains, but they wouldn't risk their lives on it. Besides that, the wild animals present in the park cared nothing for their mission. Vigilance was key.

When they found the camp, the sun had hardly moved. The smell hit first, the scent of decomposition clear. She gave Kai a look of concern. He'd gone pale, and his hand squeezed the hilt of his sword until his knuckles turned white. *Was he remembering what he'd seen on Neor?* Arlyn gripped her own bow, dread rising

341

through her. Dread that ended in vomit when they reached the perimeter of spikes, body parts of all kinds speared at the top.

The pack pushed heavy against her back as she bent to empty her stomach. Kai held her so she wouldn't topple, his fury flowing through their bond. After a few moments, Arlyn wiped her mouth and struggled to stand against the awkward weight of all she carried. Kai helped her balance and then pulled her into his arms. They stayed that way for several minutes, gaining strength.

Never in her life had she seen such a thing. Though killing Allafon had been gruesome, it had also been quick and necessary. Body parts... Arlyn forced those thoughts to a halt before she became ill again. Then she searched for her courage. Stopping Kien was just as necessary as stopping Allafon had been. More so, really. There was no telling how many camps he had established, how many people he had murdered, in pursuit of his dark spell.

Arlyn pulled away from Kai and faced the gauntlet of spikes, trying not to look at what they displayed. Feeling Kai's resolve, she started forward. Into insanity. It was impossible to avoid evidence of torture and depravity, no matter how hard she wished to dodge them. In the center of the camp, Earth-style tents sat abandoned, specks of blood staining the sides of the light green nylon. On the far end, a headless body stretched between two trees.

She glanced away quickly, but the sight had already burned into her memory. Nausea churned with every step, but Arlyn forced herself to hunt for the source of Kien's spell. An iron rod with a crystal on the end, Ralan had said. She and Kai split up, albeit reluctantly, to search faster. Arlyn snagged a stick from a pile near the abandoned fire pit and used it to push aside anything questionable. She didn't want to consider what some of those things were.

After a mercilessly brief time, Kai called from the other side of the camp. Arlyn rushed over, ready for the task to be over, and almost sobbed at the sight of the crystal the size of her fist jutting up from the short grass. This area was clear of blood, although she could see more gruesome spikes not far away.

Arlyn examined the ground, nonetheless, before shrugging off her pack and lowering herself to the grass. The energy that pulsed around the crystal added more churning to her already upset stomach, but she tried her best to ignore it. Such a beautiful thing to be a source of poison. The iron pole was short but wrapped delicately around the base of the crystal, obviously wrought to hold the stone.

She bit her lip as the iron pulled at her power. Could she convert the metal while it still held the crystal? She wouldn't be able to perform the second spell unless she did. Kai placed a hand on her shoulder, offering silent reassurance. Arlyn closed her eyes and took a deep breath as she gathered her energy. There was no choice. If the poison were to be disrupted, she would have to succeed.

Arlyn stretched out her hands, hovering them around the iron. The dark energy of the spell within the crystal buffeted her, but Kai's presence steadied her against the sensation. She shoved her energy resolutely forward. Sweat beaded her brow from the effort, from the heat of the sun pounding down. From the nausea that still rode her. Still, she pushed.

When she finally succeeded, the snap was audible, a sound like a stick breaking underfoot. The black bar of iron looked the same, but energy flowed around it without impediment.

Arlyn slumped back against Kai's legs, her breath coming in sharp pants. That was the most iron she'd ever converted, and her muscles shook from the effort. Yet she still had to activate the spell to disable the crystal. A groan ripped from her throat at the thought, but as she sat, energy began to trickle in, restoring her.

Arlyn frowned up at Kai. "Don't give me too much. You still have to guide us back to Moranaia."

"This is more important," he argued.

"If it's all the same to you, I'd rather not be stuck near this nightmare." Arlyn leaned forward, steadying herself for a moment with a hand in the grass. "I'll be okay. I already feel a little better."

Arlyn pulled a pouch from her belt and upturned the contents into her palm. An apple-sized crystal, round and almost impossibly clear, reflected a shimmery circle of sunlight into her hand. It was a powerful piece, imbued with a counter spell by Selia and Corath, but she didn't have time to admire it. She scooted close to the iron pole, her crossed legs not quite touching it. Again, she gathered her energy.

It pooled in her hands like water from a stream, and she visualized it flowing into the stone. After a few heartbeats, the crystal began to glow. The spell trapped within hummed to escape, and the force of it numbed her hands. But she held on, shoving in as much of her own energy as she dared. When the magical pressure built until she could barely contain it, Arlyn lowered the stone over the poisoned crystal. Even her breath stilled. She had only this chance.

She received another wash of energy from Kai, but she had no time to rebuke him. Her focus was on the power that clamored to be free and the moment—now.

As the spell broke, Arlyn slammed the two crystals together and did her best to hold on. From within the globe, the energy of Moranaia shot free to light the surrounding area in a golden glow. Her hair whipped about her with the force of it. From around her, she heard the clatter of falling spikes. And other things she would rather not consider.

The Moranaian energy fought for a moment with the poisoned stone, a clash that tested her strength and her stomach. Her arms trembled, and she sensed Kai behind her, steadying her. Still, the light and the battle raged on until she could see nothing but gold. Arlyn had no idea how much time passed, but finally the poisoned crystal gave way to her stone. One final push of energy from the Moranaian globe pulsed through the crystal. Then the light winked out.

Arlyn's numbed arms dropped into her lap and the globe rolled away as Kai plopped down heavily beside her. When the Neorans had entered Moranaia, the poison had been purified from their systems without any ill effects, so it had seemed a simple thing to use that same process to disrupt the spell. *So much for that.* She laughed, the odd, choked sound breaking the silence.

Incredulous, Kai gaped at her. "What?"

"I don't think even Selia expected...that." Her chuckles subsided as she stared at the dull stone now useless on the pole. "Do you have enough power to take us through the Veil?"

He paused to consider. "If I drew in energy, yes. But even with the spell disrupted, I'd rather not do so here."

Her gaze landed on an arm that had fallen a few feet away, and she almost gagged. "Me neither."

"I can return us to your house, I think. A few moments and some energy, and I'll be ready to take us through."

"Just let me catch my breath."

She rubbed her eyes with numb fingers, blocking the sight of the trophies now scattered in the grass. Her weak arms shook at the movement. Even her legs trembled, though she'd been sitting. Thankfully. She would have toppled over had she not grounded herself, physically and magically, so thoroughly before she began.

As Arlyn dropped her fingers, her ears caught the sound of crackling. Brow furrowing, she peered around the clearing but saw only trees, grass, and scattered body parts. Kai's hand closed around the hilt of his sword as he swept the area with a searching spell. Finally, he shook his head.

"I don't—"

The crackling ended with a roar, and the crystal pulsed with murky light. Her heart dropped at the odd sight. She flinched back, lifting her hands to her face as the crystal shattered. Dark magic swept through, stealing her breath. Then there was only darkness.

29

"In all my centuries of life, I have never broken my word."

Naomh paced his bedroom, his hands running through his hair until the long strands began to tangle. Caolte hadn't seen his brother so agitated since his mate had disappeared five hundred years ago. Beneath their feet, the stone floor trembled ever so slightly. If Naomh didn't gain control, he'd shake the whole place down.

"Nor have I," Caolte said. "But it seems you must choose which oath means the most."

"Perhaps not." His brother halted, brown eyes resolute. "I'll kill Kien. I never swore not to do that. Maybe then I can dismantle his work. I may not be a healer, but my affinity for earth is strong."

A slow smile stretched across Caolte's face. Finally, a plan he could agree with. "I would relish the chance to burn that one. You should never have dealt with him."

"No." Naomh strode to his wardrobe and pulled out a cloak. "Though the poison should have never seeped below. He broke his word and, in so doing, has earned his death. Come. It may not be night, but today, we ride."

Caolte followed his brother, more than ready. Naomh had raged about Meren's failures for a solid day. It was good to see him with a plan, however fragile. And once the poison was gone, they would deal with their brother. Meren's dishonor could never be allowed to stand.

⁕

Light filtered through Arlyn's consciousness with the pain. Every muscle in her body ached. Maybe even her bones. She cracked one eye open and groaned. Kai's weight pressed against her side, the contact increasing the agony where they touched. An answering moan beside her revealed that she wasn't the only one who hurt.

Kai pushed himself upright. "What the hell was that?"

Every muscle screamed in pain as Arlyn sat up beside him. "Guess we should've considered there might be a counter spell in the stone."

"Ralan should've mentioned it," he muttered.

"Must not be too serious if he didn't." Arlyn ran her hands through her hair, shaking out the dust from the shattered stone. Both she and Kai had small abrasions, but the pieces hadn't been large enough to cause true damage. "I'll live."

They leaned against one another and tried to catch their breaths once more. As Arlyn forced her muscles to relax, she began to question Ralan's idea of simple. Simple would not have left them both drained in a heap in the middle of the Great Smoky Mountains, dismembered limbs scattered around them.

"Still think you can get us back?" she asked.

Kai's arm slipped around her waist. "I'll have to. Gods only know what else that counter spell might have done. Alerted Kien for sure."

"If there was a chance he'd return, don't you think Ralan—"

"You can never rely on a seer." Kai released her and pushed himself to standing. "Not necessarily because they're cruel or dishonest. Their glimpses of future probabilities are limited, constantly changed by choices almost impossible to anticipate. Strands shift before they even know it. For most things, seers are reliable. Ralan especially, considering his power. But always have a back-up plan."

∽◯⌒

Ralan's head shot up, and the room around him faded. He heard his mother's voice from afar before even that disappeared. Unrelenting, the vision pulled him in. The bread he'd held was gone, the taste of honey replaced by the tang of fear. Who was he? Something gripped his body tight. Suspended. He could see nothing. Then another voice.

In moments, he'd returned to the small dining room where he'd been sharing breakfast with his family. They stared at him, their food forgotten. But he had no time. The chair scraped as Ralan shoved away from the table. His mother jumped at the sound, and her face lost its color. He couldn't reassure her. Instead, he turned to Teyark.

"I need you with me."

His brother stood, along with Corath. "We'll both go."

Ralan studied his brother's bonded. "Can you fight?"

"Well enough," he answered, exchanging a glance with Teyark. "We practice each day, and my sword bears enchantments."

Although panic rode him, Ralan took a moment to consult the strands. Then nodded. "Come on, both of you. There's little time."

As his brother and Corath followed him to the door, the king stood. "Where are you going? What's wrong?"

Not daring to stop, Ralan glanced back over his shoulder. "If I take the time to tell you, I doubt you'll like the future you receive."

⚬⊙⚬

Kai helped Arlyn with her pack, settling the awkward weight as gently as he could. He'd used a little more of his precious energy to heal the worst of their pain, but both of them were slow and achy. The spell in that crystal must have been a potent one. Even now, Kai struggled to pull his magical shields into place. They'd been virtually shredded. Kien must have prepared for the Moranaians to interfere in some way, for the counter had been perfect against their type of magic.

But Arlyn concerned him the most. The energy she'd gathered to release the spell had blown away with the golden light of the crystal orb, leaving her practically empty. If Kien returned, she would be the most vulnerable. Fear tightened his already sore body. The spell Selia had placed in that globe shouldn't have drained Arlyn's immense natural reserves, not even after she'd had to convert the iron.

What had gone wrong?

His bonded tied her bow to the pack she carried, since she was too weak to wield it. Her hands were still a little numb despite his healing energy, but that meant little considering his lack of talent in that skill. Kai linked arms with Arlyn, lending her his weight, and they retraced their steps through the center of the camp. Too bad he didn't have the energy to set the whole mess ablaze.

A tug on his senses had him stopping. "Did you feel that?"

Arlyn barely glanced around. He hated the dazed and exhausted look in her eyes. "What?" she whispered.

"I thought I detected a tug of portal energy. We need to move."

Kai pivoted toward the side of the camp with the headless corpse. Not his preferred route, but they couldn't go the direct path if someone was coming from the portal. As they shuffled around a crumpled tent, Arlyn staggered, and her steps became halting. When he looked down, her face had gone a pale white.

"I don't feel..." She shook her head. "Something isn't right."

He'd never get her through the portal in this state. "You need energy."

Before she could argue, he gave her more from his reserves. Arlyn straightened, restored enough to glare at him. "Too much."

"We have to go. Now."

They rushed through the camp as quietly as possible, only to be halted by a flame-haired male astride a black horse. For a moment, Kai thought it was Pol, but a second glance revealed the man to be Sidhe. A ball of flame danced in his hand as he smiled. "What have we here?"

Miaran. Was this the traitor who had helped Kien? "We have no business with you."

The male ignored him, his gaze flicking around the clearing. "Where's your master, children?"

Kai bristled. "I am no one's servant. We're not—"

"I'd believe no words from one found in this place."

"What is he saying?" Arlyn's hand tightened around Kai's arm. *"Doesn't sound good."*

Kai grimaced. Arlyn had been given the Moranaian language but didn't know that of the Sidhe. *"I believe he thinks we're part of Kien's group."*

"I could say the same," Kai answered the Sidhe, careful not to glance at Arlyn to reveal their other discussion. "You interfere in the business of Moranaia. Though considering your recent atrocities in Neor, I shouldn't be surprised."

"À sleinte!"

The voice sounded from behind him as the spell hit, cutting through his fragile shields. Kai turned his head for the source as he struggled for more energy. Lial could heal him later—as long as he could stay alive. He had to get himself and Arlyn out however he could.

Another Sidhe rode behind them, brown eyes flashing from atop his white horse. A pleased smirk crossed his face. *"Grem au."*

Even as energy began to fill Kai's depleted system, roots burst from the ground beneath them, wrapping around their ankles and curling up their legs. Kai cursed and pulled Arlyn closer as he prepared a counter spell. Branches leaned from the trees above, hemlock needles pricking as they wrapped around the arm where Kai gathered energy.

The flame-haired man rode closer. "Still yourselves, and I won't burn you alive."

Little sparks danced around them, and wood closed around their limbs. Not a good combination. Kai let his hand drop. These were Sidhe lords, ancient and powerful. He would have trouble escaping them even at full energy. Reasoning with them would be his best hope, especially with Arlyn's condition.

"You have no cause to hold us."

"I must disagree." The blond man spurred his horse around to stand next to the other. "You're coated in Kien's magic in the middle of a camp full of bloody remains. If we can't get to him, well...you'll be coming with us."

✦

Lyr shuffled through papers and tried to concentrate on the numbers. Though his muscles ached with tension, he turned to the next report with all the calm he could muster. Business, at least, was going well in the village, even if the rest of the worlds had gone mad. He skimmed through accounts of transactions for the various shops. His people primarily traded for what they wanted, only using precious metals and gems when a reasonable exchange wasn't possible. Only rarely did Lyr have to intercede to settle disagreements between the parties.

Sighing, he looked out the window to see Meli speaking with a Moranaian woman in the garden. Telia, the seamstress. Though Meli had grown comfortable with him, losing much of her hesitation, he could see her unease with Telia in the set of her shoulders. At least he'd spared Meli a formal presentation to the household, introducing her to a few and bidding them spread the word.

The door crashed against the study wall, and the reports crumpled under Lyr's fingers. Out of reflex, he shot to his feet, instantly on guard. Ralan strode through the doorway, Teyark and Corath behind him. Lyr slammed the paper he held onto his desk and leaned forward.

"A fine way to return after you ran away without a word."

"Stuff it, Lyr." Ralan stopped across from him, and for the first time, Lyr noticed a hint of fear etched onto the seer's face. "Arm yourself. We need to go."

His heart lurched as he rushed toward the door. His friend never joked about such things. "What's wrong?"

"Something happened. The futures were clear, I swear it," Ralan said, trailing behind. "I should have seen this possibility, but it wasn't there. Fucking Sidhe. By now, they probably have Kai and Arlyn."

Lyr halted so abruptly that the others almost slammed into him. "What?"

"We need to find them. Now."

With a curse, Lyr spun, slamming Ralan against the wall. His hand closed around the prince's throat. "You said there was no danger. I trusted you."

"There wasn't." Ralan made no effort to escape, his wide eyes panicked. And more desperate than Lyr had ever seen him. "I give you my word. But there are many futures from this point where they can be saved. Stop arguing with me and move."

"I don't care if your father flays me alive over a pit of iron for treason," Lyr muttered. "If they die, you will, too."

Ralan's jaw clenched, but he nodded. "There is much for us to settle. Later."

Lyr released him without comment, his focus shifting to the coming mission. He darted through the halls and ran up the stairs to his room. It took him only moments to arm himself with his sword, bow, and knives. He grabbed a small pack of camping supplies he kept in his closet for spontaneous trips he rarely got to make. When he turned back, the cloak Selia had spelled for him caught his eye. She had modified it so he could allow others to communicate, though they would still have trouble pinpointing his location. He swirled it over his shoulders and clasped it.

At a knock on the door and a shout from Ralan, Lyr suppressed a moment of satisfaction. Served the seer right to worry. But he didn't prolong it, opening the door to smirk at the prince. "Wondering where I went? Imagine that."

Ralan glared at the cloak. "We can argue my absence later. Is that thing necessary?"

"It could come in handy." He closed his eyes and triggered the portion of the spell that would allow Ralan, Teyark, and Corath to sense and communicate with him. "There. Where are we going?"

"All I can see is a Sidhe hill held by one of their lords. An old family."

Lyr scowled and headed for the stairs. "That's it?"

"I'm not a fucking GPS," Ralan spat. At Lyr's look, he sighed and ran a hand through his hair. "Sorry. Earth term. I'm not a map. I don't know the location of everything in the universe."

Lyr glanced back over his shoulder. "So your plan is…?"

"I…" The prince hurried to catch up, expression stunned. "I thought a path would come clear, but I don't know the way to this place. It could be anywhere."

"Once again, you are useless." His hands clenched to stop their shaking, Lyr glared. He knew it wasn't Ralan's fault any more than the previous events, but his sick rage had no other target. "I can't lose them. They're my only family, except for Meli." Then it hit him. "Meli!"

"What of her?" Ralan asked, eyes shadowed with a pain that made Lyr want to apologize for his harsh statement. "Is she a guide?"

"She found me when I was injured, remember? Perhaps she can use her runes."

Ralan nodded. "Find her."

Still sensing her presence in the garden, Lyr darted toward the closest exit. He looked back at his friend, who hesitated at the base of the stairs. "Ralan, I—"

"I know."

"No, you don't. I shouldn't have said that." Lyr rubbed his hand across his face, unsure how to put his feelings into words.

"I have failed you at every turn lately." The prince's expression hardened. "I will not do so again."

"Come, then. We'll save them." A grim smile lit Lyr's face. "Together."

30

Meli let out a long breath as the seamstress departed. Her first true encounter with a Moranaian who wasn't a close friend or relative of Lyr's. It had gone better than she'd hoped. At least she thought it had. Telia had been polite and cheerful, and if she was unhappy about helping with a new wardrobe, Meli couldn't tell.

A pulse of rage swept through Meli, so sudden she almost doubled over. Gasping, she wrapped her arms around her waist. Lyr. *"What happened?"* she sent, instinctively reaching out.

"Arlyn and Kai are in danger. Start walking toward the portal, and I'll meet you. I need to have a quick word with my mother."

The connection dropped, but the urgency pouring from him told her enough. Meli spun, her heart racing as she hastened through the garden. She wasn't entirely certain which path was the best, but she could sense Lyr nearing. She hadn't gone far before he emerged from another trail to her left. Her brows rose at the sight of the three princes following behind him.

"Lyr?" Meli whispered.

He skidded to a halt, grabbing her hands. "Something went wrong on the mission."

"What?" The words hit like a blow. "You said danger. Are they…?"

"Ralan believes they are alive, but we aren't certain how to find them." Lyr flicked an angry look at Ralan before his attention returned to Meli. "Can you guide us?"

Her brow wrinkled. "Me?"

"Your runes can find what is missing." His hands ran up her arms to her elbows. "We need your help."

"I…" Meli bit her lip. He wanted her to guide them? She'd almost gotten an entire group lost in the mists. "Are you sure? I'm still learning how to use the runes."

Lyr dropped his forehead to hers, and his voice lowered so the others couldn't hear. "Don't listen to doubts borne of your past. You saved me. Now help me save my friend and my daughter—the daughter of your soul."

Meli gasped at the hurt of it. Blood-souls, the fairy had said. How could she not try to save Arlyn? She grasped Lyr's arms, leaning into him for a moment, before she pulled herself away. Her back stiffening with resolve, she nodded.

"So long as you know the risk," she said. "I almost lost the others."

Ralan stepped forward. "You won't lose us. That I know."

Lyr's lips flattened into a thin line, but he only swung around and headed down the path. Meli followed, glancing over her shoulder at the prince. Ralan stared after, his expression closed and tight, and then nudged his brother forward. She had no idea what had caused the disagreement between Lyr and the prince, but there was no time to find out. They needed to focus on saving Arlyn and Kai.

When they reached the stone arch of the portal, Meli drew up short at the sight of Eri sitting calmly on a log, clearly waiting. *This can't be a coincidence.*

The child's sober gaze landed on Ralan. "I told you that you should have stayed."

"Not now, Eri," the prince snapped as he hurried over to his daughter. "We must go."

"I know." Her lower lip trembled. "Guard your right."

Ralan went pale. "How can you see so clearly? Everything is jumbled."

"Megelien." Eri raised her arms, and Ralan lifted her to his hip. Childlike once more, she squeezed his cheeks with her hands. "And other reasons," she continued, grinning. "But mostly Her."

After gathering Eri close for a long hug, Ralan finally sat her down. He swallowed hard, his eyes gleaming with unshed tears. "I'll be sure to guard my right," he whispered.

Eri hugged Ralan's legs and darted away, calling a watery goodbye over her shoulder. A lump formed in Meli's own throat at the scene. Too bad she couldn't comfort the girl. As they walked to the gate, Meli gave Ralan a sympathetic glance. His lips twitched into a half-smile, but it didn't lighten the sadness lining his face. The worry of a father.

They stepped through the portal, then, and Meli's mind went blank as the mists swirled around them. Lyr's hand squeezed hers, but she barely noted the sensation over the horror washing through her. The chill. The rolling fog. The colors she could never grasp. For one long moment, she forgot to breathe.

Take control, she whispered to herself. *You can do this.*

Trembling, Meli freed the leather pouch hanging at her waist. She almost dropped the whole thing as her fingers fumbled with the ties. But finally, the runes glowed up at her from her hands. She peered around, unsure where to cast them. She could see no ground, though there was something firm beneath her feet.

Her stomach lurched at the thought of throwing the precious stones into the rolling gray. So she sat, shivering as the mist flowed around her heavily, and pulled her robe tight around her crossed legs. She shook the runes, her mind clear of all but finding Arlyn, and cast them into the dip of cloth.

The lines that swirled across the smooth stones solidified into shapes at once, though they resembled nothing Meli had ever seen. But she didn't need to know. Light flared and illuminated a thread of color leading off into the distance. She gathered the runes into her hands instead of putting them back in their pouch. "This way."

As the others exchanged confused glances, she spared a thought to wonder what they might see. Then the magic took her over, leading her as it had the last time she'd used it. Her feet found their way through the mists even as the gray began to whip around them. Meli yielded control and followed the glowing thread.

അ൭

A scuffing sound woke her. Leather on rock? Mind still reeling, Arlyn shifted her arms. Or tried to. She froze, fear roaring through her body. Something hard and unyielding surrounded her limbs, keeping her suspended upright. She twisted her hands, trying to discover what held her. Cool rock abraded her fingers, and she discerned cold stone at her back.

Finally, she gathered enough courage to open her eyes. A few feet in front of her face, a tiny flame danced, but it cast little light. Just enough to illuminate her body, she discovered when she glanced down. Then she choked on a stifled scream. Her arms and legs were wrapped in stone as though the wall had tried to swallow her. Arlyn wiggled her feet but made no contact with the floor.

Where was Kai? She turned her head and squinted at the wall to her right. Another light flickered against his profile, and she slumped in relief at his presence. A quick check of their bond told her that he was alive and mostly unharmed. Just unconscious.

Arlyn searched her memory for what had happened, but all she could recall was seeing the flame-haired man in the clearing. She'd been so low on energy that the world had been a haze. Even now, she was weak, but power trickled in from the world around her, building her reserves once more. Slowly, like a bead of water dripping down the branches of a massive Moranaian tree.

Had the Sidhe men at the camp captured them? That seemed the most likely. The question was, where had they been taken?

Hopefully not to Kien. An involuntary shiver shook her within her stone cage.

As if summoned by her waking, the red-haired man she remembered from the clearing stepped out of the darkness, more of those tiny flames dancing around his body. He spoke, but it was gibberish to her.

"I don't understand you," she snapped.

His brow quirked up. "Moranaian, is it?"

"Yes."

"Intriguing. Most Moranaians learn the Sidhe tongue during their schooling." He stared at her with a level gaze, no sign of any intentions for her—good or ill—on his face. "Who are you that you do not?"

She lifted her chin. "I have no reason to tell you anything."

"Truly?" He chuckled. "I believe you have plenty of reasons wrapped around your limbs."

Arlyn grimaced. He had her there. Literally. "I wasn't born on Moranaia, nor was I raised there. Why did you take us?"

"Oh, no." The flames leapt as the man smirked. "I'll be asking the questions, not you. Where is Kien? We have…need of him."

"I don't know." Her breath caught. Were they working with the prince? "Dead, I hope."

The man took a step closer, his eyes narrowing. "I suppose it is no surprise that he does not have loyal followers."

"I am *not* one of his followers," Arlyn said with a glower.

Another figure moved out of the darkness, and the rock tightened just a hair around her limbs. Arlyn's heart raced at the coldness of his gaze. "Do not be swayed, brother," the newcomer said. "It does not matter who she works for. If not for him, then perhaps the Moranaians will trade their aid for her life."

"Naomh—"

"Your eye has ever been turned by a beautiful woman." Naomh's hand fell on the other man's shoulder. "But unlike our father, you are able to resist."

Who were these Sidhe, and why were they looking for Kien? Arlyn had no idea whose side they were on—if anyone's but their own. The one called Naomh had said "brother," but with his pale hair and skin, he didn't resemble their other captor. Would they use the term to deceive? She stared at Naomh but couldn't discern the truth.

Her eyes narrowed. He did seem familiar, though. Where could she have seen him?

The first man's face tightened, and the flames around him flickered and surged. "Why hasn't the male awakened?" he asked in a strained tone.

Naomh tossed a careless glance at Kai and then gave an absent wave. "The spell must have been a bit too strong. Come, Caolte. Perhaps the girl will find the truth during her wait. They hardly need guarding here."

⁘

Kien stepped through the portal, his anger barely banked by the blood he'd shed. Animals were not as satisfying to sacrifice, but he couldn't afford to upset his followers. Not now. He hadn't told them their spell had been disrupted, for they were eager to begin taking over Earth. Though none were stronger than he, together they outnumbered him. The news would have to be delivered…carefully.

The sight of his trophies, most still swaying proudly on their spikes at the entrance, calmed him. Beckett's arm waved in the wind as Kien passed by, a pleasing sight. Almost a greeting, really. He relaxed. Signs of his eventual victory surrounded him. So many of the weak had already fallen so that Kien might succeed in stopping his brother. Perhaps when he sat upon the Moranaian throne, he would honor them. Their weakness had been inborn, after all, as they held the taint of human blood. Hardly their fault.

Kien circled the outer edge of the camp until he reached the iron rod that held his greatest work. But it sat empty, the metal itself feeling…wrong. With a frown, he crouched beside it. His assistant had placed the crystal into the iron, since Kien had difficulty working magic around the stuff. He reached out a finger, surprised to discover he could touch it. How could *that* safeguard have failed? Iron was poison to Sidhe and no small number of Moranaians.

He glanced around for the stone but found only a few fragments. It had shattered? That hadn't been part of the counter spell. Something must have weakened it. His gaze caught on a flash of light, and he followed the glimmer to a smooth globe. Kien hovered his hand over it but detected no sign of a spell. With careful fingers, he picked it up and probed it with a small trickle of energy.

At the very core, he felt Moranaia.

Enraged, Kien heaved the crystal against a nearby tree, where it bounced and rolled back to his feet. Fucking figured.

Whatever had shattered that node had trickled through the connections linking them all, eating through so many that the rest were already collapsing like a spider web in strong winds. How had they known to pierce his spell with the one energy keyed to purify it? His home had to remain perfect for his rule, and they'd used that against him.

Ralan. It had to be Ralan. Nothing less than a seer could have foiled his plan so easily. He must know what Kien sought to do.

Kien stomped from the clearing and into the center of his camp, searching for some sign of who had passed through. Who could have neutralized the iron? Certainly not Lyrnis Dianore, his greatest impediment. The sharp smell of trampled grass reached his nose. They hadn't been subtle to leave such a trace.

At the other end of camp, he spotted the source of the broken grass. Fresh hoof prints circled a tangle of roots thrusting up from the ground. Kien peered up, noticing the drooping branches of the trees above. Some had broken to fall among the roots. He ran a finger over a snarled root and scowled at the lingering trace of energy. *Sidhe magic. Naomh.* Had he returned with some business and found Kien's enemies? Or had be betrayed Kien himself?

Only one way to find out.

ೲಲ

Naomh paced the spell-created forest surrounding his small estate. Meren might have gained their father's title and palace near the queen, but Naomh preferred to live in the pocket dimension under Knocknarea with Caolte, who had been left nothing. The artificial sun lighting the stones of the estate at the center was his to control, and the few who had joined them here were satisfied with his rule. Why did Meren want to risk it all?

Though Naomh rode each dark moon in search of Elerie, he liked to think he'd sense if her feet touched the ground above him. After five hundred years, he couldn't remember if he'd been able to sense her presence before. But now he was attuned to her. Watching and waiting. Provided his fool brother didn't out them all to the humans. Those vicious creatures would never let them rest.

"The Moranaians might truly be innocent," Caolte suggested from beside him.

Though protective and brash, his brother often spoke reason. But not this time. "They were coated in Kien's dark magic."

"The land felt different around Kien's former camp," Caolte argued. "Did you not notice the change? The pressure that's been gathering has weakened. Maybe they are the reason why."

Ready to prove his brother wrong, Naomh sent his power into the earth around him. The poison hadn't reached here, but he'd begun to detect stirrings, as if the land whispered its displeasure at the hurt of its distant brethren. His brow creased. The whispers had lessened— almost gone. Was Caolte correct?

The enchantment on the portal trilled a warning in Naomh's mind, drawing him from his partial trance. An intruder? Few came here to his home, and with the captives present, the timing was more than suspicious.

Naomh and Caolte approached at their ease, allowing no sign of tension to show. This was their home, the power attuned to them. If there was conflict, they would face it. No intruder would see a moment's hesitation from them. Still, Naomh lost his calm at the sight of Kien waiting imperiously in front the gate.

"You!" Naomh snapped.

The prince held up a hand. "Be at peace. I saw signs of your presence at my former camp. Did you need something? I have a couple of runaways I fear gave you grief."

Caolte's fire seared the air around them, just short of igniting. Naomh gave his brother a warning look. "We did come to find you," he said to Kien. "The spell must be stopped before Meren sends a group to the surface. I warned you it would be too much."

Kien smiled, manner easy, though no pleasure reached his eyes. "Didn't you notice I'd dismantled the spell for you? We had a deal, after all."

Naomh snorted. "You took it down yourself?"

"Just now. I thought it would be a symbol of my good intent. I would appreciate if you reward my earnest effort by giving me the servants who escaped."

Caolte's earlier words floated through his mind. Were his captives responsible for releasing the spell, or did Kien speak the truth? Naomh had no trust for the latter and knew little about the former. Perhaps they should have paid more heed to their captives' claims. Naomh would have to proceed carefully.

"If I find any servants of yours, I will send them to you, provided I know your location."

Kien's smile dropped. "I insist you return them."

"As I said, I will if I find them." Naomh dismissed the prince and strode back along the path. He had no time for the treacherous fool. He sensed Caolte's hesitation and then his brother followed. Footsteps sounded steadily behind them. Furious, Naomh spun around. "Leave here. I will find you if I have more to say."

The prince's face grew ruddy with anger. "I am a prince. You will not treat me so rudely."

Naomh smirked. "You're not my prince. I am done with your lies and false promises. From this day onward, our business together is at an end. Feel fortunate I don't kill you where you stand. Now take yourself from my domain."

"This is not finished." Kien's nostrils flared. "I trust you to honor your word. If you find my servants, bring them to me. Look near the portal in the hills close to an Earth town called Chattanooga. This time, we're in a cave."

The prince swung away, his angry steps crunching the ground beneath his feet. Naomh exchanged an amused glance with Caolte. He always honored his word. Now he just had to determine if his captives were in fact servants of Kien. He eyed the artificial sun above and calculated its passage. Surely, the male would have woken by now. As he resumed his walk to the house, he felt the portal flare once more as the prince departed.

Good riddance.

31

One moment, Lyr held Meli's hand as they walked through the Veil. The next, light speared into his eyes, almost blinding him. His bonded took another step, caught in the spell of the runes, but he tugged her back, shifting to the side to let the others follow. He blinked quickly as his vision cleared and then examined the formal gardens surrounding them. The cool air felt like spring, the flowers fresh and new under the forest canopy. Far above, he could make out the stone ceiling, though a spell masked it blue like the sky.

Meli shifted forward, still held under the magic's thrall. Tossing an annoyed glance over her shoulder, she tugged at her hand. *"You must stop,"* Lyr whispered into her mind. *"Put the runes away if necessary. We need to form a plan."*

As her face grew strained with the effort to free herself, Lyr guided her away from the portal entrance and into the trees. He headed for the wall closest to him, for the Sidhe tended to stay clear of the boundaries of their underground homes. It reminded them too much of their limitations. He only hoped that aversion would be enough if the lord of this place had detected their arrival through the portal.

This place was much smaller than the grand Sidhe cities Lyr had visited before. A private residence? That would be more dangerous than a city, in its way, for a Sidhe lord could hide many misdeeds in his own domain. Definitely a possibility they would need to be prepared for.

Lyr crouched behind a tumble of boulders that had fallen from the stone wall, the princes darting in behind him. Meli tried to pull free once more, so Lyr sat and pulled her into his lap. She stilled as his arms closed around her waist.

"What are you doing?" she sent along their link.

"Put away the runes, love. You need to end the spell."

He tensed, experiencing her struggle through their bond as she fought to conquer the magic. Like a wild thing, it resisted being contained. Lyr's own hand ached as hers squeezed around the runes, and light flared between her gripped fingers. Then the pressure cleared, and Meli dropped the suddenly calm runes back into their leather pouch. But he could still see them shining through the seams, and her dazed expression had barely altered. Her entire body shook against him.

Lyr leaned down and bit gently on her earlobe. He grinned at her startled jump as he whispered, "Meli, come back."

Another shudder shook her, this one not entirely caused by magic, before she stilled. The energy that had swirled around her faded along with the light from the pouch. After a moment, she turned in his arms to face him.

"I hope that isn't the only way to end this spell. Pleasant though it was," she said, amusement ringing along the link.

Despite everything, he found himself holding back a laugh. *"We'll figure it out."*

❧

There was nothing for Arlyn to do but dangle, worry, and try not to panic as she waited for Kai to wake. If these two Sidhe thought she and Kai worked for Kien, well…it wouldn't be good. Could she and Kai convince them of the truth? If so, the Sidhe's clear anger at Kien would be to her and her bonded's benefit. *The enemy of my enemy, right?*

Her head drooped forward, and she forced it up again. The energy that had filled her on waking was trickling out again like the water she could hear but not see. Why wasn't her body holding on to any magic? Exhaustion held her eyelids down with its weight, but there was nothing to see, anyway. Not even the little flames remained to distract her with their light.

A rustle of cloth and a low moan finally broke through the dark. *"Kai?"*

Agony passed along their bond until he blocked the pain. *"What the hell?"*

"Do you remember what happened?"

He took so long to answer that worry tingled up her spine like fingers. Or bugs. Oh, gods, was there enough space between her back and the stone for bugs? Arlyn squirmed, flattening her back against the rock. No squishing or anything. Maybe—

"Arlyn?" Kai sent, his mental voice hesitant. *"What's wrong?"*

Heat rushed into her face and down her neck. For once, she was thankful for the lack of light. *"Nothing. No big deal. Did you remember something?"*

Another pause. *"Those Sidhe. They blasted me with something. And hard."*

"I can tell." They must have been rougher on him, for the ache that had woken Arlyn was nothing like the agony she sensed from Kai. *"They were here earlier. The red-haired one had little flames around him. Just enough light to see that we're screwed."*

"I know spells to release almost any cuff but iron."

"I don't think this one is in your repertoire," she answered with a wry twist of her lips. *"They've wrapped our arms and legs in stone. We're held in the wall."*

Kai cursed in ways that tested her Moranaian vocabulary. Her father certainly hadn't combined words in quite *that* way. *"Did they say what they want?"*

"They think we're Kien's followers," Arlyn answered.

"So they implied before." She heard Kai's fingers scraping against the rock. *"Any ideas?"*

"Nothing but convincing them we're innocent. I'm growing weak again."

Concern and fear leapt along the bond. *"The energy here is clean. Whatever their intentions, the Sidhe haven't cut us off from that, though it's slow in coming. You should be getting better."*

"At first, I was. But I can't hold on to what flows through."

Could there have been something in the counter spell? Arlyn closed her eyes and tried to search within herself, but she was still learning that skill. A hint of darkness, maybe? She tried to reach it, but before she could, a burst of light shattered her concentration. Her eyes shot open to see two figures illuminated by the light of an open door. Soon that faded, too, replaced by the tiny flames that swirled around—Caolte? Was that his name?

The one she thought was Naomh strode over to Kai, a larger light preceding him. Arlyn could see her bonded, then, and gasped to observe how gaunt and bruised he appeared. The side of his face closest to her was mottled purple. His eyes met her concerned ones across the space. *"I might have resisted a bit."*

Quite a bit, by the look of it.

Kai turned back to the Sidhe. "Let us down."

Naomh's soft laugh rumbled around them. "I think not. It seems your female has lied to us."

"What?" Arlyn shifted in her stone prison. "I did not. I have been nothing but honest."

Caolte came forward, bringing more light. "Kien came looking for his servants."

Her heart seized. Kien was here? If he found them now, they were dead. He must have discovered that they'd broken the spell. "You have to let us go. He'll kill us."

"So you admit it now?" Naomh sneered at them as he pulled a long knife from his belt. "Perhaps I'll return you a bit more...damaged."

"No!" Arlyn cried as the Sidhe approached Kai.

Energy began to gather in Kai's hands, though she couldn't imagine what he would do with it. "He'll kill us because we took down his spell," her bonded protested. "We are delegates of Callian Myern i Lyrnis Dianore nai Braelyn. Harm us, and there will be war."

Scowling, the Sidhe paused. "Lyrnis Dianore, who has broken off negotiations with my brother instead of offering aid?"

"He refuses to work with butchers," Kai said, his voice shaking with fury. "I've seen the work of your kind all too recently. Sending an army of Seelie and Unseelie against your own colony. Killing the ill without thought or mercy."

Naomh's hand tightened on the hilt of his knife. "I will—"

"Stay your hand." Caolte gripped Naomh's shoulder. "He speaks the truth."

"What?" Naomh shouted, rounding on his brother.

The flames around Caolte's head flickered. "You were angry enough that Meren had lost the Moranaians' aid. I wasn't sure how to tell you the full extent of his treachery. He cleared out the Neorans. Any who were left."

For a moment, nothing could be heard but the dripping of water.

"Look," Kai grumbled. "I understand your doubts. Could you at least bind us in chains and give us some food while you debate this? My bonded is not well."

Both Sidhe spun, studying her. Naomh's brow furrowed. "We did not block energy from reaching you," he said.

The concern in their eyes had Arlyn swallowing hard. She must have looked even worse than she felt. "I can't hold on to it."

The brothers exchanged a glance—and likely mental words, as well. Finally, Naomh slipped his blade back into its sheath. "Very well. But you will remain chained until we decide what is to be done. I've a need to speak with Caolte. Alone."

✦

"Perhaps it is best if I slip through alone," Lyr said, pitching his voice so it could not be heard beyond the rocks.

"No," Ralan answered. "I have seen that we must all go. There will be trouble. That cloak will only take you so far."

Lyr rolled his eyes. "If you know what to do, why are we even bothering to plan?"

"There are many future branchings from this point. Sometimes, there is a clear way forward. Something obvious that must be done." Ralan huffed out a breath. "This is not one of those times. It is going to change—and change fast—based on the decisions made at any given time. I can't tell you which future is most likely to prevail."

"*Clechtan*," Lyr muttered. He hadn't considered that possibility, as his friend was usually so self-assured. Lyr had always known seers had limitations, but he'd never had to deal with them. "Very well. What if I scout around the area leading up to the main house? I'll find the clearest route for us to follow."

"Hmm…" Ralan paused, his eyes glazing for a moment. Then he nodded. "Just resist the urge to go in alone."

"Fine." Lyr turned to Meli. "You're sure you are free of the runes?"

"I'm certain." Her clear gaze met his, and he could sense the truth along their bond as easily as he felt her worry. "Be safe."

He leaned in for a quick kiss and then pulled the hood of the cloak over his head. Since Selia had never been to this place, she couldn't have keyed the cloak to slip through any magical defenses. But surprisingly, Lyr detected no overt shielding. Were the Sidhe here that confident, or did they simply do things differently? He could only hope the spell hiding his energy from detection would be enough to get him close without being sensed by any Sidhe he neared.

Lyr slipped from tree to tree, searching with his senses for any sign of life. He avoided the main path and angled in from another side. At first, he detected only birds and the rare deer, captive here beneath the earth. Eventually, he was forced to skirt the occasional cottage or wandering Sidhe, until he reached a fairly clear path near the back.

He spent several moments watching the large estate at the center of the cavern. A bored-looking guard shuffled his feet by the door. Servants came and went, most headed toward the large garden at the back corner. Too bad they didn't have time to wait until dark. It would be tricky to find an inconspicuous place to enter.

After studying the area a little longer, Lyr retraced his steps until he reached the stone wall that marked the boundaries of the underhill. Creeping carefully around the perimeter, he returned to the stack of stones where the others hid. After a quick, soft whistle to warn of his presence, he ducked behind the boulders.

"I found the best way," Lyr announced. "But even that is risky. I saw plenty of movement around the house itself."

"A fight is inevitable once we are inside, I know that much," Ralan said, his hand going to the hilt of his sword. "Kai and Arlyn are being held below. They must be pleasant Sidhe, having a basement dungeon."

Lyr held back a growl and stepped close to Meli. "Can you fight?"

"Maybe?" She bit her lower lip. "Not well enough to train as a warrior, but I can defend myself if you give me a knife."

His gut clenched, but he untied the scabbard to one of his blades and secured it around her belt. "I wish there was a safe place for you."

Her chin rose. "I could say the same."

Lyr grinned at his bonded, timid except when she wasn't. "Come on, then."

He led them around the perimeter, Meli behind him and the three princes ranged around her. Lyr only needed to guide them around one wandering Sidhe before their group crouched in sight of the manor. It was smaller than the palaces preferred by many Sidhe lords, but part of that might have been its construction. The entire structure appeared to be one solid piece formed from the rock beneath their feet. Everything was stone, from the open terrace that wrapped around the bottom floor to the balcony of the level above.

His eyes narrowed on the railing circling the top. Should they climb? It might be easier to avoid detection entering the building from an upper room, less likely to be occupied at this time of day. Then he glanced at Meli's long robe and decided to take their chances on a bottom entry. She would struggle with the climb, and the longer it took, the more risk of discovery.

There were few doors he hadn't seen anyone go through in his previous mission or while watching now. Perhaps it didn't matter, since Ralan had said a fight was inevitable. With a raised brow, he looked to the prince, who pursed his lips for a moment before gesturing to the door across from them. The sun above them had angled so that the terrace here was cast in shadow. It was as good as they were likely to get.

Even with the assurance that there would be a fight, Lyr took care not to be noticed. He would not invite a battle himself. Their group darted quickly but silently onto the terrace and flattened against the wall next to the door. He tested the handle. Not surprisingly, it turned smoothly, and the door opened without a sound.

With a quick gesture, he led the others inside.

32

Kai had been in worse situations—just a month ago, in fact—but not many. His entire body sang with the pain of his earlier struggle with the two Sidhe, and he was fairly certain a rib was broken. But at least he was no longer suspended in rock. With an easy wave of his hand, the blond one had removed it, a smile of satisfaction crossing his face when Kai and Arlyn fell hard upon the ground. The one called Caolte had dragged them over to a set of chains and shackled them, unresisting, once more.

Wonderful place they had here.

He'd been careful not to give them too much trouble, hoping they'd think him weakened. Not that the truth was far from that assumption. After the Sidhe left, Kai slumped against the wall and soaked in as much energy as he could. And waited. It wasn't long before Caolte returned with two small trays of food and then departed once more. Interesting that he hadn't sent a servant.

Kai's worried gaze darted between his food and Arlyn. Her weakness was increasing, her hands shaking as she tried to lift the bread to her mouth. He set down his plate and shifted over to help her. She drooped against the wall, her eyelids going heavy, and chewed each bite he brought to her mouth.

After Arlyn finished, he scarfed the rest of his own meal. Then he leaned back again, focusing within. With his meager healing gift, he knit the crack in his rib and eased some of the ache in his muscles. He didn't bother with the bruising on his face, for he wanted to waste no energy on that. He could deal with the pain talking caused.

Then Kai turned his attention to the shackles, and a chuckle slipped free. They were made of *peresten*, a metal mined and forged on Moranaia. Trapped by their own trade goods. Unlike iron, this metal caused no disruption to magic, so it was no surprise to find them spelled against tampering. Fortunately, Kai had spent some years learning counters to such spells.

A *sonal* couldn't be too careful.

He worked through the first spells easily. They were fairly common for containment, the counters not difficult to find if you knew the right mages. Then he reached one of pure Sidhe magic. Kai cursed, another favorite that had Arlyn quirking a brow, and carefully probed the spell with his own energy. It felt...familiar somehow. If he could just attune...

The snick of the shackle opening caught him by surprise. He stared down at the metal cuffs open in his lap. Why had the spell resonated with his own energy? Had they tried to use his own power against him? Kai didn't have time to consider it, turning to Arlyn's shackles to repeat the process. He expected difficulty when he reached the Sidhe portion, thinking it would be attuned to her, but no. As with his own, the cuffs fell away when he linked his own energy with the Sidhe magic. Curious.

They both rubbed their wrists, though the shackles hadn't had time to chafe. Kai met his bonded's eyes. "Think you can walk?"

"Not well." But Arlyn heaved herself to her feet. Swaying, she rested her hand against the wall. "I don't have much choice."

Kai supported her as best he could as they crossed the heavy stone floor. Dread filled him at her slow pace, for it would be difficult to escape at such a speed. Kai fed her more energy, and she straightened a little beside him. This time, she didn't argue about the energy he gave.

❧

"You should have told me," Naomh said, staring at this brother through a red haze of fury.

"Naomh—" Caolte began.

He slammed a fist into the wall beside his brother's head. "I am not a child to be protected."

Caolte's eyes narrowed. "I gave my word to Father that I would guard you, and so I have. For centuries, I have followed your lead. I haven't treated you like a child."

"Then why did you withhold information?" Naomh's entire body trembled with rage. His brother had said only that Meren had broken his promise to negotiate with the Moranaians. But a massacre? "It was no small thing."

"You have gone through enough," Caolte answered, voice suddenly soft.

Naomh turned away to pace the length of the room. "What if we captured those two in error? Delegates of Moranaia. Even if I speak with Lord Lyrnis to denounce Meren's actions, he will not work with us now. I've heard the queen herself speak of returning to the surface. Everything is ruined."

"Hardly that." Caolte tossed his head. "Ransom these two for their aid."

Naomh's brow lifted. "I have not lost all sense. This estate could hardly stand against the Moranaian army if we wrong them. Besides, there's something about the male. He seems familiar. I like none of this."

"We will find a—"

His brother's words cut off abruptly as the room shook around them. The estate shields. Naomh unsheathed his knife and pulled power to himself as they rushed for the door. He detected a small party, only five. Not the army he'd feared, then. Kien with his minions? Naomh hadn't sensed a third flare of the portal. Had Kien set up a trap?

He almost hoped so. Perhaps the prince's death would ease his own frustration.

⚬⚬⚬

For several heartbeats after they entered through the unlocked door, the building rumbled, though Lyr saw no movement down the long hallway before them. The Sidhe lord's defenses? Swords hissed from sheaths as Lyr and the others prepared for a swift reprisal to their invasion.

Quickly, he cast his mind out, searching for Arlyn and Kai. He sagged in relief when he connected with his daughter. *"Arlyn, are you well?"*

"I'm...alive," she whispered into his mind. *"We're working our way out. From below, I think. This place is a maze of levels. How did you—"*

"Later. We'll find you."

Lyr wasted no more time, letting his combat magic sweep through his body. His senses expanded, searching for attackers, until...there. Four guards rounded the corner at the distant end of the wide hall.

Teyark slipped to Lyr's right and Ralan to his left. As the guards raced toward them, Lyr lifted his sword, more than ready to make someone pay. His gaze flicked to the windows lining one side of the corridor. The terrace. If other Sidhe sought to approach from there, his magic would uncover them.

Lyr glowered at the guard in front. "We are only here to re-claim our kin. Return them, and no battle need be fought."

They slowed, the three in the back looking toward their leader, who stopped a few body-lengths away. The Sidhe's brow scrunched in confusion. "Reclaim? No one is held captive here. For your trespass, no quarter shall be granted. Our lord's rule in this is clear."

"You invite war with Moranaia."

The guard took a step forward. "You invite war by your presence."

"Very well, then," Lyr said, lifting his sword. "Come forward for your death."

The four rushed them, and Lyr bared his teeth in a terrible smile. Finally, he could act. He met the blade of the leader without hesitation, swirling into the dance of battle. The Sidhe was good, but Lyr was better. He held back, testing the other's skill, before taking the offensive. The Sidhe's face went slack with shock as Lyr advanced in a flurry of attacks. Metal rang as the guard's blade clattered on the ground, Lyr's sword at the other's throat.

With narrowed eyes, the guard lifted his hands. Lyr sensed the energy building and prepared his own shields for the attack. He shifted the knife in his left hand, ready to strike. Despite his earlier words, he had no desire to kill the Sidhe for doing his job, especially since he seemed unaware of Kai's and Arlyn's abduction. But the gathering spell might leave Lyr no choice.

"Stop."

Ralan's voice broke through the haze of combat, and Lyr realized that the hall had grown quiet. He glanced over his shoulder to see the other three guards standing silently, weapons sheathed. "What's going on?"

The guard shifted beneath Lyr's sword, drawing his attention, and his blade dug into the Sidhe's neck. A line of blood bloomed, but the man's low cry of pain cut off abruptly, the spell he'd attempted to gather winking out. Lyr's brows rose. The Sidhe's face contorted with some inner battle before his entire body went limp.

"He'll take us where we need to go," Ralan finally answered, his voice almost casual. "Sheathe your sword. They'll make it easy enough for us now."

Lyr complied. "I thought you said a fight was inevitable."

"It was." The prince smirked. "I needed a distraction to break through their defenses. Fae beings are never as easy to control as humans, and I'm out of practice."

He had been so intent on Ralan's role as a seer that he'd forgotten the prince's mastery of mind magic. It was fortunate for Moranaia that the prince was a man of honor. If he ever went rogue, like Kien…

"Come on, then," Lyr grumbled.

Lyr glanced at Meli's pale face as the princes surrounded her once more. Had she ever seen a battle? If only he could stop and comfort her. Despite Ralan's casual confidence, Lyr knew the prince's power would only last so long over four adult Sidhe. He spun away to follow the wooden steps of their unwilling guides, but he cast his mind back to his bonded.

"I'm sorry."

"For what? There wasn't even blood." A touch of amusement came through. *"That was…I have never seen anything like it. He truly has control of them?"*

Lyr understood, then, what bothered her. *"For a time. Hopefully long enough. I thought I'd scared you."*

Her huff of laughter was so slight he wasn't sure the others heard it. *"I've seen mock battles. The Ljósálfar practice daily for wars we might never fight. But controlling the minds of so many Sidhe is new. Will his hold last long?"*

"I guess we have to hope for the best."

Lyr turned his dagger so the blade ran along his wrist, out of sight. He kept his arm close to his side as the corridor emptied into the main entry. To the right, a pair of glass-paned doors revealed the gardens beyond. On the far left, huge, stone doors stood partly open as if left in haste. The guards' original station? Lyr and the others had entered under one side of the double stairs that curved up each wall of the room to meet over their heads. Another hallway opened ahead of them to continue along the terrace

The guard leading them didn't turn into the entryway but kept walking forward, down the hallway that was twin to the one they'd left. The Sidhe didn't take them far, opening the first door they came to and descending a stone, spiral staircase. Lyr gestured for Ralan to precede him. If the guards got too far ahead, they would be more difficult to control.

Forehead beaded with sweat, Ralan brushed past him. Lyr hadn't seen his friend appear so strained since he'd returned to Moranaia with his sick daughter. Lyr's anger started to crumble, then, for it was clear the prince was going to great effort to save Kai and Arlyn. It was time he remembered the trust he bore for his friend.

"Whatever happens, I am sorry," he murmured.

Ralan gave him a quick, surprised look over his shoulder, a touch of tension easing from his expression. "As am I. Thank you."

After hundreds of years of friendship, they needed say no more. Fortunate, since Lyr didn't want to distract the prince. It would be an unpleasant place for a fight if the guards worked free of their control. Instead, Lyr concentrated on keeping his footing on the smooth, slippery stone. How many millennia had these steps seen? A question he was unlikely to learn the answer to.

Finally, they emerged in a room the size of an entire house. Columns of stone spiraled at regular intervals, supporting the structure above. White, fabric-covered lumps, possibly furniture, were scattered here and there, and crates ranged along one side of the dim room. But no sign of Kai and Arlyn.

The guards stopped in the center. The leader squeezed his hands against his head as though trying to free himself, but his eyes remained glazed. "I can go no farther. I told you there were none here."

"I thought you said he would lead us," Lyr said to Ralan.

"He isn't lying. They have no knowledge of anyone being brought here." Lines of sweat trickled down the prince's face now, and his hands trembled. "My vision showed an underground room, so I had him bring us here. This basement the lowest location I could find in his mind. There must be an entrance to a secret chamber around here somewhere."

"*Miaran,*" Lyr cursed. "I spoke briefly with Arlyn. She said something about a maze of tunnels."

The four guards suddenly crumpled, and Ralan swayed, almost falling before he righted himself against a column. "They'll sleep, but shortly."

"Ralan—"

"We have to keep going. I see it now. Behind the furniture on the left wall." The prince straightened, pale but determined. "We have to go. The two lords are ahead of us, and I see plenty of things that can go wrong. So many damn decisions that could be made."

They hurried to the place Ralan had seen in his vision. Lyr sucked in a breath as the prince pointed out the slight split in the stone wall, barely large enough to slip through sideways. He never would have found it on his own. The dim flicker of light in the large room made it seem like a natural striation in the rock.

"How could the lords be ahead of us? They couldn't possibly have missed the fight had they gone down the main stairs," he mentally asked, though he hated to strain the prince further.

"I saw them take another way. A private one."

It made sense to have more than one entrance to the dungeon area. But why didn't the guards know of the place? *That* answer wasn't likely to be a good one.

33

Kai stumbled, struggling beneath the awkward weight of two packs. They'd found their belongings a few rooms away from the one where they'd been held, but Arlyn was too weak to carry hers. He had hefted both onto his shoulders before they continued their search for an exit. But after climbing endless stairs and peering into countless empty rooms, he began to question the decision.

"Is there anything of value to you in here?"

"No," Arlyn answered. *"Though we might need some of the camping supplies later."*

"I can survive in the woods without them." Kai stopped in yet another empty room and shrugged the packs to the floor. *"Making it out alive is more important."*

In short order, he'd consolidated the most important contents into one lighter bag. A bit of food, a bundle of fishing line with hooks, and a coil of rope were all he carried, besides their weapons. Arlyn had her bow and quiver, the weight of her sword too much. Every few rooms, Kai fed her more energy. It wasn't as much of a strain as it should have been, something in this place unexpectedly bolstering him.

Kai ascended yet another stairway. Had the builder been insane? They had found a few more cells with chains for holding prisoners but also plenty of rooms that were empty. Little furniture and no signs of life. But other floors had rooms like any other house. Private quarters, public spaces, and even cooking and dining areas, though those were mixed up in odd ways. To get to the kitchen, he'd climbed a set of stairs from a room containing a large stone bed frame.

Were they making upward progress? Climbing in circles? They'd retraced their steps so often, there was no way to tell. This time, they emerged in a large room lit by globes suspended overhead. Carvings of ancient scenes from when the Sidhe had ruled the surface covered the walls. The floor, though smooth, had been painted to resemble a raging stream flowing over rocks. A ballroom? Who would build a ballroom so many levels underground instead of near the surface where it could be accessed by guests?

Arlyn stumbled against him, and Kai gripped her arms. "More energy?"

"You shouldn't," she whispered, though her voice lacked conviction.

"To lose you is death. I'll not risk it." He sent more power along their bond and sighed in relief to see her straighten. "I can draw readily from this place."

"Well, then," a voice called from across the room. Caolte's smirk greeted Kai's startled gaze. "Looks like we should have blocked them from receiving energy after all, brother."

Naomh didn't answer, his incredulous stare focused on Kai and Arlyn. "How did you get free?"

Kai's lips curved up. "You should know better than to rely on spells. Too easily broken."

"Those were bound by my blood and magic. Without me, they should never—"

"Guess you were wrong," Kai interrupted, drawing his sword even as uneasiness settled in his stomach. "Just let us go. My bonded is ill, and we have no argument with your House. Since you mistook us as working for Kien, we can forgive your previous actions."

Naomh's hand wrapped slowly around the hilt of his sword, and he hesitated before drawing it. "Our home has been invaded, and four of my guards are unresponsive. Possibly dead. I find your innocence difficult to believe."

Resigned, Kai rushed forward to meet the approaching Sidhe. He sensed Arlyn pressing back against the wall and nocking an arrow in her bow. Would she be able to draw it? He sped up, hoping to ensure the conflict would stay far from her in the huge room. Caolte settled in front of the other door with arms crossed and expression inscrutable.

"This is pointless," Kai said as Naomh neared. "Your *intruders* are only here to save us."

"Enough."

Naomh gave no other warning before taking the offensive, his sword swooping down with deadly intent. Kai parried without trouble, but he worried about besting a Sidhe lord of ancient power. A power held at bay. "Not going to tangle me in more trees or rock?"

The Sidhe sneered as he spun into another blow. "Not this time. A duel in the old style, I think."

Kai's eyes widened as he launched his own attack. It was a rare honor for the Sidhe to fight with blade alone, for they were happy to dispense with those they considered weaker with a flick of magic. Ancient duels fought as such settled disputes between equals. But it was difficult to feel honored as Naomh parried each blow with casual ease. Almost as bad as sparring with Lyr.

Kai feinted low, then swooped high, tracing a thin line up the Sidhe's arm. Blood dripped down Naomh's forearm as he cursed and drew his sword back into position. Fury filled the Sidhe's eyes, and he attacked with greater resolve, sending Kai into the defensive once more. Sweat beaded Kai's brow as they circled the center of the room.

"Yield," Naomh muttered.

"Only if you free us."

The Sidhe grunted in answer and continued his blows. Clear enough. Kai had no idea how long they fought, but he was grateful for the hours he had trained with Lyr. He never could have survived against a Sidhe lord otherwise. Was there any way he could win? Naomh had few weaknesses in his guard, but...there. Next time, he had only to—

The clatter of Arlyn's bow hitting stone distracted him. Though he parried automatically, his head turned to see who'd harmed his bonded. But no one was near her. She slumped against the wall, her eyes closed as though in pain. He needed to win this fight *now*. Kai looked back, desperation overcoming sense, to see the other's sword sweeping toward his neck.

He had just enough time to avoid a killing blow. Still, the tip of the blade sliced through his tunic and into flesh. As Kai hissed with pain, the sword caught the two chains he wore around his neck, one holding Arlyn's pendant, and severed the metal. He felt both slither down, but it was the least of his concerns. He leapt back, hand finding the cut to test its severity, and sensed Arlyn stirring behind him.

"Don't shoot," he called back, knowing she didn't understand the implications of the duel.

Kai's hand shook, but he lifted his sword, ready for another attack. One that never came. Naomh stood frozen, his eyes on the chains that had fallen to the ground. Why was he hesitating? Kai gaped as the Sidhe threw his sword to the ground with a clang and dropped to his knees. Then he reached for the chain Kai had inherited on his twentieth birthday.

Naomh raised stunned eyes to Kai. "Where did you get this?"

"What is it?" Caolte asked, arms dropping to his sides as he approached his brother.

"I gave it to Elerie." Naomh gathered the chain into his hand and stood, his expression suddenly hard. "How did you come to have this necklace?"

The uneasiness Kai had suppressed returned to choke him. "My mother."

Naomh strode toward him, heedless of the sword Kai still held. "Where is she?"

"She is dead," Kai managed to get out around the restriction in his throat.

The room around them shook as rage filled the Sidhe lord's eyes. Caolte reached out to grab his brother's arm, but Naomh shook him off. "Did you kill her?"

"What?" Anger released the shock that had held Kai's voice. "You think I killed my own mother?"

"It has certainly been done before." One of the globes suspended from the stone ceiling broke free in a shower of pebbles, shattering on the floor a few body-lengths away. "How long ago?"

"I didn't kill her. I was a baby." Kai clenched his teeth, though it speared pain through his injured jaw. "Five hundred and forty-three years ago next month."

Silence fell, save the tinkling of rock shards falling from the ceiling above. Kai had never seen a Sidhe look so…discomposed. Pain pinched Naomh's face and glinted in his eyes. "Less than a year after she left me. All this time…"

Gods of Arneen. Kai's body went cold as unease solidified into suspicion. Then knowing. He'd been trying to uncover information about his father since he'd discovered he was not Allafon's son. He hadn't considered the Sidhe. But the way he'd broken the cuffs' enchantment and the ease of drawing on the energy here… He swallowed hard.

Naomh was his father.

"She meant to return to you," Kai forced himself to say. "My father—no, Allafon—held her until she bore your child. Then he killed her out of spite. He claimed me as his own."

Understanding crossed Caolte's face first, and he reached out for his brother's arm again. This time, Naomh didn't shake him off. He sagged as his eyes widened. "You mean—"

"Kai!" Lyr's voice broke through the tension as his blade rang free. His expression was furious as he sprinted across the room, Ralan and Teyark behind him. Corath and Meli halted near the door. "Stand away from him, Sidhe."

"See to Arlyn," Kai called. He had been feeding her energy despite his injury, but she wavered on her feet nonetheless. "The battle is over."

∽ৎ৫౿

One glance at Arlyn and Lyr took Kai at his word. He darted around the three in the center and headed for his daughter. She blinked, her eyes glazed. He looked her over for injury but found nothing. "What's wrong?"

She trembled so much that it was difficult to tell when she shook her head. "Don't know. Can't hold energy."

Lyr placed a hand on her forehead. Her skin was clammy, her energy lower than he had ever seen it. If not for her human blood, she wouldn't have been conscious. His anger surged as he peered over his shoulder at the Sidhe lords. "What did you do to her?"

The red-haired one lifted a brow. "I fear she came to us this way."

"Something in that crystal," she whispered.

Lyr caught her as she crumpled, feeding her energy as he held her against him. Within moments, she was able to pull back, but he could sense what he'd given already draining away. He turned to Ralan. "Did you know?"

"In the futures where the counter spell hit her, she was supposed to be in Moranaia before it took hold. The fairies can heal her."

"We need to get back." Lyr swept her into his arms, alarm squeezing his heart when she didn't protest. He strode to Kai, still standing next to the Sidhe. "If you wanted war, you have made a fine start."

"No," the blond Sidhe murmured. "I wanted Elerie."

Kai's mother? Lyr took in Kai's pallor and the shattered expression of the Sidhe. Could it be? He noticed, then, the resemblance between the two, though Kai had inherited his mother's coloring. "What business did you have with her?"

Pain-filled brown eyes met his. "She was mine."

Had they been bonded? "I am Lyrnis Dianore, Lord of Braelyn. As far as I know, Lady Elerie made no claim to such. However, I was only a boy when she returned from her last scouting mission on Earth. If she mentioned you to my father, he never said."

The room trembled around them, sending more shards from the ceiling onto the broken glass a few paces away. Lyr gave an uneasy glance upward, but everything stilled once more. The Sidhe lord stood with clenched fists, staring at him. "I am Lord Naomh a Nuall. Brother to Lord Meren, much as I wish it otherwise. This is my other brother, Caolte."

"We have much to discuss, Lord Naomh, but it will not be now," Lyr said. "Allow us to leave in peace. My daughter is clearly ill."

"There will ever be peace between our Houses if I have any say." Naomh met Kai's eyes. "For it seems we are connected through my son."

Lyr could see the turmoil on his friend's face even as he empathized with the Sidhe lord. How well he knew the shock of finding an adult child. "And his mate needs tending. I invite you and your brother to come to Moranaia as guests at your leisure." Lyr gestured to the red-haired one. "This one, *not* Lord Meren."

Glancing to Lyr, Kai wiped his sword on his tunic and sheathed it. "I'll take her."

"Not unless you want to get blood all over her." Lyr grimaced. "Can you see to the wound?"

His friend probed the cut with a wince and then nodded. But as he closed his eyes, Naomh stepped forward. "I'll heal what I wrought."

"I'm not sure—" Kai began.

"My mother was a healer. I may not use it often, but I possess the skill." Light flared in Naomh's hand. "Please allow me to do this small thing."

Kai nodded, though Lyr could tell by his stiff posture that he was uncomfortable. As the Sidhe lord healed the gash, Lyr studied Arlyn. Dark bruises shadowed her eyes, and her face was growing gaunt. He fed her more energy. And worried. When Naomh finished healing Kai, Lyr met the Sidhe's eyes again and nodded. Having almost killed his own son... Well, Naomh would have much to deal with.

"Caolte and I will journey to your land soon. I'm not sure—
" Naomh broke off and took a deep breath. "I need time to
compose myself. There is indeed much to discuss."

While Kai stooped down to get his pendant, Lyr stared at
the Sidhe lord. He had a feeling Naomh knew far more than he
would say about all of their troubles. Why else would he have
taken Kai and Arlyn had he not been involved? When these two
arrived on Moranaia, Lyr would have his household on highest
guard.

∞∞

With Lyr carrying Arlyn behind him, Kai followed Naomh up a
set of spiral steps. His body ached once more but not just as a
result of his capture. This day had been a sad, strange echo of
his confrontation with Allafon. First, Kai had been captured by
the elf who had claimed to be his father, and Kai had killed him
to escape. This time, he'd been held by a supposed stranger and
released at the revelation of his parentage. Were he not so sick
with confusion, he would laugh.

Gods, but his true father had almost killed him as surely as
his false one would have. Was there something within him that
inspired hatred? Irrational question. Naomh didn't even know
him, but it made Kai's heart pound nonetheless. For their kind,
energy was its own truth, and his power had resounded clearly
with Naomh's.

Only a close blood relation could have opened those cuffs.

"I love you," Arlyn whispered into his mind.

A little of his tension eased at her words. She would take away his pain if she could, and it meant more to him than anything. Whatever happened with his newfound father, she would support him. *"I love you, too."*

Finally, they emerged from the endless spiral into a small, circular room with nothing but a door to one side and a few windows. Kai sighed with bliss as the light washed over him, though he knew the sun outside was not a real one. At a soft chuckle from Caolte, he frowned over at the two Sidhe. "Fine place you have here."

Caolte's grin widened. "The underground section was built by my grandfather. Our father tried to talk him out of it, but he had long gone mad from being forced below Earth's surface. Naomh built the house over it when he inherited this realm."

Naomh shifted as though uncomfortable with the revelation, understandable since such knowledge wouldn't usually be granted to strangers. Family history. Kai's stomach churned, but he merely nodded to acknowledge Caolte's words. Naomh opened his mouth as if to speak, but he snapped it closed and turned, leading them once more to the door.

34

If not for Arlyn's motionless weight in his arms, Lyr would have been relieved. Freeing Kai and Arlyn could have ended in death, but instead they had gained a new ally. Kai's father, no less. When Lyr had considered possible outcomes, that hadn't been one of them.

He followed the Sidhe lord down one of the staircases in the main entry. Kai hovered on one side, his anxious gaze on Arlyn, and Meli trailed behind, next to Corath. Ralan and Teyark followed last. Why had the seer been so concerned? Considering the possibilities, the mission had gone miraculously well.

At the doorway, the Sidhe stopped. Expression blank, Naomh opened the door and gestured to the trail beyond. "It is a straight walk down that path to the portal. I trust you can find your way safely."

Lyr inclined his head. "Certainly. We will anticipate your arrival on Moranaia soon."

He didn't want to leave it at that, for Kai's and Arlyn's abduction tore at him, but it was the safest way to get his daughter to help. If these two were part of Kien's treachery, Lyr would deal with them later. Kai's family or not. As the lord met his eyes, Lyr could see understanding of that fact within them. Naomh gave a slight nod in acknowledgement.

As they stepped onto the terrace, the two guards at each side of the doorway bristled, one of them reaching for his sword. Their glares settled on Ralan, whose mouth quirked up. "It was a pleasure working with you," the prince said.

The sound of metal rang through the air, but Naomh's hand closed around the guard's wrist. He squeezed until the blade clattered to the ground. "My guests are just leaving. You will grant them the greatest courtesy."

"Guests? My lord—"

"Silence." Naomh's gaze flicked to Kai. "One among them is a son of this House. I will cast you back to the main Court if you cannot recall your place."

The guard's mouth snapped closed, lips whitening. Though he nodded, he still glared at Ralan. Lyr couldn't blame him. Having one's mind and body taken over was no small thing. "He performed his duty to you well, Lord Naomh," Lyr said. "I hope you are not too hard on him on our account."

Though the Naomh's face didn't soften, he flicked the guard's wrist away. With one last look at Kai, Naomh disappeared inside, leaving his brother to gaze after them. Caolte, too, focused on Kai, though his expression was more considering.

What did it mean that they now had a connection with a powerful Sidhe House? It changed nothing. And yet everything.

Lyr strode away, ignoring the Sidhe's regard. He barely noticed the lush gardens or the trees swaying in a spell-cast breeze. The sun was riding low, near the edge of the cavern. Would it wink out, magic exhausted, at the end of the artificial day? He had no time to find out, for both he and Kai had to give Arlyn energy now. She slept in his arms, her body jerking from time to time with some dark dream.

They were almost to the portal when he felt a flicker of danger. His combat senses sprang to life. There, near—

"Ralan!" He called over his shoulder. "To your right."

The prince twisted, barely missing the arrow that would have lodged in his throat. In a flash, Ralan had his sword free. He dodged another arrow and then sprinted toward the trees, Teyark behind him. Lyr cursed, unable to act with Arlyn in his arms. Should he give her to Kai? Before he could decide, Kien broke into the clearing, sword in hand.

Ralan's chest heaved as he pulled himself to a halt just out of attack range. "Enough of this, Kien."

"Never enough until you're dead." But the prince only smirked, lifting his sword as if in salute. "Fortunately, you brought yourself here so I could accomplish that deed."

"Why?"

Kien's face hardened. "A seer should never be king."

Ralan advanced on his brother, but a startled shriek from Meli drew Lyr's immediate attention. His heart froze to see Kien behind her, his right arm curled around Meli's throat. In his left hand, he gripped a knife, the point alarmingly close to her face.

Lyr glanced at Ralan, only to find the place where Kien had stood now empty. When he met Meli's eyes once more, they were full of fear. The same terror that burned along their bond.

"Do you like my illusion?" The prince's face twisted, a grimace of madness and rage. "I've had plenty of time to perfect it."

"Let her go," Lyr said, forcing calm into his voice.

Kien's arm tightened, drawing a yelp from Meli. "Funny how you found another soulbonded, Lyrnis Dianore. That only happens with reincarnation, you know. You did know, right?"

Wordlessly, he handed Arlyn to Kai. "So I learned. I have accepted it."

"Have you?" A gleam entered the prince's eyes. "I know a spell to recall memories from a past life. I could use it, for a price. You could have your old love back. It might erase this one's current life, but you haven't known her long. At least according to my spy."

Meli's eyes widened, and her breath came in sharp gasps. For only a second, Lyr was tempted. For almost thirty years, he had longed to have Aimee back. But as he met Meli's gaze, all the doubt and all of the past disappeared. He loved Meli for herself as surely as he had loved Aimee. His heart drummed in his ears. Or maybe…maybe more.

Lyr shoved his shoulders back and stared Kien in the eye. "You will have to name some other boon. I have no need of such a thing."

"I see." Kien trailed the flat of the blade along Meli's cheek. "How about this? Allow yourselves to be bound and guide me back to Moranaia, and I won't kill her. This blade is steel, you know."

Bound? Lyr's vision grew hazy, and bile rose up his throat. Allafon had used Arlyn to force him into chains. Gods, he'd sworn never to be captured that way again. Lyr gripped the hilt of his sword and fought to slow his breathing. Could he do it? By Arneen, he would have to. If Kien cut Meli deeply enough with a steel knife, she would bleed out before they could get her through the gate. Kai wouldn't be able to heal that kind of wound.

Then Meli whispered quietly through their bond. *"I have no allergy to iron."*

∾ଛୁଛ

As Lyr processed Meli's words, she slid her left hand slowly up her side until she could grip the hilt of her knife. By Freyr, she was tired of having others treat her as disposable and weak. She was more than they believed.

Out of the corner of her eye, she saw Ralan creeping closer. Then Teyark on the other side. Her captor shifted a little, and Teyark stilled. "Father will not have you back no matter how you gain entry, Kien," Teyark said.

"He'll have little choice with both of you gone," Kien answered, his voice loud in Meli's ear.

Teyark snorted. "I'm not a seer. What's your excuse for killing me?"

"I don't have to kill you. You'll never produce a child. It should be simple enough for me to meet that goal."

"Have you forgotten our sister?" Ralan called.

Kien's arm tightened again, startling a gasp from Meli. "She's a child."

"Maybe when you left." Teyark took another step forward. "A couple of centuries tends to age a person. I suppose you'll have to think of something else in your bid for power."

"She will step aside, or—"

A crackling roar interrupted the prince's words, and heat washed over Meli. Kien shrieked and jerked to the side, forcing her to claw at his arm with her free hand when her airway restricted. After another roar and wave of heat, Kien's grip eased enough for her to breathe. The acrid smell of singed hair and clothing wafted around them, and Meli gagged. But the distraction allowed her to draw her knife, point facing downward where it would be harder to see.

When Kien spun around, Meli saw the source of the fire. Caolte stood, another ball of flame balanced in his hand, at the other end of the path. "My brother ordered you gone from here. I would take great pleasure in killing you."

Meli's heart thudded hard as Caolte cast the flame. Would it hit her, too? But Kien danced away just in time. An odd sort of relief. "Watch it," Kien said. "Or I will kill her."

From behind, Meli heard Lyr's soft curse. Kien's knife blade pressed against her cheek, just short of drawing blood. Her breath heaved in and out, and her chest squeezed. She could do this. She *had* to do this. Loki—a God—believed in her. It was well past time she believed in herself.

Ralan lifted his sword, and Kien swung around to face him. A small diversion, but enough. As Kien called out another threat, Meli plunged her dagger backward, directly into her captor's stomach. Her ears rang with his shout of pain, and for the briefest moment, his arm loosened around her neck. With a quick wrench, she tugged free.

And ran.

∞૭&

It happened so fast Lyr almost missed it. One moment, Kien held Meli in his grip. The next, he screamed, and Meli slipped away. She dashed across the clearing, directly toward Lyr, as Kien's hands flew to his waist. Was that...a knife hilt sticking from his side?

"Do not attack," Ralan sent. *"That's an order."*

Lyr's brows rose. Seriously? But he didn't have time to ask before Meli reached him. Hastily, he shoved his throwing knife into its sheath and wrapped his arms around her. As Meli held tight, Lyr stared across the clearing. She'd stabbed Kien. *Meli* had stabbed *Kien.* She might not be a warrior, but she certainly had the heart of one.

Lyr had no more time to marvel. As Ralan, Teyark, and Caolte advanced, Kien darted between them, not even pausing when a ball of flame caught his cloak on fire. He ran toward the portal as though an army chased him. Teyark and Caolte started forward, but Ralan called them to a halt.

"Not now. I will face him eventually, but it is best not today."

"You dare to order me?" Caolte challenged.

Ralan barely glanced at the Sidhe. "If you go now, your brother will follow. In his current state, there is a chance he'll be gravely injured."

"He won't go after me," Lyr muttered, shifting Meli away and drawing his sword.

"Do not follow," Ralan snapped. Lyr turned toward the portal, more than ready to ignore his friend, but Ralan's next words halted him. "By order of your prince. Don't make me enforce it."

"Gods, you could end him." Kai's frustrated cry matched Lyr's thoughts. "Why in all the worlds would you wait?"

"The futures I can see all show negative outcomes from pursuing him now. He has subordinates who must be subdued." Shoulders slumping, the prince ran a hand through his hair. "We need to concentrate on getting Arlyn back to Moranaia."

Lyr ground his teeth together. He needed to act, but Ralan was right. Arlyn needed help. With a final thanks to Caolte, the group rushed to the portal.

Meli's hand gripped Lyr's, and her worry radiated through their bond. *"Will we encounter him in the mists?"*

He squeezed her hand in reassurance. *"Kai is a skilled guide and will take us directly along the path to Moranaia, which Kien cannot follow."*

"At least we won't have to rely on the runes."

His eyes met hers. *"You and your runes saved us, for I could not have borne the loss of Kai and Arlyn."*

Meli ducked her head in denial, but they reached the portal before she could answer. Kai studied the group, Arlyn still and pale in his arms. "Stay close," he said. "I can't spare much energy to ensure your safety."

As they gathered around Kai and proceeded through, Lyr sent more energy to Arlyn, heedless of the cost to himself. His combat senses dulled, and he could only hope they wouldn't require them. Kai needed his own reserves to see the large group through the turbulent Veil. With each step, the mist rolled violently around them. Meli shuddered beside him.

Then blessedly, they were through. The light of a real sun filled him with its glow, and the energy of Moranaia poured through him. Lyr let out an involuntary sigh, grateful to be home. He peered at Arlyn, hoping her illness would clear like the Neorans' had, but she was just as listless as before. He exchanged a fear-filled glance with Kai.

"I can still sense her, but she's weak," Kai said. "Lial might be at the Neoran camp. He can—"

"The fairies," Ralan interrupted, voice resolute. "It would take Lial too long."

Kai took off at a sprint toward the fairy pond. As one, Lyr and Meli followed.

∾⊙ℂ

Meli tried not to think of the blood drying on her hand and in her robes. The squish of knife in flesh. Bile rose, and she shoved the memory aside. There was too much to do to be paralyzed now. Would the fairies help this time? Lyr would be destroyed if something happened to Arlyn.

Maybe Meli would be, too.

She turned her thoughts away from that possibility. As the forest flew by, Meli focused on the only bright spot. *Lyr had chosen her.* She had no idea if Kien had lied about that spell, but it didn't matter. Lyr had passed up the chance to have Aimee restored to him—for her. Ameliar Liosevore, who had been considered last in most things all of her life. She who had never been good enough for any except her parents. She held the wonder close to her heart as they neared their destination.

Kai skidded to a halt at the entrance to the fairy pond, Lyr and Meli behind him, but they didn't have long to wait. The fairy appeared at once, her voice granting them entrance. Meli thought it was the same one, Nia, but she wasn't sure how fairies might vary in appearance. Perhaps they were all fond of blue.

As Kai knelt with Arlyn at the edge of the pond, the fairy floated closer, her form growing larger as it had before. Lyr and Meli stopped a few paces away, though she could feel how much her bonded wanted to rush forward. He held himself back by dint of will. And love. He did not want to interfere with Arlyn's healing even to ease his own discomfort.

"Princess Nia," Kai murmured. "Can you save her?"

The fairy placed a hand on Arlyn's brow. "This is earth poisoning most foul. It latches to her Moranaian blood the most. I will call my family."

Four other fairies—two males and two females in a rainbow of colors—popped free of the fog that rolled across the water. They grew as Nia had and surrounded Kai and Arlyn. Meli could see little then, for a green glow filled the air, blinding her. She winced away from the light. How could Kai stand it up close? Fear surged through her from Lyr, and she wrapped her arm around his waist.

When the light faded, the fairies stepped back. The four who had come forth to help bowed before Nia and left as soundlessly as they had appeared. Meli rushed forward with Lyr, his anxiety melding with her own. Then she sighed in relief to see Arlyn blinking blearily up at Kai.

Slowly, Arlyn glanced around the clearing, and her brows lowered when she spotted the fairy. "Where...how..." she started, her voice hoarse, before clearing her throat. "What happened?"

Meli stared at her, the sense of kinship she'd always felt for Arlyn blending with a new kind of affection. A friendship that had nothing to do with who they'd been before. They might be blood-souls, as Nia had said, but they would make their own relationship in this life.

Thankfully they'd now have the chance.

35

Relief poured through Lyr at Arlyn's words, and he gave a shaky laugh. *Thank the Gods.* "What do you remember?"

She rubbed a palm against her temple. "Kai fought with the Sidhe. Naomh, I think?" Arlyn gasped and reached toward Kai. "He hurt you. Are you okay?"

"He healed me," her soulbonded whispered.

Arlyn stared into his eyes, her face softening as they shared private words. "At least you know now," she murmured.

Kai must have told her what he'd learned of his parentage, but he clearly didn't want to discuss it. Instead, he and Lyr recounted how they'd escaped. Arlyn's startled gaze darted to Meli when she heard how Kien had been defeated, at least temporarily. But when she asked about the other princes, Lyr realized for the first time that they hadn't followed. He'd been too worried to think about them before.

"She needs rest," Nia interrupted, hands on hips. "Do not undo our work, for only a sound sleep will finish the job. You will have more than enough time for discussion later."

Lyr nodded, chastised. "Thank you for your aid, Princess Nia."

The fairy's hands dropped, and some of her irritation eased. "Our family owes much to yours, Myern Lyrnis. Return when you decide what to do about Alfheim, now that their kind is one of yours. We'll do what we can."

With those words, Nia shrank until her small form disappeared into the mists. Arlyn pushed at Kai until he let her stand. "I can walk," she insisted. "You are tired enough, my love."

"Arlyn—"

"But you can offer support." Eyes shining, she took his arm and leaned heavily against him. Though he groaned, he didn't argue, guiding her along the path.

Despite all that had happened, Lyr couldn't help but grin. If Arlyn was well enough to argue against her weakness, then she was going to be fine. He followed, Meli beside him, content to let his body ease further with relief. But it was short-lived, for he soon saw Lial striding down the path toward them, his face twisted into a scowl.

"Would you stop disappearing?" the healer grumbled. "If not for Ralan, I wouldn't even have known you'd returned."

Lyr glanced down. The cloak. With a grimace, he unclasped it and gathered it under his arm. "My apologies. I forgot I was still wearing this thing."

"Or to tell me when you left." Lial's mouth pinched into a thin line. "At least you warned your mother before you vanished for two days."

"Two days? *Miaran.*" Lyr ran his hand through his hair. "I had no idea time would pass so differently there."

Lial crossed his arms. "Where *were* you?"

"A Sidhe lord's private domain," Lyr answered, shrugging. "Come with me, and I'll tell you about it."

Lial fell into step beside Lyr as they continued toward the estate. Still upset, he filled Lyr in on estate business in short, clipped sentences. The Neoran children had been sent back to their queen, and the adults were almost ready to go. None remembered much of what had happened, only flashes of insanity and the Sidhe sweeping through. Frustrating, but not unexpected.

Lyr peered up at the late afternoon sky. "Do you think they will be ready to leave in the morning?"

"Yes, thankfully," Lial answered. "Try not to get injured again. I'm due a few days' rest."

With a laugh, Lyr agreed. Few needed rest as much as the healer.

ൟ

A few days later, Lyr leaned back in his chair and glared at the rippling glow surrounding his communication mirror. He'd spoken with the Neoran queen and settled a pressing dispute between two nobles along his branch. And still, there was more to be done. Next in line? Lady Vionafer of Alfheim. Sooner than expected, she had requested contact. He only waited for Meli to join him.

When his bonded walked in, his glower slipped inevitably into a smile, the peace of her presence easing his frustration. Something had changed between them, though no words had been spoken. Neither had spoken of love, but it echoed along the bond. The words he would give her later, when he had time to savor the moment.

"Do you think something happened in Alfheim?" she asked as she neared.

His gaze traveled down her body. Telia had been busy while they were away, creating a light summer dress for Meli. The thin fabric caressed her in places he wanted to explore with his hands. At her soft laugh, he shook his head and forced his attention to her eyes.

"Sorry." He cleared his throat. "I...yes, I suspect something happened."

Lyr took a moment to gather his self-control before he stood, trying not to stare at Meli as she settled beside him. Then he activated the spell to communicate with Alfheim. Almost at once, the lady mage's pale face greeted them.

"Forgive me for the delay, Lady Vionafer," Lyr said. "I was away from the estate."

"I thank you for any response, considering all that has occurred." The mage's hands shook as she gripped them in front of her waist. "Several days past, the darkened energy breached the north side of the city. I've moved those who lived there, but people are beginning to panic. And let me assure you—the Ljósálfar do not often panic."

Meli's brows pinched. "My parents?"

"They are well, though concerned." A small, weary smile crossed Vionafer's face. "It is good to see you safe, Ameliar. I always knew you would find your place. I was assured such by a charming mutual friend of ours."

"Loki?" Meli gasped.

"The very one." The mage straightened as if preparing herself. "I must admit to you that my king does not know about this discussion. He is still upset by the loss of Lady Teronver, his kinswoman, and blinded to the severity of the coming disaster. But yesterday, Freyr himself ordered me to act. I suspect we will have a new king ere long."

Lyr let out a long sigh. "What's one more possible diplomatic nightmare? I suppose if you have the support of your god, that is well enough for me. We know the source of the energy poisoning and have disrupted the spell. But finding a way to fix the damage will take no small effort. In the meantime, the fairies of Braelyn have finally granted their aid."

The mage's eyebrows rose. "The fairies? A surprise, that. Our ancestors were not kind to them."

Lyr saw no reason to explain that Princess Nia had agreed only because of Meli. "It seems you have the chance to make a better impression. I'm an uncertain of timing, as I must consult with my king, but I hope to send aid to Alfheim as soon as we can arrange it."

"You have my gratitude." The mage straightened and her hands steadied. "And I assure you that is no small thing."

"Indeed." Lyr inclined his head. "Rest assured that I will contact you as soon as possible."

After a few more polite words, the communication ended. Meli sagged against him, and he felt her concern like his own. Lyr gathered her into his arms. "We'll see the problem solved and your family safe, *mialn*."

She settled her forehead against his chest. "I know."

∽◎∾

Meli wandered the gardens while she could. Rain had fallen off and on in the day since they'd returned from the Sidhe realm. Her head tipped back as she searched the canopy, but it was difficult to see how thick the clouds had grown through the trees. Was it her imagination, or did the leaves look less green today? She had little concept of the seasons here.

She wished she was still curled in bed with Lyr, but he'd risen early to see the remaining Neorans through the portal. Her body heated when she remembered the night they'd spent and the words of love he'd said. She glanced up again, this time hoping for a nice rain to cool her. Lyr was behind on his work and had spent much of his day shuffling papers in his study. She did not want to distract from that, or he'd be busy for days.

But no rain fell, and Meli turned another corner to find Arlyn sitting on a delicate stone bench. She paused, uncertain what to do. It was the first time she'd seen Lyr's daughter since their return the previous evening, as Kai had shuffled her off to their room to follow the fairy's directive. Should she approach? Last she knew, Arlyn was still upset about the reincarnation.

Before she could decide, the other woman looked up, and her face settled into a smile. "I won't bite."

Meli gave a nervous laugh. "Bite?"

"Sorry. It's an Earth expression." Arlyn's grin widened. "I mean that I won't get angry if you come closer. You don't have to avoid me."

Meli took a few tentative steps forward. "I know you wanted time to process what you learned about me. Are you still upset?"

"Not anymore." At Meli's doubtful look, Arlyn shook her head. "After all that's happened, it just…it doesn't seem so important anymore. I can't say I don't still feel awkward about it, but we'll work it out."

"At least we know why we feel connected." She stepped a little closer. "I'm not your mother in this life, it is true. Maybe this time, we can be friends."

"I hope so," Arlyn said. "I truly do."

☙ §ℰ

Lyr tapped his fingers on his desk. This land dispute was an ancient one, the law so obscure he barely remembered it. His eyes scanned the books that lined his study, but none here would have the answer. His breath hitched. He was going to have to go into the library. Though nausea rose, he stood. There was no avoiding it.

Lyr forced himself to proceed through will alone. This dispute could not be delayed without bloodshed. In truth, it was miracle enough that he'd made it so long without needing to enter. *Clechtan*, but Lyr's mother had already braved the library. Why couldn't he?

Finally, he stood before the doors. Memories of his time in Allafon's dungeon, held helpless by iron while mentally experiencing his mother's mortal injury, seized his breath. Meli's concern filled him through the bond, and he struggled to send her reassurance. He had to do this. It was long past time.

Though his hand trembled, he pushed one of the doors open and slipped through. For almost five hundred and fifty years, Lyr had loved this room, and he breathed a sigh of relief to find that the feeling had not been erased. The spiral stairs that curled up the round room, stopping at a landing on each floor for access to the massive bookshelves, still brought back memories of childhood adventures. He'd spent many hours as a boy running up and down those stairs, pretending to be the guardian of some great trove.

Lyr could just make out the sitting area where his family had often gathered to read at the top of the tower, his parents' favorite spot. Pain stabbed him to know that his mother had fallen from there, a place so beloved. Slowly, he walked down the short set of stairs to the bottom floor. His gaze found the area where his mother had landed, and he shuddered.

At a soft shuffling sound, he spun.

"Lyr?" his mother asked from the doorway.

"How can you bear it? Being here?"

One corner of her mouth turned up. "Not always well, but I manage. There are good memories, too."

"Yes." The tension in his gut loosened, and he could breathe freely again for the first time since he'd entered. "Now we just need to bring Kien to justice."

Lynia studied the shelves of books, and her mouth curved fully into a smile. "I'll help find the answers we need. Never doubt it."

৩৩

Later that night, Lyr lay with Meli in his arms, her hair tickling his nose. He needed to rest. Tomorrow, he'd be going with Ralan to meet with the king. A few days after he returned from that pleasant task, Lord Naomh was scheduled to arrive. And once he had the king's input, he'd have to arrange expeditions to both Alfheim and Earth. He had more than enough work ahead.

Meli shifted, and Lyr's arms tightened around her. His body went hard, and he let out a sharp breath as her fingers made lazy circles on his chest.

Then again, he could sleep later.

ABOUT THE AUTHOR

Ever since finding a copy of *The Hero and the Crown* in her elementary school library, Bethany has loved fantasy. After subjecting her friends to stories scrawled in notebooks during study breaks all through high school, she decided to pursue an English degree at Middle Tennessee State University. When not writing or wrangling her two small children, Bethany enjoys reading, photography, and video games.

For more information, please visit
www.bethanyadamsbooks.com

Love my books? Come join my Facebook group, The Worlds of Bethany Adams. All news is posted there first!

CPSIA information can be obtained
at www.ICGtesting.com
Printed in the USA
LVOW12s0407120418
573117LV00001B/79/P

9 780997 532036